James Mason Hoppin

Memoir of Henry Armitt Brown

Together with Four Historical Orations

James Mason Hoppin

Memoir of Henry Armitt Brown
Together with Four Historical Orations

ISBN/EAN: 9783744642132

Printed in Europe, USA, Canada, Australia, Japan

Cover: Foto ©Raphael Reischuk / pixelio.de

More available books at **www.hansebooks.com**

MEMOIR

OF

HENRY ARMITT BROWN,

TOGETHER WITH

FOUR HISTORICAL ORATIONS.

EDITED BY J. M. HOPPIN,

PROFESSOR IN YALE COLLEGE.

———

PHILADELPHIA:

J. B. LIPPINCOTT & CO.

LONDON: 16 SOUTHAMPTON STREET, COVENT GARDEN.

1880.

PREFACE.

POLITICAL wisdom fails sometimes to perceive and make use of the fact that the spring of a nation's progress is in its youth's fresh ideas; for they are inspirations from a fountain nearer the original source of national life than the profoundest theories of scientific statesmanship. Youth's radicalism has more than once proved to be the principle of the rapid advancement of a people in freedom and civilization.

The subject of the following memoir possessed elements of greatness worthy of the best days of the republic. A power went forth from his short life (for he was comparatively a young man when he died) which will not soon cease to be felt. It was an influence for the political reformation of the land, and for a higher standard of national character. He represented, as far as in him lay, the best modern political spirit. Nobly as he had done, there seemed to be much more for him to do. Although his life's work was in some sense complete, he had not yet attained the full development of his powers. He attracted the eyes of men by his splendid promise. His life had a direction toward something lofty, rare, and beautiful,

and which, too, was all unspent when it suddenly reached
its close. The star was still ascending when the darkness
covered it. His addresses and writings will, we are sure,
do much to perpetuate his name. There are really few
things in our historical literature superior to his Carpenters'
Hall, Burlington Bi-Centennial, and Valley Forge orations.
But the fire and nobleness of his delivery, the music of his
voice, the charm of his unsurpassed oratory, these are gone
forever.

J. M. H.

New Haven, November, 1879.

CONTENTS.

MEMOIR.

MEMOIR

OF

HENRY ARMITT BROWN.

JAMES BROWNE,* from whom the subject of this biography was the seventh in descent, was one of the colonists who came over in "the good ship Kent," and laid out the town of Burlington, New Jersey, towards the latter part of the eighth month, 1677. This was five years before the landing of William Penn and his peaceful company on the banks of the Delaware. James Browne was the son of Richard and Mary Browne, of Sywell, in Northamptonshire, England. His father, Richard, having been converted to the Quaker doctrine, had removed to Bedfordshire, where the family was living when James, then a young man of twenty-one, came to America with others to settle on that portion of territory purchased of Lord Berkeley by the Society of Friends.

In 1679, James Browne married Honour Clayton in "the primitive meeting-house, made of a sail taken from the Kent," being the first marriage recorded in the State

---

* The terminal " e " was afterwards dropped to satisfy Quaker simplicity.

of New Jersey. He removed from Burlington once more "into the Wilderness," dying at Nottingham, Pennsylvania, in 1716. His descendants, with the exception of James Brown, who, near the close of the last century, returned to England and lived on his estate at Snaresbrook Manor, in the neighborhood of London, were mostly residents of Philadelphia, and fairly represented the mercantile intelligence, respectability, and wealth of the old Quaker families of the "City of Brotherly Love."

Charles Brockden Brown, author of "Edgar Huntley," and, it may be said, the originator of American novel literature, who was born in 1771, and died in 1810, belonged to this family. He was own uncle of Henry Armitt Brown's father, and his grand-nephew, in some points of character, strikingly resembled him. They were both men of sensitive natures, and were both bred to the law; but having early a strong bias toward a literary life and to that of political essayists, this literary bent in the case of the first drew him away entirely from the legal profession, and in the case of the last exerted a powerful influence that was gradually separating him from his practice at the bar and leading him into a broader political career.

This mild strain of Quaker ancestry was mingled in the subject of the present memoir with Revolutionary blood. His great-grandfather upon his mother's side, Colonel Benjamin Hoppin, of Providence, Rhode Island, passed through the seven years of the War of Independence as a captain of the Rhode Island Continentals, and was present at Princeton, Red Bank, Monmouth, and other battles of the Revolution; while another maternal ancestor, Thomas Weld Philbrook, of Rhode Island, served at Ticonderoga, and also suffered incredible hardships on board the "Jersey prison-ship."

Henry Armitt Brown was born in Philadelphia, December 1, 1844. His father, Frederick Brown, was a representative business man in Philadelphia, whose character for integrity and public spirit need not be enlarged upon, especially to those of his townsmen who, for half a century, so well knew, and honored, and loved him; and, although his commanding presence is seen no more in the streets, he will be long remembered for his geniality and sterling worth.

Although Henry exhibited mental traits of both parents, yet from his mother, whose maiden name was Charlotte Augusta Hoppin, it has been remarked by his friends that he inherited literary tastes; for such tastes are, perhaps, as frequently a matter of temperament as of education.

He was a sweet-tempered child, delicately strung, and extremely sensitive to the touch and sight of harsh things as if unfit to be stretched on this rough world, imaginative, curious in his questionings, sympathetic and affectionate, but stubborn of will, and apt to see things in a very independent and ludicrously odd light.

When an older boy, his favorite pastime was studying the histories of great battles, especially those of Napoleon, and also at the time those of the Crimean war, and in arranging and moving companies of tin soldiers and parks of artillery according to the changing plans of the battles. This play was carried out on so large a scale as to attract the attention of the neighbors and of older people to the extent of the combinations. One whole portion of the garden thus employed would become the scene of a wide and hurrying conflict, platoons of soldiers shifting across the field, forts blowing up, dwellings in flames, rivers crossed, and discharges of artillery from the flying batteries. "On one occasion," his younger brother relates, "I, being the representative Russian, had to build my

tower and raise my parapets in order to prepare for the
defence of the Malakoff. Hal, as the besieging force, dug
his intrenchments. We each had little brass cannon, and
loaded them with one pellet of lead and a few grains of
powder, attaching to each a train of powder, so that at the
appointed time the fuse could be lighted, and we could
step off and await the result. The attack commenced.
Harry brought out some forty or fifty of his men as the
attacking column, and while doing so was endeavoring to
start his cannon in order to cover and assist them, but his
punk would not light the fuse. I, however, was more
fortunate, and trained up my cannon on the assaulting
column, and the fuse ignited. Three or four of the enemy
were demolished, and the majority of them knocked down.
Harry, immediately on surveying the field of battle, said,
' Well, Lardner, we have *reversed* history. The Malakoff
cannot be taken this afternoon. Let us get some dinner.'"
This boyish play, in fact, grew to be an absorbing passion,
turning a childish amusement into a thoughtful and fore-
casting exercise of the reasoning powers; and his early
taste seems to have long clung to him, for until he was
fourteen years old his principal ambition in life was to be
a great captain. His letters were full of military matters,
organization of companies, marches, and courts-martial, as
if they were very real things and the fate of empires hung
on them. He besought his father over and over again to
send him to West Point Academy. This throws some
light upon his character, which, as it sometimes happens,
beneath an almost feminine delicacy of organization hid a
nature of sinewy ambition fitted to leadership.

Harry, even as a child, had a peculiar sense of personal
dignity, which was disturbed at anything which seemed
unfairly to lower him in the eyes of others. But he was

brimful of life, and his mimicry of animals and funny performances at school were sources of infinite satisfaction to his schoolmates, and sometimes the laughter bore away on its tide both teacher and scholars. He seemed unconscious of the pleasure he gave others. Although not domineering, every one naturally fell under his control. He was director of the mock orchestra and captain of the juvenile battalion, and also a champion cricket-player, difficult as this is to reconcile with his quiet habits in after-life.

His excessive fondness for sport was commenced at an early age, when, as a little boy, he brought in the cedar-birds and small game in abundance. This love of "gunning," as we call it in America, was carried into later life, and it was increased as he grew older by his love of nature, leading him into the woods and fields in rambles, accompanied only by his dogs, or along the picturesque banks and silver stretches of the Delaware River, the home of the duck and the little reed-bird, and the habitation of innumerable bright plants and flowers.

Like most lively boys he fell to rhyming, inditing verses to the young ladies at the Burlington St. Mary's School, or lampooning "ye unpopular tutor," or writing burning patriotic odes, or composing German ballads "in the manner of Longfellow or some other fellow." Some of these effusions in point of lively wit were quite up to the mark of juvenile performances of most of the great poets that are published.

His first instructor, outside of home walls, was Miss Lucy A. Lerned, who taught school in the basement of St. Luke's Church, in Philadelphia. A warm, mutual esteem was always kept up between teacher and scholar, as their correspondence shows. Harry's later school-days were passed at the Burlington Academy and at the boarding-school of Dr. James Gilborne Lyons, in Haverford, Pennsylvania. He began to study Latin at the age of seven, and obtained a "first honor" in the summer term of 1853; and when he went to college, his master, Dr. Lyons, wrote a letter, in which he speaks of him as "a student of industrious habits and good abilities." He appears to have taken captive his instructors, not only by his faithfulness to his studies, but by his exceedingly winning qualities of heart, for they follow his career with words of affectionate praise.

He came up to be examined for admission to Yale College in July, 1861, an unspoiled youth. If truthfulness, sincerity, and purity were ever expressed in a countenance, they shone on his open brow. Yet it was a thoughtful and serious face. His great, blue eyes asked searching questions of all. Then, as always, he looked at you steadily, and grasped your hand with a firm grasp. He seemed at first to be half-amusingly and half-actually dazed by the new responsibilities and, to him, immense vistas of a great college, but it was not long before he cast himself into the current of student life with an unbounded ardor. He here found a congenial field for his varied talents. It was into the brotherhood of young men he had come, and his sympathies went out to all in whom he recognized an honorable and sympathetic heart. There has not been graduated for a long period—perhaps never, socially—a more thorough-bred Yale student, one inspired by a more genuine college spirit, who more whole-heartedly identified himself with college life, and who infused into that life a more genial influence, than he of whom we write. Though both were popular men, the true Harry Brown of Yale was a vastly higher order of student than the fictitious Tom Brown of Oxford. This is the testimony of his classmates, and his college career is too recent for us to forget it.

He was soon felt to be a social and, in some points of view, intellectual power in college,—a leaven to leaven the whole with the enthusiasm for true brotherhood. While more ambitious of class than of scholarly distinction, there was no envy or spirit of intrigue about him. He never wrought nor wriggled himself into an influential position. Whatever honors he won were freely accorded to him. While he did not make a positive mark as a scholar, he succeeded in obtaining an excellent intellectual discipline. Yale did wonders for him. He did not lose sight of this object. He gained more from his college course than many higher-stand men in substantial improvement. He had "sensibility," which, Emerson says, is even better than talent; and he had also a remarkable power of intellectual appreciativeness, though not always operating in regular ways. In merriest and maddest moods he studied his own powers, his mental aptitudes, the character of his instructors and companions, and the best methods of influencing men. The jest was succeeded by the thoughtful mood and by the air of intense abstraction. Those deep-sunk, glowing eyes underneath the square, bold forehead did not bespeak a frivolous nature. Concentration, intense purpose, were strongly marked. As in the legend of taking Calais castle by disguised English knights, under the silken robe was hid the coat of mail. He was already preparing himself for life. He read much, but independently and rather scatteringly. He was fond of the classics,—the Latin poets especially,—and also of history, of political economy, and, to a certain extent, of philosophy, so that the studies of

Senior year were particularly agreeable to him. But he was soon recognized as an off-hand speaker,—lithe, graceful, never at a loss for something witty, brilliant, and telling.

Some irregularity into which he was led by an untempered zeal for college customs (many of them more to be honored in the breach than the observance), caused him to spend a part of Sophomore year in seclusion, which, however, in his case, did not hurt him in the estimation of his classmates, nor, it might be said, of his instructors, for the reason that no moral taint was ever breathed upon him. He was no rioter or deep drinker. His life was irreproachable, and his sense of honor exquisite.

When fun was in order he was assuredly "Master of the Revels." As humorist there was no end to his exuberant drollery, his sportive fancies, and his witty invention. The "Pow-wow" of June 7, 1862, in which he largely participated, will ever be memorable as being the best of its kind. The motley chorus of his racy songs roared by the throats of sturdy Sophomores struck the level of the occasion much better than something more fine would have done. In resolutions drafted by class committees; in speeches delivered at class suppers; in Delta Kappa, Alpha Sigma Phi, and Psi Upsilon lyrics; in debates and war-songs of the Brothers in Unity; in the organization and carrying out the Thanksgiving Jubilees of Sophomore, Junior, and Senior years; and, above all, as one of the illustrious "Cochleaureati" in the now defunct "Wooden Spoon" celebration, his pen and voice were foremost. He was class Mercury and Apollo—orator and poet. He was Momus too. His acting was excellent in every rôle, comic, tragic, and sentimental, and was much praised. A newspaper writer thus spoke of it in noticing the "Wooden Spoon" exhibition of June, 1865: "The colloquy of Virginia did not refer to the unfortunate State somewhere down South, but was a comic rendering of the old tragedy of Virginius. The author, Henry A. Brown, of Philadelphia, is the best actor in the college, and personated old Virginius to perfection." Another said: "The announced poem by Henry A. Brown was omitted on account of the lateness of the hour, much to the regret of the audience, as Mr. Brown's poetical talents are widely known in New Haven, and are of no common order. Two of the songs of the occasion are from his pen, and are sufficient evidence of his superiority in this line."

The "Wooden Spoon," as is known to those acquainted with Yale life, was originally a grotesque custom instituted as an award to the biggest eater, but it had lost its coarse associations, and came to be highly prized by the students as conferring social distinction upon those who received it. They were the most popular men in the class, and who deserved to be so because they were men of genuine kindness and unselfish character, who, sunny-hearted themselves, made "sunshine in a shady place" to others,—in a word, they were heart-crowned. Well did Harry Brown merit this unrecorded college honor; and the big wooden spoon, wreathed with ivy, now hanging on the wall of his silent study, is a memento that to his old friends would ever speak pathetically. The heart's fruits are unfading. In no evil sense, but, as time went on, in a true sense, and bearing many a divine fruit, he held to the poet's words, though put in cynic lips,—

" Und grün des Lebens goldner Baum."

In the November (1864) number of the *Yale Literary Magazine*, Harry Brown contributed a versified story entitled "The Lady of Katzenjammer," in the style of the

"Ingoldsby Legends,"—a very clever performance, commencing and travelling on in the free-swinging pace of those rollicking Irish poems. Indeed, much of his intellectual energy was spent in these literary excursions and by-paths, and especially in the life of student societies.

At a time when Yale was swarming with societies, open and secret, partly derived from the German universities and the old customs of the Burschen *Pennalism,* and partly a home product, Harry Brown was a great Society man. The societies did much for him, perhaps more than they would do for a hundred other men of different mental make. They were most assuredly not an "unmixed evil" in his case.

It will not be denied that our American university system, which, in some respects, is the child of our wants and a truly marvellous result of our civilization, is not as yet ideally perfect or practically complete. The old system, which had some excellent features and turned out men of strong individuality, is giving way to the new, while the new is not yet attained. We are in a transition, and thus chaotic state. We aim at the universal and fail in the particular. We glorify and perfect the system, and leave the subject of it imperfectly educated. Too much is attempted for it to be thoroughly done. The result, therefore, is sciolism rather than science. It is like grasping too large a handful of which little or nothing remains in the hand. "Modern education," another says, "is the beginning of many things, and it is little more than a beginning." It certainly becomes a serious question whether an elementary knowledge of many things is worth as much as the mastery of one rugged art, which necessitates such a toughening of the mental fibre as to enable the student to grasp any subject. Power balanced by character is the highest aim of education. The culture that teaches the mind its uses, that gives capacity for affairs, that develops a harmonious and vigorous personality, should be the common resultant of the various forces of a university education. Mere specific training of one set of faculties is not the theory of a scientific education. The severest discipline of the critical powers, or of the memory, which goes to make scholars, and is of the utmost value in laying the foundation of a true, intellectual training, leaves untouched some of the richest parts of the manifold nature of man, the æsthetic and moral powers wherein, more than in others, potential manhood exists. " Experience has shown that the intellectual qualities which insure success in the discovery of truth are rarely combined with the qualities which lend these truths their greatest practical efficiency. The habits of the study are not the best discipline for affairs." This truth, so tersely put by one of our younger writers on educational matters, should be a hint to those who desire to make a university system of education the most practically effective as well as the most thoroughly scholar-like. The waste of mind is too great a price to pay for the experiment of theories. " Culture," says Principal Shairp,* " is not the product of mere study. Learning may be got from books, but not culture. It is a more living process, and requires that the student at times should close his books, leave his room, and mingle with his fellow-men. He must seek the intercourse of living hearts, especially in the companionship of his own contemporaries, whose minds tend to elevate and sweeten his own. It is also a method of self-discipline, the learning of self-control, the fixing of habits, the effort to overcome what is evil, and to strengthen

---

* Now Professor of Poetry at Oxford.

what is good in our nature." It is laying the plan of life in human intercourse, in the knowledge of human nature, in self-knowledge, in self-reliance, in thought as in study. It is the drawing out of the energies in strife with living forces, wherein what is slavish and useless is stripped away and a free manhood is the result. We once came across an officer, high in rank in the American army, who had distinguished himself in the last war for his business capacity as well as gallantry in the field,—by brains as well as bravery,—who, in a familiar conversation upon a hotel stoop, remarked, emphatically, that the qualities and acts which won him success in his professional life were just those which caused his expulsion from college. This was putting the matter in a way where truth is sacrificed to point; but it is a question whether such a man, or a man powerful in another career, like Henry Armitt Brown, would have been what either of them was if they had restricted themselves entirely to the prescribed course, and had been mere scholars while in college, or continued to be mere scholars out of it. It seems, sometimes, to be regretted that such force could not earlier be recognized and turned into right channels. These men, in their secret heart, lamented the time they may have spent in social life that should have been given to thorough study: nor would severe scholarship have done them more injury than polish a steel blade; but to do what they and other manly intellects ought to do, and do it well, requires a longer time than four crowded years, and a broader, scholarly preparation for college, with a more free and professional course of study in the university, ending in a definite concentration upon some department of study best suited to their powers. This should be accomplished by the culture of their varied capacities, none of which should be starved with meagre diet, but, by being generously nourished, should develop them into knowledgeable, genial, alert, strong, and useful men, fitted to serve the State in any position to which they might be called; for, though we would not entirely give in to the Socratic axiom that the highest good of life is "practical wisdom," yet a wisdom which is unserviceable to living is but a transcendental philosophy. In these remarks no encouragement is meant to be given to the neglect of scholarly duties, for the university is the place where scholarship is *the* duty and the inexpressible privilege never to be regained if lost. Not that good scholars are always made in college (for it is a lamentable fact that they are not), but while there should be good scholarship, if our colleges could turn out ready men as well as ready scholars,— serviceable men,—who are "a measure and rule to themselves," as fit for the pursuits of public life as for critical research in private study, it would be a marvellous gain. This, perhaps, is what Matthew Arnold and other writers mean when they vote that Greek shall not be a condition to entering the university; not that Greek is not a grand attainment for a man and a gentleman, which nothing else, and certainly no modern language, can take the place of, but that the man should come before the scholar.

There is another danger difficult to define threatening our universities, in which we seem to hear the warning voice of a man so full of earnest purpose as was the Armitt Brown of Yale days,—of ardent glow of manly intellect, however irregular its flashes. The athletic epoch, chastened in his time, has had its uses; it was a much needed reform; it has done great good and will do more; but it were a lamentable triumph if, while it brought back the Greek type of physical strength, it quenched the Greek type of mental force. The roystering muscularity of a vast deal

of English modern university life bordering on the brutal
we would by no means have transferred to the American
college.

> " I past beside the reverend walls
>   In which of old I wore the gown ;
>   And roved at random thro' the town,
> And saw the tumult of the halls ;
>
> " And heard once more in college fanes
>   The storm their high-built organs make,
>   And thunder-music, rolling, shake
> The prophets blazoned on the panes ;
>
> " And caught once more the distant shout,
>   The measured pulse of racing oars
>   Among the willows ; paced the shores
> And many a bridge, and all about
>
> " The same gray flats again, and felt
>   The same but not the same ; and last
>   Up that long walk of limes I past
> To see the rooms in which he dwelt.
>
> " Another name was on the door :
>   I linger'd ; all within was noise
>   Of songs, and clapping hands, and boys
> That crash'd the glass and beat the floor ;
>
> " Where once we held debate, a band
>   Of youthful friends, on mind and art,
>   And labor, and the changing mart,
> And all the framework of the land."*

It is often said that young men at college learn more
from each other than they do from their teachers. Harry
Brown, who, at an impressionable age, possessed in an un-

---

* Tennyson's " In Memoriam," lxxxvi.

common degree the capacity of friendship, as also the passion of hero-worship, was keenly alive to the influence of his college-mates, since from the nobility of his soul he recognized what there was of superiority in them, and this good he constantly drew from by a manly friendship.

There was one classmate who exercised a supreme power—it might be called fascination—over him, and who, in fact, was the worshipped idol of his soul. Joseph Appleton Bent was a man whose intellect consumed his body, and while the flame burned it was with excessive brightness. It was electric light too bright to last. In the history of the class of '65 Harry Brown pays a hearty tribute to the memory of his friend, who died three years after graduation, having already made his mark as a lawyer and orator.

There was a sympathy between these two young men that enabled Harry to know his friend. His slumbering energies, and the final direction that their activity took, were fired by the inspiration of Bent's genius acting on a kindred spirit; and this influence, as is sometimes the case with contemplative men who have lost the heart-friends of their youth, continued to hover over him like a light, like a spiritual presence. What follows may seem to be an enthusiastic tribute, but Bent, tried by any true standard, was no common man, as he was not who thus eulogizes and laments him as David did Jonathan.

"His style of speaking varied with each occasion, and seemed naturally to adapt itself to all. He could be grave or gay, witty or serious, solemn or animated, with equal grace; and there was, at all times, a stateliness in his manner and a reserve of power remarkable in one so young. His readiness and skill in debate were unsurpassed. Brilliant as he was in attack, he was greatest in reply, and to more than one of his admiring hearers, his slender form, sloping shoulders, high forehead, and long straight nose bore a striking resemblance to the portraits of the younger Pitt, while his stately manner and sonorous voice seemed to complete the likeness. It may, perhaps, be thought that the impression which he made upon his associates was deepened by their youth and enthusiasm, and that their high opinion of his powers might not have been confirmed by the judgment of maturer years. To a limited extent, no doubt, the first remark is true; but Bent's powers may be judged, not only by comparison with those of the foremost of his contemporaries, whom he so far excelled, but by that highest test of the orator, the effect which they produced on so many occasions in and out of college. He often turned the balance of a question and carried a point against what was, at the outset, a hostile sentiment. His speaking not only controlled the feelings and charmed the ear, but it changed conviction and overcame the will; and, if it be objected that the one was perhaps not the strongest, nor the other the most fixed, it may be added that his was a mind which to a remarkable degree was susceptible of continuous and healthful growth, and his powers would, without doubt, have kept more than equal pace with the years. No one who has seen him in the full exercise of his great gift can doubt that, when he died, a light was quenched that burned with the fire of real genius.

"Born as he was for leadership, keeping ever from earliest boyhood before the eyes of men, his true character was not always appreciated. He had a natural shyness which took the form of reserve, and many thought him cold. This was a great mistake. To those whom he admitted into his affections there was no friendship warmer or more sincere than his, and no one had to a larger extent than he the faculty of grappling to his own the hearts of others. The class was proud of his reputation; the world in general admired, but his friends loved him. To most, even of his classmates, he was the skilful politician, the graceful writer, the brilliant wit, the unrivalled orator; but to the few to whom he revealed himself, he was the rare companion, the true and tender-hearted friend.

"And in that character I, who write these lines, which do his memory such scanty justice, love best to think of him. I am not able, even now, to feel that Joe Bent is dead. Five years of close companionship growing ever closer,—of friendship, strengthening with each day, gave him a hold upon my heart which Death itself has not had power to break. Across the interval of twice that length of time the face and figure of my early friend rise, often, now before my eyes. I see that slender form erect,—one foot advanced,—the head thrown back,—the long right arm outstretched with open hand, sweeping the air with graceful gesture,—the cheek flushed with excitement,—the eye flashing beneath the smooth white brow,—the short lip curling with the pride of conscious power,—and on my ear seems still to fall the ring of that inspiring voice! Oftener still, I walk with him in the busy street and hear the shrewd, epigrammatic comment on men and things. I sit beside him in some quiet place and go over again the thousand great schemes for the future of which his mind was full. We talk—we laugh—we argue—we debate;—just as we used to do so long ago. I share in all these hopes and fears of his; he enters into mine. Nor can he change. I may grow old and alter, but Death has conferred on him for me immortal youth.

"Ten years have passed since we left old Yale together,—seven since we parted not to meet again: new ties have bound me; new friends won my regard; new associations formed around my path;—but thy place cannot be taken by another, nor shall my heart forget thee, O my friend."

Both these brilliant careers have been quenched, yet the harmony of their lives and the memory of their friendship, and the incitement of their manly ambition to lead men up to something higher, and their country on to something better, burn in many hearts.

Harry Brown was chosen to be the class poet, a substantial tribute to his popularity, if not to his poetical genius. He had a vein of true poetry in him, but it is rare that poetry "made to order" is of high order. Laurelled Tennyson drops a leaflet or two from his crown when he writes a laureate ode. The poem delivered so gracefully on Presentation Day, 1865, was not adjudged to be below the mark of such performances, perhaps above the ordinary standard, and, with excellent taste, it was natural and sincere, without attempting the sublime. His classmates were satisfied that a great poet had spoken, and what more could be asked? It was altogether an interesting commencement season, that of 1865; and the regatta at Worcester and Yale's naval victory, counting in time seventeen minutes forty-two and a half seconds, in which another of his classmates, Wilbur Russell Bacon, distinguished himself as stroke-oar, illustrating the strenuous motto of the class, *Οὐ λόγοισι 'αλλ ἐργουσι,* added to the glories of the occasion. At this commencement occurred the ever-memorable patriotic memorial of Yale's dead soldiers, at which William Evarts presided and Horace Bushnell spoke.

Henry Armitt was also selected to be one of the class historians, a more honorable than, it would seem to be, desirable office, and while, as is the custom at this occasion, he thrust men through and through with his historic blade, he also managed to bring them to life again and to make them laugh heartily without making them angry; for his wit was not that sort of which Jeremy Taylor speaks, "which hath teeth and nails to bite and devour thy brother." His graceful little "Ivy Song," sung by the class under the walls of the library building, fitly closes his college career with its thoughtful ending.

He spoke afterwards thus humorously of his class at their triennial meeting:

"It may not be known to you, ladies and gentlemen, that the class of '65 was always a remarkable class. It is true we were not distinguished for accurate scholarship. I remember on one occasion a prize was offered to us, but there was no mathematician in our class to claim it. For the class of '65 turned to other things the attention which some of its predecessors had given to mathematics, and the only mathematicians among us are certain of our married brethren, who have made examples of themselves by coming here to-night increased to two, and some of them with one to carry. No, we were never distinguished for our scholarship. In calculus we found incalculable trouble; conics delighted us not;

we saw nothing to admire in analytics but its first two syllables. We knew little Latin and less Greek. We sought to read the stars by other methods than those which astronomy teaches, and we were more familiar with the courts of the Areopagus than with the philosophy of the Academy. We were, in fact, the Samaritans of the college, for ' we feared the faculty, and served our own gods.' "

If there be truth in this jesting language, both as respects others and himself, it is a wrong judgment to suppose that in the speaker's case the stern nurse, Yale, did nothing for his real growth. This has been emphatically denied. On the contrary, she did everything. No college in the land could have done better for him. Where he seemed careless he drew constant nourishment and strength. It was at Yale that he acquired the power to think, to write, and to speak,—three great acquisitions for a man. But, as has been said, he learned what he did in pretty much his own methods, seeking what he thought he needed most, not always judging rightly, but retaining his individuality, and steadily, even obstinately, refusing to be run into the common mould. The teachers who nourished, for better or worse, the intellectual young men at that time, were Motley, Macaulay, Emerson, Matthew Arnold, Herbert Spencer, and John Stuart Mill. It was then, as now, a conflict of free thought, but of transition, we believe, to a higher or more productive philosophy. It was also then, at Yale, about the beginning of the struggle (*Kulturkampf*) after a broader literary and scientific culture than had before existed. Thackeray bore away the palm from Chauvenet, and Auerbach from Ueberweg; but no young man of good mind could remain during a college course, under the solid training of President Woolsey and other instructors of old Yale, without gaining sturdy intellectual growth, enriched scientific knowledge, and disciplined habits of mind. The career of Henry Armitt Brown after leaving college confirms this assertion; and if his *Alma Mater* has reason to be proud of him, he often expressed himself as proud of her, and he was ever a most loyal son of Yale.

We made a reference to the triennial meeting of the class of '65, at which meeting Harry acted as chairman, and, as this in some sense belongs to the period of college life, although it is anticipating three years, we will speak of it here again. It was held in New Haven, July 22, 1868, and just sixty-five of the members were present and sat down to dinner. Harry presided with genial dignity, wit, and grace. The "silver cup presentation" to the first-born child of the class formed not the least interesting and mirth-provoking part of the doings of the evening. The president introduced the ceremony with some happy words. The "Cup Song," in honor of the "class-boy," the son of Henry Clay McCreary, of California, was sung with heartiness. We give it as a reminiscence of college days and of Yale customs, which, perhaps, to some readers, may be novel and will amuse them:

SONG.

BY HENRY ARMITT BROWN.

Air—*"John Brown's Body."*

Like bees with honey laden that are crowding to their hives,
We have gathered here to-night, my friends, our children and our
  wives,
To make a *little* noise, if ne'er before in all our lives,
       For Yale and Sixty-five.
              Chorus.—Glory, glory, hallelujah, etc.

We have longed to see this evening since our Freshman year began,
And how often have we wondered which of us would lead the van;

But to-night the question's settled and McCreary is the man !
　　　　　Hurrah for Sixty-five!
　　　　　　　Chorus.

You're a lucky man, McCreary, and honor you we should :
You've done us all great credit, and the best a fellow could.
There are some of us yet single,—your example will do good
　　　　　To your friends of Sixty-five.
　　　　　　　Chorus.

We all one day will follow in the course that you have run,
And if Fortune smiles upon us, we shall do as you have done ;
And each one ere his setting see the rising of his son,
　　　　　Like this boy of Sixty-five.
　　　　　　　Chorus.

Then fill your glasses, classmates, for a bumper ; while ye sup
Give three cheers for McCreary and his lady ! shake it up ! !
All honor to the fellow who has won the silver cup
　　　　　Of the class of Sixty-five ! ! !
　　　　　　　Chorus.

May the God who watches o'er us smile on the little boy,
Pour in this cup His blessings till it runneth o'er with joy,
And make his years like links of gold, untarnished with alloy,
　　　　　Is the prayer of Sixty-five.
　　　　　　　Chorus.

Accept, then, blessed baby, in the name of Mother Yale,
Your hundred uncles' loving gift ; grow noble, brave, and hale ;
And when you quaff its contents, may remembrance never fail
　　　　　Of Yale and Sixty-five.
　　　　　　　Chorus.

May it keep your head forever clear, your heart forever true ;
And as long as you will stick to it, be sure we'll stick to you ;
And now, you small McCreary, we'll give three times three for you,
　　　　　Cup-boy of Sixty-five !
　　　　　　　Chorus.

We cannot leave Harry Brown's college life without giving an extract or two from a letter of one of his own classmates and most intimate friends:

"Harry, while in college, studied the languages with an appreciation and enjoyment that belonged to no one else in the class. This was evidenced by the thorough familiarity with the style of each author, by the ease with which he could, at any time, recall passages remarkable for some fine shade of thought, imagery, or delicacy of expression. He would often astonish us by quoting at length, and with no hesitation whatever, from Homer or from the Latin poets, and when we expressed surprise and asked how he could recall them, he would answer that he did not know, and that he did it with no effort. He was particularly fond of Horace, and apt at repeating passages from him. These quotations were never for show, but always came in pat, suggested by some little every-day happening. From the study of other branches, such as metaphysics, history of English literature, and of civilization, political economy, etc., I know he acquired great good, and why he did not show this in his recitations to a greater degree I never could quite understand. I have thought that perhaps it might be that he grasped *principles* rather than the words and detail with which they were expounded by an author. Then, too, we know that he was strikingly original,—fond of following up his own thoughts,—and no doubt often, when he sat down with his Wayland, his Hamilton, or Hopkins, would find himself thinking in directions suggested by what he read, rather than mastering what he read with special reference to a recitation.

"He was a keen observer of human nature, and he caught intuitively the peculiarities of mind and character of each of his classmates. Recognizing this, we made him one of our class historians, and a better choice could not have been made. When on Presentation Day he rose to read what he had written, there came a treat to those who heard, which will always be remembered.

" He had a quick sense of the ridiculous, and a vein of quiet humor that enlivened all his talk and writing. He enjoyed exercising this gift, and might have done so in after-life to the expense of the higher fame which he achieved, but for an incident which, I believe, changed his current. A rather heavy subject for composition had been given out, and when he was called upon he read a production which from beginning to end kept the class in uncontrollable merriment. Our instructor, however, partly because he considered the proprieties violated, and partly because he saw the danger that the gift of wit brings to the bright mind by the temptation to indulge it at the cost of higher faculties, criticised him severely. Being of an exceedingly sensitive nature he took the thing to heart, as was shown by the restraint he placed upon himself in all class exercises of like nature afterwards. Not long before his death, and when he was in the midst of his fame, he complained to me that he had entirely lost this old-time appreciation of humor; but he was wrong here. His letters and his conversation always sparkled with wit, as did his response to the toast, 'The Junior Members of the Bar.' His standard was simply higher, and his themes were of too noble and heroic a character to admit of its indulgence.

" I remember Harry most pleasantly in college for his love of nature. Sometimes he would gratify it by long, lonely tramps, when in peculiar moods, but he generally craved companionship. A cloud-picture, or unusual appearance of the sky or light upon the hills, a fine sunset or a gathering storm, never escaped him or failed to bring him vivid pleasure.

"I distinctly remember my first meeting with him. It was at the beginning of Freshman year. I had secured board at the table of two maiden ladies, near the Sheffield school. At my first meal a thin, pale boy, with large gray eyes, came in with me. He had just graduated from some military school, which was evidenced by the semi-military cap he wore looking more warlike than he did. We were all Freshmen at the table, and before long the restraint of newly coming together wore away. We all passed a most pleasant year together, for which we were indebted to Harry's vivacity and good company more than anything else. He was of a uniformly happy temper, and always showed the kindest consideration for others' feelings.

"I loved Harry, was proud of his successes, proud of his friendship, and I cherish his memory."

Soon after their graduation Harry, with his friend Bent and others of his classmates, joined the Columbia Law School, in New York City. Here, with a great enthusiasm for Professor Theodore Dwight and a moderate enthusiasm for the study itself, and with many interruptions and breaks by other pursuits,—literary, social, and political,— he read law for a year. On December 8, 1865, he was admitted to the membership of the Union League Club of Philadelphia, for which association he afterwards did knightly service. In July, 1866, in company with Mr. Adolph Borie's family, he sailed for Europe, where he passed sixteen months in travel, during which time he visited the countries of Europe, with the exception of Russia, Sweden, Norway, and Spain. The following winter he spent in going up the Nile, sailing for Egypt from

Brindisi. He ascended to the second cataract in his own boat. He went from Egypt to Palestine, riding from Jaffa to Jerusalem, and through Palestine and Syria to Damascus, returning to Italy by the way of Smyrna, Constantinople, Athens, and Sicily. He came home improved in health, having before suffered from dyspepsia. In a letter replying to one from a committee of his class, he answers categorically several questions in relation to his manner of life since leaving college. Among other things he says: "My future expectations are moderate and modest. I do not expect great success, but I do not anticipate failure. So far as I can recall I have married no one; from which you may conclude that, as to children, 'I have none to speak of.'"

About this time he relates in a letter to a clerical friend of his family (which letter we subjoin) a remarkable dream, worth recording as a psychological phenomenon:

"May 3, 1869.

"Rev. and dear Sir,—After many delays I send you a short account of the dream which excited your interest last summer.

"In the fall of 1865, I think it was in the month of November, while I was studying law in the city of New York, I retired to my room about midnight of a cold blustering evening. I remember distinctly hearing the clock strike twelve as I lay in bed watching the smouldering fire until drowsiness crept upon me and I slept. I had hardly lost consciousness when I seemed to hear loud and confused noises, and felt a choking sensation at my throat as if it were grasped by a strong hand. I awoke (as it seemed), and found myself lying on my back on the cobble-stones of a narrow street, writhing in the grip of a low-browed, thick-set man, with 'unkempt hair and grizzled beard,' who, with one hand at my throat and holding my wrist with the other, threw his weight upon me and held me down.

"From the first I knew that his desire was to kill me, and my struggles were for life. I recall distinctly the sense of horror at first and then that of furious determination which took possession of me.

"I did not make a sound, but with a sudden effort threw him half off me, clutched him frantically by the hair, and in my agony bit furiously at his throat. Over and over we rolled upon the stones. My strength began to give way before the fury of my struggles,— I saw that my antagonist felt it and smiled a ghastly smile of triumph.

"Presently I saw him reach forth his hand and grasp a bright hatchet. Even in this extremity I noticed that the hatchet was new and apparently unused, with glittering head and white polished handle. I made one more tremendous fight for life; for a second I held my enemy powerless, and saw with such a thrill of delight as I cannot forget the horror-stricken faces of friends, within a rod of us, rushing to my rescue. As the foremost of them sprang upon the back of my antagonist he wrenched his wrist away from me. I saw the hatchet flash above my head, and felt instantly a dull blow on the forehead.

"I fell back on the ground, a numbness spread from my head over my body, a warm liquid flowed down upon face and into my mouth, and I remember the taste was of blood, and my 'limbs were loosed.'

"Then I thought I was suspended in the air a few feet above my body. I could see myself as if in a glass, lying on the back, the hatchet sticking in the head, and the ghastliness of death gradually spreading over the face. I noticed especially that the wound made by the hatchet was in the centre of the forehead, at right angles to and divided equally by the line of the hair. I heard the weeping of friends, at first loud then growing fainter, fading away into silence. A delightful sensation of sweet repose without a feeling of fatigue —precisely like that which I experienced years ago at Cape May, when beginning to drown—crept over me. I heard exquisite music; the air was full of rare perfumes; I sank upon a bed of downy soft- ness—when, with a start, I awoke. The fire still smouldered in the grate; my watch told me I had not been more than half an hour asleep.

"Early the next morning I joined an intimate friend, with whom I spent much of my time, to accompany him, as was my daily custom, to the Law School. We talked for a moment of various topics, when suddenly he interrupted me with the remark that he had dreamed strangely of me the night before.

"'Tell me,' I asked; 'what was it?'

"'I fell asleep,' he said, 'about twelve, and immediately dreamed that I was passing through a narrow street, when I heard noises and

cries of murder. Hurrying in the direction of the noise, I saw you
lying on your back fighting with a rough laboring man, who held
you down. I rushed forward, but as I reached you he struck you
on the head with a hatchet, and killed you instantly. Many of our
friends were there, and we cried bitterly. In a moment I awoke,
and so vivid had been my dream that my cheeks were wet with tears.'

"'What sort of man was he?' I asked.

"'A thick-set man, in a flannel shirt and rough trousers: his hair
was uncombed, and his beard was grizzly and of a few days' growth.'

"Within a week I was in Burlington, New Jersey. I called at a
friend's house.

"'My husband,' said his wife to me, 'had such a horrid dream
about you the other night. He dreamed that a man killed you in a
street fight. He ran to help you, but before he reached the spot your
enemy had killed you with a great club.'

"'Oh, no,' cried the husband across the room; 'he killed you with
a hatchet.'

"These are the circumstances as I recall them. I remembered
the remark of old Artaphernes, that dreams are often the result of a
train of thought started by conversation or reading, or the incidents
of the working time, but I could recall nothing, nor could either of
my friends cite any circumstance 'that ever they had read, had ever
heard by tale or history,' in which they could trace the origin of this
remarkable dream.

"I am, dear sir, very truly yours,
"Henry Armitt Brown.

"P.S.—I may add that these friends of mine were personally unknown to each other.

"The first one, in New York, dreamed that he was the foremost
who reached the scene, the other that he was one of the number who
followed; both of which points coincided with my own dream."

Mr. Brown resumed his study of the law in the office
of Daniel Dougherty, Esq., of Philadelphia, and was
admitted to the bar as an attorney in the District Court
of Common Pleas, December 18, 1869. According to a
note of congratulation from Mr. Dougherty, "he passed
the best examination of all those who applied at that time."

He devoted himself faithfully to his legal studies; but in April, 1870, he went again to Europe, in company with William P. Pepper, Esq., and travelled through Sweden, Norway, and Russia, countries left unvisited in his former trip, returning home the following November. In Russia the constant society of his friend, Eugene Schuyler, Esq., not only added to his pleasure but his profit as a traveller. While absent he wrote several letters to the *Philadelphia Press*. These letters show descriptive power without any clap-trap. He gives in one of them an account of "The Derby Day" of 1870:

"A thousand notorieties around. There is the famous turfite So-and-so, and yonder the celebrated jockey who won the Derby of such a year. That man in a white hat and a gray coat, with a field-glass hung over his shoulder, who gesticulates so violently to a circle of the sporting gentry, is Tom King. Every man about you is shouting to his companion. Fellows with bands on their hats, and books and pencils in their hands, are offering bets here and there in all directions. On the stand above you a number of ladies have already taken their seats, and are gazing down upon the crowd with interested faces, hushed into silence by the confusion and wild disorder. There is royalty close by you, for in that corner of the box of the Jockey Club the King of the Belgians is chatting with the Prince of Wales. But you turn suddenly from royalty as you hear some one exclaim, 'Look, there's Gladstone!' and recognize in the box above you, in the tallest of the three men who have just entered, the strong, grand, thoughtful face of the prime minister. It is whispered that he was never before seen at a race, and thousands of curious eyes are fixed upon him."

While battling about in the English Channel, he thinks that, though a hundred recipes and drinks have been invented, "there is no cure for sea-sickness like smooth water." In one of his letters from Northern Europe he gives a bit of description of Swedish scenery on the ride towards Stockholm:

"Frederickshall lies between two lofty hills at the mouth of a little river that pours into the sea. From it to a point in Sweden called Strand a new road has just been opened through a lovely country. We started in carioles early in the afternoon. The cariole has been often enough described to me, and it answers perfectly the description. For the first hour or two the motion was dreadful, especially when we had to go slowly. You sit in a sort of leather box hung between two long springing shafts, and when the horse walks or trots slowly you are tumbled up and down, this side and that, all at once. When he goes rapidly and down-hill, or fairly runs, the motion is more regular and your misery less acute. However, in the course of a few hours' driving the disagreeableness disappears, and I fancy that cariole driving may become with practice easy, just as camel riding in the East. One could hardly imagine a more picturesque road than that which leads from Frederickshall to Strand. For a time it follows the rocky banks of the torrent which meets the sea at Frederickshall, and then turning aside between two lofty hills descends to the banks of an exquisite lake, in the bosom of which lie twenty bright green islets. Now it winds around the shoulder of a rugged hill, and again sweeps down into a peaceful valley filled with fields of grain, and then, as if tired of civilization, plunges suddenly into the depths of a dark forest. On every side gigantic trees of great girth interlace their dark branches, wrapped in a drapery of moss that clings about them and sweeps upon the ground, till they look like ghosts of the old demi-gods, clad in the mouldering garments of the grave, shaking their hoary arms threateningly at the adventurous traveller who dares invade their solitude. Deeper and deeper your narrow path winds into the forest. Great rocks lie scattered around, and the thick branches overhead make a perpetual twilight. Suddenly the scene changes. You come out upon the shores of a little lake, and a flock of ducks rise in haste and fly off with loud whistling of their wings. You have left the whispering pines and the hemlocks, and the bright sunlight shines down upon the dusty road. So the scene changes again and again until you have passed the lovely lakes and begin to descend into a valley, in which, by the shore of an eleventh one, you see the smoke rising from the smoke-stack of a steamer. Here you bid adieu to your cariole."

In another letter there is a sunny picture of Elsinore:

"One of the loveliest spots in all Europe is certainly Elsinore. The sun was shining brightly on the old castle, and the blue sea was whitened with sails. The coast of Sweden, wooded to the very shore, with here and there the towers of a chateau peeping above the trees, looked smilingly across the narrow straits, and on the Danish side the white beach with a strip of meadow, and then tall banks, waving with their dark-green trees, stretched from the town far away northward. Kronberg is a fine old pile with pointed towers, and, standing on the point where the straits are narrowest, looms up imposingly, especially when looked at from the sea. But that which fills the mind at the mention of Elsinore is not the old castle, nor the older town, nor the beautiful streets, nor the enchanting picture of land, sea, and sky. At first I was disposed to be merry with the Hamlet idea, and sent a servant to inquire if the Lord Hamlet was within. One fellow had never heard of his lordship, but his more learned comrade answered that he was dead and buried in the rear of the hotel. But the very air of Elsinore fills you with thoughts of the sweet prince. I thought and dreamed and talked of Hamlet, until I felt like a walking edition of the play bound in cloth. How easy to imagine that yonder orchard, sloping to the sea, was the scene where the old king was sleeping, his 'custom alway of the afternoon,' or that in the church-yard close by occurred the stormy meeting with Laertes; and I found it hard to realize, as I looked out that night to where the moon, struggling with the clouds, touched with silver the castle battlements, that it was not upon that very platform, on just such a night, that Hamlet trembled before the apparition of his father."

He speaks of the pleasing character of the voyage from Stockholm to St. Petersburg, descending the river-like gulf with its countless islands, until you emerge into the Baltic and soon enter the archipelago, which, under the name of the Aland Islands, stretches almost continuously from the Swedish to the Finnish coast. In Russia he visited Moscow and Nijni-Novgorod, giving crisp touches of life as well as of scenery:

"The hotter the weather the more the Russian clothes himself. Even the boys go about muffled in heavy coats, and at noon on the warmest day, when the heat is intense, the Russian is to be seen on the open squares of St. Petersburg wrapped in his enormous overcoat. He is much more indulgent to his legs, for they are often clad in white linen trousers, the effect of which, peeping beneath a heavy overcoat, is rather odd, and gives the appearance of a figure draped to illustrate the changes of the seasons, with midwinter about the body and midsummer at the extremities.

"Had the famous tea of Boston been Russian 'chai,' brought overland instead of being tossed half a year on the ocean, our forefathers, who threw it into the harbor, would have been patriots indeed! Perhaps they thought the sacrifice enough as it was, though 'they fought and bled and died' without having known the purpose for which tea was created. In Russia it is no thin watery liquid, pale with milk or cream, handed about in tiny cups to be sipped by gossiping lips; it is a rich, clear amber, poured while boiling hot into tall tumblers of thin glass, and delicately sweetened. It is the Russian beverage day and night, and everywhere you find it of the best.

"But the most interesting spot, and the first sought by the stranger, is Mont Plaisir, where the great Peter died. It is a little low villa, consisting of a large hall, with a row of small chambers on either side. It stands on a terrace, close by the water's edge, and it was while watching the bay with his spy-glass from the terrace that the Czar saw a boat in trouble, and hastening to the rescue caught the cold that cost him his life. He died in a little room opening out of the great hall. Behind a tall screen is the iron bedstead on which he breathed his last; the sheets and pillow lie upon it, and his faded silk dressing-gown is folded at the foot. His slippers are on the floor close by, and everything is preserved as it was on the day of his death."

At the famous fair of Nijni-Novgorod he seemed to think that it was indeed a great "sell," since things of no value were exposed for sale as well as valuables; that it was "a matter of degrees," as the French judge said to Dumas when the latter was hesitating to describe himself as a dramatic author. He pictures one old fellow, "bearded, venerable, and indescribably dirty, sitting in the sun by a piece of old cloth, on which a few rags, some broken glasses, and an ancient newspaper or two were tastefully arranged for sale. I may do his stock injustice,—there might have been a nail or two."

Upon Mr. Brown's second return home he settled himself down to his professional studies. He shook off the slight *dilettantism*, which was the mingled product of a fondness for society and the cherishing, in a time of life betwixt the ideal and the actual, of something of a Hamlet-like spirit of thoughtful inaction, or "scruple of thinking too precisely on the event." He was a dreamer, though an earnest one. As in college, while ever pondering it, he had not found his work. He had not heard the bugle-call. He talked of the "*palmam non sine pulvere*," but he did not descend into the dust of the strife. The associations of early years clung about him, and he was more of a loiterer in those green imaginative meads than a laborer in the real field. But he was ready to do whatever was congenial to him. He became greatly interested in the organization of the Yale Alumni Club of Philadelphia, in 1871, of whose executive committee he was a most executive secretary, writing, speaking, and laboring in every way for it; and to the end of his life he was one of its most efficient members, diffusing much of his enthusiasm into this and other similar associations which were founded one after another throughout the country. He frequently spoke in his neat, sensible, but modest style at the dinners given in Philadelphia, New York, and other cities; and when he did not speak, he sang, or rather, furnished the songs.

This leads us to notice a more extended flight of his muse in the poem delivered at Providence, Rhode Island, before the Thirty-eighth Annual Convention of the Psi

Upsilon Fraternity, held with the Sigma Chapter of Brown University. This was, perhaps, his best poetic effort. It is bright and pure, as everything he did was. It is musical, and deals with difficult metres such as young poets are apt to mesh themselves in, with an easy mastery of rhythm. It is well conceived, too, and has a more earnest ring than anything heretofore. It awakes a faint recollection of Edgar Poe's "Raven" in its changing melody, its vague and fanciful plot. It won a kindly word from Bret Harte, who pronounced it "clever," as well as praise from others, which he valued not less.

Among the many institutions of a highly cultivated and literary city like Philadelphia, there is none more quaint than the "Shakspeare Society," which, it is enough to say, numbers among its members Horace Howard Furness, Esq., editor of the New Variorum edition of Shakspeare. Meeting together in an upper room, hung around with historical pictures, and provided amply with the best Shakspearian editions, dictionaries, and commentaries, this truly "worshipfull societie" (mostly composed of lawyers) do excellent work, which, it is to be hoped, will not all be lost and "turne to ashes" with the smoke of their pipes. Mr. Brown was an active member of this club, and the thorough philologic drill of these critical evenings in contact with Shakspeare did his style no injury. It grew more Saxon, nervous, and idiomatic. The influence of his study of Shakspeare, as well as of Horace, after leaving college, is perceptible in its power upon his oratory, giving it elegant finish, condensation, and tactical dexterity in dealing with mind. At the annual dinner of the society, 26th of April, upon the birthday of "*Gulielmus Filius Johannes Shakspere*," his hand is seen in the culling of choice citations, like spicy flowers, from that portion of the bard's works which had been studied during the preceding winter.

> " The yearely course that brings this day about,
> Shall never see it, but a holy day."

Leaving these lighter intellectual excursions, wholesome as well as pleasant though they may have been, we come to the professional and legal period of Mr. Brown's life. He buckled himself to his work in right man-fashion. We find his name in the courts doing the tasks and the drudgery that usually fall to the lot of the young attorney. He had begun to appreciate the sensible words of another: "Of all the work that produces results, nine-tenths must be drudgery. There is no work, from the highest to the lowest, which can be done well by any man who is unwilling to make that sacrifice. Part of the very nobility of the devotion of the true workman to his work consists in the fact that a man is not daunted by finding that drudgery must be done; and no man can really succeed in any walk of life without a good deal of what in ordinary English is called pluck. That is the condition of all work whatever, and it is the condition of all success. Lawyers acquire the faculty of resolutely applying their minds to the driest documents with tenacity enough to end in the perfect mastery of their contents; a feat which is utterly beyond the capacity of any undisciplined intellect, however gifted by nature." He plodded patiently through the " briefless" desert that leads to the Promised Land. He, however, acquitted himself with credit whenever an opportunity came for him to speak as junior counsel in the conduct of cases. Thus, in the trial of his first murder case, before the Oyer and Terminer Court, in the month of April, 1871, he showed, for a young man, according to the testimony of the legal gentlemen engaged, uncommon ability and acumen. It was a case of identification. There was some variation in the evidence, which was skilfully seized upon and made use of by the defence. Mr. Brown's conduct of the case, as well as that of his colleague, were complimented highly by the opposing counsel for the Commonwealth, and were characterized as "worthy of older practitioners"; and this was said in reference to notably shrewd Philadelphia lawyers, to each of whom, doubtless, the words of Juvenal would apply:

"Qui juris nodos et legum ænigmata solvat."

In the report of the case, the close of Mr. Brown's argument was characterized as "affecting, and was listened to with marked attention." His admirable conduct of the case and his strong speech doubtless saved the man. After this Mr. Brown was engaged from time to time in criminal and other cases of more or less importance, always acquitting himself well and giving his best efforts to his work. Whether, if he had lived longer, he would have come under the category mentioned by Rufus Choate that "case-losing lawyers would have no cases to lose" we know not, but he assuredly made an uncommonly successful beginning, and awakened high hopes of future eminence at the bar. One public speech of his deserves fuller notice, as bringing him at once into prominence in the profession as a man of brilliant oratorical powers.

On the 19th of December, 1872, a complimentary dinner was given at the Continental Hotel, by the Philadelphia Bar, to the Hon. ex-Chief-Justice Thompson. There was a very large assembly of the bar, and of the judges of the various courts. The best legal talent of the city was represented. The guests numbered some three hundred. It was, in fact, one of the most marked and impressive occasions of the kind which had ever taken place in the city. Peter McCall, Esq., who presided, responded to the first regular toast, and was followed by Chief-Justice Read, Hon. George W. Woodward, Hon. Morton McMichael, and many other distinguished gentlemen. While the speeches now and then scintillated with humor, they were mostly solid addresses, befitting the dignified and thoroughly professional character of the occasion. The eighth and last regular toast of the evening was:

"The Juniors of the Bar."
—"illi turba Clientium
Sit major."—*Hor. Od.*

"We are all engaged in the same ministry,—we are one brotherhood,—members of one common profession, of which we have a right to be proud."—*Mr. Justice Sharswood, Bar Dinner*, 1867.

"Et vosmetipsos sic eruditos ostendite, ut spes vos pulcherrima foveat, toto legitimo opere perfecto, posse etiam nostram rempublicam in partibus ejus vobis credendis gubernari."—*Just. Proem.*

This was responded to by Henry Armitt Brown, Esq., in the following words:

"Mr. President,—Somewhere in the varied reading of a boyhood, from which, as you have no doubt observed, I have but recently emerged, I remember to have found an anecdote of the elephant. In a truthful work, compiled by a philanthropic lady, called 'Anecdotes of Animals,' you will find it somewhere written that it is the habit of those sagacious brutes, when they come to a deep and rapid river, to send over first the smallest of the herd, assured that if he ford it in safety the largest may attempt the crossing without inconvenience or danger. To-night, sir, you have reversed this proceeding. One by one the leaders of this company have passed this current of good-fellowship with firm footsteps and majestic tread, and now, safe upon the other side, you summon to the crossing the smallest of you all, that from your places of ease and security you may enjoy his flounderings. I represent that portion of the Junior Bar which may be called the " great unemployed." I speak for those unfortunates to whom, thus far, the law has seemed less of a *practice* than of a *profession.* I am well aware, sir, that in the early days of our seniors at the bar things were quite different. I am credibly informed that in their time the client did the waiting, not the lawyer. When they had crammed into two years the work of seven,—when they had skimmed through such text-books as chance and their in-clinations had suggested,—when they had satisfied the inquiring minds of the board of examiners as to the action of assumpsit or the estate in fee-simple,—they doubtless found an impatient *turba client-ium* awaiting their coming from the examination-room, burning to seek their counsel and cram their pockets with glittering fees. The times are changed; clients are changed, and we have fallen on de-generate days. We sit long years in solitude. Like Mariana, in the moated grange, 'He cometh not, she said.' Day follows day, and months run into years. No tender-hearted corporation is moved by our condition; hardly an assault and battery attacks our leisure; rarely does even the voice of the defendant in an action for slander startle the stillness of our lives. And we are often condemned to the experience of Tantalus. One sees a stream of clients pour into the office of a friend near by; another is kept in a chronic anxiety by the knock of prosperous-looking laymen, who mistake his office for another man's; while a third finds it part of his daily trial to see the most promising processions in full march for his office diverted from their purpose and turned aside by the wickedly enticing wide-open doors of an envious neighboring savings-fund. Thus, sir, we seem doomed to sit solitary and alone, while our offices, like the unhappy country of the patriotic Irishman, 'literally swarm with absentees.' But we are not altogether without hope. The flower that is born to blush unseen may cherish in its petals the hope of being plucked by rosy fingers; the gem of purest ray may still expect to glitter on the broad shirt front of some prosperous capitalist. I have seen it re-cently asserted, on no less an authority than a daily evening news-paper, that it is in the nature of mankind to hope. Shall we despair? There may be those among us to whom dulness is not dreary nor idleness irksome. There may be in our midst mental dyspeptics, of whom some one has wittily said 'that they devour many books and can digest none.' We may have among us ingenuous youths like the

New York law student who thought the feudal system was lands, tenements, and hereditaments, and originated in New York City; or when asked whether a husband's infidelity was a ground for divorce, did not exactly comprehend the question, and begged to ask, 'Am I to understand by that word "infidelity" that the husband of the woman denied the existence of a Supreme Being?' We may be good and bad, yet there are brains among us that will be working, and tongues that will not rest forever dumb. In the solitude of our offices,—a solitude broken only by the visits of men rightly termed men of assurance, who seek unselfishly to induce us to lay up treasures beyond the grave, or by those of beggars, whose theory seems to hold that the office of the youthful lawyer is the chosen abode of that charity which is kind, no matter how much or how long it suffereth,—in that rarely invaded solitude we are nursing hope. Do we not right, sir, as we sit there without even the memory of a client with which to people our cane-bottomed chairs, to dream of knots that may need our untying, of shadowy corporations of the future seeking for counsel, of railroads not yet enjoined? May we not expect the day when the tread of the client will resound through the entry, and his voice clamor for admittance at the door, when we, too, jostled by a *turba clientium maxima*, shall sally forth into the forum to argue points yet undreamed of, and puzzle jurors yet unborn?

" But if it be a long time before we become entitled to the duties and responsibilities of our profession, to some of its privileges we are admitted at once. From the moment of our adoption into its ranks we are made to feel the influence of that fraternal feeling which is one of the chief glories of the Philadelphia Bar. We feel it everywhere, at all times,—in the forbearance of the elders; in the respect of equals; in the veneration of the young. It is proof against all attacks, and survives the bitterness of every contention. I see around me men who were yesterday, and perhaps will be to-morrow, arrayed against each other in intellectual combat. The passions of the fight have vanished; the heaviest blow has made no bruise; the fiercest thrust has left no scar. And here, where the united bar has assembled to honor one whose learning and character has so long added strength and lustre to his great office,—here among the leaders of the bar, even the youngest feel that there is room for them. And following in their turn, they too may press forward to lay at his feet their tribute of veneration and respect.

"In the words of another honored guest, whose courtesy and thoughtfulness and unfailing kindness have done so much to impress upon the juniors of the bar their sincerity and truth,—in your words, sir, fitly quoted here, 'We are one brotherhood.' Old and young alike. Yoked in the same ministry, cherishing the same traditions, inheriting the same history, taught by the same examples! Long may Providence preserve those honored lives! Long may you both shed the light of living examples on your younger brethren! Long may you taste the reward of your labor in the calm enjoyment of completed fame! *Vivite felices quibus est fortuna peracta!*

"The years are fleeting; and on us, in our turn, must fall the responsibilities and trusts of life. Then when time shall have made us stronger, and suffering more patient, if we have been earnest in endeavor, firm in purpose, honest in emulation, true to our exemplars and ourselves, the bar that has so often found them in the generations of yesterday and to-day may not search hopelessly among her servants of to-morrow for the skill, the learning, the eloquence, the strict integrity, the calm devotion to his threefold duty which make the perfect lawyer; nor our Republic seek in vain among her younger children for that broad and generous statesmanship which embraces all humanity, is firm, benevolent, consistent, which, lifted above the passions of the hour, acts not for to-day but for all time,—tried though it may be by both extremes of fortune, still stands four-square to all the winds that blow.

"I am but one in this company, and stand on the threshold of professional life. I am altogether unworthy to speak for my brethren of the younger bar, and yet, to-night, I feel their hearts beating with my heart, and hear their voices ring in mine, bidding me tell you that we seek no higher glory and cherish no loftier ambition than to tread worthily in the footsteps of our fathers, and at the end of lives of usefulness, and it may be of honor, to hand down unspotted and unstained the institutions they committed to our care into the keeping of their children's children's sons."

There had been some slight astonishment expressed, and perhaps a little touch of prejudice excited, by the announcement of Mr. Brown's name as one to fill this, in some respects, responsible position; and this might very naturally be accounted for from the fact that he was so recent a member of the bar, and as yet comparatively unknown. But all such feelings were dispelled like mists the instant the clear and calm tones of his exquisitely finished elocution fell upon the ear. The modesty, the manliness, the wit, the good sense, and the elevated closing sentences of the address confirmed the good impression made, and there was but one opinion, most enthusiastically expressed, as to its merit. Although coming at the end of a long and exhausting evening of speaking, it was listened to with absolute delight. The *Legal Gazette* of December 27, 1872, in noticing the bar dinner, remarked: "The last-named gentleman (Henry Armitt Brown), in response to the toast, "The Juniors of the Bar," made an excellent and appropriate speech, reflecting credit not only upon himself, but the young members of the bar in general. It was decidedly one of the best speeches of the evening." Another paper (*The Legal Intelligencer*) said: "The effort was an able one, and during its delivery received the attention of every person in the room." The *Public Ledger*, of Philadelphia, characterized it as "one of the most marked orations of the evening, calling forth from the seniors as well as the juniors the heartiest applause." The *London* (England) *Law Times*, of February 15, 1873, thought the lesson of the speech, as commented upon by the *Pittsburgh* (Ohio) *Legal Gazette*, "would be a lesson that should be taken to heart by the junior bar of England." One of the young lawyers present wrote a note on the spot to a member of his family, containing these warm words of praise: "I cannot go to bed without writing a line to tell you what a triumph Harry has had. There has been no speech in my time, by a Philadelphia lawyer, that has made the impression his did to-night. His audience, to a large extent, had to be *conciliated*, and, what was worse, he knew it; but he conquered every prejudice, and when he finished there was not one dissenting voice. A more perfect and complete success was never achieved by any orator, and it was the best men of the bar who were the loudest in his praise." In fact, it was discovered that he could speak.

This discovery that Henry Armitt Brown could speak was not a new one to many. In the Municipal Reform Association of Philadelphia, which had been established previously during this same year, he had already taken an active part, which involved much public speaking, and of a kind to test a man's metal,—but before alluding to this a word should be said of his entrance on the field of popular lecturing. It came about in a natural way, and from a wish to help on good objects. His first lecture, " Hundred-Gated Thebes" (one of a course of four lectures), was originally delivered for the aid of a benevolent enterprise, and was heard by large audiences in Philadelphia, Burlington, and many other places within and without the State. One of the notices of this lecture, in the *Daily Miner's Journal*, ·Pottsville, December 31, 1872, falls into an amusing error about his antecedents: " A fine audience assembled last evening at Union Hall to hear Mr. Brown, son of the late David Paul Brown, Esq.,* who is a rising young lawyer of Philadelphia, and who was requested by Daniel Dougherty, Esq., to come up and fill his engagement to lecture,—Mr. Dougherty being too unwell to come. Mr. Brown's subject was 'Thebes,' and for nearly two hours the lecturer held his audience absorbed and interested in it and his delightful delivery. He is a fine speaker, superior even to his father in his palmiest days."

* It is hardly necessary to state that David Paul Brown was a Philadelphia lawyer of celebrity, especially in criminal cases. He was born in 1795 and died 1872.

Mr. Brown prepared other travel lectures, with the titles of "A Pilgrimage to Jerusalem," "From Dan to Beersheba," "On the Acropolis"; and he delivered them first in the chapel in the rear of St. Andrew's Church, and afterwards at other places. In these performances he showed marked descriptive power and mother wit, but his mind was an earnest one, his imagination kindled at solemn themes, and the thoughtful aspects of his semi-poetic topics were not set aside for sensational effect or mere amusement. He would have risen to the first rank in the popular esteem had he followed out this career. He had every qualification for it, and would have rivalled the most shining names in this field. As it was, he generally spoke for some philanthropic object, and he went upon the principle, Touch the feelings and you touch the pocket; arouse the imagination and you ennoble and enlarge the sympathies. But there was something better than this for him.

Since the days of old Rome great cities have been centres of power and also of corruption. They form in themselves political units. Immense social forces are concentrated in them. The municipal privileges possessed by corporations, having at their control large revenues and extensive patronage, are strained to the utmost. The irresponsibility of corporate powers presents a temptation to extortion from the taxpayer. The taxpayer suffers from the immunity of the tax-maker. It does not much matter what political party is dominant, and unless there is honesty somewhere, and honesty of the most fearless and independent sort, there is apt to be outrageous abuse of political power. Such a state of things leads to the most monstrous frauds and rapacities. The desperate contest in the city of New York, which cannot soon be forgot, differed in some of its phases and in its gigantic proportions from that in Philadelphia, which city not long before had been declared by good authority to be " the best governed in the Union, and whose local legislators were distinguished for their integrity and devotion to duty," but in its main aspects the conflict was the same in Philadelphia as in New York, and was none the less needful, determined, and bitter. Those who demanded reform were confined to no class of society or shade of political sentiment. The vast power of " Municipal Rings" demanded the most extraordinary efforts to bring about their overthrow.

The call for a change in the methods of political action in the city of Philadelphia culminated at the beginning of the year 1872 in the formation of a Citizens' Municipal Reform Association, with ward organizations and central committees. The principles of the association struck at the root of political abuse, viz.: the matter of the purity of elections. They declared that important offices should be in the hands of trustworthy men of whatever party. To prove the unselfishness of their motives they pledged themselves not to hold office or to be candidates for office. They meant to do thorough work. It was a dispassionate movement made at a time when there was no great political excitement, and in a lull between the national elections. The association embraced principles like these : a non-partisan registry law; salaries and not fees; no interference of the Legislature in local affairs; an examination by the people into the city departments to learn where their money goes; public officers to be the servants not the masters of their constituents; a determined and continuous opposition to all rings and corrupt politicians of both parties; and a devotion to the best interests of the whole city of Philadelphia and the Commonwealth of Pennsylvania.

From the earliest beginning of this Reform movement Mr. Brown identified himself with it. His moulding hand is seen in all its principles and acts. His energizing spirit constantly urged it on. In fact, he had found something to do worthy of him. This was a real evil to attack. It was a work that called for strong men. He was fairly woke up. We date his public life and his public greatness from this moment. He was obliged to enter the fight with able, but in some instances uncongenial, allies. He did not shrink from any fastidious feeling of this sort. He was willing to endanger his own political reputation and chances. He struck hands with all who were resolved on purifying city politics, cost what it might. He threw his whole force into this agitation. He was the life of it while his connection with it lasted, which was essentially to the end of his life. He was active in organizing the different ward associations. He was a frequent and fearless speaker in all parts of the city. He and his associates had to contend with formidable foes, and with those elements of unprincipled force to be found only in great cities, and nowhere more reckless and ruffian than in Philadelphia. He sometimes spoke when missiles flew, but he calmed the excited crowds with a word. His self-possession was perfect. The tones of his voice exerted a wonderfully soothing influence, and he was never seriously interrupted. In one great mass-meeting in West Philadelphia he was the first speaker. He charged that outrageous abuses existed in the city government; he declared that the time had come for radical reform; he affirmed that the men then in office had sought their places hampered and tied by promises with which their nominations were bought, and that they wrongfully administered the offices to which they were chosen. He boldly dissected

the characters of office-holders. He exhibited a power of
rapid character-analysis. It was the clean and fatal rapier
thrust. He said the severest things without coarseness or
harshness. He said what every one felt to be true. Whenever a political demagogue fell writhing under his thrust,
as boys say, "he did not know what hurt him"; but it was
simply truth spoken in the keenest manner. He did not
appeal to men's passions, but to the best that was in them.
His style was eminently "sweetness and light," the per-
suasiveness of a consciously honest soul. While he could
be scathingly sarcastic, his real sweetness rarely permitted
him to be so. He preferred the weapons of truth and
calmness. "The gentle mind by gentle deeds is known."
Some of his colleagues were noble idealists; others were
ennobled by the idea of reform; but there was no one
who was more thoroughly, unselfishly, and practically a
reformer than himself. By the testimony of his friends in
this struggle no one felt what he was doing more deeply
than himself. He acted on his convictions of duty. He
thus rose up at once to be a leader. Everybody recognized
him as such. One of his colleagues said, "He was worth
a whole army corps to the cause." He gave no pledges;
he resorted to no partisan tricks. If he aspired to political
leadership he scorned political office. His speeches grew
more and more weighty. At first with reluctance, but
then with delight and an ever-increasing sense of power,
he took up, at the request of one of his friends who saw
what there was in him, the practice of extemporaneous
speaking. He came to like it immensely, to grow easy
under its difficulties, and to rejoice in its freedom. His
voice, action, and thought adapted themselves readily to
this change of style, and many a crowded and turbulent
assembly acknowledged the sway of his off-hand address

and cool, finished elocution. By this means he acquired something of the gladiatorial power of Wendell Phillips and other reform speakers, of meeting the changing exigencies of assemblies, and of prompt repartee. He said of a political and notably self-opinionated opponent, who on one occasion was accused by a speaker of his own party of being an "infidel": "An infidel,—not so; he is a self-made man, and he worships his creator."

He has been blamed for acting at times against Republican nominees and the Republican party, while he was himself an avowed Republican. His aim was higher than party. He might have answered in the words put in the mouth of Savonarola by the author of Romola: "The cause of freedom, which is the cause of God's kingdom upon earth, is often most injured by those who carry within them the power of certain human virtues. The wickedest man is often not the most insurmountable obstacle to the triumph of good."

But there was a new field beginning to present itself to his claims and oratorical powers, which served for a time to draw off his attention, though not his heart, from the cause of municipal reform,—it was the opening Centennial epoch of memorializing the great events of the country's history. From his intense love of the past and of the memory of his ancestors, he had always been drawn to historical studies; and he had the qualities of an historian, patience in original research, love of exact statement, the imagination which comprehends and clothes the past in life, and a picturesque style; and if he had become tired of political life, it is the opinion of friends who knew him best that he would have devoted himself, as he often talked of doing, to historical investigations. The splendid career of Motley attracted him, as it has other young men; and, to our own knowledge, for some time after leaving college, he was casting about for a fit theme of an historical nature to which to devote his attention.

There were two occasions of a more or less historic character that led his mind naturally to take a vivid interest in the Centennial campaign that followed. The first of these was an anniversary meeting of the Lincoln Institution, established for the children of those who had fallen in the civil war, which was held January 17, 1873. Mr. Brown was called upon to speak in memory of Major-General George G. Meade, the recent president of the institution, who had died a short time previous. The closing sentences of this address were as follows:

"I think not of Meade as the gallant officer stemming the tide of disaster at Seven Pines or Gaines's Mill, nor as the skilful general driving his routed foe from Gettysburg, but rather as that quiet, self-contained man, who, in the stillness of his tent, received the order that made him commander of a demoralized army wearied with forced marches, to overtake, on its own soil, its triumphant enemies, and took up the burden without a murmur. I think of him in the last years of his well-spent life, not as the laurel-crowned hero of a tremendous victory, but as the patriotic citizen moving in our midst without ostentation or display, respected, honored, and beloved. And to-day, speaking of him in this place, I love to picture him as one in whose heart charity had found a refuge, who 'comforted the widow and the fatherless, and kept himself unspotted from the world.'"

The second occasion to which we allude was the great mass-meeting held on the 19th of April, 1873, at the Academy of Music, under the auspices of the Women's Centennial Committee. This was the opening gun of the Centennial Exposition campaign in Philadelphia, which afterwards filled the world with its rumor. The vast assemblage on this occasion was called to order by Mr.

John Welsh. The venerable Eli K. Price, a representative of one of the oldest Quaker families of Philadelphia, presided. Mr. Brown was the first speaker. His remarks were brief but pertinent, and applause greeted the conclusion of his speech. The *Philadelphia Press*, in a notice of the prominent addresses of the evening, says: "The speeches of Henry Armitt Brown and Daniel Dougherty were finished orations. Mr. Brown is young in our legal public circles, but will live to an old future, judged by his present promise. Mr. Dougherty is always young in heart; and it was pleasant to see that the ripening mind, while it gives him wisdom, does not moderate his love of country. These two really fine orators made some striking points, and in style and ideas they made a capital aggregate. What they said will be remembered, as it ought to be. Brown starts out as a more quiet rhetorician, a sort of young-old man, and Dougherty, after two decades of impulsive public speaking, adorns middle life as the teacher of a highly chastened style. In the audience sat two great-granddaughters of Benjamin Franklin,—Mrs. Gillespie, chairman of the Ladies' Centennial Committee of Thirteen, and Mrs. Emory, wife of General W. H. Emory, now in command of the Department of New Orleans. A fact like this shows how near we are to the Past; how close we stand to the leaders, inventors, and heroes who, by their wisdom, genius, and patriotism, gave and preserved us a nation."

There were other notices not so flattering. It was said that Brown's speech was too "fine" for a mass-meeting; that he was young and had a great deal to learn. This criticism caused amusement among his friends, since the meeting was simply a gathering in the Academy of Music of the prominent people of the city, and, in fact, the assembly was entirely lacking in the element which goes to make up mass-meetings generally. The *Catholic Herald*, while praising the address as "evincing culture," blamed his allusion to "liberated Italy," and said that the idea was a "stench in the nostrils of every Catholic." It may be that there was a grain of truth in the criticisms of his style. Mr. Brown's tendency was to elaboration and great carefulness in what he said on a set occasion, having conscientious fear lest he might not do full justice to his theme. He so prepared himself as to insure success, and perhaps sometimes over-prepared. But criticism was patiently received, and did him good. He never attempted to defend himself against criticism, but silently weighed its worth, and suffered it to have its corrective influence. He learned from his foes.

In the incessantly busy life which he now led, he had, to cheer him, a bright home-life. He was married December 7, 1871, to Miss Josephine Lea, daughter of John R. Baker, Esq., of Philadelphia,—a union of rare happiness and congeniality of mind. His house became a centre of hospitality seasoned with wit. His own companionable qualities, his literary culture and reading, his incomparable skill as a *raconteur*, not seeking to display himself but to give pleasure to others, made him sought for in the most influential circles; and where he was, though ever modest, he was sure to be the centre of conversation as naturally as a hearth-fire in winter draws around it all in the room. It was a heart-glow at which all warmed themselves. Like Tom Hood he could electrify a circle by his stories, his improvisations and humorous representations of character, transforming himself into Daniel Webster, Edwin Forrest, an Eastern Shore countryman at pleasure, or leading on to questions of political and public moment; and as he grew older the last predominated, and here was seen to be the treasury of subjects in which he had garnered up his inmost thoughts. He grew to be a nobler patriot with the growth of his reflective powers.

But the place where his soul dwelt, and shone, and glowed like a luminous lamp fed by odorous oil at midnight, where he gathered together all his wandering fancies without fear of criticism, was his own room in the upper part of his house. It is now just as he left it, with the same papers lying on the table where he last sat. It is a low-studded apartment immediately under the roof, and poorly lighted from without at mid-day. Heavy beams painted red, as in old English houses, run across the ceiling. Thick tapestry curtains hang before the windows, so that it is easy to exclude the daylight or to turn day into night. It was probably of these curtain-hangings that he wrote to his mother, then in Europe, " Be sure and send me some curtains that are mediæval, feudal, griffony, and dragony,—you know what I mean." In the wide-jambed fireplace the gaping chimney lets in a beam of outside sunshine upon a great bed of white ashes, wan relics of many a magnificent wood-fire whose flames danced upon the hearth and the uncouth fire-dogs. On the mantel-piece stand curiously-twisted brass candlesticks from Norway, bronze gods from Egypt, small marble obelisks, tall mugs of Bohemian glass with colored heraldic devices. Over these in the centre are suspended a Russian Byzantine painting of a long-bearded Greek saint, and on either side large photographs of the heads of Goethe and Rufus Choate; the last a gift from Mr. Choate's family through James T. Fields, Esq.,—a powerfully life-like portrait. A portrait of Shakspeare and a mask of Garrick (taken from the mask in the possession of the Garrick Club of London) occupy the right hand of the fireplace, and between them, wreathed with ivy, is hung an immense wooden spoon, trophy of college days. A big brass Norwegian kettle on a tripod of antique form stands near, and by its side next the wall is a long-cased clock. A sideboard, black with age and·highly carved, is filled with spoils of European travel. Three or four other carved Norwegian cabinets and chests stand in the room. A bronze cast of Napoleon's face after death, statuettes of Henry Clay and Daniel Webster, and many other small works of art occupy the shelf of the bookcase, which runs breast-high around the apartment. On the red-papered walls are large groups of palm leaves and brass sconces; in the corners are shields of family arms. The door is mounted with massive brass hinges and locks. Louis Quatorze high-backed and stamped leather-covered chairs stand around the room, which is carpeted with rugs and skins of different animals. Upon the writing-table stands a small but spirited bronze of William Pitt, taken from the statue erected in Hanover Square, London, and by its side lie a miniature edition of Shakspeare and a Bible. The last opens more readily than anywhere else to the Old Testament prophets, whose lofty imagery and burning sentences against national crimes formed his favorite reading. The library itself, for a young man's, is large and well selected, showing a manly taste. The books are chiefly historical and political. There are the standard works on Greek, Roman, Italian, French, English, and American history, the speeches of English statesmen and orators, various editions of Shakspeare, a good though small selection of Latin and Greek classics, the English poets, some of the French essayists, and some works on government, political economy, and industrial and social questions, together with his law library. In his last years his reading tended to a solid kind, and if he could not say precisely in the words of Frederick W. Robertson, "I read hard or not at all, never skimming, never turning aside to many inviting books; and Plato, Aristotle, Butler, Thucydides, Jonathan Edwards, have passed like the iron atoms of the blood into my mental constitution," yet he could speak of his real working years in much the same way. We do not claim for Mr. Brown that he was a "terrible worker" during all his intellectual life, but he was growing ever more and more severe in his tasks, jealous of his time, careful in the selection of his studies, self-denying and self-disciplining in his reading. He fed his mind upon substantial food, and perhaps he felt the necessity of making up deficiencies that would strengthen and consolidate all, and would make a firm foundation on which to build a statesmanlike superstructure. He was beginning to learn the lesson

> "Of labor, that in lasting fruit outgrows
> Far noisier schemes, accomplish'd in repose,
> Too great for haste, too high for rivalry." *

The question might be asked, How can a lawyer become a statesman? In Germany this is answered by the establishment of schools specially devoted to the sciences of government, of State-law, but in our own land a young man is compelled to make his way alone to something broader in political knowledge and life. By the prompting of his own genius, if at all, he is led to study the science of government, the government of towns and cities, and the practical working of these. He is led to study commerce in its multiform relations; manufactures and the various industries and arts that have a bearing upon the welfare of

---

* Matthew Arnold.

the people; political economy and financial questions in their practical as well as theoretical aspects; history, ancient and modern; religious systems and their influence upon popular character,—in fine, everything that has a direct relation to national interest. In this way, by independent effort, and by study directed to a high aim, he may expand himself from the professional type of man—the lawyer who is a man of precedents, and whose aims are personal—into the comprehensiveness of the public man and statesman. In fact, no book or school can teach this. Genius for such studies, original observation, and a tireless energy that leaves nothing unknown, nothing unexplained, —the energy of Charles Sumner, or of greater men, like Bismarck and Abraham Lincoln, the last of whom educated himself into a statesman from being a very narrowly-trained lawyer,—these are the pursuits and qualifications which, in the place of a more systematic European cultivation in statesmanship, go to educate the man who is to make laws and guide the State. Into this field of self-training for something larger and broader Mr. Brown was continually pressing with an intense earnestness,—but these matters and questions we must defer to a somewhat later period of his life.

The Centennial epoch had commenced. Philadelphia, as being the central point of the proposed national commemoration, was in the beginning of its excitement and stirring preparation. All Pennsylvania was to be aroused to share in this patriotic feeling and in the work of procuring funds for this colossal enterprise. Popular orators were sent out to all the chief country towns. It was a time of *flux de bouche,* but of all who spoke, none, we are of the opinion, had a truer idea of the importance of the opportunity to promote pure patriotic sentiments than

Henry Armitt Brown, as certainly no one more distinguished himself as a speaker than he during this fervid epoch. Speech was to be the Teucrian bow with which he defended the ships of his country's hopes and treasures from irreverent hands. He made one of his first addresses September 18, 1873, at the large town of Reading, Pennsylvania. It was an immense citizens' meeting to which over two hundred vice-presidents were chosen. The *Philadelphia Press* said of it: "At the Grand Opera House, H. Armitt Brown, of Philadelphia, delivered one of the best addresses on the Centennial enterprise heard this year."

The succeeding week he spoke to a great gathering of the people at Bethlehem, Pennsylvania, in the Moravian Day School Hall. He commenced his speech in these words:

"For the first time in my life it is my privilege to visit Bethlehem, and if I were here for any other object than that which has brought us together to-night, it might seem to me necessary to introduce myself to you with some words of apology or excuse. But when, as a Pennsylvanian, I come before Pennsylvanians; when, as an American, I am speaking to Americans, endeavoring as far as in me lies to arouse my countrymen to the discharge of a great patriotic duty, I feel that apology is unnecessary; I forget for the moment that I am a stranger; I seem to be at home looking into the faces of friends."

During the months of October and November, 1873, Mr. Brown delivered at various towns in Pennsylvania and Ohio an oration entitled "The Centennial, the Story of an Hundred Years." This address seemed to strike audiences differently. In one place it was pronounced tedious, and it was said of the speaker that while "his manner of delivery is attractive, his diction clear and faultless, and his whole appearance that of a true orator, yet he failed to comprehend his subject, and spoke more of the Centennial to be than of the Centennial that had been." In another place the prophetic feature in the speech was considered the most attractive one. The special character of this address may be gathered from a brief notice in an Ohio paper: "The speaker on the 'Story of an Hundred Years' dwelt particularly upon the past of our country's history, contrasting the beginning of this century with the ending; comparing our present standing as a nation, our wealth, prosperity, strength, and greatness as a people, with the weakness, poverty, and insignificance in the eyes of the nations of the earth, of the United States in 1776. For Mr. Brown, like all good Americans, counts the ending of the century *not* with an 18 and two unmeaning ciphers, but with the magic figures 76, and we believe inspired every hearer with a desire to live and see the true centennial of this government, and witness the consummation so long foreshadowed by the preparations of President and people for the grand ceremonial at Philadelphia in that year.* He had a worthy subject and fully did it justice. His manner is pleasing, his voice thrilling and in the heroic parts moves every heart; while, whether he be interested or not, he impresses all with the conviction that he is, and that every word is the inspiration of the moment. No monotonous repetition of an 'oft-repeated story' is suggested either by word or manner. His enemy, had he listened, would have been stung with envy, while his friend would have been made glad."

It is with oratory as with music, sometimes it raises and sometimes depresses our hearts. If men tell us what we are ready to receive they are eloquent. "Nothing," says a French author, "is so uncertain as eloquence."

New England was catching the Centennial enthusiasm.

---

* This was written in 1873.

There was the hundredth anniversary of the throwing overboard of the tea in Boston harbor to be celebrated on December 16, 1873. To this "Boston tea-party," given by the Boston ladies,—some of them lineal descendants of the "Mohawks" who did the deed,—Philadelphia was invited to send guests, and one of the two whom she chose was Mr. Brown. The celebration was held in Faneuil Hall, or, as Daniel Webster and the old-fashioned people used to call it,—and it would have been peculiarly appropriate for this occasion,—"Funnel Hall." The crowded assembly was addressed by Hon. Josiah Quincy, Hon. Robert C. Winthrop, Henry A. Brown and Frederick Fraley, of Philadelphia, Rev. Edward E. Hale, Hon. Thomas Russell, and Samuel M. Quincy, with a poem by Ralph Waldo Emerson. Amid these veteran speakers Mr. Brown seemed slender and untried, but he did nobly. He was Greek Glaucus among the old heavy-armed gladiators. He was introduced by the president, Mr. Quincy, in these words: "Boston does not stand alone in the controversy which the Tea-party aroused, and of all places most immediately connected with us was the largest city of our Union, as it then existed,—Philadelphia. The moment the act was done Boston sent Paul Revere to tell that the tea was in the water. We sent a messenger one hundred years ago; and though the Philadelphians are slow in some respects, they have now sent their representative after the lapse of a century."

Mr. Brown spoke as follows:

"LADIES AND GENTLEMEN,—A few days ago a stranger stood in the new museum in the State House at Philadelphia. Around him were the relics of colonial times and the portraits of our ancient kings, from Charles II. down to George III. Approaching him, a gentleman said, with courteous inquiry, 'You are a foreigner, sir?'

'Bless you,' was the reply, 'I am no foreigner; I am an Englishman.' [Laughter.] And in his spirit so I feel to-night, sir, though I stand for the first time in Faneuil Hall. I see about me no familiar countenance; I am in an unaccustomed place; I have journeyed far from home; and yet this is Boston, and this Faneuil Hall. Here hang the likenesses of men whose portraits since my childhood I have seen in Independence Hall,—John Hancock and John Adams, Samuel Adams and Elbridge Gerry (Robert Treat Paine is not there yet, though the place is waiting), and I feel that here at least I am no stranger. [Applause.] I rise in this presence and on this anniversary to speak to you the words of Philadelphia,—the fraternal greetings of your brethren assembled there. Would that the messenger were more worthy; would that there might come to me to-night a voice of fire—an inspiration born of the memories of this place—that I might drink in the spirit of this anniversary, and tell in fitting words the message which I bring! It is in keeping with your ancient kindly feeling for Philadelphians that you ask to hear from her to-night. Boston has heard her voice before; not only in 'piping times of peace,' of prosperity, of sunshine, but in days of doubt, and danger, and distress, of suffering, of trial, and of want. In season and out of season, in joy and sorrow, in peace and war, you have more than once turned to her for sympathy, and you have not found her wanting. When your fathers asked her help and counsel in the dark hours that preceded the great struggle, she sent them back no uncertain action. You protested against the stamp acts, and so did she; you destroyed the hateful tea, and when the news reached Philadelphia her inhabitants assembled to applaud your act, and, if need be, to follow your example. The sounds from Lexington roused her as well as you, and the story of your triumphant defeat on yonder heights awoke in Philadelphia an echo that shook her iron hills. She opened wide her arms to greet the great men whom you sent to her first Congress; and, when the British held Boston in their grasp, she heard the clanking of your chains, and that Congress, assembled in her State House, sent you Washington. [Applause.] As she was then she is to-day. Still, on her busiest street, stands the old State House,—preserved with pious care,—holding up, as this thrice-sacred building does, the old time and the new time face to face; and from its walls your great men, as well as hers, look down upon another spot made holy by their patriotism and virtue. There, in the centre of her busy life, lies Independence Square, its corners resting on her crowded highways, 'a sacred island in a tumultuous main;' close by she guards the relics of the dead—your own as well as hers—whom fate confided to the keeping of the land for which they died; and in her bosom there, to-day, she bears the dust of Franklin. All around her are reminders of the time when Philadelphia and Boston stood in the very front; when Pennsylvania and Massachusetts held up the hands of Washington. Before her roll the waters that wash the feet of Trenton and Red Bank; beside her lies the smiling valley of Whitemarsh; still, in her suburbs, stands the old stone house round which the battle raged at Germantown. She sees the sun set behind those peaceful hills—unconscious of their fame—between which slumbers Valley Forge, and by her southern borders flows a placid stream that bears the immortal name of Brandywine! Here stood the sons of Boston and her children side by side. There your blood and hers commingled stained the cruel snow; together you shared the sufferings and the sorrows; together the danger and the toil; and the victory, with its blessings, was for both! Her tongue may cleave to the roof of her mouth and her right hand forget its cunning, but she will remember this! And it is peculiarly appropriate that she should speak to you to-night. When the news reached Philadelphia that year—1773—that the tea-ships were on their way, her citizens met in the State House on the 17th day of October, and unanimously resolved 'that the attempt to levy taxes without the assent of the people was an infringement of the inherent right of freemen, and an attack upon the liberties of America'; 'that resistance was the duty of every true American'; 'that whoever should directly or indirectly aid or abet in landing, receiving, or selling the tea was an enemy of his country,' and 'that the consignees should be forced to resign.' On the 2d of November following the Bostonians met here and adjourned to the 5th, when, having appointed John Hancock moderator, they unanimously adopted as their own 'the resolutions of our brethren of Philadelphia.' Six weeks later they met again. The fate of their country hung upon their acts. The excitement reached Philadelphia. Her tea-ships had not yet arrived, and she awaited, breathlessly, the news from Boston. The days came and went; a week glided by and still there were no tidings; when suddenly, at two o'clock in the afternoon of

December 24, a courier came riding in, post haste, bringing great news. By five o'clock that day the town was all alive. Men gathered in the streets to tell, with glowing cheeks, how their brethren of Boston, coming in from twenty miles around, had packed old Faneuil Hall as it was never filled before, until it became necessary, owing to the crowd, to adjourn to the old South Church,—to that building which, but the other day, saved from destruction as if by miracle, has earned another title to your gratitude and veneration, —and there, as the winter's afternoon wore on, counselled together what to do; until at last, finding no other course left open, and roused by the eloquence of their leaders,—above all, sir, by the burning words of him whose honored name you bear,—they poured into the streets, and through the early dusk to Griffin's wharf to make the night immortal! Two days after Christmas the tea-ships anchored near Philadelphia. At an hour's notice five thousand men gathered in town-meeting. The consignees were forced to resign, and the captains, alarmed at the steadfastness of the people, turned their prows seaward and sailed away forever. Thus did Boston follow the example of Philadelphia, and again Philadelphia that of Boston, both animated by a noble devotion to the common cause. A century has passed away, and I confess, Mr. Chairman, that that seems to me a beautiful sentiment, and one which savors of the spirit of that olden time, which has led the Philadelphians to choose to celebrate this night, and gather, as they soon will do, in a gigantic tea-party in memory of the glorious deed of Boston. It is in the power of Boston, sir, to reciprocate this feeling and return this compliment; and of this—in the few moments which remain to me—I wish to speak. As it was your fortune to rock the cradle of liberty, it was Philadelphia's to guard that of Independence. Here, in your Faneuil Hall, the corner-stone was laid; there, in her State House, the edifice was crowned. This anniversary belongs to you; another anniversary belongs to her. And now that we are face to face with the one hundredth birthday of the nation, Philadelphia has been chosen as the spot of its celebration. She is, so to speak, the trustee for the whole country, and the guardian there, as you are here, of our common treasures. The President, by direction of Congress, has named the time and place. He has appointed commissioners for every State and Territory; he has authorized them to raise money for the purpose of holding a great exhibition: he has invited all the nations of the earth. In Philadelphia, on the 4th of last July, in the presence of the chief men of the nation and of many States, of representatives from every corner of the Union, and of tens of thousands of the people, were solemnly dedicated to the Centennial four hundred and fifty acres of land. There, in less than three years, will an international exhibition rise, more remarkable than any which the world has seen. Not London in 1851, or Paris in '67, when the doomed empire put forth its might to show to the world the wealth and power of France, nor that exhibition which has drawn the eyes of all men to Vienna during the present year, will compare with it. They represented nothing but internal progress; the Centennial will commemorate a great principle and an era in the social, political, and moral development of man! There will the past and present meet and converse; there will be spread before you the products of agriculture and the mine,—of industry and skill,—the discoveries of science, the masterpieces of art, the riches of all nations, the treasures of the earth and sea! There will the rice and cotton of the South, the grain of the West, Pennsylvania's iron, and the manufactures of Massachusetts be displayed before the world, where, beneath a gigantic roof more than forty acres in extent, the men of every race and clime jostle in the crowded avenue! I remember that Alciphron, the sophist, declined the invitation of his friend King Ptolemy to make his home in Egypt in these words: 'For where in Egypt shall I behold the things which I see daily around me here? Where else shall I behold the mysteries of our holy religion, the straits where the ever-memorable battle was fought that delivered Greece,—the neighboring Salamis,—in a word, the whole of Greece concentrated at Athens?' How much more will the American of 1876, standing in the birthplace of the nation, and beholding the monuments of her power and her greatness, seem to see the whole history and progress of his country concentrated at Philadelphia! But besides the exhibition, which will illustrate the progress of the century and be but temporary, there is to be erected a memorial hall,—a monument of the first centennial. Beautiful in design and of enduring materials, it will stand there forever, a national museum, the pride of Americans, the wonder of strangers, the admiration of posterity, until, perhaps, at a second centennial, its beauties will pale before the glories of that distant time. But not in these alone will the American centennial be complete. There

will be a solemn commemoration of the great anniversary. Of this
I dare not trust myself to speak. What tongue shall tell the story
of that day? Who shall paint the picture that will then be spread
before the nations? Thirteen little colonies grown to thirty-seven
sovereign States,—a weak confederacy, held together by pressure
from without, become a mighty republic, taming the new world in a
century! Man's capacity for self-government no longer an experiment,—three million men increased to nearly forty million, gathering at their country's birthplace on its one·hundredth anniversary!
What voice shall worthily describe the scene when the dawn of that
day shall at last have broken, and the heavily-laden hours pass on
towards high noon, and the American people, reunited, return
thanks to God and to its fathers? Will it not be a grander consummation than they ever dreamed of who used to stand here where I
stand to-night and teach their countrymen the path that led to it?
Will it not far exceed the picture which their fancy painted when
they sought to stir the hearts around them with visions of the time
to come? Will it not seem to fulfil the prophecy of your own John
Adams, when, on the evening of that eventful day, while his great
mind—as Bancroft says—' heaved like the ocean after a storm,' he
sat down and wrote to his devoted wife: 'This will be the most
memorable epoch in the history of America,—to be celebrated by all
succeeding generations as the great anniversary festival; commemorated as the day of deliverance by solemn acts of devotion to
Almighty God, from one end of the continent to the other, from this
time forward for evermore'? Do you ask me what results we may
expect from this? I need not tell you of the advantage that will
come to all alike; to every man and woman and child,—in opening
new avenues for enterprise and industry and skill. I need not
speak of the knowledge we shall gain when we shall have compared
ourselves with each other and with other nations, nor of the increased
wealth which that knowledge shall bring. I need not talk of the
reputation we shall achieve when the world shall have seen us as
we are, nor of the power and influence that will flow from all this.
I love rather at a time like this to speak of nobler things. I look to
this centennial for grand results. I look to it to bind up the days
of old with those to come, and teach Americans that, henceforth and
forever, they are not only a nation of promise, but also a nation of
fulfilment, not only a people of the future, but also a people of the

past. It will join the corners of the land in friendship; it will re-unite this people as nothing else can, and blot out the memory of calamitous times; it will arouse us from the apathy which weighs upon us, and remind us that we owe a duty to our country as well as to ourselves; it will arm us against the temptations that are luring us to destruction, the love of ease, the appetite for power, the lust for gold; it will awaken in us a truer spirit, and purify our pride; it will teach us how much that is good, how much that is grand and noble other nations have accomplished for humanity; it will make us a better people. It will soften the national heart; it will broaden the national view; it will deepen the national thought; it will strengthen the national life! And these results alone will be worth all the labor or the money that can be expended. I could name as many more, but I have already spoken quite too long, and I must close. Such, in a word, my countrymen, is the task which Philadelphia has undertaken. She has begun the work, and there is no turning back. But she cannot do it solitary and alone. It is the duty of all the States of the whole country. It concerns them all alike. It is a great national undertaking. Now, at the very outset, she asks your sympathy and aid. Of all her sister cities, she turns the first to you. You can help the Centennial in a thousand ways,—in your families, among your friends, and in the communities in which you live, as a people, as a city, as a State. You can talk of it, give to it, work for it, pray for it. Philadelphia asks it not for her sake, but for your own and for our country's. She asks it in the name of all that you have endured together in the days gone by, in the name of that progress which the Centennial will illustrate, of those labors which it will complete, of those virtues which it will commemorate, of those sacrifices which it will sanctify; in the name of that freedom whose anniversary it will consecrate,—which came to us from God.

"I know, my countrymen, that she does not appeal to you in vain. I might doubt in other places, but not here. I do not forget to whom, nor where I speak. I look into the eyes of men who have the blood of the leaders of our early times, and the spot on which I stand is holy ground. I have an abiding faith in this people and in this place. The air is full of waking memories. Whatever in this dying century there has been of good, of noble endeavor, of self-sacrifice, of honor, of truth; whatever, in a word, has contributed

to the greatness and happiness of man seems, at this moment, to rise
up out of its grave instinct with life.   In the august presence of this
anniversary the spell that holds them dumb is broken, and, from
each crevice in this ancient hall, come forth ten thousand tongues
to plead with mine!   They speak to you, to whom it has been
given to share the blessings of the century that is about to close.
They speak to you, to whom it may be vouchsafed to see the glories
of the century that is about to open.   They tell us of a past, honorable, sanctified, complete; and on this threshold of the future they
teach us, with the voice of inspiration, that He whom our fathers
worshipped will hear the supplications of their children, and—truer
than the imagined gods of pagan story—maintain, through all the
generations yet to come, the virtue, happiness, and power of the
republic."   [Applause.]

This speech, even among addresses of more distinguished
men, was characterized as "brilliant."   In the language of
a correspondent who had good opportunity to study the
audience, "it made a delightful impression."

We must now turn aside for a while from the current of
the great Centennial to notice some other events and oratorical labors.   The first of these, occurring at the beginning
of the year 1874, is of a very pleasing character.   Having
made the discovery of Mr. Brown's gifts, his fellow-citizens
seemed determined to call them into constant requisition;
and his next service was in behalf of The Merchants' Fund
of Philadelphia, an association incorporated in 1854, whose
purpose, as defined in the second article of its charter, is
"To furnish relief to indigent merchants of the city of
Philadelphia, especially such as are aged and infirm."   The
twentieth annual meeting of this society was held on the
evening of January 27, 1874, before a large assemblage at
the Academy of Music.   Mr. Brown was the third regular
speaker on the occasion, and was thus introduced by Mr.
Frederick Fraley, the chairman of the meeting:

"We have heard the Church speak for our charity, we have heard the Merchant speak for our charity, and now we are to hear the Law speak for our charity. I know that merchants depend often upon the lawyers for good counsel and good guidance through their troubles, and I know that the eloquent gentleman whom I am about to introduce to you can represent properly the much-abused profession of the law. I have the honor of introducing my friend, Mr. Henry Armitt Brown." His address was a thoughtful and elaborately prepared production. Among friendly notices was the following from the *Philadelphia Press:* "Our young orator talked like an old statesman. He applies what he draws from the past to the necessities of the present. He has an axiomatic style. Few men of his age have gone back to borrow from the old examples, and forward to welcome the new inspirations, with a happier faculty. There is in the address a model for the young men of our day, and the merchants for whom he spoke could have had no better interpreter of their splendid benevolence."

But more stirring times in politics were at hand. Reeling blows were to be given and received. The Municipal Reform question once again rose to prominence and agitated the whole community. The efforts of the party of reform, who were ever steadily at work, had already brought about positive results. The contest in Pennsylvania over the new constitution had been fought and won by the friends of reform by a majority of over one hundred and forty-five thousand. The introduction of needed changes by the new State constitution had, as was supposed, made the municipalities comparatively independent; had destroyed the capacities for evil of the Legislature; had rendered fraud more difficult to perpetrate; had insured fairer elections; had lessened the opportunities for plunder. Their success, however, injured them.

The Reform party, "unused to being on the winning side," had grown lax. The party in power thereupon had redoubled their efforts, and had renominated the whole ticket of those who were then incumbents. The boldness of this movement, in the face of all that had been established by reform, together with the detecting of actual frauds in the recent election, reawakened the energies of the independent party, and, after much discussion, they nominated Alexander K. McClure for the mayoralty of Philadelphia. This nomination aroused enthusiasm and opposition. Mr. McClure was well known to be a man of great force and of unusual power of attack. He was distasteful to some of the leaders of the independent movement itself, but he was supported heartily by the great majority of the Reform party, composed of Republicans and Democrats, who were determined to break the "ring" by using a powerful instrument. Enormous mass-meetings were organized, which were characterized by unexampled enthusiasm. At these meetings, and especially at the great ratification meeting held at Horticultural Hall on the evening of March 31, 1874, McClure was the principal speaker; and his speeches were really wonderful specimens of boldness, originality, sarcasm, and a kind of resistless Dantonesque eloquence. No less weighty, though calmer in tone, were the speeches of Mr. Brown, who threw himself into this election contest with all his strength. If the best men of the Republican party held back and demurred at coming up to the mark as candidates, he did not wait for them nor spend time "in searching for angels," but, taking whom he believed to be the most available man for aggressive reform purposes, he fought for him with all his might. Thus on the evening of February 4, he made a rough-and-ready speech for reform at Oxford Hall, in the Twenty-ninth Ward, in which he declared that

the world-wide reputation of Philadelphia for being a clean
city, "so clean that you could eat your dinner in the streets,"
was a bygone tradition, and the only ones who could eat
their dinners in the streets now were the hogs. These were
the city scavengers. He showed the gradual multiplication
of abuses, the steady increase of municipal indebtedness,
and the peculiar method of taxation to secure the largest
revenue from the taxpayers. He set forth the excessive
valuations upon property, the steady growth of the tax-rate,
the undue increase of taxation as onerous, both upon the
rich property-holder and the poor tenant, because the latter
was obliged to pay the tax in rent, and the fact that there
was no due return for this increased taxation, the city being
more badly kept, the water facilities being poorer, and the
lighting more defective, and that while each citizen was entitled to the seven hundred and fiftieth part of a policeman,
yet not more than the one-fiftieth part of that fraction
was allowed him. But the two principal speeches that he
made during this short and sharp campaign for Centennial
mayor deserve to be more fully recorded: the first, at Germantown, Pennsylvania, February 7, from its boldness,
pungency, and wit; and the second, at Horticultural Hall,
in Philadelphia, a week afterwards, a briefer speech, from
its incidental exhibition of character. We have only space
for the second shorter speech:

"FELLOW-CITIZENS,—I shall not speak to you at length to-night, for
I am not well, and there are many other speakers on this platform.
It seems to me impossible to exaggerate the importance of this contest.
It is all very well for our opponents to tell us that there is nothing
to be decided on Tuesday next but whether Mr. Stokley or Mr.
McClure shall be mayor of Philadelphia. It is to their interest to
tell us so, and try to make the people believe it, but it is all a great
mistake. [Applause.] The men who tell you that don't think so
themselves; they don't understand the people of this city, and have

not understood them for a long time past. They have taken mildness for cowardice, patience for fear, forbearance for stupidity. They have underrated you and overrated themselves, and the time for believing them has long passed away. [Here a disturbance broke out in the gallery. One of Mayor Stokley's policemen having expressed his disapproval of the speaker's sentiments, there were loud cries of "Put him out!" Mr. B. called out, "Let him alone; he'll vote all right on Tuesday." The audience laughed and the speaker proceeded.] That wonderful meeting of the 31st of January was something more than a political demonstration. It was the outgrowth of the times. It was the natural result of years of misgovernment; it was the protest against a corrupt tyranny of an abused and plundered people! It was the uprising of honest men against a system which had fastened itself upon them until it seemed as if there was no shaking it off; it was the beginning of a new era in Philadelphia. [Cheers.] And so I repeat, as I look this vast audience in the face, that it is impossible to exaggerate the importance of this contest. There is not a man within sound of my voice who doesn't know in his heart how important a day to him, and all of us, the 17th of February will be. It is not a question simply of the mayoralty, of the success of this man or the other; it is a question whether the people shall have its own again, or whether this great city shall forever hereafter be absolutely governed by a few bad men. [Applause.] This is the question for you to decide. You cannot escape it; it is a responsibility you cannot shirk. You must perpetuate the present state of things or destroy it now forever. [Applause.] And while the contest seems to me to be the most important in the history of Philadelphia, there never was a greater contrast between two parties. It is a battle between regulars and militia; but the regulars are demoralized and disheartened, and the militia have enthusiasm and overwhelming numbers. [Cheers.] It is a struggle between the politicians and the people, but Right and Virtue are on the people's side. [Applause.] You have, in the first place, on the one hand, a non-partisan nomination. [Cheering.] The event of thirteen days ago, which made this place historic, was the spontaneous outburst of a general sentiment in this community. The people, outraged and betrayed, found here at last a leader [applause], and the great effort to lift the affairs of Philadelphia out of the field of national politics took then a form. You have, I say, in Colonel McClure's nomination an attempt to break up partisan control and rally the honest men of all parties on the side of good government. And how has this canvass been conducted? Night after night he goes about from hall to hall in every part of this great city to talk to the multitudes who cram them, even on such rainy winter nights as this,—to talk fairly and frankly,—to tell them why they need reform (if any men can be found in this city to believe that we do not need it), and to point them to a safe deliverance. [Cheers.] He is supported in this by men of both parties. At every meeting at which I have had the good fortune to be present I have heard Democrats and Republicans talking to the people, side by side and shoulder to shoulder in the common cause. He is supported by a newspaper which has not yet contained a falsehood or an unfair argument, or an ungenerous personal attack. Day after day in every part of it you see the same thing; in its editorials, in the speeches which it contains, and which I believe the people read [applause], unanswerable arguments in favor of reform. It is frank, it is honest, it speaks the simple truth, and if there should be no other result in the contest Philadelphians should thank *The Press* for showing them the rare example of an honest, independent newspaper. [Great applause.] Money we have little, barely enough to pay from day to day the expenses of our meetings and the advertising bills of hostile newspapers; but the money that comes hourly in small sums from the people proves that there still lingers in this community a love of courage and independence, and that the people of Philadelphia know well enough in whose victory their safety lies. [Applause.] Thus, day by day, night after night, the fight goes on; the people read, and listen, and reflect, and the cause of their enemies grows steadily more desperate. [Applause.] The nomination of Mr. Stokley is a partisan nomination forced on the party by a few of its managers. And how do they conduct their part of this campaign? They have control of every office and all the patronage of power. They command a small army of office-holders, and boast that they own a large contingent force of colored voters. They draw immense sums of money for all imaginable expenses from innumerable sources. By a skilful use of every means they scatter broadcast partisan newspapers and false tax receipts [applause], and, as I see to-night, beautiful engravings, accompanied by biographies. [Laughter.] The carefully prepared accounts of their meetings, with immense lists of vice-presidents,

many of whom are openly supporting Colonel McClure, are distributed by the policemen in every portion of the city. They rake
up stale slanders, dead and buried fifteen years ago, and parade
their mouldering relics in the charnel-house of a Sunday newspaper,
and, notwithstanding that the refutation comes at once from the
author of the slanderous article himself, they continue to slip the
paper, marked with colored pencils, under honest men's doors while
they are asleep. In place of arguments they give you slanders;
they answer reason with abuse, the protest of the people with a party-
cry [applause], and not content with announcing themselves at every
meeting as the exclusive possessors of every virtue, each one cling-
ing desperately to the much-abused prefix of 'the Honorable,' they
unite in calling the independent movement of the people of this
great city to destroy the power which has made their city government a disgrace among their countrymen and choose a ruler for
themselves—the audacious attempt to seize power of 'the criminal
classes.' [Cheers.] They harp forever on a single string; and, as
many a fellow in a scrape has done before, they think to divert
attention from themselves by calling out 'Police!' [Laughter.]
It is not surprising, my friends, that they should take this course.
The men who have governed Philadelphia for the past few years are
capable of anything but good. [Cheers.] They have crept into
power through the apathy of some men and the partisanship of
others. They have grown to believe themselves the natural rulers of
the people, they have used their offices for their own good and that of
their associates; they have ruled you with an absolute sway. What
wonder is it then that they should use every means, and with the
lowest means they are the most familiar, to defeat your effort to
throw off their weight and try to perpetuate forever their ill-used
power! What wonder that the men who were caught in the act of
defrauding you but a few weeks ago, who have persistently declined
to investigate that 'hole' [laughter], who have the audacity to ask
you to prolong their power by the very votes of which for years they
have deprived you [applause], should go but a step further and call
themselves honorable and the people of Philadelphia the criminal
classes! [Cheers.] Do they answer our arguments? No. Do
they reply to our questions? No. Do they deny that our debt is
steadily increasing; that our taxation has quadrupled; that rents
are forced up and great industries driven from our city; that the

people are deceived and plundered right and left; that great public improvements are often turned into great private jobs; that the offices of the city are in unworthy hands; that they whom you have trusted have deceived you; whom you have honored have betrayed you; whom you have made your servants have sought to be your masters? Do they deny any of these things? Fellow-citizens, no. They content themselves with one general answer: That the safety of this city demands the success of the Republican party, that Mr. Stokley is not at all the kind of man for mayor, but that he has given you a good police. [Laughter.] The safety of Philadelphia depends upon no party, and upon the success of no party candidate. [Cheers.] It rests on the character and intelligence of its citizens, and if they be content to be ruled by men of neither ability nor character, to intrust the control of their public affairs to those to whom few of them would commit their private business, no Republican nor any other party can save their city from destruction. [Applause.] Corruption is a disease of rapid growth, and for it there is but a single cure. [Cheers.] I don't object to Mr. Stokley as a man. That he has raised himself to a place of prominence in this community, if the means he has always made use of have been beyond a question, should be in this country especially an honor to him. It is—or let me say it *should be*—the peculiar pride of Americans that here, under our free institutions, there is for every man a chance, and no aristocracy is recognized but an aristocracy of brains and character. [Applause.] Nor do I object to Mr. Stokley because he is a politician. I do not share the usual contempt of men for that much-abused title. It is in itself an honorable name. There can be no profession more honorable, short of the ministry of Christ, than the profession of politician; but of politician in its nobler, better sense. To devote great talents and lofty character to the common good, to consecrate great powers to the service of the State, to stand up in her defence unmoved alike by the fickle winds of favor or the tempests of adversity, to act from no motive but love of the common weal,—this is to be a politician and a statesman [applause], though small men, by the practice of low, selfish arts, have dragged both names down into disgrace. I say I object to Mr. Stokley not because he is a politician and has taken an active part in the affairs of his division and his ward, for that is what every patriotic American should do. [Applause.]

"But I do object to him because he is identified with bad government in Philadelphia. [Loud applause.] Because he is an instrument in the hands and to-day the chief representative of a band of politicians who have been tried and long ago found wanting [applause]; who have plundered this people and lowered the tone of public morals; who have done more to drag down the name of politician, and prevent the rise of talent and of honest worth, than any class of men who ever ruled a city. [Great applause.] Talk of the old Greek tyrannies, of oligarchs, and the thirty tyrants who poisoned Socrates and banished honest men from Athens! This is a more frightful tyranny. This is an enlightened age. These are the days of newspapers, the teachers of morality to the people, of common schools, of the railroad and the telegraph. It is a tyranny over mind as well as body; it is an organized attempt to exclude all independence, all character, all ability, from any share of power, and prostitute the highest offices to the lowest purposes. [Cheers.] This is why the Ring rulers of Philadelphia draw the line so low,—they know that to lift their standard half an inch on the scale of ability or honesty would be forever to exclude themselves. [Great applause.] This is why they shut up every avenue to honor in this city and force all aspirants for power to follow in their train. This is why they fight all good reforms; why they conduct this canvass with slander and abuse,—because they have determined that no man of character, ability, or independence shall ever rule in Philadelphia. [Applause.]

"Between him and them they know there must be warfare unto death, and they are bound, if it be possible, to drive such men forever out of public life. It is a necessity of their being,—it is their only safeguard in the future, to make a canvass so low, so degrading, so revolting to every sense of right, that no man in the future whom you may ask to serve you will be willing to subject himself and his family to the horrors of a canvass before the people of Philadelphia! [Applause.] I remember to have read that when a great man was attacked by his enemies who sought to banish him from Athens, he met a citizen who asked him to write his name on a vote in favor of his banishment. 'What has he done to offend you?' asked the statesman. 'Nothing,' replied the man, who did not know the other; 'but I want him banished because I hate to hear a man always called the Good and Just.' It is this state of feeling among the people of

Philadelphia which these men hope to foster and to cultivate,—in spite of good examples,—in spite of schools and newspapers,—in spite of all the teachings of the past. And it is this system which you will perpetuate if you re-elect Mr. Stokley. [Applause.] You will say amen to all the past and set the seal of your approval on the present municipal government and postpone deliverance perhaps for a generation or perhaps forever. [Applause.] And think, my friends, what a lesson you teach the young men of Philadelphia! Remember, you who are old men, that your children did not see the times when this city was governed by her best and ablest citizens; when (it is but thirty or forty years ago) you sent to your Councils men like Joseph R. Chandler [applause], and Frederick Fraley [applause], and Joseph G. Clarkson [applause], and George Sharswood [applause], and Henry J. Williams [applause], and Peter McCall [applause]; when they were presided over by James Page [applause], and Joseph R. Ingersoll [applause], and William Bradford [great applause], and your Select Council for nearly sixteen years by no less a man than William Morris Meredith. [Great applause.] Remember, I repeat, we have never seen such times as those, and you know the influence of bad example upon youth. Perpetuate this Ring and you say to the young men of Philadelphia,—' Honesty is not the best policy; it is all a lie. The lust of power and greed for gold,—these are the noblest sentiments that can move the human heart. The people of Philadelphia want nothing better than selfish politicians to rule over them. Purity is weakness,—honest men are fools. To be patriotic is to be insane,—to have ability is to be over-burdened in the race of life. To be a man of culture is to be a snob!' [Great cheering.] This is the lesson which Mayor Stokley's re-election will teach; and on you will rest the responsibility of teaching it. [Applause.] And do not doubt that your children will better the instruction. My fellow-citizens, in less than three years the eyes of all men will be turned to Philadelphia. The celebration of a great event will bring to your city the representatives of every race. Then, when they shall gather reverently about the birthplace of your liberty,—when, on that great anniversary, men of all nations shall stand in Independence Hall and gaze upon the portraits of Adams, and Jefferson, and Washington, Benjamin Franklin, and your own Robert Morris, will you have them say: ' Begun and ended in an hundred years! This people had every blessing which Providence could bestow,—and threw it to the winds; Prosperity,—and they trampled it under foot; Power,—and they bartered it away; Liberty,—and they sold her into bondage; Virtue,—and they drove her from among them! In all things they were fortunate, and in all things unworthy. What is gold without honor? What is America without that which chiefly constitutes a State,—an honest man?' [Continued cheering.] My fellow-citizens, it is for you alone to decide the future of your country. But if you would be true to the teachings of your fathers, true to your duty to posterity, decide aright the question now hanging on your acts, and let the sun go down next Tuesday afternoon upon a redeemed city, in a regenerated Commonwealth." [Great and continued applause.]

The result of this hard-fought election is given in Mr. Brown's words in the March number of the *Penn Monthly*, 1874. He writes:

"It was a struggle between enthusiasm and organization, and the latter triumphed, as it generally will. On election day the First Ward and the Tenth were literally taken possession of by repeaters, and the Democratic districts, under the lead of statesmen like Mr. —— and the Hon. ——, declined to give the usual Democratic majorities. The command of unlimited means enabled the party in power to scatter messengers and extras of newspapers with imaginary returns in every quarter of the city. A panic was thus produced, and the innumerable company of men upon the fence, hesitating how to exercise the inalienable right of freemen, jumped down with one accord upon the Stokley side. In a poll of nearly one hundred and eleven thousand the Republican candidate had about eleven thousand majority. It has become so customary after elections in this country for the defeated party to raise the cry of fraud that it has quite lost its significance, and seems to be a sequel to every political contest. In this case, however, the fraud was not of the kind with which we have become familiar under the registry law; it was perpetrated rather through personation and repeating than by false count, though in some cases where the minority in-spector could be bought, that also was indulged in, but it is not reas-suring to find that the safeguards which the new constitution was supposed to throw about the ballot do not avail to secure to Philadelphia a fair and free election. It is doubtful, however, whether an election can be held in a large city without the commission of fraud, for we hear at the present time of much trouble arising from it in England, and in France elections are no purer than elsewhere. So ended the most brilliant contest of which Philadelphia has been the scene, and at this writing the triumph of those who opposed the new constitution and were sixty days ago wearing sackcloth and ashes, their knees knocking together under them for fear, seems complete. The most peculiar feature of the case is the want of enthusiasm with which the success of the Ring is hailed by its most respectable supporters. It is a victory over which there has been little exultation, a triumph over which there have been tears."

The *Penn Monthly Magazine* had for many years been carried on by a number of young Philadelphians in the interest of social, political, and educational science, aiming, above all, at the thoughtful diffusion of true principles of government and political rights. Mr. Brown found a corner in this publication, and for four or five years of his life he was editor of the department entitled the "Month." This consisted of disconnected articles, sometimes only paragraphs, upon subjects of passing but not fleeting interest, as he often headed his remarks, " It is not designed to discuss here all the chief topics of current interest, but only those upon which we have something to say." Here, as learnedly or lightly, just, in fact, as he felt at the moment, he touched the salient points of characters and events. Up to this period a great variety of subjects (though they grew to be more and more of a political nature) had been treated in a crisp way,—the new German empire; the old Catholic congress; financial questions and paper money; English high-churchism; Mr. Froude and Father Burke; republicanism in Spain; the epizootic; the Siamese twins; the electoral vote for President; Agassiz; Bismarck; McMahon; government appointments; Grant's administration; *Crédit Mobilier;* the currency bill; strikes in England; municipal reform; civil service reform; the coming Centennial Exposition; and a vast many other themes of more or less importance. We shall have occasion to quote from the "Month." Two or three specimens of these literary improvisations may give some idea of their character. Their estimate of men and things is not always as "all think."

"The death of Charles Sumner ends at once all controversy in reference to his recent unpopular course in the Senate, and recalls only his great services to the nation in his earlier and better years. He was a thoroughly educated man, and his whole life was an instance of the result of culture in a man of not uncommon gifts. Besides a fine personal appearance, nature had not bestowed on Mr. Sumner many strong qualities either of mind or judgment. He was from the outset, and he remained to the last, a diligent, patient, exhaustive student, and his work at the bar, in the Senate, and on the stump.—though it seems to class his elegant oratory with the effusions of our ordinary politicians,—was always the result of hard, steady application. As a lawyer he reported and edited the opinions of others; he lectured on law at Harvard College, and wrote a pamphlet on the Oregon question, but he gained no great distinction at the bar. His entry into political life was in opposition, and he showed to best advantage in his persistent advocacy of the abolition of slavery and in the establishment of equal rights to the colored race. His addresses in and out of the Senate were labored, careful, and thorough, but had little of the fire of eloquence or the force of conviction in them. But in them, as in his whole life, he was honest, open, straightforward, and persistent. He alone in the Senate of the United States maintained the traditions of the orators of an earlier day, as one who had united scholarly eloquence with active political partisanship, and with him the race of great public speakers seems at an end. Contrasted with Clay and Webster, it is clear that he had little of their innate fire and genius, but measured by the standard of the colleagues of to-day, there is no one of them who could cope with him in the sort of studied oratory which he made his own to the very last. But his best and highest quality as a citizen and as a Senator was his inflexible honesty. It never occurred to him that he could be asked or expected to do anything that would sully his character, and no man ever suspected him of any but honest motives in all he did. IIis love of literature led him into kindred pursuits of art, and his collection of books and pictures, of rare engravings and sculpture, was such as showed the nicest taste and the most refined culture. In this, too, he stood almost alone, for his colleagues in Congress are too deeply immersed in the business of politics to have any time for the cultivation of their intellects. As a representative, therefore, of the best culture of the country, his loss will be felt in Washington and in Boston. The incidents of his life are too well known to be rehearsed here, and his death is too recent for an impartial judgment of his merits as a statesman and of his services to his country. IIis example of honesty in the midst of corruption, of courage in the face of bitter hostility, may well efface the painful recollections of the later years of his life, embittered by ill health and domestic griefs."

There are many published statements and utterances of Mr. Brown which show that he held in high esteem the memory and character of him whose "empty chair" was for so long the most eloquent speech in the Senate of the United States.

"The counting of the electoral vote for President and Vice-President has brought to public notice the dangers and absurdities of the present system of choosing our Chief Magistrate, and the consequent propriety of sweeping changes in the Constitution. The main purpose of the authors of our present arrangements has been entirely defeated by the shape that partisan organizations and methods have taken, and the cumbersome machinery of the electoral colleges now serves no purpose whatever. It is to be hoped that this is not the only part of the Constitution that will be changed. Let the Presidential term be extended to ten years and a re-election forbidden. Bring all civil officials, except members of the Cabinet and foreign ministers, under the tenure of office that now applies to the judges— 'for life or good behavior.' And abolish all the local restrictions that prevent citizens of one State from being elected to the service of another, either in the State government or in Congress. This last amendment would do much to give breadth and true nationality of spirit to our public men. It would deter men of foresight from giving themselves up to the petty and selfish aims of a district, by the hope that their self-denial and really public spirit would meet with appreciation elsewhere; 'a prophet has honor save in his own country and in his father's house.' It would relieve our younger and weaker States from the necessity of sending ——, ——, and other corruptibilities and vacuities to the United States Senate, without impairing beyond measure the care exercised by Congressmen to promote the special interests of their constituents. As it is, Congressmen are mere local errand-boys to the national struggle for the loaves and the fishes, and Ruskin's gibe was not without its truth: 'There is no *res publica* in America, only a multitudinous *res privatæ*.' "

"Governor Dix, of New York, has fully justified those who built their hopes upon his firmness and manliness of character. In refusing to commute the sentence of Foster he resisted as terrible a pressure as ever sought to sway a man's judgment. In a calm and earnest letter to Dr. Tyng, who was foremost in seeking to save Foster's life, the governor gives his reasons for doing what he conceives to be his duty. They are such as one would expect from him. With a tenderness that is morbid, for which we are remarkable in this country, we forget that when a jury has pronounced upon a man's guilt, and the courts have determined that he has been lawfully tried and found guilty, his punishment becomes a question of the execution of the laws. A jury is not required to consider the consequences, but the act itself, and to find, not whether a man shall be imprisoned for life or put to death, but whether or not he is guilty of the offence with which he is charged. For certain crimes the wisdom of mankind, directed and modified by experience, has fixed certain punishments, and he deserves well of his country who, unmoved by fear or favor and undismayed by responsibility, stands firmly by his duty, as he understands it, and executes the command of that law which is the safeguard of us all."

"The Connecticut election is full of significance, and at the same time it is not. Connecticut is always an uncertain State, and this year the feuds among the Republican leaders, coupled with the strength of Governor Ingersoll and the prestige of his excellent administration, would have made the result doubtful in any case. But, on the other hand, the prize for which both parties were contending was not the governorship, which is open every year, but the seat in the Senate occupied for the past six years by Governor Buckingham. Under these circumstances the defeat of the Republicans is a severe blow. Their candidate this year was an excellent one, the leader of the bar in New Haven, and nothing was left undone to win success. But in Connecticut, as in some other States of the Union, many of the best men in the Republican ranks have become disheartened and disgusted; and in such a state of feeling there seem to be worse things in this life than the defeat of one's party. Some stayed away from the polls, and others even voted against the ticket from the belief that a defeat, perhaps, would be beneficial punishment to the leaders of the party. It must be added, too, that the Democracy of Connecticut is of rather a liberal and practical kind. It is very apt to place good men before the people, and is not entirely incapable of taking advantage of its opponents' mistakes. It has courted, too, rather than repelled the advances of the Liberals and of discontented Republicans with evident benefit to itself. Should the re-election of so admirable a governor as Mr. Ingersoll be followed by the choice of some equally good man as Mr. Buckingham's successor, there will be no occasion to regret this Republican defeat; but there is great danger, from what we hear, of the election of some one who will strengthen neither the State, the Senate, nor the cause of reform."

"The French Assembly has had one or two strong debates. One of these occasions gave M. Gambetta an opportunity, which he improved, to make a brilliant speech. But the day has gone by when a speech can affect the result of such contests. Where the feeling is marked, a striking figure or appeal may deepen it, as in the debate in which D'Audriffet-Pasquier likened Alsace and Lorraine to the lost legions of Varus, and roused the feelings of his hearers to the utmost; but it is to be doubted if it is possible for any orator at the present day to overcome prejudice, or break to pieces by any power of speech the chains forged and riveted by political management and intrigue.

"The system adopted here at home of carrying on legislative business forbids the cultivation of oratory by robbing it of practical effect; the habit of writing speeches is death to debate, and the customs now so successfully practised of lobbying and log-rolling put on the finishing touches. The gift of eloquence is apt to be undervalued in a country where money is the standard of worth, and is sure to be despised by those who have it not. The taste of the age, too, is growing less favorable to speech-making, and the orations of M. Gambetta, and of Señor Castelar, are far less effective now than they would have been fifty years ago. Oratory is going out with the romantic and the picturesque."

That oratory is "going out," or has gone out, we do not believe. Mr. Carlyle may tell us that "silence is the eternal duty of man"; but oratory is a fact of human nature. Macaulay suggests that the scientific intellect has usurped the place of the primitive emotions, and therefore great poets and orators are no longer the power they were. But it is the occasion which brings out the orator. In our recent stormy history, at one of the great war-meetings, a plain Connecticut governor, who had no conception that he would be called an orator, made the most eloquent address it was our fortune ever to hear. He cast rhetoricians behind his back. He turned men's minds as rivers of water are turned. In the time of need the orator or prophet appears. The man of heroic will, of cheerful hope, of the ready hand and the ready speech, who speaks out of a passionate heart, who speaks wisely as well as courageously, then becomes the master influence. All obey because God breathes through him, and the truth is with him as a visible sceptre. Emerson says that "it is rare to find a man who believes his own thought or who speaks that which he was created to say"; but when such a man appears there is the power to sway minds which we call eloquence. Our own orator, at all events, in spite of his *Penn Monthly* theories, had not yet won *his* greatest triumph. That was to come, and was soon to come.

It was now nearly approaching the time when another important event in the country's history was to have its centennial anniversary; and this time the scene was at home in Philadelphia.

On the 5th of September, 1774, the first Continental Congress that had been called to deliberate upon the troubles which were growing more and more serious between the colonies and the parent country, met at Carpenters' Hall. This venerable building, so intimately associated with the Revolutionary period, was erected in 1768, by the Carpenters' Company of Philadelphia, which still occupies it, preserving its relics and its appearance, as far as possible, both within and without. "It stands in the centre of a little court, or *cul-de-sac*, approached from Chestnut Street by a narrow alley, between Third and Fourth Streets. It is of cruciform shape, two stories in height, surmounted by a cupola, and is constructed of red and black bricks, in a style in vogue a century ago,—its checkered walls being in curious correspondence with its history. In general architectural style it closely resembles Independence Hall. The plainness of the façade is relieved somewhat by balustrades under the upper windows, and by a portico in Doric style, which is called 'a frontispiece' in the old minutes of the company. For 'turning the columns of the frontispiece' Samuel Fletcher was paid, according to the minutes, the sum of two pounds and three pence. The lot attached to the building originally extended out to Chestnut Street, and was leased at an annual ground-rent of ' 176 Spanish milled pieces of eight,' but it became too valuable for the company to retain, and they now hold only a few square yards of grass-plots and walks in front of the hall, and a narrow strip at the sides and rear. The huge bulk of the buildings in front, upon the street, eclipses entirely the modest, quaint old hall, and its eventful history was almost as effectually eclipsed by the throng of recent events until the approach of the Centennial of American Independence brought it to notice." The chief interest attached to the hall arises from the fact that the first Continental Congress met there, and held its first and second sessions in the large room on the ground-floor of the building. The carpenters have a tradition that the Constitutional Convention met in the same room in 1789, and held there the whole of the four months' session during which the Constitution was formed. But this cannot be substantiated; and probably Carpenters' Hall is not entitled to the honor claimed for it of having sheltered the Fathers of the Republic while they were engaged in forming the Constitution; but notwithstanding this doubt it is an historically interesting edifice. In the hall itself are the desks and chairs used by the fifty-four Continental delegates, and they are in about the same position as they were one hundred years ago. It seats some four hundred persons, and, on the day of the celebration in 1874, it was closely packed, while a patient crowd stood without during the speaking. A profusion of flags decorated the interior, and upon the walls hung the portraits of Peyton Randolph, President of the Congress, of the Rev. Jacob Duché, its chaplain, who offered the memorable prayer (how great the pity that he should have afterwards turned Tory!), and of Thomas Mifflin, an early governor of Pennsylvania. On the platform, during the speaking, sat Vice-President Wilson, General Hawley, of Connecticut, members of Congress, and other dignitaries. John Welsh, Esq., of Philadelphia, presided, and made a short and forcible speech, which was followed by Mr. Brown's oration. This is printed among the addresses at the end of this volume. It is certainly not too much to say that in its matter and manner it was the most elegant speech delivered in any part of the country during the Centennial period, and its immediate impression was truly extraordinary. The orator's portraitures of Revolutionary characters, especially of Patrick Henry and Washington, were so vivid, that whole ranks of persons in the audience rose and turned around to look in the direction where he pointed, as if expecting to see those men of a hundred years ago sitting in their places. It was a triumph of the imagination seldom witnessed. It was, too, an earnest and soul-full address, fired by the noblest sentiments. It struck a deep chord. The *New York Tribune* spoke thus of the occasion: "The ceremonies at Carpenters' Hall in Philadelphia stir the popular heart with a feeling of patriotism and pride of country which in these days is not as common as it might be. The national holiday has degenerated into a noisy nuisance. The lives of the heroes of the Revolution have been turned into cheap jokes. It is well that at least once in a hundred years, if no oftener, we consent to reflect seriously for a few moments upon the early scenes of our history, and compare the statesmen of the ancient time with our own. Philadelphia was fortunate on Saturday in the choice of an orator. If all the speeches inspired by the Centennial are to be even half as good as Mr. Brown's, we shall be unexpectedly blest." In a more elaborate notice the same paper added: "The oration delivered on Saturday at the centennial anniversary at Carpenters' Hall of the first meeting of the Continental Congress, was a worthy tribute to the principles and the men that were represented on that ever-memorable occasion. Those who listened to the burning words of the young Philadelphian at Faneuil Hall on the hundredth anniversary of the Boston tea-party, will remember the affluence of historical knowledge as well as the broad and earnest patriotism with which his views were enforced, and will be prepared for the exhibition of similar characteristics in his latest production."

The *Philadelphia Press* said: "As the exercises continued, and the oration of the day was being delivered, the whole aspect of the assembly changed. Those there seated were no longer men of business, but sons of liberty who had suddenly realized the grandeur of their birthright. The thrilling oration fanned into a white heat the long-smothered embers of patriotism until the air seemed heavy with the magnetic influence of deep emotion and mental excitement. Time and again the speaker was enthusiastically applauded, and, when at last he bowed himself from the platform, the whole audience unconsciously arose, the better to express their admiration of and gratitude to the orator for once more rekindling the fires of early patriotism. The scene was one never to be forgotten. Old men whose years overlapped the nineties stood erect with a renewed youth and waved their hats in the air, and the young men, to whom the word liberty had long been so familiar as to have become an empty sound, seemed suddenly to realize the deep significance of the term, and to long for some way of proving their devotion to a government which had cost such precious blood to gain."

The *Philadelphia Evening Herald* was very enthusiastic. We will quote a few of the more moderate sentences:

" No description can reproduce the impression which the orator made upon his audience. He spoke upon a remarkable occasion to a remarkable assemblage, and his most intimate associates who knew the man and expected nothing little from him, heard him to the end with increasing surprise. They knew that what they had heard was not the fruit of protracted study under favorable auspices, but the labor of three brief weeks, wherein research, composition, and elocutionary preparation were necessarily blended into one, and because of that knowledge the achievement was to them a still greater one than to the ordinary listener.

"Of Mr. Brown's method of delivery it is impossible to speak as its exceptional character warrants. Artistically it cannot be excelled. It is powerful without being crude; it is inspiring without being inflammatory, teaching the mind as well as the heart. It possesses all the variations of running water, now musical as the brooklet, now sonorous as the cadence of the river. Nature gave him a voice, and art made him an orator. Herein lies the secret of his oratory, —a perfect mastery of himself. His fine voice is not more penetrative or powerful than that of many a speaker, but it is in wonderful subjection. It is absolutely free from monotone, which is the distressing feature hardest to shun in oratory, as it is the most difficult to unlearn. To sum it all up in a word, the charm of Mr. Brown's delivery consists in his absolute naturalness.

"The subject-matter of this oration deserves a more scholarly analysis than can be made in this review, inasmuch as it will henceforth be a part of our history, and because while the few will always remember it as spoken, the many will only know it in its written form."

It is not necessary to quote further from journalists all over the country, who vied in speaking well of it, to show the estimate at the time of this address. It must speak for itself. The first thought of it may be found in this extract from a letter of Mr. Brown's, dated August 12, 1874:

"I have been puzzling myself this afternoon—after my custom—about an invitation I received to-day. September 5 is the centennial of the first meeting of the Continental Congress, which was held in Carpenters' Hall. One of the committee of the Carpenters' Company called on me this morning to ask me to deliver the oration on the occasion. I told him I would let him know to-morrow,—for the time is very short,—and meantime have been wondering what to do. The occasion is, perhaps, as good as any I have had, and the subject worthy of effort. But I know just as well as you how much I shall have to pass through in these three weeks of hot weather in the agony of preparing such a speech as will reflect credit on myself and do the occasion justice, and I am almost inclined to let the chance go by. Perhaps, however, I may yield to the admonitions of the still, small but ambitious voice within me, which bids me accept this invitation."

The address was certainly not a random effort shot at an occasion, although composed, as the above letter shows, in an incredibly short time; but it had heart and toil in it; it was a production thoroughly wrought as a work of art, with much careful research, exquisitely true to fact, clothing past fact with new life and color, and flooding it with warm light like a great historical picture, despising the superficial, the vulgar, the smart, the boastful, and evincing a manly conception of classic oratory of an earnest aim, such as is now seldom heard. Its delivery (so it is said) was exceedingly powerful, and even entrancing. Perhaps it would not be too much to say with another (at a time when some critics were talking of the young-mannish rhetoric of Greece and Rome, a suspicion of which appears in the oration), "He is a young man, it is true; but his address on Saturday night has made him famous."*

---

* An interesting fact in regard to this address was communicated to the family by the mother of two young men living in New England. While members of a preparatory school they were desirous of procuring a scholarship in Harvard College, which they were about to enter. They translated the Carpenters' Hall oration into Latin, one of them taking the first half and the other the second, both of them, by this means, succeeding in their object.

Before plunging again into the subject of politics, we subjoin an extract from a humorous letter sent to the writer about this time, on the occasion of the playful proposal to make the joint purchase of a "Castle on the Rhine," just advertised for sale in the *New York Tribune:*

"The 'castle' suits me perfectly. I can imagine the satisfaction I should find in sitting down to dinner 'with my helmet on' in that huge dining-room beneath that heavy-beamed ceiling. How solemn the feasts would be at the beginning! until the flowing Rhenish (and other mediæval bowls) would wash away the bounds of etiquette, and the vassals would begin to be uproarious at the farther end of the table. With what satisfaction, too, would I go bare-headed to the gate to welcome you, Herr Professor, when you would arrive in pomp and circumstance! Think of the magnificent banquets we should serve up, with the stately dances afterwards, to the sound of harps, in the flaring torchlight, our 'mutual' and 'individual' serfs meanwhile careering around big bonfires in the court-yard! I say the castle suits me perfectly. But the price,—there's the slight difficulty. Twenty-seven thousand pounds may be a small sum for a prince, or a nobleman, or a 'gentleman of position' on the Rhine, but here in Philadelphia it is large. At all events, I shall have to deliberate before I agree to purchase. Perhaps we might buy a castle or two and set them up in Litchfield. You remember that we agreed that pleasant afternoon, when we walked up to Prospect Hill, that something of the kind was all that the scenery there needed to make it European."

Politics had now a sudden revival, and another brief but sharp contest was waged, in which the party of Reform in Philadelphia gained a positive triumph. It was on the occasion of the election of district attorney, and, more particularly, upon the question of the re-election of William B. Mann, Esq., who, for twenty years, with but a short interval, had been in office. Mr. Mann was the Republican candidate, but had already been strongly opposed by the Union League and the party of Reform on grounds of public welfare. A great meeting was held in Horticultural Hall on the evening of October 30, 1874, at which many of the leaders of the Reform movement spoke, not only with freedom and force, but with considerable personal virulence. Mr. Brown was the fourth speaker. It was one of his most effective efforts, calm in tone, but incisive and unsparing in its dealing with persons and facts. There is every evidence that the election was influenced, and, in fact, decided, by this spirited meeting at Horticultural Hall. The Republican candidate for district attorney was badly defeated, running behind his ticket, so that for a time the cause of municipal reform was in the ascendant. In an extract from a private letter written the next morning by a prominent Reform politician, this result is foreshadowed: "I am told that our meeting has done its work, and that the feeling in the streets has undergone a decided change."

About this time Mr. Brown delivered his lecture on "The Story of an Hundred Years" in Boston, as one of the Bay State course of lectures. He was introduced to the audience by his friend, James T. Fields, Esq., who asked for him "the warmest welcome." He gave this and other lectures at many places during this period. He related a funny mistake which happened to him, similar to the one that occurred to Mr. Froude in Boston. Mr. Brown and Edith O'Gorman, the escaped nun, lectured in a town the same night. The next day he was invited to dine out. The lady of the house, in arranging the table, happened to mention the name of Mr. Brown as one of the guests. "An' who is Mr. Brown?" asked the waitress. "The gentleman who lectured last night." "An' is he the escaped nun? Sure, I'll not work another lick in this house." With that exclamation she bounced out of the room, and it required quite an explanation to induce her to come back. On those lecturing tours his letters home were very amusing, and are good transcripts of the similar experiences of others. At one place he writes:

"The hotel where I am staying is a two-storied shanty of unpretending exterior. My home has been the bar-room, a small apartment, twelve by fifteen, in the midst of which around a stove have been sitting a gloomy company toasting their cowhide boots in melancholy stillness, and enlivening the occasion only by constant expectoration against the unoffending stove. No sound has broken the stillness since my last vain attempt to organize a diversion, save the sputtering remonstrance of the insulted stove, and I have been generally left to my thoughts. It will take a large and enthusiastic audience and a handsome fee for the intellectual food I have prepared for them, to repay me for what I have thus far endured."

In the following month of December he seems to have done some shooting down in North Carolina, since we find this minute (what the Germans would call *Jagd Rapport*) among his papers, showing good sport:

Thursday, from 3.30 till sunset,	2 covies.	H. A. B.,	4;		B. W. R.,	2	— 6
Friday, all day,	9 "	"	22;		"	7	— 29
Saturday,	7 "	"	30;		"	15	— 45
Monday, from 11 till sunset,	7 "	"	17;		"	7 & 1 snipe	— 24
Tuesday, all day,	8 "	"	22 & 1 snipe;		"	12	— 34
			95			43	138

At the beginning of the year 1875, Mr. Brown was engaged in aiding in the formation of an International Collegiate Alumni Association, inspired by the Centennial Celebration, of which he was made one of the executive committee. We also find, in addition to his *Penn Monthly* contributions, an article from him in a Philadelphia paper upon the qualifications of civil magistrates. Its stress is a plea for the adoption of the clause in the conference bill of the phrase "learned in the law." The line of argument may be gathered from this extract:

"But it is said that young lawyers, or such members of the bar as will seek to take these places, would spend their time in searching for legal points, in settling the law and not the case. This seems to us an unfair assumption, and no sound argument against the lawyer's eligibility. These courts are created for the people's convenience. The more speedy the trial, the more exact the administration of justice, the better for all parties,—save the criminal. Now, the law has certain rules by which its business can best be managed and justice done. There are rules of practice and rules of evidence. They have been suggested by wisdom and tried by experience. And the lawyer only is familiar with them and can apply them safely. Then, too, a certain amount of education is required at the bar. The lawyer can always do more than read and write. He must pass more than one examination before he can enter his profession, and the restriction of which we speak will secure for us, as magistrates, men of at least ordinary education. Then, too, we have a control over him which we have not over the layman. A lawyer is amenable to the censors of the bar. He is a sworn officer of the courts. The one may present him for misdemeanor; the other may throw him over the bar. If, then, we were to provide that our new magistrates should be learned in the law, we would be sure, at least, of men of some education, of ordinary intelligence (which ought not to be too much to ask), learned enough—not to embarrass a question, perhaps, but to decide a claim with promptness and according to law, and sufficiently familiar with the rules of evidence and procedure to expedite the business of their offices and secure justice,—over whom we would have a control such as we possess over no other member of the community. And then, besides all this, by restricting these offices to the comparatively few men in this city whose business in life it is to understand and study their powers and duties, we would elevate it in the popular eye and give the magistrate himself a higher dignity. Restrict the choice to members of the bar, and you will stimulate among lawyers a new and honorable ambition. Undoubtedly there are many excellent men of that profession to-day who would willingly take an office, which thus might be made a professional one and full of usefulness and honor, who would not consent to go into the scramble with the multitude for a share of powers, scattered among incompetent and unworthy hands."

Mr. Brown interested himself in the organization of a "Social Art Club" in Philadelphia, and also a "Penn Monthly Association," to include men of literary, scientific, and artistic taste in the city. We must be allowed to say that Philadelphia has a marvellous facility for organizing social and literary clubs, and perhaps that accounts for the exceptionally genial culture among its professional men. She fences herself in with her own institutions, draws from her own life, honors and loves her leading men with enthusiastic affection, is beholden to no other city for her intellectual life. Philadelphia swarms with these good things, and in some points puts other cities to the blush in the fidelity with which she cherishes home talent. Before the "Penn Monthly Association" Carl Schurz was invited to lecture upon "Education Problems." He was introduced by Mr. Brown in these off-hand words, "That in performing this act he was introducing to them one who would have been foremost in any Senate of the United States in any period of American history, but one who, in the past ten years, had shone with especial brilliancy in those things which used to be in the past, ought to be in the present, and he trusted would be in the future, the only titles to political distinction,—great learning, great ability, unsullied character." The friendship with Mr. Schurz, which had been already begun before this time, was one of those influences imperceptibly drawing Mr. Brown into a broader field of political life. Their correspondence shows the reliance Mr. Schurz had upon his friend's judgment, courage, and capacity. Shortly after this, Mr. Brown joined with others in giving a complimentary dinner in

New York (April 27, 1875) to Mr. Schurz, at which time he made a speech. He was also an invited guest and speaker at the celebration of the battle of Lexington in the same month, and shared the toils of the journey between Lexington and Boston on that highly interesting but somewhat confused occasion.

In the month of May the merchants of Philadelphia gave a dinner to the merchants of New York at Belmont Mansion, in Fairmount Park, on the occasion of their visit of inspection of the preparations for the Centennial Exhibition, the Hon. Morton McMichael being in the chair. John Welsh, Esq., introduced as the "father of the Exhibition," spoke, as did also Messrs. McMichael, William E. Dodge, S. B. Chittenden, Henry A. Brown, and Erastus Brooks. The playful opening of Mr. Brown's speech put the assembly in excellent good humor:

"Mr. Chairman,—If anything could increase the natural embarrassment which I feel on being thus called out it would perhaps be the reflection that my friend, Mr. McMichael, has introduced me in terms which I cannot hope to justify. And more than that, he has assigned no good reason for having called upon me. I find myself on this, as I have been on other occasions, somewhat in doubt about my identity. I do not think, frankly, that that is altogether due to the fact that the name which I have inherited from my fathers is far less of a designation than most other names. I do not know exactly to-day whom or what I represent. I had the honor once on a very solemn occasion to appear to some of my audience in the character of the Hon. Morton McMichael, many times mayor of Philadelphia. And every now and then I have the privilege of addressing in the country audiences of my fellow-citizens, who cling persistently to the belief that I am the late eminent David Paul Brown. Under these circumstances, sir, do you wonder that I am in doubt about myself? Is it surprising that I remind myself of the story of the Dutchman who went down to the hospital after Gettysburg to find his son? 'Dere vas many tents,' he said, 'mit voundets, und I feels very bad. I say "Vare is mine sohn?" und dey say "In de bed at de ent of de tent." I goes to de ent of de tent und der vas voundets all around; und some he got no legs und some he got no arms und some he got no heads,—dere vas all kinds of voundets. I go to de bed und I say "John," und he say "Vas." Und I say "Stood up," und he say "I can't stood up because mine legs is shoot avay!" Und I say "Come home! come home!" und he say "I can't come home because mine legs is shoot avay!" Den I sit on de bed, und I say "Sit up!" und he sit up, und I put my arms around his neck und he put his arms around my neck, und I begin to cry und he begin to cry, und I looked into his face,—und it vasn't him!' Gentlemen, if you hope for one-half of the things Mr. McMichael's introduction may have led you to expect put your arms around my neck and look me in the face: I tell you I am not the man."

We cannot now realize the enormous labor and anxiety, the uncertainties, hopes and fears, which accompanied the organization and the carrying out to a successful termination of the whole gigantic Centennial enterprise. Some few did the work, and some few inspired the enthusiasm to do it. Mr. Brown did both, and his hand, his purse, his voice, were never lacking. He had the pride of a Philadelphian in it, and, as his speeches always show, he had the principle of love of country, seeing in this peculiar time as hardly no other man seemed to see it, the golden opportunity to renew patriotic ideals, to lead back the people to original sources of national life and honor.

These were troublous times in the Union League. This noble association, which did such admirable service during the period of the civil war, was suffering from an internecine war. Its "committee of sixty-two," as it was called, which had in April, 1874, been appointed and endowed with plenary powers, had by its action awakened the suspicion of some of its Republican members upon the ground of party measures. Acting under the authority of resolutions passed by the Union League itself, and especially under the direction, "That the influence and support of the Union League and its members should and will be given only to candidates of unexceptionable character," on grounds of public welfare and pure Republican principles, the committee had lent their influence to the Reform party in the election of city magistrates and other measures of the Municipal Reform Association, for which action they were called to task in a special meeting held October 14, 1875. This was a most acrimonious and violent meeting, very nearly breaking up in a disorderly scene, in which confusion, however, Mr. Brown made his voice heard in firm opposition to the preceding motion that dodged the question, holding the convention to a decision upon the action of the committee of sixty-two.

Soon after this a large Republican mass-meeting took place (October 29) in Horticultural Hall, for the purpose of conferring upon political questions of the hour, and especially the nomination of General Hartranft for governor of Pennsylvania. The two speakers were ex-Governor Edward F. Noyes and Mr. Brown. The remarks of the last-named orator, who came out squarely upon the Republican platform, were commented upon by one of the leading papers of Philadelphia in these terms:

"The speech of Henry Armitt Brown on Friday evening, advocating the election of Governor Hartranft as the representative of hard money principles, was the finest political argument of the campaign, and it is likely will have a large influence with those who, while they deplore the follies of the recent Republican administrations, fear to trust their future to a party which, at the same time that it clamors for honest government, incorporates dishonest principles in its platform. Mr. Brown has been the ablest as well as the most conscientious of our reformers, and his action has, therefore, a special significance."

A touch of character must not be lost, for it is refreshing in these pushing times to find a modest man. The modern Diogenes ought to have another pane to his lantern. A letter had been addressed to Mr. Brown urgently requesting him to add his picture to the portraits of "a hundred representative men of Philadelphia" in the way of a memorial. This reply was among his papers:

"November 9, 1875.

"GENTLEMEN,—I have received your kind communication informing me of your purpose to prepare for exhibition next year a collection of portraits to be entitled 'One hundred representative men of Philadelphia,' and asking me to sit for mine. I appreciate the honor, but cannot believe that I have been able to do anything which entitles me to a place in such distinguished company, and, as your number of subjects is necessarily limited, I ought to make way for some worthier person.

"You have already honored me beyond my deserts by including my name among those from which your list was drawn.

"I am, gentlemen, very truly yours,

"H. A. BROWN."

The record of the years 1874 and 1875 would not be complete without copious extracts from a "journal" or "note-book" of Mr. Brown's, which seems to have been kept during these years only, and which, it is to be regretted, was not longer continued. Sketches of interviews with the great lawyer, the venerable Horace Binney, form the main subject.

"*December* 30, 1874.—Met Mr. Carey by appointment and went with him to see Mr. Binney. Instead of going to the front door and ringing the bell, as I expected, Mr. Carey entered the little entrance, and, reaching the inner door, knocked sharply twice. A slight noise, succeeded by unbolting and unbarring, followed, and the door was opened. Mr. Binney himself stood before us. He seemed about the middle height. On his head he wore a black skull-cap, as if to conceal his baldness. A large folio lay open on the table, and his spectacles lying beside it showed what he had been doing. Greeting Mr. Carey pleasantly, and shaking me by the hand when introduced, he asked me to sit down, and, having taken up the big folio, walked over to the end of the room and placed it carefully on the lower shelf,—then, returning, took a chair facing and between us. After a few general words, Mr. Carey spoke of the near approach of his ninety-fifth birthday. 'Yes,' said the old man, 'I shall be ninety-five in a few days. I don't know how it is that I have lived so long. It has stolen on me unawares. Up at Cambridge they want to make a great deal of it, but I tell them they shan't. I tell them they shan't (repeating it). Survivorship is the meanest thing in the world. When I was at the bar I never could make anything out of a case that had nothing but that to recommend it. In my case, the fact is, —as I tell them at Harvard,—I have happened to outlive—not everybody, thank God!—but a great many dead people.' Mr. Carey presently began on the Reciprocity treaty. Mr. Binney heard him for only a moment. 'Come,' he said, 'now I want to talk to Mr. Brown;' and, moving his chair near me, he asked something about my living in England. I told him that I was a Philadelphian. Another question followed, which led me to say that I was a member of the bar. Suddenly his face lighted up. 'Oh, now I know you,' he said. 'I thought Mr. Carey said something about your being a stranger. I have read some speeches of yours. I knew your father well,'—and so on for some minutes. When we had been seated about a quarter of an hour, there was a pause, when he drew out his watch, and, in a very courtly tone, said, 'You must excuse me to-day; I have an engagement to drive with a lady. The next time come earlier;' and, turning to me, 'I shall be glad to see you soon again. I will let you into the secret way of getting in. Did you notice the way in which Mr. Carey knocked? (knocking with his knuckles, as he spoke, on the table). Well, come to the side door and give that knock, and if I'm here I'll let you in. That was the old Phi Beta Kappa knock we used to have in Cambridge in '93. Come about ten o'clock in the morning.' With a few words like these he ushered us out in the most lordly manner. I have never seen an old man who seemed so much the master of his faculties. I had imagined him much feebler and more broken. In repose his face looks old, but when animated, in conversation, not remarkably so. His teeth, however, are gone. I shall call soon again.

"*February* 10, 1875.—Peyton told me in the cars this morning several interesting anecdotes of Mr. Clay. Manner, he said, was everything with him. He related an incident of his power which, he said, he himself witnessed. Some unfortunate gentleman, while sitting at table in a hotel in Kentucky, happened to look around sharply at a drunken scion of the first families who came staggering into the dining-room. The latter at once shot him dead. Clay defended the murderer, and, in the course of his speech, declared that the insults which could be conveyed by a look were sometimes more terrible than either words or a blow, accompanying this with an expression of face so insulting that the jury winced at it and soon afterwards acquitted his client, Peyton believes, simply on account of the impression this conveyed.

"On my arrival at the office I took advantage of the hour, and the fact that nothing pressed, to call again on Mr. Binney. On knocking with two raps at his office-door it was opened, and, to my surprise, he recognized me at once. He wore as usual his velvet cap, which hides the top of his forehead. He drew a chair before the fire and bade me do the same. A glance at the table showed me that he had been reading John Quincy Adams's Memoirs. I began to speak of them, when he started off at once. 'Adams,' he said, 'was in Congress with him in '33 and '35,—an admirable man, —I confess I have never quite made up my mind on the question of the bargain charged as made between him and Mr. Clay, though I think the friends of both parties must have had an understanding.' He contrasted—with some degree of earnestness—Adams's refusal to appoint a relative to office, even at the request of the President, with the practice of great men of to-day. He spoke of the change for the worse in public men,—mentally and morally. 'When I was in Congress there were many men of ability and honor in public life, but the bad ones were getting the ascendency very rapidly, and it has been growing worse ever since.' I said I thought that General Jackson had done much to debase politics. 'Yes,' he replied, 'undoubtedly.' To my question whether he knew the general (which was a very foolish one to make) he answered, 'Oh, yes; did you ever see him?' I replied, quickly, 'Oh, no, sir, he died before I was born;' and was sorry I had made the remark, for a shadow passed over the old man's face as he seemed to be reminded of the difference of sixty years between us, and said, half to himself, 'Very likely, very likely.' He then went on to tell me with much animation that the day after he closed a two or three days' speech against the removal of the deposits, he received an invitation to dine at the President's. 'Of course I went. He put me on his right hand at the table, and kept me by him all the evening; he told me much about his personal history. His early education had been very defective,— he had to ride a long way to school and take his dinner with him,— and the teaching was of the rudest kind. I was curious to know why he paid me these especial attentions. I learned that he had sent his nephew, Donelson, down to the House to hear my speech, and report to him. When he went back the general said, "Well, what does he say?" "He is pretty hard on you," said Donelson, "and pitches into you severely; but it's the speech of a gentleman; he treats you like a gentleman." And so the old man at once invited me to dinner.' Mr. Binney told the story with evident pleasure. 'Clay,' he said, 'was a delightful man to talk with and hear speak. He had a fine voice and manner, but his speeches did not read well. Webster, on the other hand, sounded sometimes dull, but the next day what he had said seemed excellent in print. He had extraordinary power. I have heard him sometimes when he seemed to lift me up to my tiptoes. He was not a great lawyer. He had not thorough training or deep learning, but in the argument of constitutional questions he had no superior.' I spoke of the Girard will case as one in which he had not sustained his reputation. 'He had the law against him,' was the reply; 'and, besides that, he didn't understand the law in that case. Had he done so he would have been in a far worse position than he was.' But in the Dartmouth College case,—'Ah, there he had the law with him.' I spoke of Webster as being the best model among American authors, though not to be mentioned with Burke. The latter's range was so much greater, etc. We talked of this a little and then of Webster's character, but he came back to him as a lawyer. 'In constitutional questions,' he repeated, 'he was unequalled. I have always said that he was superior even to C. J. Marshall, and you know I heard his speech in the Jonathan Robbins case when I was a law student.' Indeed, I said, at Sixth and Chestnut, in March, 1800! 'Marshall and Webster,' he went on, 'were, of course, very different. The former seemed to make link after link, until he had joined two points with a perfect chain. IIis logic was wonderful. But Webster seemed to strike a succession of ponderous blows. IIe bore down everything before him by his weight.' I spoke of Everett. 'A very remarkable man,' Mr. Binney said. 'IIis industry was extraordinary. IIe sat next me in Congress. One day he called at my lodgings and asked me if he might read to me a report which he had prepared on a question which was purely legal. I have forgotten the subject, but I remember that it involved several difficult points of law. It took him three-quarters of an hour to read, and when he had done I told him that I had no comment to make; that he had correctly stated the law and quoted the authorities, and that I had no comment to make upon his labors. And yet he was a man who had never studied law.' In illustration of a remark called forth by something I said about party discipline and the narrowness of party spirit, the old man then told me, as he said, 'a remarkable circumstance.' 'When Tom Benton brought in his bill to debase the gold coin to keep it from flowing to Europe, and supported an elaborate scheme based upon that idea, I examined the matter with some care, and was clear that it violated some truths of history and finance, but I hardly expected to speak, until J. Q. Adams came to my seat one day and said, "Mr. Binney, are you not going to speak on this subject?" I replied that I thought speaking would do no good, but the next day, I think it was, I took the floor. The IIouse was not more than a third full at the time, but they listened to me with great attention in a speech of perhaps an hour and a half. When I had done a gentleman took the floor to speak on the same side. The IIouse suddenly filled as if by magic. Every member was soon in his seat, when they commenced such coughing and scraping of feet that the member could not go on. Then they called for a vote, and passed the measure without a pause. IIere was an organic conspiracy to carry through this party measure without reference to argument or the honor of the country. It made an impression on me at the time, and showed how thorough party training had even then become.' Further talk about Mr. Webster led Mr. Binney to speak of Jeremiah Mason, 'one of the greatest lawyers and greatest men this country has produced.' 'He was a giant in size, and, by the way, the chief justice of Massachusetts was here to see me the other day,—an enormous man, too; nearly as tall as Mr. Mason,—Mr. Gray.' He asked me if I had read his (Mason's) Memoir and Correspondence, prepared by Mr. Hillard, of Boston. I had not. With that the old gentleman rose and searched for a moment in one of his bookcases, but could not find the volume, giving it up at length with the remark that his daughter arranged his books when they got in disorder, and that he would send it to me. He asked me if I had received an invitation to go to the celebration which they are to have at Lexington on the one hundredth anniversary of the fight. I answered that I had, and hoped to go. 'I am too old for such journeys now,' he said. 'At ninety-five and over I cannot go so far from home. I don't know how it is that I have lived so long. It has stolen upon me unawares.' He then told me of his passing a year—from 1792 to 1793—at a place now called West Cambridge, waiting to grow old enough to enter college. There was a pond there called Menotomy. Years afterwards he went with Mrs. Binney, who wanted to see the place, but couldn't find it. More than forty years after his residence there he tried again, and, driving out from Boston, found that he could direct the coachman how to go, and at last found 'Menotomy Pond.' But it was then called 'Spy Pond,' and he could find no man, woman, or child who had ever heard the old Indian name which he had spoken and heard a hundred thousand times.* 'Tell them this story, and say that they do wrong to change the names of their towns and villages. The Indian names are beautiful and ought to be preserved.' I mentioned the wicked change in the Adirondack Mountains, of the tallest peak from 'Tahawus,' 'cloud-splitter,' to 'Mount Marcy.' The old man laughed and said, 'The Secretary was not much of a cloud-splitter.' After more than an hour's talk I took my leave. The interview was most interesting in every respect. There is nothing to indicate great age in Mr. Binney but the loss of teeth, which often makes his words a little indistinct. He is

---

* This is like the story which is told of another great lawyer, Alexander Wedderburn, who was Lord Chancellor of England in 1793. When an old man he went to Edinburgh for the purpose of visiting "Mint Close," where he used "to play at the bools" as a boy, and to see if it was still just as he left it sixty years before.

neither blind nor deaf, and every faculty seems unimpaired. He stoops considerably, but his eye—a deep blue—is still bright, and does not look like that of a man of sixty. In everything he says you notice the man of power. His language is always correct and beautiful.

"*February* 19, 1875.—I talked with Dr. Allibone at some length. He thinks very highly of Everett, and also of Webster, but denounces, with perhaps justifiable warmth, the attempts to compare the latter with Burke. Dr. Allibone said some very kind things of my speeches which were gratifying, but ought not to be written down, at least by me. I can hardly bring myself to believe them: I am certain it would not be honest to have them even set down.

"*March* 6, 1875.—At the 'Junior Legal Club' this evening, Judge —— and —— were talking of the timidity and nervousness which men feel in court. —— said, to the judge's evident surprise, that he had never quite recovered from the feeling. —— agreed with us that it was a matter of temperament. Another of the company quoted to me a remark which I made at the meeting at the Penn Monthly room on Thursday, in my first speech. I was speaking of the proposed club and of that scheme for a 'Century Club' which —— and Dr. —— —— had in charge. The danger, I said, is that they start at the wrong end. They have too elaborate ideas, and make the great mistake of trying to make the Century plant bloom at the beginning instead of at the end of a hundred years. As he recalled it I remember how much it seemed to strike the men as I let it fall, for that, after all, is the danger we generally encounter, and nearly always with fatal results, in the formation of these clubs. Men are not content to wait, while such things should always be in great measure a growth. I think that the 'Penn Club' will succeed because it will start modestly, and money will be out of the question. I doubt the success of the 'Social Art,' as I did that of the now defunct 'Æsthetic.' Some one recalled to my mind ——'s joke about the new House of Correction. He was passing in the cars the huge building, when a man near him asked, 'Is that a distillery?' 'Oh, no,' was the answer, 'It's a rectifying establishment.'

"*March* 7, 1875.—Went to the Continental to-day at one o'clock, though it was snowing heavily, and passed an hour or more with ——. He talked very freely and as strongly as I have talked, having apparently come entirely around to my way of thinking. He said that the Republicans would undoubtedly renominate Hartranft, perhaps unanimously. I said that his administration had, on the whole, been satisfactory. He didn't think that anything could be done, and added that we must all sit down and wait. 'Your position,' he said, 'is perfectly understood, and couldn't be better. I shall make my independence known. I thought last winter, in the McClure fight, that you were wrong, but I think now you did just right. Your course has been consistent and bold; all you have to do is to keep quiet. But I will take an opportunity to speak or write about these tests, that are not tests of Republicanism, that will leave no doubt about my views with regard to them.' I remembered as he said this our former conversations, when he thought that I was all wrong and going astray, and the letter he wrote last winter to —— urging him to save me from perdition,—that perdition which he sees now is the way to security and a strong position. —— was the first to come over to me, now ——. Both of them two years and less ago the strongest administration men. As I said to ——, I feel and think as I did two years ago, and men like me are strengthening in our independence every day, while men like you are weakening daily in your party loyalty. I think, perhaps, that he is right, and that nothing can be done this fall to better things,—because the men who could are timid, or half convinced, or doubtful of their strength. But the change will surely come.

"*March* 15, 1875.—J. —— ——, of Kentucky, lectured at the Academy to-night. Pugh sent me a stage-ticket, and I found a seat between Richard Vaux and Samuel Dickson. The lecture was in many respects better than I had expected, being full of satirical points and many fine passages. —— has the common fault of the Western speaker, of dropping his voice at the close of a sentence. The majority of the best things were thus lost to the audience and fell flat. He said that men were holding high and responsible positions who were no better able to discharge their duties 'than a gorilla would be to vindicate his race from the Darwinian theory.' After the lecture we sat down, to the number of twenty-five or thirty, to supper at the Reform Club. —— is quiet, genial, and appreciative. Story-telling and good things kept us all amused until twelve, or nearly that, when, to my disgust, speech-making was begun. We all had to speak in turn, and one or two did not see the necessity of doing their part conversationally. —— in particular was oratorical to a degree which, in a small company, is trying enough.   ——— was amusing and mimicked others, to ———'s evident delight.

"*March* 16, 1875.—Dined with ———. We had much talk of a political turn.   ——— believes that Grant will secure the Republican nomination without a doubt. He thinks that Kerr, of Indiana, would be the candidate for the Democrats. He told us many good stories, especially of the South-Western politicians, many of which, though rough, I enjoyed greatly. Walked home with him and ———. I like ———, who strikes me as a kindly-tempered man and one of culture. He told an amusing story of General ———, a local celebrity in his State. The general was running for office, and his opponents determined to beat him. Among others they engaged Mr. W———, a lawyer and famous orator, to speak against him. W——— made a great speech before an immense audience, and when he sat down the general saw that unless something was done at once to counteract its effects his fate was sealed. He rose slowly, and said, 'My friends, you know me well. You have known me long. I have lived here right among you ever since I was a boy. It may be I have many failings, and you know 'em all. Everything that this gentleman has said of me may be true, and if you choose to believe him you must think tolerable mean of me. But this, I say, my fellow-citizens, I never *done*,—I never embezzled my client's money ; I never forged a check for sixty-four dollars and seventy-two cents; I never ruined my friend's sister.' Up jumped W——— in a fury. 'Sit down, sir !' said the general. 'I say again, my fellow-citizens, I never embezzled my client's money ; I never forged a check for sixty-four dollars and seventy-two cents ; I never ruined my friend's sister.' 'Do you mean to accuse me of these crimes?' broke in W——— again, beside himself with rage. 'I say,' went on the old general, and he repeated the three offences with great deliberation, 'that I never *done them things !*' The meeting broke up in the midst of great excitement. A challenge from W——— was at once accepted by the general ; but, of course, the duel could not take place till after the election. The general was triumphantly returned, and then sent a humble apology to W——— for his 'mistake,' and was never weary of protesting that if he could only lay his hands on the 'feller' who told him 'them lies,' he would flay him alive.

"*April* 30, 1875.—Samuel Hollingsworth entertained the 'Junior Legal Club.' Had a very pleasant talk with Judge Mitchell and

David W. Sellers. The latter told of his remembrances of J. R. Ingersoll and others of the old bar, of the courtesy, dignity, and attention to details of the leaders.

"*June* 7, 1875.—Called this morning on Mr. Binney. He was in his back office, the window of the front one, and indeed of the whole house, being closed tightly, because, as he said, 'they were putting in coal.' The back office is a large, pleasant room, with straw matting on the floor, and two large windows opening out upon a broad garden full of trees and flowers. Mr. Binney wore his little cap, as usual, and seemed to me at first rather feeble for him, or, to speak more correctly, less vigorous than usual. He had been reading the *Spectator*, and told me, with some animation, of the 'extraordinary spectacle,' mentioned in the last number, of the people crowding out to the Alexandra Palace during the Whitsun holidays in such numbers as to make it impossible to move the railway trains, and compelled more than twenty thousand to pass the night out-of-doors. I told him of the experiences I had had at Lexington, where the crowd was so great, and of the strange scene at the depot. This led him to speak to me again of the year he spent in that neighborhood, at West Cambridge, or Menotomy. I turned the subject presently upon Mr. Adams's Memoirs, the sixth volume of which he had just commenced, and remarked that I thought it strange that so able and learned a man as Mr. Adams, living in the period in which he filled so large a place, had taken no part in the discussion of the great constitutional questions which arose. He seemed to have contributed nothing to constitutional law. Mr. Binney replied that 'the reason was that Mr. Adams did not take naturally to legal questions, and was not a well-read lawyer. He practised a little in Boston, but not much, and he did not feel much interest in, or enthusiasm for, the law. But he had a natural gift for politics and government, and they had the wisdom in Massachusetts to perceive this political capacity very early, and to send him to the Senate. He acquired in time a thorough knowledge of European and American affairs, and in some things he was the fullest-minded man I ever knew. But he was no lawyer. When Mr. Cheves was president of the bank (of the United States), the question arose as to the duty of the bank to redeem the notes of various States in government notes at Philadelphia, and Mr. Cheves, who was not much of a banker and stayed here but a short time,—

but a very estimable gentleman,—came to me for an opinion. I gave him one, and said that the bank had to do it, and pointed out that the arrangement as made by General Hamilton was one mutually advantageous for the bank and for the government. He was not satisfied, and Mr. Adams insisted that the opposite view must be correct. Together they got an opinion from Mr. Pinckney, in which he agreed with me. I think they got six opinions and all the same way. Even then Mr. Adams said he supposed it must be the law, as it was so stated by gentlemen,—about whom he made some complimentary remark,—but he couldn't be satisfied. I remember, too, another instance of his stubbornness. Mr.——, whom you don't remember, was a China merchant. He imported immense quantities of tea, and under the bonding law as then existing he had it placed in the storehouses, and whenever he pleased he could take out as much as was necessary and bond it. Well, he made an arrangement with the keeper of the storehouses, and took out great quantities without putting it in bond at all; for then, too, as has been more frequently the case in later years, it was a question of "who should watch the keeper." Of course this was all discovered. He had borrowed largely in New York, and given as security the bills of lading, etc., of cargoes that were coming to this port. Mr. Adams had the ships libelled at once on arrival here as property, and I was engaged by the insurance companies, the holders of the bills of lading. The law was clear, of course, but Mr. Adams insisted on his view, and sent Mr. Wirt up to fight me. I did not mind Mr. Wirt much, because I had the law with me; but he made a fine argument, and I won the case. So little did Mr. Adams know of commercial law that he insisted on taking the case up to the Supreme Court. I argued it there against Mr. Wirt again, and, *nemini contradiciente*, the court held in my favor. So the government was put to all that expense by Mr. Adams's obstinacy and ignorance of the law.' Mr. Binney then told me of the suit which he conducted as the counsel of —— against —— for slander. —— had alleged that ——, as consul at St. Petersburg, had knowingly admitted English goods as American. Mr. Binney was opposed to J. R. Ingersoll, and John Quincy Adams was a witness. 'I suspected,' he said, 'that he had prepared himself the questions that were to be put to him, and I asked him this question directly on cross-examination, and he could not deny it.'

"He then spoke of the Memoirs again, and said 'no one could read the opinion which Mr. Adams set down in his journal of Mr. Clay, and then notice the latter's appointment as Secretary of State and the silence about it, without the conviction that there had been a compromise,—not by Mr. Adams, but arranged and managed by his friends. Again,' said he, 'Adams was in some things a narrow man and an unforgiving. He was honest always, but full of prejudices.' I asked Mr. Binney if he had known Mr. Pinckney. He answered, never; he had never seen him. But he was a man of great power, undoubtedly. He then went on and told me of a case in which Mr. Pinckney had defended a ship that was brought in as a prize,—the first case of the kind, and the principles of maritime and prize law were new to us then and the questions that arose unsettled. I won the case here, and it went to Washington. I won it also, I remember, at the Circuit Court before Judge Bushrod Washington. For some reason I did not go to argue it in the Supreme Court: I don't remember why. Mr. Pinckney was engaged on the other side and made a great argument, and she was condemned. Judge Washington dissented, but gave no opinion; but he spoke to me afterwards of the matter, and said I ought to have gone down, that Mr. Pinckney's argument had carried the court.' He (Mr. Binney) alluded to the stories about Pinckney's affectations of dress and manner. 'I believe he was a good deal of a coxcomb.' We then talked of the old bar, and he spoke of Tilghman, Lewis, and the elder Ingersoll. 'The first,' said he, 'was an accomplished, thorough lawyer,—a remarkable man. The second, Lewis, a great rough man, with a rough education, who became finally a thoroughly educated man by his own exertions. In the higher capital cases he was very powerful. Mr. Ingersoll was in some things the most singular man I ever knew. When unexcited his mind was slow to work, and if left to himself he would work out his arguments very imperfectly, and often made mistakes, apparently showing much less knowledge of the law than he possessed; but in the excitement of a trial or argument, when once aroused, his mind was keen and powerful, and his knowledge seemed to come out. His mind was like a sensitive paper written over with a chemical preparation that required to be heated before the characters would come out clearly.' The old gentleman continued to talk most delightfully of the leaders of the old bar. I spoke of Mr.

Sergeant. 'Ah,' he said, 'he was a good fellow. The trouble with him was that he wouldn't prepare himself properly. But he had great readiness, and while he spoke thought out his case. He would ravel out his adversary's case and knit up his own while he was speaking.' I spoke of the change in the bar and the want of ambition among its members to become accomplished lawyers in the highest sense. I said I knew of but few men of my time who seemed to me to have a very high ambition. Mr. Binney continued: 'I am so much retired, and see so little of the world in my privacy here, that there are many things which I do not see in which I would take interest. Doubtless you are right, and the bar has degenerated. All that I have seen and heard confirms your opinion. But you must remember that the times have changed, for Philadelphia, up to 1806 and even much later, was the commercial metropolis of the country. All the underwriting was done here; the great cases arose here or came here for settlement. It is not so now. We have necessarily grown provincial; and with the decline in the relative importance of the cases which it tries, the bar has fallen off. But,' he went on with much animation, 'remember that the more commonplace the bar, the better is the chance for ability and industry; for there is always work enough in Philadelphia, and important work too. If the general run of lawyers do not strive for the first places there must be all the more room in the front rank. Cherish an honorable ambition. Be strict in attending to your business. Prepare yourself with care. Be industrious and study hard, and resolve, no matter what the temptation may be, never to do an unworthy action or take a mean advantage, and by all means'—here he leaned forward and placed his hand upon my knee—'cultivate your talent for public speaking; then, take my word for it, the reward will come.' Continuing in this strain, he spoke next of the changes in the condition and prestige of the bench. 'To think that there should be chief justices of Pennsylvania by the score! But we mustn't slander any one; there are some excellent gentlemen among them.' I asked him 'if he did not attribute the decadence of the judiciary to the elective system?' He said, 'No; I don't think that to return to the appointive system would entirely cure the trouble. Governors are partisans and are apt to appoint partisans, and, on the whole, I think the people may be trusted to choose men as fit as those whom governors would

select; but the office should be held for life during good behavior,—
that would make the incumbent independent of all political influence
for a re-election. When the late convention met I urged these views
upon several gentlemen without avail. But to make our judges
dependent every few years on the favor or fancy of political con-
ventions is all wrong. Too much cannot be said against it.' After
a two hours' interview I rose to go. He shook me very warmly by
the hand and said I must come again soon. I said I might go to
Europe, and in that case would call again before the end of June.
With this I took my leave. The impressions made on me by previous interviews were deepened by this. · It seems quite impossible,
as you hear Mr. Binney talk and watch the changing expression of
his intellectual face, that he is within five years of being a hundred
years old. His voice is not weak, and were it not for the loss of
teeth would not sound like that of a very aged man. His eye is
bright. When I came in and he saw me, it kindled with a pleasant
light of recognition as many a much younger man's might not have
done, no matter how friendly his feelings to me. He is not deaf.
The instant I knocked at the door I heard his prompt 'come in.'
He stoops very much, but it is rather the stoop of a scholarly habit
than of age. The most remarkable thing about him is his conver-
sational power,—if I pass by the extraordinary memory which shows
itself in all he says,—for he remembers everything (even the name,
to-day, of the vessel which he defended,—the first prize brought in
in the war of 1812, and which I have forgotten already). In what
I have written of his conversation I have tried to recall his words,
but I have been able to do so very imperfectly. He reminded me
all the time when he spoke of what Chesterfield says of Bolingbroke,
that his eloquence was of so pure and fine a character that were his
ordinary and familiar talk taken down as it fell from his lips it
might have been printed without correction either as to method or
style. It is without question the purest, smoothest, most dignified,
and elegant conversation I have ever heard. May I hear more of it
next fall and winter!"

Mr. Brown's political opinions were not held, as has been
hinted, without the sacrifice of other things. As an illustration of this remark, after conducting for three years an

editorial department in the *Penn Monthly Magazine*, he resigned from political differences. So great, however, was the desire to retain him on the staff that several times his articles were published through the other editors generously waiving their right of control, because, in the language of one of them to him, "You felt sure that you were right." It was finally on the Bristow question that the split was made.

In the month of March, 1876, Mr. Brown sent to the *New York Tribune* the following letter, which indicates his feelings in regard to public affairs at that time:

"To the Editor of The Tribune.

"Sir,—The fall of Mr. Belknap has precipitated a crisis. Men knew before that public affairs were corrupt from low places up to high, but this event has convinced even those who hated to believe, and brought the thing in all its ghastliness before their eyes. It has stirred this country as nothing has done since the death of Lincoln. 'We must be rid of politicians,' is the cry which goes up on all sides, as if we could dispense with politicians in a government like this. The fault lies, indeed, directly at the door of that class of men, but it is not wholly theirs. A large share of it belongs to those who are the first to impute it to the politician. Nothing can be more unjust than to brand with obloquy a class of men and set them apart for scorn because of the sins of a portion, however large that number. And nothing, surely, is more fatal under institutions like ours than this disposition, to-day, to stamp office-holders with distrust and frighten out of the public service all who are best fitted to discharge its duties. How can we improve the condition of our affairs if, because many men in place are unworthy, we make the very act of holding office, in advance, dishonorable? The politicians, it is true, are in the main to blame for this unhealthy sentiment, but the people themselves have suffered to grow up the things from which it takes its rise. Nowhere in the world is politics so plain a duty as in the United States; nowhere else can the neglect of it breed more fatal consequences. For one, I do not share the usual contempt of men for the much-abused title of politician. Office-seeking may be one thing and politics another. There is no profession more honorable, short of the ministry of Christ, than that of politician, in its truer, better sense. To devote great talents and lofty character to the common good, to consecrate great powers to the State, to stand up in her service unmoved alike by the fickle winds of favor or the storms of adversity, to act only for the common weal,—this is indeed to be a politician and a statesman; and there can be little hope for the future of America when such a career shall have ceased to be possible, and such an ideal to stir the ambition of her youth.

"One cause of our present evils is not far to seek. The American people are still virtuous and patriotic. They have shown their devotion to both honor and their country under the severest ordeals that ever tried a people. But, the war over and the Union saved, they turned to their private affairs with an eagerness born partly of necessity and partly of disgust with politics, which, in its false meaning, they had come to think the cause of all their troubles. A few wise counsellors warned them that to neglect politics utterly was dangerous. 'No,' they said among themselves, 'politics is not the art of governing, but of getting rich by plunder. We are tired of faction and worn out with party strife. We have done our duty to our country and want no personal reward. Let others take the offices if they wish. We have business to attend to. Let us alone.' They have now so long neglected their public affairs, or intrusted them so often to selfish and unworthy hands, that there has come to be a class, distinct from and even sometimes hostile to the people, with which subserviency to party is the single test of merit, which holds in its hands all the paths to power and commands every avenue to office, dictates its own terms, issues its own decrees, sets up candidates and knocks them down, with little sense either of responsibility or honor, giving to those who cast the votes and pay the taxes small share in shaping party or national policy, and so little voice in the selection of their rulers that, in most cases, there is nothing but a choice of evils. And what has been the logical result? Bad men creeping into high places; party spirit preferred to patriotism; public honors the spoil of faction; political patronage the reward of dishonesty; the glory of great deeds put to the basest use; high powers prostituted for gain; great places bought and sold; the gates of office shut to honest men; the service of the State no longer an honorable career; confidence shaken; faith undermined; trust betrayed; the people plundered;

the State disgraced; the nation dishonored; old age disheartened; youth made corrupt; manhood put to shame. There have been exceptions, it is true, and they have shone all the brighter by the contrast, but such things have we all seen as this first century of our national life draws to a close. Were they not dangerous to ourselves we cannot ignore the influence of such examples on those who are growing up among us. If we show them bad men in power and a people apathetic, can we doubt that our children will better such instruction ?

"And these evils, of which all patriotic men complain, are long past being corrected by party platforms, however adroit, or party promises, however eloquent. For years we have been fed on such things, and we suffer still. No disease like ours was ever cured by aggravating and perpetuating its cause. We need a radical medicine. Nor can we hesitate to take it. When things that have long been dangerous become disgraceful, honest citizens have no longer any choice. Under our institutions duty goes hand in hand with privilege; we cannot shirk the one and hope always to enjoy the other. The people of this country must shoulder their own burdens, choose once more their own rulers, take their affairs again into their own keeping, and teach the politicians that they propose to carry on this government by their aid, perhaps, if they can, without it if they must. They should use every honest means within their power— and who can limit the means and power of an aroused and determined people ?—to secure, this year at least, the purification of public affairs, the faithful discharge of public duties, character and brains in public place, prompt and impartial enforcement of the laws, economy, honesty, and ability in every department of the government. To do this, or even vigorously attempt it, will indeed be worthily to celebrate the Centennial year. But they can do nothing without the election of a President of their own. Left to themselves, the managers of both parties will set up men for the people to vote for, whom the majority of neither party would select. For any new organization the time has both gone by and not yet come. The formation of one (formidable as it might be even at the outset) before the Cincinnati Convention shall finally have refused to satisfy the longings of the people for better men and things, would throw the prize at once into the Democratic camp, and strengthen in advance the worst elements of that distrusted party.

What, then, can we hope for? The Republicans will not nominate Mr. Adams. He represents everything that is most desirable in a President,—character, capacity, training, experience, traditions. But men say he cannot be nominated at Cincinnati. Well, what then ?

"We have within the ranks a good Republican, who was faithful in the darkest days under circumstances which put his courage and conviction to the sharpest test. No Democrat turned Unionist, like Andrew Johnson, only to change again, but a Republican from the beginning, bred from an old Whig stock. A soldier during the war, active and distinguished in the field; a lawyer who has won reputation and high position at the bar; a man of administrative ability as well as a sagacious counsellor, who has not only opinions, but is ready to enforce them, and who, while putting his duty to his country first, has been all the truer to his party, because he has refused to let scoundrels, who have robbed the people, make use of its prestige or take refuge behind its glory; a Southerner who was loyal,—a Kentuckian who fought in the Union army; a Western man, right and outspoken on the currency; a Republican official who has been the foe of corruption and the punisher of thieves. Mr. Bristow is comparatively young in years, but not in the service of his country. He has been long enough in public life to show his ability, his patriotism, his courage, his sense of honor, his self-reliance, his strength of will. A month ago the President feared and was hostile to him; to-day he bears the whole Administration on his shoulders. When men heard that Belknap had fallen in dishonor, from Grant down they turned to Bristow as the only man to trust. He, at least, has had no connection with the things that have disgraced us, nor shown sympathy with those who have. Here is indeed a candidate fit for the place and time. Leaders have been raised up for us before, but rarely so evidently as this man to-day. But how can he be nominated? Only by that without which little that is valuable has ever been accomplished,—hard work. Mr. Bristow can be chosen by the organization of the sentiment in his favor, now so apparent, into a force so strong without the convention as to cause alarm, so strong within as to command a hearing. His friends must work as those of other men are working. They must organize at once. They must use the party machinery to secure delegates wherever possible. They must get together in city, town, and village, form clubs, open correspondence, write to the newspapers, argue with the hostile, convince the doubting, teach the ignorant. They must use every hour they can command until the 14th day of June, and then be represented well at Cincinnati, outside as well as inside the convention. The majority of the present leaders would prefer any man to Mr. Bristow. What advantage to them would be the choice of such a man? Better for their purposes the election of a Democrat. They build, as usual, on prejudice, and count on the mistakes of their antagonists. They expect to win this time, as they have before, not because their candidate is better, but because that of their adversaries is worse. Those who have so often profited by Republican partisanship and Democratic blunders see no necessity for the nomination of Mr. Bristow. But they will not control this next convention in the old-fashioned way. The majority of delegates will not, it is true, be Bristow men from choice, but they will desire victory above all things, hoping, with the election of any Republican, to keep their places undisturbed. The rumors of revolt will not have touched their ears in vain, nor will their eyes be blind to signs of independence. Such an organization as honest work will make all over this country, in the present temper of the people,—if it will but announce beforehand, frankly, its determination to work for Bristow with all its might, but to support no candidate below the plane on which he stands, and even, if driven to the choice, to acquiesce in the election of an honest Democrat rather than help that of a doubtful Republican,—cannot fail to influence a convention composed of men who desire most of all success. That is the great step in this business. Convince the delegates that distrust of Democrats alone is no longer sufficient to elect Republicans, and the fight is won.

"And what may not such a nomination do? It will bring back into the ranks the best of those who have gone out since '68. It will awaken enthusiasm that has not been felt since '64. It will place the party on the safe and honest ground of principle. It will be a guaranty for the future, and recall what is best and most honorable in the past. It will stop dissensions, close gaps, heal wounds that might be fatal. Liberals, Independents, Republicans of every grade and kind, save only those whose leadership is death, will work together with a will for such a candidate, and we shall at last have a President who can be relied upon to crush corruption and give us such an administration of the highest office as shall satisfy the aspirations of a free, intelligent, and patriotic people.

"Very truly yours,

"Henry Armitt Brown.

" Philadelphia, March 27, 1876."

This letter was the first gun of the Reform movement in relation to the Presidential election. Bayard Taylor, in an editorial notice of the same day, says of it: "It is a most encouraging sign when a young man of talent and increasing reputation, like Mr. Henry Armitt Brown, whose communication we publish to-day, shows himself clearly awake to the difficulties and duties of our present political situation. He describes them with an earnestness which does not obscure the impartiality of his vision, and which, we trust, may carry with it a potent infection for good. The sooner the young men of our country, recognizing the extent and verity of our disgrace, shall thus analyze its causes and find one of them in their own apathy, the more speedy and sure will be the needful political reaction."

The famous Fifth Avenue conference of those who desired to bring about the reformation of our national affairs, which was called by William Cullen Bryant, Carl Schurz, Martin Brimmer, ex-Governor Bullock, Horace White, L. F. S. Foster, Parke Godwin, and J. W. Hoyt, and which was presided over by ex-President Woolsey, was held in New York, May 16, 1876. To this meeting Mr. Brown was appointed delegate, and took part in the speaking. Although nothing definite in the way of political nomination was proposed, yet the principles set forth in speeches and resolutions were of a positive kind. They pointed to the speedy resumption of specie payment; a thorough non-partisan civil service, where fidelity and capacity should constitute the only real claim to public employment; the supremacy of the civil over the military authority in every part of the land, and total non-interference on the part of the general government with the local affairs of the States; retrenchment and reduction of the public expenses; the earnest effort to have a man chosen for the Presidency who was not a mere politician but an honest man, whose very name would be a sufficient guarantee of honest government and a rigid enforcement of the laws. The manifesto of this conference was a noble document. It ended with these words: "Our generation has to open the second century of our national life as the fathers opened the first. Theirs was the work of independence; ours is the work of reformation. The one is as vital now as it was then. Every true American must have the courage of his duty." In a narrow sense, it may be said that this movement was a failure; but who can tell the influence that a bold effort like this—a thunder-storm in the political firmament—had upon the political condition of the country? Huss and Latimer were burned at the stake, but the words they spoke have purified, for centuries, the religious life of Protestant and Catholic alike. The words of an earnest young man like Henry Armitt Brown, spoken fearlessly at the time of his opportunity, are not lost; they are felt now, and will always be felt.

The singular prominence (for a young man) that he had at this time, the fact that his native city and State put him forward on every public occasion, the frequency with which his name came before the people, the many speeches he made here and there, before all kinds of societies,—political, philosophical, social, and literary,—have led some to say that he was ambitious of distinction,—a frequent charge against young men who take a leading part in affairs. He doubt-

less was ambitions; he did aim at a certain kind of power
which is the fair object of political striving; but ambition
is to be viewed with intelligent discrimination. Ambition
is a sentiment of the healthy mind just as is the law of
happiness. If a man have power, he is forced to try it in
competition with others. If a man have a gift like oratory,
he has a lawful delight in its use, which is also a means of
its development. The desire to unfold one's powers, like the
wings of an eagle, is the spring of achievement. If it end
merely in this self-development, it becomes ignoble. But
a young man without ambition is like a tree without sap.
He lacks the principle of natural growth. His restlessness
may be the spirit of God stirring in him.

> " The noble hart that harbours vertuous thought,
>   And is with childe of glorious great intent,
> Can never rest untill it forth hath brought
>   The eternal broode of gloric excellent."*

But, if ambitious, Mr. Brown's well-regulated will and
balanced nature kept these fires under control. He loved
well-earned praise as noble men always do, but he never
bought praise by the sacrifice of his principles, though
ready to suffer for them. He declined offers of official
position. He did not seek prominence in any way, as he
did not seek office. He might have been a mere social
celebrity. He might have belonged to the *jeunesse doré*
of a great city. But the only reward he asked for doing
well was to have more work to do. He did delight in this
taxing and filling up to the utmost of all his energies with
public work put upon him, and he cheerfully spent " laborious days" without personal reward in this kind of service.

---

* Edmund Spenser.

He flung himself into the Presidential contest with the greatest ardor, and no one man toiled more incessantly, both in public and private, to bring about what he considered a higher political result than had yet been attained, at least in these last days. But, before speaking of this, let us go back to a characteristic of Mr. Brown's mind, which has already been alluded to,—his love of nature. He had the poetic sense, but his busy life did not permit him to indulge this taste, for politics and æsthetics do not inhabit the same house. But he lost no opportunity to catch a smile from nature's face. He wearied of the city; he longed for the free, open country. He delighted to pass the summer months in the picturesque hill region of Litchfield, Connecticut, where, with his dog and gun, he roamed the fields and woods about blue Bantam Lake, and filled his mind with fresh thoughts. He was keen in his notice of scenery, and his letters are full of expressions of pure joy at new scenes. He was observant of trees. He loved an oak as he did an oration of Demosthenes, or any other strong and beautiful product.

In a letter, dated August 22, 1875, to his mother, who was then in Europe, he describes the changes that had taken place at the family's "summer home" in Burlington, New Jersey, which had been unoccupied for many years, and especially in the transformation time had wrought on the trees there. Surely none but a lover of such things could have written the following:

"In vain does one look for the smoke-stack of the steamboat from that porch, or from the chamber window out of which you used to watch the coming storms; the big willow, and the linden, and the mass of trees that grow out of the 'forest,' effectually shut out the view. The maple-tree in the kitchen-yard has thrown up such enormous roots as to raise the pavement several inches. The grapery is in reasonable condition,—thanks to Woodie Hancock. The walks are neat and well trimmed. Some few of the trees ought to have been taken out years ago, but most of them are magnificent and have thriven wonderfully. The evergreens are superb. In the back lot several spruces are models of beauty. We walked about to-day and examined several which ought to be taken down,—the shapeless and scraggy ones which interfere with the growth of better trees. But it is so hard to raise and so easy to cut down that we shall be careful. The summer-house remains unchanged, and the pines about it are now big trees. The arbor-vitæ hedge is still fine, but roughly so,—no longer trim and smooth. Not a bush, however, seems to have died or become sickly, and its height in some places will reach eight feet. Do you remember the row of pear-trees that never would bear much fruit, that stood near the hedge? There were some quinces that stood in front of them. They have now grown great, and seven of them are Seckels, and are hanging full of fruit. They are fifteen or eighteen feet high and very promising. The wistaria that you planted around the little arbor at the entrance of the vegetable garden has become of extraordinary size. It covers the side of the barn,—stretching across the roof, runs under it and appears on the other side of the stable-yard, and swings about the chestnut and maple trees in the most generous fashion. The dwarf pears in the little orchard have ceased to be, the stocks gradually dying from age. The little cherry and evergreen that were hardly noticeable there five years ago are tall and vigorous trees, and you cannot see the stable from the house. I am glad to find that the birds are very numerous, and still more so that the place has become the resort of many beautiful red squirrels, which apparently have their home in the big maple that took ten horses and eight men to move, for the base of that tree is heaped with gnawed walnut shells. While we were at dinner one of the little bright-eyed fellows came up to the piazza and gambolled about to the great delight of Nannie. The grass in many places is worn, and in many places it is a mass of soft green moss. So, too, are the banks on the side toward Aunt Mary's house. The big honeysuckle still blooms in fragrance at the corner of the veranda where you used to sit in hot mornings, and at the front steps is the other vine, in which I notice a bird's nest as of old. There are but few flowers about except the roses, which are blooming in great bushes here and there. I feel that you have been in communion with us this afternoon as we walked about and recognized the different treés, and talked of them and those they have sheltered once on a time. Here is the maple that was planted to replace the one snapped off in the great storm of '54; there is the locust, once but two or four inches thick, where we used to get the great thorns for antlers when we 'played deer,'—now a tree eighteen inches in the butt; another tree as thick as my body, which I planted as a seed picked up in the circle in front of the house on the little grave at the foot of it, still a mound a foot high, where 'Bluff' was buried; and yonder is the giant chestnut in Aunt Mary's back orchard, now a cone of yellow blossoms! The ancient crab-apple smiles a sickly smile, the 'Kentucky coffee-tree' has thrown his head skyward forty feet, and the twin chestnuts at the corner of the house are two feet thick at the stern. One of the larches has begun to die at the heart and shows now about six feet of dead top above the purple magnolia, but the other, its mate on the other side of the 'arch,' is tall and sturdy. The copper beeches stand as of old. The pair of yews, spreading over a diameter of twelve or thirteen feet, still guard the front walk; the smoke-trees are feathered with pink cloud from top to toe as they were wont to be, and the constant chattering of robin, blackbird, thrush, and wren keep up the concert all day long."

In another letter, dated June 10, 1877, written from Lebanon Springs, New York, he gives utterance to a wish that his old friend, Horatius Flaccus, would certainly have joined him in, and they two would have tramped out with immense pleasure to survey the spot, to look up the capabilities of the place, and to discover the qualities of the trees, the soil, and the springs. No snow-powdered Soracte, it is true, was in sight, but the Catskills must do for the nonce. He says:

"And yet I think if I were a millionnaire and could indulge a passing fancy, I would buy fifty or a hundred acres that I know of, two or two and a half miles from here, on the summit of a hill from which the views surpass anything I have seen except Rigi Culm. There is a natural terrace between two knobs of rock on which a cottage could stand. Behind it is a large dense wood of chestnut, oak, and pine trees. From the front of a house built here you could take in three-fourths of the horizon. You look eastward into Berkshire County and see half a dozen villages with their dividing ranges of hills, while to the southward beyond the valley of the Hudson the Catskill range stands up like a purple wall. The hill is not very high, but peculiarly placed, and I would buy some acres and build a cottage here had I the needful."

Mr. Brown went to Cincinnati in June of 1876 as a delegate of the "Bristow Club of Philadelphia" to the Republican convention, to use all honorable means to secure the nomination of their candidate. The history of that famous convention, of its wirepullings, schemings, skirmishings, votings, changing phases like Naseby fight, and its (to the country at large) unexpected result, is well known and need not be repeated. He, who had been among the first in the field for his candidate, made a brave stand for him. He delivered a vigorous speech at Pike's Opera House, Cincinnati, Tuesday, June 13, Hon. Job E. Stevenson in the chair. From this speech we make but one extract:

" What is it that the people of this country desire to do? What is it that they demand in a candidate? Character? Is that much? Capacity? Is that much in an intelligent people? Courage? Is that much in a people that has shown the bravery of the American people? Character, capacity, courage: those things they ask. They ask fidelity to trust, fidelity to republican institutions. They ask an honest government, an honest and able administration of their public affairs. They want to see men in the highest as well as the lowest offices of this government, who are honest, faithful, capable, and who can be trusted. They ask this not as a favor, but as a right, and they are bound to have it. The politician of the hour, be he reinforced ten million times, cannot make the people of this country any longer vote against their will for dishonest men. [Applause.] You may take the horse to water, but how many does it take to make him drink? They may nominate, but it is the people who elect.   They must give us a different kind of men from the sort that we have been threatened with, to say the least.   And, more than that, the people, I say, demand these things of a candidate. They demand, also, a man who has been tried; who has shown his courage; who talks not about reform, but does reform; who promises nothing, but who performs;—a man who has given pledges; a man who has proved his sincerity; a man who has passed through the fire and has not proved himself a tallow candle.   They want that kind of a man; they want a man born with a backbone; they want a man who has a backbone born in him and developed; they want a man who has a backbone that has been strengthened by the practice of standing up; they want a man who can resist temptation.   These are not great things to ask; and the American people, as a patriotic, as an intelligent people, demand and will have these things.   [Applause.]

" Now, is it impossible for the Republican party to furnish this? Is there not, in that great party that went into the war and crushed rebellion, such a man as that?   Is there not in the party that saved the Union and held up the hands of Abraham Lincoln such a man as that?   There are many, but there is one to-day raised up for us as a leader by the hand of God himself.   In crises, in dangerous times in our history, God has raised up leaders before this.   When he raises up before us a leader to-day who stands pointing out the path, shall we be blind?   In all parts of this country to-night, in little hamlets by the sea-board, in huts in the mountains, in the mechanic's shop, by the forge, by the furnace, wherever in this country the honest and patriotic American longs for honesty in power, and purity in national affairs, his eye turns, as if by instinct, to the south bank of the Ohio, and his voice utters the name of Bristow. [Prolonged applause.]

" My friends, there is no doubt of this.   Poll the American people to-day and they would say Bristow—eight out of ten of them.   Poll the Republicans in all parts of this country, and Bristow is their choice to-day.   [Cheers.]   Even here in Cincinnati—I don't mean even here in Cincinnati, but I mean even here in Cincinnati among the politicians—go and ask them about the candidates, and one will say Mr. A., and some will say Mr. B., and a very few—chiefly from the State of New York—will say Mr. C.   [Laughter.]   They declare for this and that one as their first choice, but they say, after all, that Bristow would carry the people. Even among the politicians who are the managers of the machine, while they prefer one man from this State, or another man from a different State, and so on, yet they all agree that the second man is Bristow." [Applause.]

The speech was thus commented upon in the papers:

"Another of the events of the night was a speech of the young Philadelphia orator, Henry Armitt Brown, before a Bristow meeting at Pike's Opera House. Mr. Brown reviewed the situation of the party in 1872, when it controlled so many States, with a man in the opposition whose candidacy was a comedy, until it passed over the narrow limit between the comic and the pathetic, and the farce ended in a tragedy. Then he described the present hazardous condition of the party in the country, and its dependence on the character of the candidate to be put forward by the convention. The qualities the people now demand, he said, are character, capacity, and courage; and Mr. Bristow, he thought, filled the demands. Mr. Brown's speech was a really brilliant one, and was enthusiastically received by the friends of Mr. Bristow."

"Mr. Brown's beautiful diction, close logic, and admirable bearing on the platform were brought into their best play in the presence of a large audience assembled. Job Stevenson presided. Dr. Bellows of New York, James Freeman Clarke of Boston, and others spoke. Mr. Brown, in concluding, said: 'In a time like this America wants not the representative of any particular section, nor the favorite son of any State. What she wants is a man. Sixteen years ago she found him in Illinois; to-day she finds him in Kentucky.'"

Mr. Brown's liking for Mr. Bristow was reciprocated by the latter gentleman. Neither sought the other's friendship, and it was only a strong similarity of political views that brought them together. They became confidential correspondents, and recognized in each other many of the same characteristics. Mr. Bristow has freely declared that Henry Armitt Brown was born to be a political leader, because he not only had political insight, but because he acted on his convictions; and that he was sure, if he had lived, to take a high position in the nation. He was equal to any post in the gift of the people.

The Cincinnati Convention over, the months of June and July, 1876, were taken up with that long looked for event, the national commemoration at Philadelphia, when, in presence of a mighty multitude from all parts of the land, the one hundredth anniversary of the Declaration of Independence was celebrated by song, speech, and the united and reverent acclaim of joyful hearts. In the wording of Mr. Evarts's oration, "The event brought its own plaudits. It did not hang on the voice of the speaker, nor depend upon the contacts and associations of the place. It was the serene commemoration 'of a new State, of a new species,' which showed the marvellous wisdom of our ancestors; which struck the line between too little and too much; which walked by faith, indeed, for things invisible, but yet, by sight, for things visible; which dared to appropriate everything to the people which had belonged to Cæsar, but to assume for mortals nothing that belonged to God."

We subjoin Mr. Brown's account of his personal adventures on that multitudinous occasion in a letter addressed to his mother. It is a pity he could not have finished the narrative. He writes:

"The great event, however, was the scene on the 10th. Having received no invitation, I presumed I was to see the ceremonies with the democracy, and expected to go out towards noon and spend the day with my wife in the grounds, having no relish for the scrambling and pushing of such a vast swarm of people.

"On Monday, the 8th, however, I received an invitation from General Hawley asking me to act as his aide-de-camp. At first I thought I would refuse. There had been trouble about invitations, and Philadelphians generally had felt slighted. D——, C——, and others had not been asked, and I felt disinclined to go except on my own merits. On second thoughts, however, I reflected that it was foolish to take that view, and —— agreed with me, strongly advising me to accept. I did so, and on Friday went to report myself. I found that the staff was to consist of four army officers, four brigadiers of Pennsylvania militia, and four civilians. The preparations were being pushed with an energy that seemed like frenzy, and the rain fell in torrents from a leaden sky. At five in the morning of the 10th, I was awaked by the din. Whistles, cannon and bells, made such a racket that it was impossible to sleep. After a peep at the weather, which was most unpromising, the rain continuing to fall, I breakfasted in haste, and dressed in my evening suit, with a ribbon across my manly bosom, sallied forth at seven, met William McMichael, and started for the grounds. We had to walk the entire distance. Wagons, carriages, cars, all were crowded even at that hour, and when we reached the gates they were already, an hour before the opening time, besieged by an impatient mob. Arriving at headquarters, we found that the four officers, two of the brigadiers, and McMichael and myself constituted the staff. About half-past eight, being told that we had three-quarters of an hour to spare, McM. and myself started off to get a cup of coffee. Hurrying back first, I found, to my dismay, that Hawley and his staff were gone. Throwing my overcoat into a corner I followed, and after twenty minutes of vigorous pushing got through the crowd that was rapidly forming below the circle of seats, and gained a place on the platform. You know how the seats were arranged. A huge amphitheatre facing the main building had been erected against Memorial Hall. A large gallery on the north side of the main building served for the choristers and orchestra, and beneath and between the two stood packed the people. It was now half-past nine o'clock. The sun, which had been struggling with the clouds, burst through and the morning became clear and beautiful. For nearly two hours the crowd kept streaming in unbroken. Judges, Governors, Senators, Congressmen, Diplomats in court costume, Foreign Commissioners in all sorts of dress, with a great multitude of women, poured through the alley, kept by ropes and soldiers from the main building to the stage, and mounting the steps took seats assigned them. By half-past ten o'clock there must have been a hundred thousand people grouped between the buildings. About that time the Emperor of Brazil arrived with the Empress, and a large number of ladies of the Cabinet and of the Senate, and took the principal seats. It must have been half-past ten when General Hawley asked me to get McMichael and go with him to the back door of Memorial Hall, and remaining there, to let him know when the President arrived. We hurried to our place. By chance I recognized Hudson Rich, of Burlington, as a captain of the Centennial Guard. 'Can you detail a man to me?' I asked. 'Yes,' was the reply, and presently I had a man posted at the back gate with orders to let me know the instant the President came. The scene from the back of Memorial Hall was beautiful—— Here unfortunately am interrupted. It occurs to me that a very interesting account of the opening might be taken down from my lips, but must close."

Mr. Evarts was, on this occasion, the guest of Mr. Brown, and it is an interesting though trivial circumstance that, at Mr. A. J. Drexel's reception on the evening of July 4, Mr. Brown introduced Mr. Hayes (then candidate for the Presidency) to Mr. Evarts, afterwards his Secretary of State. It is remarkable (for so young a man) what a number of friendships, unmixed with a shade of servility, but characterized, on the other hand, by a stiff independence and self-assertion, Mr. Brown already sustained with leading men of the nation. He met them, though modestly, on equal terms, and in the most natural way. We find among his correspondence letters which bespeak much more than an incidental acquaintanceship, and some of which contain a free interchange of ideas and opinions with such men as President Hayes, Wm. M. Evarts, Carl Schurz, Charles Francis Adams, Wendell Phillips, Josiah

Quincy, B. H. Bristow, E. R. Hoar, Chief-Justice Waite, Robert C. Winthrop, Benson J. Lossing, Parke Godwin, Longfellow, Whittier, James T. Fields, Bret Harte, Oliver Wendell Holmes, Wm. Walter Phelps, Eugene Schuyler, George Wm. Curtis; and, outside of the country, with Thomas Hughes, Lord Houghton, Sir Charles W. Dilke, and others prominent as writers and politicians in England and France. He seemed to have the faculty of attracting to him men of ideas and power, and he in turn was attracted by them.

Among the *Penn Monthly* jottings of the year just ended are to be found discriminating sketches of Hans Christian Andersen, Andrew Johnson, Gerrit Smith, Horace Binney, a lawyer *pur et simple*, and Benjamin R. Curtis, with many other articles that show a more confident power in the discussion of national politics. His article upon Mr. Binney, which fitly closes what he has already written of him, ends thus:

"The future critic of our institutions glancing through the list of obscure and sometimes ignoble names which Pennsylvania has sought to honor, will wonder why men like Sergeant, and Meredith, and Binney were never made governors, or chief justices, or secretaries of the United States, and will see in that fact, perhaps, one explanation of the smallness of her influence on the country, in comparison with that of South Carolina, or Virginia, or New England. 'By their fruits ye shall know them;' by the worth and character of their men cities and commonwealths are rightly to be judged. More than one Bostonian has become famous because of his surroundings. Horace Binney was great in spite of his. But now that he is dead, Philadelphia, perhaps, will appreciate what manner of man he was, and realize, when too late, that she will probably never again possess or lose so great a citizen."

This memorable Centennial year of 1876 was calculated to awake deep thoughts in many breasts. In a "leader" written for the New Year's number of the *Philadelphia Times,* which shows how he felt on the subject, Mr. Brown says:

"But what has been our moral and political growth? We are more intelligent generally than we were a hundred years ago. We are richer, more powerful, more skilful, more learned, more enlightened; but are we a better people? Are our merchants more public-spirited, our lawyers more patriotic, our men of capital less selfish, our politicians purer and less partisan? Do we choose for rulers the best men in each community? Is it still an honor to serve the people and the State? Does the office seek the man, and political power rest only in tried and trusted hands? Are our cities better governed than they were in earlier days? Does the public service draw out the best talent and character, and open, as it once did, careers of usefulness and honor to the worthiest citizens? Are public duties more faithfully discharged? Are the liberties of the people guarded with more jealous eyes? Is the national honor dearer to us than it used to be? Or is it true that we have not striven to grow better; that we have been content to praise the past with fulsome eulogy and then forget it; that we have turned from the examples of our fathers and devoted our energies to the service of ourselves; that we have constantly sacrificed the common good to private gain; that in our hunger for wealth and petty power we have so systematically neglected the simplest public duties, that politics are at last synonymous with vice, and statesmanship with incapacity; that office has become too often the avenue to dishonor, and political power the path to infamy?"

These questions poured out with impetuousness show the thoughts that were boiling in his mind. He had outgrown the partisan, and had caught the spirit of the time and become national in his aims. For a time the law, that "most jealous mistress," lost its hold on him. Charles Sumner at about the same period of life wrote to one of his friends: "For myself I become more wedded to the law as a profession every day that I study it. Politics I begin to loathe; they are of a day, but the law is of all time." It was not so with Mr. Brown. He was more absolutely interested in politics than in law. He was irresistibly led to take up a political career because he had in him the root of larger things than of a mere professional life. He might be called, if such an expression were allowed, a classic Republican. He made (a better way still) a party to himself.* But he seemed to be born with principles of a hundred years ago. Considering his youth and social environment, he was singular in retaining amid modern culture some of the rugged sentiments of an older type of American republicanism. One of these was reverence. It is no exaggeration to say that he could have mingled, without one shadow of incongruity, in any congregation of serious-visaged New England pilgrims in their plain "meeting-house" on top of Plymouth hill, or have kept hushed silence in an assembly of old-fashioned Pennsylvania Quakers, waiting for the moving of the spirit, or have sat in the grave and courtly company of our early Constitution-makers in "Independence Hall." His Puritan blood would not yield to much of the so-called progress of the day which sneers at ancient customs. He was conservative in his principles though radical in his measures. He was too earnest to be greatly swayed by fashions. Though a product of the times he lived in, yet he "carried a measure in himself," independently of the opinions of others. There was not in his manners that

---

* "Si ch' fia te a bello
Averti fatta parte per te stesso."
La Divina Commedia: Paradiso, Canto xvii. t. 24.

familiarity which breeds contempt. He knew the distinction between things God had made honorable and those he had made base. He recognized law, or the principle of authority founded on right. He was sturdy in such primitive notions as honoring parents, showing deference to the aged, paying respect to office and to religion. This reverent spirit of which we speak was partly a matter of taste, but more of principle. Delightfully genial as he was in society, reminding one of Anthony Trollope's description of George Lewes as a companion, and leaving behind him no equal for an hour's chat, there was still something about him of the antique. He would go to a certain length only with the custom of the day, and he halted in firm but modest protest at whatever offended a manly sense of honor.

Another of his old-time sentiments was patriotism. This was his passion. He fed this sentiment in his thoughts like a sacred flame. Literature, poetry, travel, did not satisfy him; he had the discontent of one seeking his work. There was a duty to his country that called him. His political life fell upon times of anxiety and dreariness, when the old spirit burned low on the altar. He had to be a reformer in order to be a patriot. The two streams of tendency had met in strife. Never was there a time when good political leaders were more in demand. A short time before, military chiefs were needed. Young Napoleon was the cry. Now, statesmen, or, if the word be too large, honest politicians, are the want. Our country, though young among nations, is passing through a time of development, which, if not betokening weakness in its constitutional principles, nor giving proof of inherent disease in the body-politic, is showing signs of an enormous strain put upon its political system by new emergencies, and the necessity of a much broader and more skilful adaptation of its principles of government to these crises. The nation is no longer "in its gristle." It feels growing pains. It is fast maturing. It has, at all events, outgrown its babyhood, and perhaps its first youth, and is entering upon its manhood, with manhood's burdens and perils. The time of tutelage is replaced by the time of action. Reared in rustic seclusion, our country is now introduced into the family of nations, to take its position and do its work, and is also beginning to experience the seductive influence of Old-World civilization and ideas. Europe is pouring its myriads upon us of those whose characters and opinions are irrevocably shaped in anti-republican moulds. The Corinthian brass which we hope will be the result, is now in a state of violent fusion of its various elements. The end of all is, that in the present transition period the unity of the national idea is undergoing change. Greatly diverse forces are rushing in, and it is a time of danger.

> "The juggler's hand is in the ballot-box,
> While office wins by tricks."

Old ideals shine less and less clear. Republican faith grows dimmer and dimmer. Even as the primitive simplicity of the Christian faith was gradually lost under the influence of materialistic forms, so the pure republican idea is obscured. The moral tone of the nation is also lowered. The germinant truth of self-government, moral in essence, has been opposed by an uprising immoral custom, and powers of evil let loose by the immense expansion of the material prosperity of the country, are assailing the country's life. Our nation at present has more to fear from internal demoralization than from any external foe. The love of gain is the root of all popular as well as personal evil. Wherever there is gold, though guarded like the Nibelungen treasures, there is the hissing and writhing of office-seekers. The history of political reform in this country is that of a small and determined group of men who have entered upon the disheartening labor of delivering the nation from the evils of official corruption. It needs some element of the heroic to carry on such a work. Charles Kingsley said, "We are growing more and more comfortable, frivolous, pleasure-seeking, money-making; more and more utilitarians; more and more mercenary in our politics, in our morals, in our religion; thinking less of honor and duty, and more of loss and gain. I am born in an unheroic time. You must not ask me to become heroic in it." True reformers have had, so to speak, to take their life in their hands. They have had to assault those powerful organizations which, in the strong language of the *North American Review*, "rob the people annually to the tune of millions and tens of millions, through its whiskey rings, its Indian rings, its custom-house rings, its railroad rings, and other legalized machinery which it manipulates." The tide sets strongly towards a reckless development and waste of our national resources instead of steady reform and economy. The theory is present aggrandizement instead of future permanent prosperity. It is the doctrine of spoils, of the sale of offices, of bad faith in government agents, of partisan interference in the business and patronage of government, of the betrayal of sacred trusts, of the farming of the highest civil, educational, and religious interests for purposes of gain, and of social corruption. While many of the charges against public men have been manifestly false, yet there can be no doubt of the dead apathy and actual obstruction in regard to true reform in civil matters of those who hold power in Congressional and governmental circles. There is too much government.

There are too many offices, too many incumbents in government pay, who might earn their livelihood in private life and add something to the country's strength. Above all, honest and able men are wanted,—political leaders who will not rely on expedients, but principles, who regard the future results of political opinions, who do not look so much to party success as to national existence, who model themselves on Alexander Hamilton rather than Aaron Burr. Abraham Lincoln, with all his shrewdness as a keen-sighted Western politician and rail-splitter, believed in the old ideas of right, honesty, and freedom. The progress of liberty was not a catchword with him. Henry Armitt Brown, though a young politician, was building himself upon true models. He was a man of uncorrupted life. As was said of another, "of a simple, frank, unconscious character, he had in him the possibility of heroic action." He was courageous without making a display of it. Seeking boldly for mastery, he still followed Edmund Spenser's words:

> "In vain he seeketh others to suppress
> Who hath not learned himself first to subdue."

And he was like one of Spenser's own heroes,

> "For he loathed leasing and base flattery,
> And loved simple truth and steadfast honesty."

Mr. Brown did not confess to "the new gospel of non-reform." He believed that the rational basis of government was moral, was laid on individual rights, and that its object was the best good of society. Where, therefore, there existed a civil abuse, he felt it to be his duty to attack it. This was an instinctive feeling. He had an intuitive dissatisfaction with whatever was wrong in society. He naturally allied himself with reform. He began at once to act with that party of uncompromising men who were almost hopelessly in the minority. He accepted the American theory of "the omnipotence of a platform," and he prepared himself for a life-long contest with demagogism. He felt deeply, *deeply*, as he often expressed it, the deplorable condition of public morals, of public and private faithlessness, of social and civil mismanagement. The great questions of labor and capital, of poor-relief, of socialism and communism, of the finances, of free-trade and national credit, were seething in his mind. It was for educated men with educated wills to take up these questions. "Politics as a profession," and "the scholar in politics," he often said, were phrases he cared little about, but the times were perilous and his country needed her best men,—"men of clear intellects, strong convictions, high purposes, and honest minds." The questions before the country were not to be settled by the mob or by a happy chance. They were the most difficult and complicated of questions, even intellectually viewed. Such things would not right themselves. He held that society needed reconstruction in some of its first principles. Men should be taught to "mend their manners, and to cultivate their own free will as the arbiter of their own destiny." He felt the need of "new noblenesses, new generosities, new conceptions of duty, and how duty should be done." He would set his face like a flint against the public decadence, and call for the making of a new order, with fresh blood in it, bold thoughts, culture directed by patriotic purposes. He believed that we must have good government, and that the one intolerable thing in this country is anarchy.

We hasten to speak of the Presidential campaign. When it had fairly opened Mr. Brown was early in the field, and, although he had been disappointed in the nomination of a candidate other than his own, he accepted with heartiness the choice which had been made by the Republican party, and girded himself to the task of helping on Mr. Hayes's election as a man "who had rather be right than be President," and one also pledged to reform views. To show how his efforts were estimated, a prominent member of the Cincinnati Convention has, in so many words, publicly declared that no one Eastern man did more at the West to insure Hayes's election to the Presidency than Henry Armitt Brown. His labors were chiefly concentrated in Ohio and neighboring States. Perhaps nothing could give a livelier account of his "stumping tour" than the following extract from one of his familiar letters, dated November 6, 1876:

"It is the eve of the most important election that has taken place in this country for many years. I reached home last night after my third journey since September 24. On that day I left town for the West, remaining till the 12th of October. On the 17th I started again, and was absent till the 23d. On the 27th I spoke in Burlington, and on last Tuesday—the 31st—I began my last pilgrimage. I made six speeches in Ohio; seven in Indiana; one in Wilmington, Delaware; one in Burlington, New Jersey; and eight in Pennsylvania; a total of twenty-three; and have been engaged either in speaking, or travelling for that purpose, thirty-three days out of the forty-three since September 23.

"I must have spoken to a great many thousand people in that time, for my smallest meeting must have numbered six hundred, and from that figure they ran up to ten thousand and twelve thousand. I was fortunate in my associates as well as in sometimes being alone. In Ohio I held three meetings with Mr. James Tanner, of New York, and two by myself. In Indiana I spoke five times with Senator Morton (though he held the afternoon and I the evening ones); once with General Harrison, the candidate for governor; and once (to a torchlight procession) with Governor Woodford, of New York, and Mr. Kasson, member of Congress from Iowa. Here I had Mr. Brosius of Lancaster, for a colleague at Scranton, Pittston, and

Bloomsburg; and Major Wilson Norris was with me at Easton; but at Burlington, Wilmington, Gettysburg, York, Chambersburg, and Carlisle, I was alone. My shortest speech was half an hour, my longest two hours and a half, and generally I consumed more than an hour and a half of my hearers' patience and time. I mention all these things to show you how much I have gone into the fight which comes to an end to-day, and it may perhaps excuse me in your eyes for writing so little to you within the past two months.

"I have read your letters to P. and myself, acknowledging the speech sent from Columbus, and K.'s of a similar date. As for the reported speech, I can only say that I knew you would want to see it and would judge it leniently, but it was hardly up to the opportunity I expected to have, and my later speeches were very much better in all respects. I have learned many arts and wrinkles in this long campaign. As for the general result, I can hardly venture a prediction, although prophecies of defeat are liberally made on every side. Long before this meets your eye we shall both know the result, and prophecy is useless. But I think that the Republicans are going to be beaten. The canvass has been shamefully mismanaged by the 'regulars' and 'machine-men' of the party, who insisted on carrying it on in their own way. Instead of bringing the best men to the front and fighting the battle on Hayes's letter of acceptance, they preferred to believe that it was won without a struggle, before a shot had been fired, and when they did wake up it was very late in the day. Bristow, Schurz, Evarts, and men like them have done their utmost, and made a gallant fight. My own position is clear enough. I have supported Hayes because I believe him to be honest and sincere. I am in the party and yet not of it, and, personally, men like me may be more benefited by its failure than by its success. The time may then come when we shall be needed. As long as the party continues to enjoy unbroken power such men as I are treated with no consideration, and indeed little respect. But I earnestly hope to see Hayes elected. I saw him several times when at Columbus. He is an educated, cultivated gentleman, and his wife is a charming woman. We had much pleasant conversation, and if the thing turn out as I fear it will, I shall feel personal regret and disappointment. But I have learned to take political defeats philosophically, and shall accept this as I did McClure's and Bristow's,—with serenity and composure. But if we defeat the

Democrats,—who in little persons have been too large for their clothing for a week past, and in larger ones have been unendurable from their boasting and noise,—I shall lift up a sound of rejoicing that shall be heard afar.

"I could write you a column a mile long of my Western experiences. Such things as this I saw: imagine a little, new town, perhaps ten years old, its houses common, its streets full of dust. Through the streets pours an unceasing procession of wagons, carriages, carts, buggies, and horsemen, with a mass of pedestrians on both its flanks. Many of the wagons, etc., are decorated with colored muslin, flowers, flags, and evergreens. Young girls dressed in white, with tri-colored scarfs and garlands of country flowers, fill them. Youths in a sort of improvised uniform ride in the crowd in companies. Here there is a huge wagon filled with girls, who go by singing, while from an elevated place in the centre a young woman, gotten up in spangled dress as a Goddess of Liberty, waves a flag or banner. There a log cabin with live 'coons on top, and corn and pumpkins hanging from the eaves, is drawn along on wheels, while two fellows dressed up are at the door,—one as an old woman knitting, the other a man chopping wood. Every sort of decoration and device is resorted to, and the ingenuity and versatility of the people are remarkable. At length the procession reaches a grove, where it winds about a speaker's stand built between four trees, and there in a little while, seated in a chair,—for his legs are paralyzed,—Senator Morton talks to a countless multitude for two hours or more. In the evening I speak to them as long from the same place, by the light of torches; or, if the night be stormy, in the court-house or town-hall.

"General Harrison, our candidate, who ought to have been elected, is a gentleman of ability and character,—a grandson, too, of old Tippecanoe. Hence, of course, the log cabins and 'coons, which will remind you of the campaign of 1840. Here are some facts to interest you. There were made during the last week of the campaign in Indiana, by gentlemen from all parts of the country, —invited by the State committee,—eight hundred and thirty-eight speeches in each of the counties of the State. Those made by candidates or volunteers were too numerous to be counted. At one place the crowd that came to hear Governor Morton—but remained to hear us both—was estimated to be twelve thousand, and at Indian-

*

apolis the torchlight procession had five thousand torches in line, many of them borne by lawyers and merchants and business men of standing; our carriage, drawn by four horses, was escorted by about three hundred cavalry, or mounted torch-bearers, and through the street of the city we moved in the glare of continuous fireworks. When I rose to speak afterwards at the base-ball grounds, it seemed to me that I overlooked a lake of fire in which ten thousand red-shirted men were striving to keep afloat.

"In this State the features of the campaign are tamer; but at Gettysburg I had an enormous meeting and a very enthusiastic one. Anthony Higgins presided at Wilmington in the opera-house, which was packed. L. and P. and P. went down with me, and we dined at Tony's bachelor quarters, and supped after my speech at a friend's,—Mr. Buck's. At Burlington I spoke to a crowd packed into the old lyceum, such as neither Signor Blitz nor Dr. Valentine nor Mungandaus, the Chippewa chieftain, ever drew; and when I spoke of what I had seen on the stage on which I stood, and described the latter scalping his fallen enemy, and, amid a profuse spilling of red-flannel blood, braining him with a brand-new tomahawk purchased for the occasion at Page & Thomas's, and decorated with eagle feathers wrung from a turkey that might have hung in state in the old market-house in Union Street, many a man in the audience remembered things he had not thought of perhaps for twenty years. So much, then, for this matter of the stump. I know you will be amused to hear these things."

In describing one of his Western talks, he says: "I delivered last night a speech to a crowd of between three and four thousand in the Capitol Square. Of course, in the actual delivery I varied it with remarks and 'stories,' which are omitted in the report." His address at Columbus, Ohio, September 26, 1876,—one (as he said) of twenty-two,— would serve as a good specimen of these campaign speeches. It draws the lines of party politics with bold strokes. It reviews the financial question acutely; the political situation of the South is seriously and yet candidly treated; and, lastly, the subject of governmental reform of the civil service is discussed in a way that convinces one that the speaker is not a merely theoretic but a practical reformer.

At the beginning of the year 1877 the Reformers were again at work concentrating their efforts on a nomination for the mayoralty of Philadelphia. Both William S. Stokley and Joseph L. Caven were prominent and honored Republicans, but the latter was run as an independent candidate, sustained by Republicans, Democrats, Liberals, and all shades of Reformers. He had made a decided record against municipal extravagance and corruption, and had done faithful work in building up a powerful public sentiment in favor of retrenchment, economy, and a general reform in finance and the public service. A great meeting of citizens and tax-payers was held at Horticultural Hall, under the auspices of the Reform Club, on the evening of January 20, 1877, William Welsh, Esq., in the chair. Several gentlemen spoke, though Mr. Brown's was the principal address of the occasion, and, by some of his friends, was considered the most powerful political speech he ever made. Its closing sentences were solemn in their simple impressiveness:

"My countrymen: 'Time makes no pauses in his march.' The moments are swiftly passing, and you who make up this mighty multitude will presently have scattered to your homes. Great opportunities come but once and stay but a little while. Days quickly make the weeks, and soon this battle will be lost or won. Change is ever going on about us, and you who listen, and I who speak, shall in brief time pass from the stage on which we are to-day the actors, and our places be taken by our own children. Let it not then be written, that while the sounds of your great festival still lingered in the air, ere yet that pleasant city which Penn founded, where Jefferson wrote, and Washington lived and Franklin died, had filled her second century, self-government was already an outcast, and true liberty could find no stone to pillow her head. Let them rather say that then, as always, in every crisis of her history, though leaders were weak and parties wanting, the heart of the people did not falter, and the sons of those who had so often protected others still had the courage to protect themselves."

As this is the last of his public efforts in the work of municipal reform, it should be emphatically stated that its effect upon public opinion both at the moment and onward was great. It has been declared by a prominent public man whose opinion is of great weight, that the local Reform movement in Philadelphia began and ended with Henry Armitt Brown. He certainly embodied the best there was in it, and his mantle has fallen upon no successor. Would that his example might continue to be influential, so that he might be, as it were, the founder or the type of a race of politicians in this country who, keeping themselves pure from personal aims, might make politics the noblest of sciences! Then something like a broad impulse might be given to public affairs, and a theory of national government might be carried out, which would put the labored absolutistic systems of a Stein or a Bismarck, colossal as they are, to the blush.

During these busy years of public life his early friends, and his college friends especially, were not forgotten. One of these during this period came to Philadelphia in a state of despondency so profound that it ended in mental derangement, or something nearly bordering upon it, so that he became an inmate for six weeks of the Pennsylvania Asylum. During that time Mr. Brown visited him constantly, sometimes every day, talking with him, encouraging him, amusing him, fairly lifting him out of his dreadful condition by the force of his indomitable affectionate will, so that he was, mainly, as it would seem, through this instrumentality, restored to his normal state. One closely

related to the poor sufferer, during this trying period writes:
" As one of ——'s dearest friends I thought it my turn to
render thanks for your great kindness to him.   We all feel
most tenderly grateful to you, and deeply appreciate that
noble friendship which prompts you to take upon yourself
so much trouble for his sake.   —— desires me most heartily
to express her thanks to you for your labor and success in
persuading him to send his letter,—a truly 'great thing' for
him to do, and no one else could have induced him to do it.
I think that 'Harry Brown' is the only link which binds
him to what is pleasant, and to life."

At a meeting called by the Union League to endorse the
administration of President Hayes, held March 12, 1877, Mr.
Brown made a short speech, in the course of which, considering his political status, these very generous words occur :

" I am no prophet, and political prophecy is the most dangerous
of all. But I have no fears for this government or people. I am
one of the youngest in this company, but I have seen extraordinary
things. If I look back less than a year in point of time, I behold
enough. I have seen in that short space the most marvellous dis-
plays of patriotic spirit and common sense. I have seen two great
parties alike demanding a safe and honorable policy in their platforms, and expressing in their candidates, each as well as it was
able, its idea of Reform. I have seen a long and heated contest
followed by four months of uncertainty and doubt as to who should
be our ruler and what the controlling power in our government. I
have seen a free people, where suffrage is universal and liberty absolute, remain tranquil and self-controlled in the midst of things
that might have shaken to pieces the strongest despotism. I have
seen forty millions of freemen intrusting to fifteen individuals the
question who should govern them for four years to come. I have
seen those fifteen persons decide by a majority of one that he should
be chief magistrate who claimed to be chosen by the smallest majority possible in the electoral college,—a single vote ; and those
forty millions yield a perfect obedience to the law. I have seen that

man, standing uncovered in the presence of the people, declare him-self their servant rather than his party's,—the lover of his country rather than himself. I see him to-day, in the Presidential chair, proclaim a broad and generous policy; a brave, benevolent, consist-ent statesmanship, fulfilling the definition of Edmund Burke, that he is the true statesman who 'unites the ability to improve with the disposition to preserve.'"

In the crisis immediately succeeding the election, Mr. Brown, with other prominent politicians, had been "inter-viewed." He was modest in giving his opinion, but while fully prepared to support a legitimate decision either way, he was decided in his belief that Hayes had been duly elected. He thought that both parties were not without blame, that no man or party could afford to profit by a fraud, and that parties themselves were not an end, but only a means to an end,—the prosperity and honor of the country. The laws must be sustained at all events. The constitutional forms of law must be carried out. There must be a conscientious settlement of the electoral question. He wished the electoral college were abolished, but it was not, and its rules must be implicitly followed. He did not fear the local trouble that threatened the Presidential in-auguration. A system which could stand the strain it was then undergoing could stand anything. "We have plenty of patriots," he said, "if we have few statesmen, and, after all, the situation doesn't demand statesmanship as much as it does common sense and self-control. I don't think it perilous, because, though I'm not very old, I've lived long enough to have seen an abundance of those qualities in my countrymen."

These activities were interrupted by another visit to Europe in the summer and autumn of 1877. During this journey he wrote many letters for the newspapers, in which he spoke of European politics and described prominent men whom he saw. One of these letters is taken up with a graphic portraiture of Thiers; another with an account of a French election, and how the voting is done in Paris; but we will quote from these letters only his narrative of an eventful and perilous passage home on the steamship "Pennsylvania," during the early days of November.

"I think it worth while to try and give the *Times* some account of the recent remarkable voyage of the 'Pennsylvania.' We left Liverpool about 4 P.M. on the 31st of October. The night before had been dark and stormy, and when evening fell, as we came out of the Mersey, the prospect was not favorable. But the next day broke pleasantly enough, and there was nothing in the western sky as we steamed out of Queenstown harbor and along the Irish coast to suggest the dangers that were in store for us. Friday, the 2d of November, was a pleasant day, and we spent most of the time on deck. Our company was not a large one. Exclusive of the servants and children, I think we numbered but twenty-five. Friday night when I went to bed we were steaming along at eleven or twelve knots, with the sky partially overcast and a stiff but not unfavorable breeze. During the darkness we encountered the storm. I thought the old ship was rolling rather heavily when I awoke on the morning of the 3d, but I did not imagine the true state of things. Those who had been on deck told me after breakfast that it was stormy and wet up there, and I amused myself below. About three o'clock, however, I concluded to go up and take a look.

"The sky was full of clouds, angry and savage-looking, though there were patches of blue sky to be seen, and through one of them the sun was shining brightly. But the wind was dead ahead and blowing a gale. I stuck my head out, and it seemed as if the wind would blow it off my shoulders. The sea was magnificent. In five previous voyages I had never seen it so high. Great waves, longer than the ship, and, as it seemed me, higher than the boats on her sides, followed one another swiftly, tossing their white-caps into spray as they split in two on both sides of us. The 'Pennsylvania' would rise up like a living creature over the tops of the highest, and then rush down into the boiling valley that lay between them with incredible speed. One after another I could see great ridges of water approaching us at a terrible rate with strange regularity, and each time as they struck our bow the ship would shake herself and make a rush and pass over them in safety. I hung on to the side of the door and watched the waves break at the bow, and sometimes come rushing back over the deck, with intensest interest. Presently the chief officer, Mr. Dodge, came sliding along, and stopped for a minute's chat. 'A heavy westerly gale,' he called it, and 'a very bad sea,' and presently he slid off to his duty and I went downstairs to dinner. Very little was said about the weather at the meal, which was pleasant enough in spite of the rolling, and after an evening passed in chat we all turned in, as we thought, to sleep. But by ten or eleven o'clock slumber was impossible. The motion was a combination of all that is disagreeable in the movement of a ship. At one minute the vessel rolled, at another she pitched, now she seemed to be climbing skyward, and in an instant pitched into an abyss, to be brought up suddenly with a terrible thump. By midnight I felt sure that the sea which I had watched with such admiration was nothing to what we now encountered. Slowly the hours dragged along, and we struggled through them.

"At last day came, and with it an increase of fury in the storm. Of course there was no going on deck and little comfort in the 'social hall,' for the windows and doors had to be tightly shut. All day we watched and waited, comforting ourselves with the thought that so furious a storm could not last many hours, but the wind and waves knew better. Sunday evening repeated the torments of the night before, but about midnight the wind went down somewhat, and Captain Harris, with characteristic thoughtfulness, sent word to the ladies of the fact. After that, for a few hours, almost every one slept a little; but Monday morning broke in storm and disappointment. As if it had only been resting to renew the attack more furiously than ever, the gale came on with daybreak. From that time until sundown, and from that till Tuesday morning and all Tuesday and the night that followed, it raged with fury. On Wednesday morning it had long ceased to be a gale and become a hurricane. The wind (they estimated on the bridge) blew with a velocity of one hundred miles an hour, and the sea was lifted up into mountains. All that day and the next, until Friday morning, the 9th of November, it blew a hurricane. It is as impossible for me to describe those

days as it is for me to forget them. They were dark and terrible.
From morning till night, from sundown until daybreak, for six
nights and days, there was no change. As one looked out from the
windows of the social hall, or through the tightly-fastened ports, the
scene was indescribably awful. Beneath a leaden sky, far as one
could see, raged the tossing ocean. Without a lull the wind howled
and hissed through the rigging, and lashed the sea into a mass of
foam. In every direction, on all sides, the waves broke, dashing the
spray until the air seemed full of rain-like clouds.

" So the stormy days crept by and dragged the gloomier nights
after them. About ten o'clock on the sixth night,—Thursday,—
when all hands in the cabin had retired, not to sleep, but to watch
for daylight, the ship gave an unusually heavy lurch to the starboard, and for the hundredth time shipped a heavy sea. In a second
followed a crash that shook her from stem to stern, and sounded like
a thunderbolt. It was made up of three distinct sounds in one,—
the dull fall of a heavy weight on the deck, the splintering and
crushing of wood and glass, and the pouring of a large stream of
water into the cabin. It was a deafening, terrifying sound. I
bounded into the saloon and beheld a memorable sight. Beside my
door sat a lady with her hands clasped together, gasping with fear.
Across the saloon were three others as white as a sheet, in various
attitudes of alarm ; the startled face of one of the men appeared at
the door on my side of the ship; and down the companion-way, as
the vessel rolled to port, poured a huge torrent of water. In a moment we rolled to starboard, the stream stopped pouring in and
dashed furiously against the tables and piano, wetting me in an instant above the ankles, and splashing to the ceiling. Half a minute
later everybody was in the saloon,—no one had apparently undressed
and gone to bed,—and for a little while we were busy in picking up
our luggage from the floors of the cabins, into which the water at
once penetrated. The unhappy stewards rushed to and fro, bailing
out and mopping up the water, and in half an hour the wet carpets
were taken up and the water dried from the floor, the broken windows, through which the water had come, nailed up and closed, and
nothing remained for us but to talk the thing over and wait for daylight. I must say that it was a plucky company,—no tears were
shed and no hysterics indulged in by the ladies, and, as far as I saw,
every man was quiet and ready and self-possessed. But it certainly

was a startling incident, coming to us as it did after so many days and nights of anxiety and apprehension.

"'We had taken on board,' said one of the officers to me, 'a hundred seas as bad as that on that day alone, but they struck us fair.' This one came as the wind began to fall a little on the starboard quarter. It struck the right end of the bridge and carried away the canvas covering, broke in and ruined the second boat, lifted the third boat out of the davits and hurled it into a thousand pieces on top of the skylight over the engines, twisted the fourth boat out of the davits (breaking one of the latter, a piece of hammered iron four and a half inches thick, like a pipe-stem) and smashed it to bits against the corner of the social hall, breaking two windows and letting in the water, and, besides damaging two other life-rafts, tore the last one on the starboard side out of its place and laid it snugly over the skylight on the saloon. Omitting details, this was the result of one wave. There were some of us who, as we crawled about on deck next day and witnessed the destruction, could not help thinking what might have happened to us had anything in the steering apparatus broken or become disarranged. When Friday morning came the wind had fallen greatly, though the sea was still high, and we had some music in the cabin. The storm seemed at last to have spent its force, and our spirits rose with the barometer. About ten o'clock we dispersed, the ship had begun to run smoothly, and, for one, I expected to get a nap, the first for a long time. All had become quiet, when suddenly the engine stopped. I sprang up and climbed the stairway. 'A steamer is signalling us,' said a fellow-passenger. Looking out, I saw a curious light close by on the port side, and then hurried down for my hat and overcoat, for it was wet and very cold. When I got up again in a minute afterward the light was close under the stern. 'It's a wreck,' said a dozen voices in the darkness, and then faintly through the blustering storm came the cry, 'Steamer, ahoy!'

"As I crept along the deck, feeling my way, I could see a bright light burning close to the water's edge. Captain Harris commanded silence, and called in stentorian tones, 'Have you got a boat?' No sound came back but the roaring of the wind, and the light grew fainter and more distant. 'Close to the water's edge,' 'the masts torn out of her,' 'a big wreck,' passed in whispers as the captain tried to make her out with the glass,—and we stood in a group near the wheel-house watching the fast-fading light. Suddenly it disappeared, suggesting to my mind a horrible possibility. 'Call for a volunteer crew,' came from the captain's lips, and he ran forward to the bridge. In a few moments the wreck's light again appeared, faint and flickering, and where we stood holding on to the bulwarks we could hear Captain Harris's voice giving orders even above the whistling of the wind. In a few moments the forward boat on the starboard side swung clear. Mr. Shackford, the second officer, and the six seamen who had promptly volunteered, were on board; the order was given, and down the frail thing descended with them into the black, seething abyss below. For an instant I thought they would disappear beneath the ship as she rolled heavily over on them. But the next they were tossed in the air as high as the bulwarks. A faint light made them visible to us as they pulled for their lives. Once, twice, thrice, as we watched them, they were sucked back under the great ship's side, as if doomed to be crushed beneath her, but at last a huge wave caught them, and away they went. And Heaven favored that gallant crew, and Captain Harris understood his business. By keeping the ship in motion and moving her around in a circle he got to leeward of the wreck again, and in about an hour the boat came sweeping back toward us again. Around the bow she swept and away off into the darkness, whirled about as if she were a feather; at last they managed, after several efforts, to catch the rope, and one by one as the life-boat rose to the sea they were picked out and set firmly on deck again. They had got near enough to hear voices on the wreck cry, 'Come alongside.'

"No one had asked to be taken off nor called for provisions, and the sea ran too high to get near, so Mr. Shackford answered that we would lay to till morning, and after trying to communicate further returned to the 'Pennsylvania.' I pass over the inconveniences of the night that followed. Its physical discomforts were the worst of the voyage, as we lay till daybreak rolling slowly to and fro in the trough of that tremendous sea. At last the long-delayed morning began slowly to break, and the horrible blackness of the sea and sky gave place to a cold and cruel gray. But with the hidden sun the wind began to rise. By seven o'clock it was blowing another gale, and the impatient sea was being whipped into its old fury again. There, as we steamed towards her, was the wreck, a trim, staunch-looking bark of three or four hundred tons, riding the waves buoyantly, with two short jury-masts bearing a storm-sail, and holding her well to the wind.   Except for the disproportionate shortness of her masts, she looked to my landsman's eye all right.   Two or three men could be seen on deck, and the smoke that came out of the stove-pipe in the cabin roof told that she had the comfort of a fire.   But we could do no more than see her.   Help her we could not.   No boat could live in such a sea, and we lost our fourth boat in the attempt.   As a last effort, about ten o'clock, Captain Harris got as near as he dared go in such a sea, and launched a life-raft with a long cable, hoping that he could get it towards the wreck by the aid of the sea.   But repeated efforts availed little, and by eleven o'clock in the morning our own safety compelled us to head to sea. The weather thickened up, and presently we lost sight of the unfortunate vessel.   Further efforts were useless, and we crept slowly towards the westward.

"Such was this memorable voyage.   Of the severity and length of these storms there seemed to be among the officers but one opinion.   Rarely had any one seen so fierce a gale, never so bad a sea, and the way both lasted was beyond precedent.   Had the 'Pennsylvania' not been the best of ships, exceptionally staunch and strong, and from her peculiar model riding the waves with wonderful buoyancy,—and had she not been commanded and officered as she was by men of great experience and skill, and extraordinary courage and endurance, her career would undoubtedly have ended in those words, 'lost at sea,' or 'never heard of,' which stand against the names of many a noble ship, and are the curt epitaph of many a gallant company.   Henceforth these words will have for me a new significance.   I think I can imagine now, perhaps, some of those unseen tragedies,—the anxiety, the hope, the sudden crash, the gallant struggles, the roaring wind, the cruel, overwhelming sea, the wild confusion, the terror, the despair, the short but awful agony.   Certain it is, that never did my eyes rest on a pleasanter sight than when, on Thursday morning last, I stood on the deck of the 'Pennsylvania' and beheld a broad and noble river flowing majestically to the sea between long lines of low and level shore, and before me the spires and steeples of a placid city beginning to rise out of the marshes and meadows of League Island.   For not stately London, nor brilliant Paris, nor quaint old Nuremberg, not the green fields and woods of England, nor the magnificent scenery of the Alps, nor all the hills and dales that lie between, could offer me the charms that dwell in those narrow streets, with their monotonous rows of formal, pleasant homes, which, but a week before, I had more than once thought I should never see again."

Mr. Brown, in fulfilment of an invitation received some time before his visit to Europe, immediately after his return, quietly, but diligently, set himself about preparing his Burlington bi-centennial Historical Address. His labors and investigations were indefatigable. He strove to combine amplitude of detail with accuracy, and no hound ever tracked his prey more unremittingly than he followed up an historical fact, however minute, that added life to his history. He went to first sources. His accustomed seat in an alcove of the Philadelphia Historical Society Library is pointed out, where for days and weeks he labored in the compilation of his materials. He spared himself no pains. He read extensively and yet selected with severest care. He corresponded widely with those from whom he could derive the least information. Days of incessant research were considered by him as not lost if they brought but the slightest historic matter to his store. Family memorials as well as public documents were ransacked. The result was something of rare and permanent value.

The opening services of the occasion are thus described in the *Philadelphia Weekly Times* of December 15, 1877:

"The old Quaker town of Burlington, New Jersey, celebrated on Thursday, the 6th of December, the two hundredth anniversary of its formation. The morning opened clear and cool. The river-banks and pine-lands gave up their population, and Burlington's own seven thousand people let it be known that they could act the host with the old-fashioned Fourth of July spirit. The one hundred guns sounded faintly in the dawn because a stiff breeze swept up the curve in the Delaware and bore inland all the noise of the early morning. Chimes from St. Mary's and all the steeples of the academic city were half drowned by the flap and flutter of the decorations which stuck around everywhere, from stores, dwellings, and trees. The rallying-point for the crowd was at the intersection of the two wide thoroughfares, Broad and Main Streets, and when, at ten o'clock, General E. Burd Grubb, the marshal, and his aides brought it into order, the procession was formed and moved out of Main Street. Following the cavalcade of citizens came the militia companies of Burlington, Beverly, Camden, and Mount Holly, the fire companies in gorgeous array, and a number of civil societies. Meanwhile, the crowd enjoyed itself on the sidewalks, and bands of young men in fantastic attire wandered about and added to the excitement and the racket. The church-bells rang out more clearly above the din about noon, because the wind blew less sharply, and the mid-day salute quickened the step of such of the tramping soldier boys as were in earshot.

"At three o'clock the commemorative services were begun in Birch's new opera-house. Steady-going, well-to-do folks of Burlington, Trenton, Mount Holly, Beverly, Camden, and many Philadelphians formed the audience. On the stage were a dozen circles of distinguished gentlemen. The Right Rev. William H. Odenheimer, Bishop of Northern New Jersey, sat in his episcopal robes in the chair of honor. By his side was Vicar-General George Herbert Doane, of Newark, and behind them were ex-Governor Parker, tall and sturdy, ex-Governor Newell, Congressman J. Howard Pugh, Hon. John F. Babcock, a score of well-known clergymen, and members of the State Legislature and the Burlington City Council.

"Bishop Odenheimer made a short prayer. A musical piece suggesting the heroism of the early Quaker pioneers was sung by the Orpheus Glee Club, and the president of the bi-centennial committee, Congressman Pugh, stepped forward. The address of the day, he said, belonged to another man, one pre-eminently fitted to make it, yet he would congratulate his townsmen upon the unity of interest, fervor, and enthusiasm which was manifestly characteristic of the occasion. Dr. Pugh said: ' And now here is one whom we claim as a Burlington boy, for most of the time since his boyhood, at least, he has made his summer home with us, Henry Armitt Brown, Esq.' "

The address itself must be estimated upon its own merits. After its delivery, notices eulogistic and letters congratulatory poured in. We give a few of these letters, dated two or three months later, from those at a distance, whose judgment might be presumed to be cooler, in acknowledgment of printed copies of the address, and which naturally find place here:

"Boston, March 19, 1878.

"My dear Mr. Brown,—I have read with as much delight as instruction your eloquent and noble Burlington oration. I was especially impressed with the passage relating to the Quaker petitioners to Parliament, who offered themselves as hostages for their imprisoned brethren. I agree with you in thinking it one of the most pathetic instances in English history. But the whole of your address is admirable in spirit, in tone, in command of novel facts.

"Renewing my thanks to you for enabling me to indulge in the luxury of reading such an oration,

"I remain, very sincerely yours,

"E. P. Whipple."

"Boston, March 19, 1878.

"My dear Sir,—I thank you for the pleasure I have had in reading your very elaborate and interesting oration. Plymouth Rock, we shall have to confess, has not sent forth all the heroes, or called forth all the eloquence. I only wish that as much knowledge, as much taste, as much lively description could be found in all the addresses in which the anniversaries of our historical epochs are commemorated.

"Believe me, my dear sir,

"Very truly yours,

"O. W. Holmes."

"Boston, March 25, 1878.

"Dear Mr. Brown,—I thank you for sending me your oration on the 'Settlement of Burlington.'

"I had skimmed it over in the newspaper, but I have given it a worthier perusal in the pamphlet.

"It is an interesting and eloquent discourse, and I congratulate you on your success. I hope you will have spared a copy for our Massachusetts Historical Society.

"Believe me, with kind regards to your wife,

"Yours very truly,

"Robert C. Winthrop.

"P.S.—I did not fail to observe with interest the classical tribute to the memory of your father."

"Oak Knoll, Danvers, Mass., March 26, 1878.

"Hon. H. A. Brown.

"Dear Friend,—I have read with great satisfaction thy instructive and eloquent address. As a member of the Society of Friends, I heartily thank thee for it. I hope the perusal of it will have a good effect upon a class in our

Society who make it a point to disparage and undervalue
the early Quakers.

"With high regard, thy friend,
"JOHN G. WHITTIER."

" CAMBRIDGE, March 26, 1878.

"DEAR MR. BROWN,—I have received and read with
great interest and pleasure your oration on the 'Settlement
of Burlington.'

"It is a very stirring and eloquent production, and very
picturesque in its details.

"Please accept my cordial thanks for your thought of
me, and for making me one of your hearers at second hand,
—that is to say, one of your attentive and sympathizing
readers.

"I remember Burlington in the old stage-coach and
steamboat days; and remember passing the entrance to
Joseph Bonaparte's grounds. It was in May; and the
scenery seemed, and still seems to me in memory, very
lovely. Your words bring it all back to me. It is like
presenting me a bouquet.

"Be kind enough to give my best regards and remembrance to Mrs. Brown, and believe me,

"Yours very truly,
"HENRY W. LONGFELLOW."

" WASHINGTON, D. C., March 28, 1878.

"MY DEAR SIR,—I have received your oration and
have read it, as I always do what you write, with great
interest.

"You inquire respecting unprinted accounts of the
winter at Valley Forge. I apprehend that there is very
little, or nothing, to be added to the printed material that

relates to that subject. I do not know of anything relating to it in the public archives that is nòt already before the world. Among my own manuscript collections, I have one journal of the time, and at least one allusion to it, made by German officers who were there. These shall be perfectly at your service if you chance to come to Washington; but I am bound to say there is nothing in them which would repay the time and trouble of the journey.

> "Very truly yours,
>
> "GEO. BANCROFT."

These letters may possibly appear to be the courteous expressions of those who knew how to say kind things to young men of worth and promise; but that they were more, and were genuine words of praise, we think the address will show, when candidly read. The charge of prolixity does not hold against this oration. Its style, while finished, is not highly rhetorical. It is in quiet good taste as befitting the peaceful old Quaker town about which its loving memories linger. It has more of the unpretending plainness of perfect speech than is commonly found. It is not wordy, but terse and solid with facts. Whole periods of history are analyzed and comprehensively summed up. Without dwelling minutely upon them, an event, a character, a scene, are painted in a few vigorous strokes. The address has that picturesque life and freshness which is the result of the most thorough study, and of a genuine interest on the part of the speaker. As it draws near its close, there are touches of delicate pathos quite inimitable, and best understood by those to whom it was spoken. It is an eminently sensible address throughout,—homespun, we would call it, if it were not so beautiful;—and, above all, there is an appreciation of what is genuinely noble in principle weakened by no conventional narrowness or mere sentimentalism. The manly ring of righteousness is in it. It exhibits the character of one who sees the true greatness of the beginnings of a State which is established in justice.

Political matters at that time, when the financial question, the Southern question, civil reform, and other great subjects awaiting the action of a new administration were agitated, mingled with professional business, seem to have taken up the early part of the last year of Mr. Brown's life. He was, as one of his friends writes, "still dreaming of reform." He held on to that idea, not disheartened for a moment, urging it constantly upon such men as Mr. Schurz, Mr. Bristow, and other leading politicians of his own school, and pouring out to them what he had in his heart. He would do his part to give a decided trend to the political current. He was earnest in the hope of the advancement of the main object of his life, believing as he did that government itself was the best instrument of political reform. He had indeed no Quixotic conception of perfect justice being done, but he thought that an organization already established—viz., the State—was one of the most powerful means of securing the redress and protection of the rights of all, and the greatest good of the greatest number, which is the end of true government. He had more confidence in men than others had, and he wished to make trial of all who promised anything. At the same time he was keen-sighted, and was not deceived by appearances. He was already suspicious of some " whose leadership is no rebuke to wrong even if it does not discourage the right." He prophesied " the biggest fight, within six months of Governor Hayes's inaugural, that ever tried the courage of a President." He longed for "the more positive assertion of the reform principle, which would give courage to honest men in the nation." He thought, with a few others, that "bold leadership" and "heroic treatment" were sometimes required. These, and not "good intentions" alone, could inspire courage at a time when national affairs looked so dark.

On the questions of hard money, of Southern pacification, and kindred topics, he thought the government at that time had made a fair record, or, at least, had made a fair show, but there were peculiar difficulties arising from organized opposition in the Senate, and feeble support in the House, on the question of the reform of the civil service, and here he felt that a united effort by the purest and best men in the nation, and especially in the Republican party, was demanded. He was restless under the silence and supineness of the Reform party in the land, and, if he had lived, his voice would have rung out in unmistakable tones, urging on what he considered to be the cause of civil purification.

On the subject of the tariff Mr. Brown differed with many good men, and with some of his best friends, and, true to his Yale training, was strongly inclined (though not yet entirely given over) to free-trade views, as being, on the whole, better than even a temporary system of protection which necessitates governmental intermeddling with trade; in fact, he had been chosen, about a year before, to the membership of the Cobden Club, London, and had been asked to contribute a paper upon free trade.

At a bar meeting held March 14, 1878, in memory of an eminent lawyer, James H. Castle, Esq., Mr. Brown was one of the speakers. His remarks were brief but to the point. He said:

"Mr. Chairman,—Before these resolutions are put to a vote I want to say a word. I have no wish to make a speech, for I am not unmindful that that privilege belongs to those who are older at the bar and older in friendship with Mr. Castle than I can claim to have been. But I grew up within the sunny circle which his nature threw around him, and for more than a third of my lifetime I have enjoyed a friendship with him as close as was possible, perhaps, between two men separated, in point of age, by more than a quarter of a century. I should be sorry to mar the harmony of this most harmonious meeting by any attempt to add words of mine to what has been already said in eulogy of him, but the allusions made by my friends, Mr. Morris and Judge Mitchell, to the melancholy prediction written on his photograph, have suggested to me, as I sat here, that I should tell you what happened when I saw him last. Less than three weeks ago—a fortnight ago on Saturday evening—I was told that Mr. Castle was in the parlor. When I hurried down-stairs he greeted me as heartily as ever, and told me that he had heard that I was engaged in something in which perhaps he could help me. He had, he said, a map drawn by an officer of Lafayette's staff, of the retreat from Barren Hill, which he wanted me to see. It was an original, and unique. I said I would call at his house and get it. 'No,' he replied; 'I will leave it at your office on Monday morning as I go to mine.' I repeated that I had rather call on him. 'Let me have my way about it,' he interrupted; and I acquiesced. He did not wait until Monday, but, characteristically, brought the map and left it for me the next evening at my door. I noticed that he spoke in a husky voice, as if he had a cold. It was not that, he explained, but something which had begun to grow in his throat and gave him trouble. He had just come from his physicians, and, said he, 'They are going to cut my throat.' He answered my anxious questions with a half-serious, half-jocular manner that was natural to him, and presently arose to go. I went with him to the door. As he stood for a moment on the steps he turned, and, taking my hand in his, said, 'Well, I sha'n't see you again, so we had better say good-by.' 'Oh, Mr. Castle,' I exclaimed, 'don't talk so!' 'Yes,' he repeated, 'you will never see me again. Good-by, my boy;' and, with a warm squeeze of my hand, he passed quickly down the steps and vanished into the night.

"I know very well, sir, that the life of man is short. 'The life of man,' said the old Saxon thane, ' is like the flight of a sparrow in the winter-time, that comes in at the open door, flutters for a moment in the firelight on the hearth, and, on a sudden, darts out again into the icy darkness.' I may be the next one of this company to follow him whom we lament to-day. But should my life be lengthened to the years of the venerable gentleman who sits before me, I shall never forget that manly form as it stood there for a moment, for the last time, on my threshold. I shall never forget that beautiful countenance and the warm grasp of that honest right hand. I shall never forget that dead gentleman who was my friend; and the tones of that prophetic farewell—for such it has sadly come to be—touched a chord in my heart and memory that will ever vibrate at the mention of his name."

Near the beginning of the last year of his life, Mr. Brown had been asked to deliver an oration on the anniversary of the occupation of Valley Forge. The following is a letter from Benson J. Lossing, Esq., who was consulted by him upon this historic theme:

" THE RIDGE, DOVER PLAINS,
" DUTCHESS Co., N. Y., April 1, 1878.

"MY DEAR SIR,—Your esteemed favor of the 23d March reached my desk during my absence from home, and this is my excuse for seeming discourtesy in not promptly responding.

"I really have no knowledge of facts concerning the history or incidents of Valley Forge other than what may be found in the books you have mentioned. I gathered all I could find, at the time, for my 'Field-Book of the Revolution,' and nothing new that seemed authentic has fallen in my way since.

"I suppose the time chosen for your oration (June) implies that the central historic point in your discourse will be the departure of Washington from Valley Forge to pursue Clinton across New Jersey. I have prepared a paper for the June number of *Harper's Magazine* on the battle of Monmouth. It will be issued about the middle of May. I do not know that you will find much that is new in it. I made brief extracts from a diary, or rather an orderly book of a British officer, that was found on the field of Monmouth after the battle. The orderly book was deposited in the Historical Society of Pennsylvania by Mr. Buckelew. Through Professor Samuel Lockwood, of Freehold, New Jersey, I got permission to make use of it, and Mr. John J. ——, of the Historical Society of Pennsylvania, kindly sent it to me. At the request of Mr. Buckelew I returned it to Professor Lockwood, and I presume it has been sent back again to the Historical Society. Have you 'The Treason of Major-General Charles Lee,' by Dr. George H. Moore, late librarian of the New York Historical Society? It casts light upon the incident noted in my Field-Book of the hesitation of Lee in taking the oath of allegiance at Valley Forge, and of other incidents of his official career, to which I have alluded in the paper for 'Harper.'

"I am sure the author of the oration at Burlington last December, and at the Centennial Celebration of the meeting of the First Continental Congress, needs no suggestions from me as to the treatment of *any* subject. I cannot tell you how much I have enjoyed the perusal of your Burlington oration, not only as an historical address, but as a literary composition. I am specially pleased with its pictures of the Quaker settlers in that region, for I am of Quaker descent on my mother's side,—Long Island settlers. The oration must have been specially pleasing to the old families of West Jersey, and particularly of Burlington, because of its wealth of information upon local topics and honored citizens.

"Your kind avowal of your appreciation of my ' Field-Book of the Revolution' is very grateful to me, for it is another testimonial added to many, that the object I had in view in the peculiar *construction* of that work has been accomplished, namely, to induce *young* people to read and become acquainted with the period of our history which, as Paine said, ' tried men's souls.' It gratifies me to know that it turned the attention to that history of one so gifted, patriotic, and zealous as Henry Armitt Brown. I have placed your letter in the copy of the oration, which you kindly sent me, as a legacy for my children.

" With sentiments of cordial esteem,

" I am, dear sir, your sincere friend,

" BENSON J. LOSSING."

This oration at Valley Forge, delivered June 19, 1878, was the last of Mr. Brown's public efforts. He was, physically, in no sort of condition to undertake it. His system was run down by hard work, and it was only his resolute will that enabled him to go through the labor and excitement of the occasion. His brother, Frederick Brown, Esq., gives this brief account of the day so far as it relates to him personally:

"Early on the morning of the 19th June, 1878, I met Hal at the Norristown Railroad depot, and we started for Valley Forge. For forty-eight hours the rain had poured down, but this morning was clear, though warm, and the rain had freshened the earth and made all nature rejoice.

" Arriving at Norristown, we found a carriage waiting for us, and my brother enjoyed the drive of seven miles. It rather improved his condition. After driving down to see the review we took our lunch in the carriage, and then went to Mr. Todd's mansion, where we were most kindly received, and Hal had an hour's rest, and then to the tent. Three hours elapsed, and then Governor Hartranft introduced the orator of the day.

" He commenced, as was his usual practice, very slowly and distinctly. His voice had not its usual power at first, but gradually cleared, and after holding the audience completely in hand for some two hours, the last words were delivered with immense effect, and in perfect stillness. He turned, took three or four steps back to his chair, dropped into it, and almost fainted. Then cheer on cheer broke out, and a large number rushed forward to shake hands with him; but the first who neared him noticed his condition, and one kind soul called out to his fellows, ' Boys, this man is used up to-day. We'll wait till he is better to shake hands with him;' and the crowd fell back.

" Alas! the day that he was better was never to arrive. After he recovered sufficiently we started for Norristown, and then took the cars again, two good friends of Hal's accompanying us.

" When we reached his house it was 9.30 P.M., and he was ready for bed. After one day's rest he commenced writing the Monmouth Address, and finished it in bed on the 28th of June,—being taken with typhoid fever from which he never rallied, dying on the 21st of August, after fifty-eight days of steady fight between natural strength and science and the fever."

No one ever engaged an audience under greater difficulties. In the first place his voice was impaired by a cold, and then there was the constant banging of the band, the cracking of board benches, the cries of venders of all kinds of things, and the absence of any effective police regulations. But, in spite of all, the interest was held for two hours unflagging, and without the slightest manifestation of weariness, to the end. A detailed narrative of the scene and the oration has been written by a college friend. From this paper, which was originally prepared to be read before the Chicago Library Society, we give the following extract:

"The day itself was singularly beautiful. The crowd began to gather from all the adjacent country early in the morning. They visited with reverent interest the little stone house on the immediate banks of the river where Washington was quartered; dispersed themselves over the historic hills; traced out the old earthworks on the upper ridges, which the constantly renewed growth of the woods has preserved in nearly their original character; pointed out to each other from some stand-point of advantage the places where, over the fair fields of grass and grain, other lines of defence, long since obliterated, had once been located, and looked down the old Gulf road, glistening now under the clear June sunlight, over which the little army marched exactly a century ago full of the spirit of victory.

" Nothing could be finer than the sight, as toward midday the crowd, swelled now to large proportions, began to mass itself in and about the great tent, pitched by the side of what remained of an old redoubt that formed the key to the original line of defence. The most commonplace soul among them seemed to catch some of the inspiration of the spot and its memories.

" The horizon of those whose life had been most circumscribed must have been a little widened with the thought of what had been done and suffered where they stood.

" Before such an audience, filled with the subtle influence of the day, the occasion, the memories, and the visible history about them, our young orator stepped forward to pronounce the oration which was on the whole the greatest, as it was the last work, of his short life.

" Pale with the natural excitement of the occasion, and with what was known afterwards to be the unnatural excitement of encroaching disease, he stood before them, an ideal, youthful, manly presence. Gifted with a rich voice, using with consummate art the grace of oratory, of which he was a master, he held the vast crowd as by some enchantment, while he reproduced the scenes of one hundred years ago, and made the hills and woods alive again with the patient heroic figure of the Continental soldier. Who that was present can forget how the crowd visibly thrilled, as he said,—

" ' If my voice be feeble, we have but to look around. The hills that saw our fathers suffer look down on us; the ground that thrilled beneath their feet we tread to-day; their unmarked graves still lie in yonder field; the breast-works which they built to shelter them surround us here ! Dumb witnesses of the heroic past, ye need no tongues ! Face to face with you, we see it all. This soft breeze changes to an icy blast; these trees drop the glory of the summer, and the earth beneath our feet is wrapped in snow. Beside us is a village of log huts,—along that ridge smoulder the fires of a camp. The sun has sunk, the stars glitter in the inky sky, the camp is hushed, the fires are out, the night is still, all are in slumber except where a lamp glimmers in yonder cottage window, and a passing shadow shows a tall figure pacing to and fro. The cold silence is unbroken, save when on yonder ramparts, crunching the crisp snow with wounded feet, a ragged sentinel keeps watch for liberty.'

" Having quickened their imagination with such pictorial and heroic suggestions of the scene, and having
12

stimulated their patriotic enthusiasm and impulses with the natural contrast between the nation then and now, he brought his oration to a close with this solemn vision of the future:

" ' The age in which we live is but a link in the endless and eternal chain. Our lives are like the sands upon the shore; our voices like the breath of this summer breeze that stirs the leaf for a moment and is forgotten. But in the impenetrable to-be the endless generations are advancing to take our places as we fall. For them, as for us, shall the earth roll on, and the seasons come and go, the snow-flakes fall, the flowers bloom, and the harvests be gathered in. For them, as for us, shall the sun, like the life of man, rise out of darkness in the morning and sink into darkness in the night. For them, as for us, shall the years march by in the sublime procession of the ages, and here, in this place of sacrifice, in this valley of the shadow of death, out of which the life of America arose regenerate and free, let us believe with an abiding faith that to them union will seem as dear and liberty as sweet and progress as glorious as they were to our fathers and are to you and me, and that the institutions that have made us happy, preserved by the virtue of our children, shall bless the remotest generations of the time to come; and unto Him who holds in the hollow of His hand the fate of nations, and yet marks the sparrow's fall, let us lift up our hearts this day, and unto His eternal care commend ourselves, our children, and our country.' "

From the delivery of this oration Mr. Brown went home, it might literally be said, to die. Low in strength, and using up all the physical energy he had in speaking, he contracted a fever at or about the time of the celebration of Valley Forge. The day itself was very hot, and the tent in which the speeches were made much hotter. He came home utterly exhausted; nevertheless, within twenty-four hours of his return he commenced work on the Monmouth oration, which he finished while on his bed. This, his last literary production, will not be thought to be unworthy of him, or to show any signs of failing strength. It is full of vigor and oratorical fire. It was not until the *evening before* the day appointed for the celebration at Monmouth, that he finally consented to allow his family to telegraph that he could not perform the office. From that time the fever increased, and before many days its symptoms were unmistakably those of typhoid. For eight weeks there was a succession of hopes and fears. At one time, when strong confidence of his recovery was aroused, the good news gave joy to all good men throughout the country. It was touching to observe during this long period when he was struggling with the disease, how intense was the interest manifested everywhere and by all kinds of persons, and, above all, by the laboring class. Relatives and family friends would be waylaid at all hours of the day and night to be questioned by strangers who did not give their names—chiefly working-men—in regard to his condition. He had struck into human sympathy. At first, in his rarely occurring moments of delirium, his mind seemed to be taken up with the act of speaking. When fully himself again, he questioned his physicians as to the nature and duration of his disease. He wished to know precisely his condition. Just at the turning-point, at the end of three weeks, when the fever was almost gone, there came a terribly hot day, and he was again prostrated. After that he was conscious only at intervals of a day or two, but when thus himself, though suffering much mentally, all impatience had left him. He seemed to be communing with thoughts of higher things. His religious nature was looking from the earthly away to God. He expected, indeed, to recover; and his recuperative powers were so great that it is no wonder his friends hoped to the last. In order to give him the benefit of a change of air, however slight, he was removed to his brother Frederick's house, a few streets off. He surprised those who were carrying him in an apparently unconscious state by giving a direction as to the way in a calm voice, showing that he knew perfectly what they were doing. Observing that most of the accustomed furniture of the room had been removed, he uttered a protest that so much trouble should have been taken on his account. His voice, whenever he spoke, remained strong, and his eye clear.

That night, however, he began to sink, and he died at half-past eleven o'clock on Wednesday morning, August 21, 1878, at the age of thirty-three years.

The funeral, which took place at his brother's residence, was largely attended by members of the legal profession. There was a brief service at the house, and then the remains were taken to the church of St. James, the following gentlemen acting as pall-bearers: Samuel Dickson, Wayne McVeagh, Daniel Dougherty, Henry Hazlehurst, Theodore Starr, E. Hunn Hanson, Samuel W. Hollingsworth, Victor Guillou, and John J. Ridgway.

At the church religious services were conducted by the Rev. Dr. Morton, in conjunction with Drs. Claxton and Paddock and other clergymen. Dr. Morton spoke a few words in a feeling and appreciative way of the deceased. The interment was at Laurel Hill, at the gate of which cemetery the funeral procession was met by all the workmen employed upon the grounds, as their mark of respect for the dead.

In a quiet spot, overlooking the great city at a distance with its toiling myriads, and the picturesque and beautiful Schuylkill River which flows close by beneath, life's work over, he peacefully rests. The life is ended, and the river still runs its ceaseless course. But could we look into those things that are unseen and eternal, the river would cease to run, and the life in ampler majesty and joy flow on.

Henry Armitt Brown, though a man of uncommonly varied gifts, was a born orator. This was his highest manifestation of power by which he impressed himself on men. This, therefore, must be our chief word concerning him; and with some thoughtful and loving words of others respecting his eloquence and his character we take leave of him.

There can be no question that he exercised an extraordinary influence over audiences, even more than his published speeches would seem to bear out. The orator's power, mysteriously connected with his personality, evades our attempt to perpetuate it. The voice, eye, gesture, the subtle magic of the presence, vanish. Music lingers in its characters, but eloquence, like the wind, never recedes nor stays. The charm perishes along with the speaker. That which came like a divine breath from the soul, departs with it. Slight as was his form, his speech " wielded the fierce democracy." With the exception of Patrick Henry, Henry Clay, Daniel Webster, and a few of our greatest orators, no speaker in the land ever had moments of completer triumph than he over the minds and feelings of his hearers,—as at Carpenters' Hall, Valley Forge, and the occasions when he mastered rude and hostile assemblies by the spell of his eloquence. Wherein lay that spell? Not in rant, clap-trap, and stormy declamation.

Not in a massive style like Bright's oratory, nor in cumulative epithet like Sumner's, nor in "epigrammatic brilliancy" like Beaconsfield's, nor in broad philosophic discussion like Gladstone's, nor in the magnificent marshalling of fact and phrase like Macaulay's, nor in a coarse passionate vigor like O'Connell's. He did not have all forces combined,—who does? His speech was more like that of the great French orators, finished, classic, evenly sustained, without display of violence or undisciplined imagination. He had an elegance of style not incompatible with the highest vigor. He won by a forceful but steady pressure. He had three qualities of an orator,—a masterful will, personal magnetism, and an exquisitely finished elocution.

His strong, masculine will, was itself a pure force in his oratory, that thus became, in Emerson's words, "the appropriate organ of the highest personal energy." He was filled with his theme. He became a complete instrument of the word he spoke. He poured himself out upon his speech with the whole energy of his being. Yet the flow was regular and calm. There was intense feeling though under control, and this communicated itself, as reserved power does, imperceptibly, to the audience. They felt its gentle but resistless sway. They felt that the man, body, soul, and spirit, while obedient to the higher intelligence informing them, was in the utterance. Hence sympathy and magnetism,—a fire that fused speaker and hearers in one. He took quiet but entire possession of his audience, and in apparently effortless ways often produced wonderful effects; for while the speech was smoothly flowing, claiming no undue advantage over his hearers' minds, chording in and going along with their convictions, appealing to the best that was in them, with no attempt at eloquence, there was opportunity generated for ample power, and the divine afflatus sometimes came, lifting him and his hearers into higher regions of thought and feeling. The wind blew evenly along, but now and then the tempest filled the sails with a heaven-sent inspiration.

His delivery was a constant charm. His voice was one of great flexibility and compass, and his articulation was singularly distinct, rounded, and musical. He had not particularly trained his voice by elocutionary methods (that was something he was always going to do), but it was a natural gift with which he could, as upon a lute, sound all the notes and stops of passion. While there was somewhat too much of rhythm and he was not sufficiently abrupt, in many points his speaking resembled the oratory of Grattan, —the same finished style and harmonious delivery, the same brilliant fancy and incisive wit. He had not yet been tried in the severe school of parliamentary debate, but his readiness in extempore speech, though developed late, showed what he could have done in Congress if he had lived to cope with others in the halls of national legislation. For, as we have said, he was a native orator. Everything was spontaneous. He had in him the hidden resources of oratorical genius. He was, above all, a political speaker. He delighted in those broad themes which concerned the welfare of the State and the administration of the laws. He had a manly intellect. As we have said, he grasped after power in order to control men in their relations as citizens to the best good of the State, which, Dr. Arnold thought, was the highest ambition of a man. While, like George William Curtis and Wendell Phillips, he was fully able to apprehend the morality and greatness of these political questions, he aimed, more than either of them, we think, at the methods of a true state-craft, and the actual establishment of a pure and noble government. He was not only a politician in theory but science. He did not speak for momentary impression, but as a means to a higher end. He sought to raise the political spirit of the nation. Thus, with grit and manhood to back him, exceptional purity of spirit, self-possession, vivid imagination, fine and ready popular humor, an expressive countenance and a noble gesture, and an exquisitely modulated voice,—when filled with the subject he was speaking upon, he was transformed far beyond what his slight frame and quiet manner would ever have given the expectation of his being, his words vibrated in men's souls, and they recognized in him the divine gift of the orator. Beyond all these, his character was one of manly modesty, calm in its equipose and strong, courageous to speak and act its honest purpose.

> " Self-reverence, self-knowledge, self-control,
> These three alone lead life to sovereign power."

To say a word or two of his more familiar traits. If he allowed himself two or three weeks to prepare an oration, he would pass the first two in fruitless efforts to write what suited him, becoming more and more discouraged as each day passed; and, finally, when he had barely time to do the work, he would seem to strike a fresh vein, and would write almost steadily, with interruptions only for slight meals and sleep, until he had completed the whole.

Sometimes he would finish the peroration, or other parts of the address, and then spend his time in putting them together satisfactorily, but he never did any real work—anything he could make use of—until very nearly the time appointed for the delivery.

He always read in advance of his writing, and would search indefatigably in any direction for matter bearing on his subject; he liked to read what he had collected to his wife or to a friend, and their interest would stimulate him; and, while talking it over, his mind would become more thoroughly aroused. The committing to memory never seemed to give him the least uneasiness, and one day usually sufficed for that, no matter how much matter there was. He thus filled his mind with the subject, and spoke, though from memory, with the inspiration of the theme.

When he first began to be prominent in Philadelphia, unkind articles concerning him would be occasionally published in the papers; for a time these annoyed and pained him, though he would say but little about it; afterward he schooled himself so as not to seem in the least affected by such notices, and would laugh when speaking of his former sensitiveness. He treated his critics with undiminished courtesy. But he was by nature very sensitive to such things, and would be much grieved if he thought that those he cared for, particularly the members of his own family, misunderstood or were displeased at anything he did. Being unusually fair-minded and free from prejudice, he could not understand the reverse in others.

Mr. Brown was not what some would have considered a religious man, though there was a strong religious element in his character. The actions of some men, done under the guise and in the name of religion, which he regarded as wrong and unworthy of the Christian name, had greatly shaken his faith in professions of belief. That his *heart* was right we have good reasons for knowing; and if forming a lofty ideal of the requirements of life, and trying to live up to it as nearly as he could, counts for anything, he has not come short. That he was, in the latter part of his life, meditating upon a more positive attitude in regard to Christian faith, there is proof.

Among his letters are found a great many from all kinds

of persons, thanking him for all sorts of favors received. He was overrun by men out of employment and in difficulties, and he almost always made efforts to relieve them, in many cases obtaining for them relief or substantially benefiting them, so that his friends sometimes thought he was quite too sympathetic.

He never thoroughly enjoyed anything *alone;* if it were a beautiful landscape, fine music, or a notable occasion, he always needed some one to partake of his enjoyment to make it perfect. Fortunately, he had a most happy faculty of making friends wherever he went, inherited, he thought, from his father, and in that way he would often find congenial companionship when on a journey, or absent from home, in other cities. But one thing that runs through all his correspondence and conversation was an intense love of home, and a desire to be there. His purest pleasures were away from the strifes of public life, and to be with those in whom he found sympathy of mind and rest for his spirit.

After the news of his death, the letters of condolence which came pouring in bore on them all the proof of a spontaneous sympathy. From classmates, and men of his own age, the expressions were of the most poignant grief, as if they could not believe, or bear to believe, the sad intelligence. The staff of their honor seemed to have been broken. From political friends the lamentation appeared to be not less heartfelt. One of them, a conspicuous member of the Reform party, writes, August 23 :

"I am shocked at this announcement. All men who shared his high aims have lost in him a friend and champion. His wise counsel and perfect courage will be sorely missed, and this void will keep his memory fresh in hearts to which his rare personal traits were unknown. My thoughts have run back to-day to many and many an hour passed with him, never to be forgotten."

G. S. Cannon, Esq., of Bordentown, New Jersey, sent to Frederick Brown, August 22, these few words, which, coming from a lawyer and an elderly man, are affecting:

"Your fond anticipations have not been realized, and your noble, pure, gifted, and eloquent brother lies enshrouded for the tomb. Thousands of hearts outside of your family will be touched and troubled by this great bereavement, and will not soon forget, but will again and again recall to their recollection, his gentleness, sweetness, and the wonderful endearments which were his."

The following letter from Alfred C. Lambdin, Esq., to Frederick Brown, contains a reference to the Monmouth address:

"I send you herewith the MS. just as I received it on the night of the Monmouth Celebration. I held it subject to your brother's orders, hoping that it might receive the revision he meant to give it, but it was not God's will.

"I cannot tell you, and I do not need to tell you, how intensely we all feel the shadow of this great loss. I think that all his friends felt toward him as toward a brother, and therefore can enter in some degree into a brother's sorrow.

"He was a man whom we must be thankful to have known, whose influence was invigorating, whose memory will be helpful."

Dated from "Gambrel Cottage, Manchester-by-the-Sea, Mass., August 22, 1878," Mr. John R. Baker received these swift lines from James T. Fields, Esq.:

"I have just read in a morning paper the sad intelligence. How strange it seems, and how hard to believe!

"After receiving yours of the 8th I felt easy, and was waiting day after day to learn of the dear one's recovery from his long illness.

"What a mystery! It seems like a vision that cannot be true.

"My heart goes out to those left weeping behind, and I mingle my tears with theirs, grieving that I cannot do anything or say anything to help them.

"God bless you and help you all in this unlooked-for loss! I had been looking forward to many happy meetings with dear Harry, for I loved him and had high hopes of his successful career as a patriotic and most talented citizen.

"At a proper time give our love to your daughter and granddaughter, and tell them how saddened we both are by what we hear to-day.

"There is no sunshine in my cottage here to-day, although the sun is shining on the shore."

General George B. McClellan wrote to Mrs. Brown from Orange, New Jersey, August 23, as follows:

"Not many months ago when my family were in sorrow, I received a most kind note from your husband, and little thought at the time that the occasion would so soon present itself for my writing to you. I do not seek to intrude upon your grief, but desire in briefest words to tell you how sincerely I and mine sympathize with you in your sad hour of trial, how cordially we esteemed and admired your husband, and how deeply we feel that the loss is not simply that of his family, but that the community in which he lived has reason to deplore the untimely

death of one whose past gave the most excellent promise
for the future.

"My family unite with me in sincere sympathy."

A cherished friend of Harry's and of his family, Bishop
Clark, of Rhode Island, expresses thus his sense of personal loss in a letter dated August 26, addressed to Frederick Brown, Esq.:

"I hardly know how to express my profound and earnest sympathy with you, your mother, and all the household,
in the sad calamity that has now fallen upon you.

"I have thought that there was no man of his age in
the land who showed a higher gift in certain departments
than your brother. I have been anticipating for him a
long and brilliant career. But the Almighty had some
higher work for him to do in another field, and so He took
him.

"The loss to the public is great, but no one can tell
what a terrible void has been left in the family circle.
Only time and the nearer prospect of meeting those who
have gone before, in their new homes, can assuage such
grief.

"This bereavement seems to be very strange and inscru-
table now, but by and by we shall see that your brother,
after all, was not taken away prematurely. He may have
been spared some great trials, and as he had ripened early,
he was early transferred to a world where no further trials
or disappointments can reach us."

These words, from over the sea, are from Sir Charles
Reed, M.P., dated September 2:

"I have had a note from Julia Lea this morning, and
straightway I have had a long look at the lovely portrait

you gave me in 1876.   The sight of it intensified my grief when I imagined the face I saw, shrouded in sorrow for the loss of one who, though but slightly known by me, was greatly admired for what he was, and for the promise of what he was to be.   How little we know!   At Childs's dinner-table he was the centre of interest, and full of vivacious wisdom.   He looked firm and strong, and I marked him as one of your country's foremost men, for he spoke of liberty and corruption as I like to hear the patriot speak, and we forgathered then in true sympathy.

"In Paris and in London I tried in vain to see you both, and I heard of your terrible voyage and sent messages.

"In the midst of your great loss I will refrain from saying more.   Human sympathy avails but little in the hour of such crushing sorrow, but it may please you to know that there are those who feel for you, and some who desire, from a distance, to bring their wreath of friendship and lay it on the tomb of Henry Armitt Brown."

The poet Longfellow wrote the following note to a member of Mr. Brown's family, September 9, 1878:

"I thank you for counting me among those who sympathize with you in your great loss, and for sending me the photograph of Armitt Brown, and the various eulogies called forth by his death.

"I had a great personal regard for him, and a high opinion of his character and abilities.   When such a man dies it is not only a private loss but a public loss, and such it is felt to be by the whole community.

"I beg you to convey to Mrs. Brown my warmest and deepest sympathy, and to your own family my best regard and condolence."

Another letter from across the sea, dated Monnetier, Savoy, France, September 12, 1878, is from John Welsh, Esq., our recent minister to England, and is thus feelingly expressed:

"Here, in a recess in the mountains, with Lake Leman below me, whose waters are ever flowing onward to the ocean as our steps are moving towards eternity, and Mont Blanc above me, whose peaks rise toward heaven clothed in garments radiant with purity as resplendent as the hopes of the future which fill our hearts, I desire to express my sympathy for you in your affliction, an affliction so heavy that there is only one who can lighten it, and to Him I trust that you have been able to turn in humble submission.

"In common with all who knew him whom we mourn, I have looked with pride and pleasure on his rising progress, marked by the manifestation of the purest principles, the manliest conduct, and the highest aspirations, and had assigned for him a future of great usefulness and honor.

"It is otherwise, and he has left us. We mourn his loss. He was beloved. Your heart must be full of sadness, and yet what joy there must be mingled in it that you are the mother of such a son, one whose life was marked by so many virtues and whose death is so universally mourned.

"Pardon me for my intrusion, but I cannot withhold from you this feeble tribute to the memory of one who was possessed of my warmest regard, and the expression of my deepest sympathy for all those who are now suffering under the bereavement caused by the death of my friend, Henry Armitt Brown."

We add but one more of these "words of friends,"—

from the venerable Judge John J. Pinkerton, dated West Chester, March 31, 1879:

" My absence at the Supreme Court has prevented an earlier acknowledgment of your kindness in sending me the Valley Forge oration.

" I am under special obligations to you for it, as I had already received from Harry all else that he had printed, and this only was needed to make my collection complete.

" My relations with your brother were exceedingly cordial, and my affection for him great. His death created a personal grief not easily put into words. To the State it was a loss hard to repair; as a common friend wrote me about him, 'I cannot help feeling that our moral forces are diminished.' To all of us, who knew him, he was an example of the supreme value of noble conduct and high demeanor."

The formal notices which succeed, are culled from a great number of similar expressions of public regard. In them there will be seen to be the same manifestation of an unfeigned sorrow for a great public loss, and a desire that the lesson of such a life might not all be lost. We print them, as we have done the letters which have gone before, because they show unconsciously, and better than we are able in any other way to bring out, the profound impression made on the community of the character of a genuine man. While eulogistic they have the stamp of thorough sincerity.

The "In Memoriam" verses of Miss Caroline L. Mitchell, of Burlington, New Jersey, which were composed the very hour that the sad news reached her, and which have in them a heart-glow, merit the first place:

" Only a short while since a voice sublime
  Told of the deeds of mighty men of old,
Waking fresh echoes from the ancient time,
  Telling a story—never idly told—

" Of the brave warriors and their deeds as brave;
  Of wrong and suffering, sorrows sad, yet grand;
Of freedom conquered and the freemen's grave,
  Link'd with the deathless story of our land.

" And they who listened felt their pulses thrill
  And joyed to follow on that clear-voiced call,
For thousands hearkened, in a hush as still
  As that which follows on the thunder-fall.

" But now ! oh voice sublime, oh voice most true,
  Break through this silence which now seals your tone;
Tell those who know that honor is your due
  Of the fair life,—of death which you have known.

" Tell us, oh voice sublime,—from out the light
  Which floods this silence,—why our feet are set
To stumble lonely in this awful night,
  Where all things but our weeping we forget;

" Tell us why, for a time, upon the plane of life
  Your tones rang clear, in swift, responsive call;
And when death came, and, after solemn strife,
  Wrapped silently your joy and grace from all;

" Tell us from Paradise, in words of love,—
  The God we worship knows and shares our grief,—
Oh, tell us of His cross; that through His wounds,
  To our sad hearts, may come some sweet relief.

" God keeps His own ! Then let His blessing fall
  On you—in death at rest—in measure large.
Life loses and Death wins ! His bugle-call
  Warns the brave warriors of the coming charge.

> " Peace be your portion, till the voice of God
>   Calls on His own to leave the grave and live,—
>   Then, voice sublime, make answer,—while the ' rod
>   And staff' of God 'support and comfort' give."

New Rochelle, New York.

Hardly less promptly appeared the following appreciative article in the *Philadelphia Evening Bulletin* of August 22, 1878:

"No sadder news has been chronicled for many a day than that which announced yesterday the death of Henry Armitt Brown. The terrible nature of the disease with which he wrestled so long made this catastrophe seem very probable; but anticipation of the end has robbed it of none of its mournfulness now that it has come. It only remains for those who have to note the removal of this gifted young man from the places that have known him, to give expression to the sense of loss which is felt by every one who had an opportunity of estimating his character and his intellectual ability, and of observing the promise that the future had for him of high achievement and honorable fame. The language of eulogy too often is strained when the dead are spoken of; but here was a man for whom the warmest epithets of praise alone are fit, and who deserves a kindlier epitaph than any that can be written for him. It was one of his best qualities that the praise which was heaped upon him during his life never ministered visibly to his pride. He died at thirty-three, after having won by sheer force of intellect and character such triumphs as few men in middle life can boast of; and yet he bore his honors meekly. His head was never turned by his successes. His manner was always suave, his courtesy to the humblest was never less refined than when he mingled with the greatest. If it happened that he could help some less fortunate man who struggled upon a pathway which he had climbed with ease, there was always an extended hand and a word of cheer. He had too large a soul for flattery to hurt. He was far too great a man to permit the littleness of vanity to make him heedless of the obligations of his kinship with the lowliest of his fellows.

"To most men who read of his death he was known only as the scholar and orator; and none who ever heard him doubted the fairness of his claim to the distinction which came to him. His natural gifts were extraordinary; but he used them well. He made so close approach to perfection because he strove valiantly to reach a high ideal. He was a hard student, a toiler who realizes that the best consummation follows ever with the greatest effort. His style seemed the most fitting that could have been chosen for his purpose. He wove the fabric of his speeches with daintiest skill, accompanying the cogent argument with pictures which were full of vivid power. Some of his descriptions of scenes that have come to us famous from the old time are elaborated so artfully, with so much picturesque detail, that the figures are rounded before the eye and crowned with a semblance of reality. The reader of his speeches feels his power to conjure up the people and the things of the past; but the full value of his ability in this respect can be estimated alone by those who have heard him when he was his own interpreter. He was a great orator. If he had lived it is possible that he might have taken rank among the very greatest. There was a grandeur of method, a largeness of style, an excellence of gesture, and an exquisite intonation which enabled him to move an audience deeply. The unskilled who heard him marvelled at his power, but he numbered among the warmest of his admirers men who themselves had no mean skill in the art of eloquence.

"But he was far more than a charming writer and a noble orator. He was a man who had high aims from his early youth. Not only did he covet for himself, at a time when most young men are pursuing pleasure, such distinction as he attained, but he determined within his soul that he would strive for better things for his country. He loathed the corruption and trickery that have poisoned our politics, and one of the first aspirations of what may be called his public life was toward reform. Perhaps the method he preferred was not the wisest or surest to attain the desired end. But his wish was ardent and his effort was sincere. He never surrendered his hope of better things to come, or yielded his purpose to expend his energies in their behalf. He had the intensest scorn for those who play upon passion and prejudice to gain promotion in public life, and he hated the methods which enable the trickster and the demagogue to climb to the high places of the nation. If he had lived, a time surely would have been when the people, acting independently of partisan machinery, would have chosen him to speak for them in the national councils. And there were those who believed that the statesman of the better days to come might be such as he. He was the kind of a man who would have made the profession of politics worthy of the adoption of the pure and the wise, and would have shown to the country how there might be politicians who should be moved by high principles and lofty conceptions of patriotism and duty. It is nearly certain that he looked forward to such a career; certainly his friends believed that it awaited his ripened powers and the combination of events. No man more worthy to conduct such a reform, or better fitted to stand as the representative of a higher code of political morality, has ever in recent years commanded public attention in this city.

"But these great possibilities are past. There is no future for him excepting in that world where all wrongs are righted, where the best and the purest are always crowned, and where that which defiles and makes unclean has no abiding-place. The Divine hand that led him onward here toward noble things, and that appeared to be shaping him for a great and splendid destiny, has smitten him while his task seemed hardly yet begun, and the life that was so full of promise is ended in the grave. If we cannot fathom the mystery of such a dispensation, we can be glad that so much as was done in the brief span of this man's existence was done well; and it must be a consolation to those to whom the bereavement brings greatest sorrow, that the life which has closed had no stain upon it, but that there remains among those who observed it a memory that will be forever fragrant."

A special meeting of the Executive Committee of the Municipal Reform Association was held August 22 at the office of John J. Ridgway, Esq., Mr. P. Morris Perot presiding, and Mr. L. P. Ashmead acting as secretary. The following resolutions, presented by Mr. Henry C. Lea, were unanimously adopted:

" *Whereas*, Providence has seen fit to remove from among us our friend and associate, Henry Armitt Brown.

" *Resolved*, That we deplore his loss as a matter not merely personal to ourselves, but as a misfortune to the community at large, which can ill afford to spare one whose brilliant intellect, richly-cultured mind, lofty aims, and chivalrous courage were always at the service of the public, with a rare disregard of self. Spurning the baser arts of the politician, he was content to win his way by the force of his high gifts and purity of character, preferring that success should be delayed rather than obtain it by means inconsistent with the nicest sense of honor. Time alone was lacking to win for him the high place that was his due in the councils of the nation, and the career which is now cut short would have been a conspicuous example that mediocrity and unscrupulous self-seeking are not the surest requisites for success in our public life. For what he was we mourn him ; for what he would have been we grieve for our city and our country.

" *Resolved*, That the officers of the Citizens' Municipal Reform Association be directed to convey these resolutions to the family of our late colleague, with the assurance of our deepest sympathy with them in their irreparable loss."

The following is a report taken from the *Philadelphia Times* of August 26 of a bar-meeting held August 24 :

" Never, probably, in the history of the Philadelphia bar has there been such an assemblage of the lawyers of this city as gathered together on Saturday morning in Room C of the Court of Common Pleas to do honor to the memory of their late associate. It was not the congregation of the friends and professional intimates of the deceased alone, nor a meeting held simply to comply with the etiquette of the Bar Association, but rather the clustering together of legal gentlemen of all degrees and stations to pay an earnest, heartfelt tribute to the memory of one who had endeared himself to all by his honor, his manliness, his culture, and his manifold accomplishments.

" Long before the hour of meeting, eleven o'clock, the members of the bar entered the court-room, and with solemn countenances and bated breath quietly recounted reminiscences of the life of Mr. Brown, and told and retold instances of his many excellencies and good qualities. There seemed to be a feeling of sadness pervading all present, which fully betokened the love and admiration held for the young and gifted lawyer and orator who had died.

" A thing was noticed about this bar-meeting which has

probably never, certainly very seldom, occurred before, and that was the presence of many gentlemen outside of the profession, who had come to testify by that presence their respect for the object of the meeting. Leading merchants and bankers with whom Mr. Brown had been associated in the Reform movement were there. Several clergymen and members of the medical profession were in attendance. Among these last none was more conspicuous than the tall form and fine head of the distinguished surgeon, Professor Gross. He was accompanied by a leading member of the Baltimore bar, his son-in-law, Mr. Benjamin F. Horwitz. The judges of the Common Pleas and Orphans' Court were there,—all who were in town,—Judges Peirce, Thayer, Biddle, Hare, Ashman, and Penrose, while Judge Sharswood, of the Supreme Court, came to preside and speak the first words. A few of the members of the bar who clustered around these gentlemen may be mentioned: George W. Biddle, Isaac Hazlehurst, W. Heyward Drayton, William B. Mann, John K. Findlay and his partner Mr. Thomas, Morton P. Henry, Samuel A. Dickson, Wayne MacVeagh, George Tucker Bispham, Henry Hazlehurst, Richard L. Ashhurst, Daniel Dougherty, James H. Heverin, Samuel W. Pennypacker, John J. Ridgway, A. Haller Gross, J. Parker Norris, Max McIntyre, Charles W. Warwick, John R. Read, Henry C. Townsend, Pierce Archer, Jr., Thomas J. Ashton, Francis Brewster, Victor Guillou, James Lynd, Sussex Davis, Robert N. Willson, Samuel B. Huey, Charles B. McMichael, E. Hunn Hanson, and Lewis Waln Smith.

" Judge Sharswood in taking the chair spoke but a few moments. He said:

"' My brethren of the bar and bench, I do not feel like saying anything to you of the cause of our assembling this morning,—the death of Henry Armitt Brown. To me it is one of the saddest occasions at which I have ever been present. We are often called upon to express our regret at the death of men who have attained their three-score years and ten. On such occasions there has always been the consolation that a full sheaf has been gathered to the eternal garner. We looked upon a perfect arch, and were only called to lay a cap-stone upon it. Here it is different. We have a broken column, of elegant proportions, promising to be a glorious structure, suddenly arrested, and we are only left to fancy what it might have been. We bow to a mysterious Providence, and all that the survivors can do is to kneel in submission to the will of Him who seeth the end from the beginning. He has done this, as all things else, in wisdom and love. I shall not under-take to anticipate anything regarding the life, character, and public services of our brother, and will leave that to those who knew him more intimately.'

"At the conclusion of Judge Sharswood's address Samuel A. Dickson presented a set of resolutions, as annexed:

"'The members of the Philadelphia bar having received with profound regret the announcement of the death of Henry Armitt Brown, and being desirous of expressing their appreciation of his virtues and their sense of the loss that has fallen upon themselves and upon the community, have

"'*Resolved,* That in the death of Mr. Brown the profession has lost one of its most brilliant members, whose success in the field of eloquence has not only gained a high reputation for himself, but has added largely to the renown of the Philadelphia bar.

"'*Resolved,* That Mr. Brown's career has exhibited one of the most striking instances in the annals of the bar of the early and rapid attainment of high and honorable distinction. In less than ten short years he made himself one of the first orators of the country, one of the foremost citizens of the community in which he lived, and one of the prominent figures to which all lovers of good government and unselfish patriotism instinctively turned for advice, encouragement, and aid.

"'*Resolved*, That while it is true that Mr. Brown's eminence was chiefly gained by his labors outside of the immediate sphere of professional exertion, it cannot be doubted that the same high qualities would have brought success had circumstances and choice inclined him to give himself up to the practice of his profession. The leisure afforded him by inherited wealth was not spent in idleness nor sloth. He lived laborious days to fit himself for his work. His learning was wide and liberal, and his mind was stored with "the great thoughts and fine sayings of the great men of all ages;" but the ripe culture gained from foreign travel and classical studies did not dim nor dull his love for his country nor her institutions. In all of his orations and addresses he never spoke for self nor thought of self, and it was this that lent the most irresistible charm to his oratory. Through all his words there shone the clear, brave spirit of the courageous and high-minded gentleman, who was pleading for the cause of good government, or seeking to revive the memories of the loftier and purer patriotism of the past. To those who will turn again to the orations delivered in Carpenters' Hall and at Valley Forge, it will not seem extravagant to apply to him his own eulogy upon the great orator of the Revolution: "Through all descending time his countrymen shall repeat his glowing words, and inspire in the hearts of men to be that love of liberty which filled his own."

"'*Resolved*, That we tender to the family of our departed friend the assurance of our profound sympathy, and that a committee of seven be appointed to communicate a copy of these resolutions.'

"Daniel Dougherty, with whom Mr. Brown studied law, seconded the resolutions at considerable length and with much feeling. He said:

"'The sad and solemn duty devolves on me, gentlemen of the bar, of formally announcing to you the demise of Henry Armitt Brown. Struck down by typhoid fever, he struggled for two months, alternately rallying and relapsing, until Wednesday last, when his brief yet bright career terminated on earth, to begin, I hope, an endless home in heaven. The journals of the city have given full details of his birth, parentage, and education. As a man he was familiar to all of us. Philadelphians, not only at home but who are sojourning in different parts of our country and abroad, will learn this deplorable intelligence with sorrow deep and heartfelt. I knew him, Mr. Chairman, from his youth. I watched with affectionate pride the bright boy develop into the brilliant man, and looked forward with fond anticipations to see him one of America's illustrious citizens. He was the most conspicuous young man in Philadelphia, and the one most likely in the future to fill a large space in the general eye. Though not officially announced, it was well known that Secretary of State Evarts had offered him the position of Second Assistant Secretary. As a writer he was concise and elegant, adapting his style to the subject, light and airy if the theme were so; severe and grave if the importance of the composition demanded it. His speeches in his few important cases at the bar elicited encomiums from the bench and ranked him as a rising orator. His lectures, and his political and miscellaneous addresses, extended wide his popularity, and were earning for him a national reputation. His oration at Carpenters' Hall, in the effect its delivery had upon his hearers, and its glowing eloquence, mark it as, without a single exception, the most masterly effort called forth by our Centennial anniversaries.'

"Speaking of Mr. Brown's earnest advocacy of municipal reform, Mr. Dougherty said:

" 'The emoluments of office had no charm for him. He was without the weakness that attends ambition; he would not stoop that he might rise; he would not court the schemers that, alas for our country, stand between the people and public honors. He neither could be flattered by the smiles nor bribed by the favors of those who have usurped the distribution of offices. He would not sacrifice his independence by shaping his opinions to suit the designs of partisans. He was conscientious in his convictions, and fearless and defiant in battling for the right. Over all his public and private traits there shone the serene beauty of the gentleman. Many years ago I heard his father say that it had been his aim to give his children a happy childhood. He did more,—he implanted in his sons the seeds of noble manhood. If Harry, as his intimates endearingly called him, had lived, he would have filled a lofty niche as one who joined to the possession of shining talents, sterling qualities that recall heroic days, and who dedicated all to truth, virtue, and patriotism. I dare not dwell on his home and his mother's home, both now desolate. I cannot trust myself to speak of our more than friendship, and close by seconding the resolutions.'

"Hon. Wayne MacVeagh next arose. He was so completely overcome by his feelings that it was with difficulty that he could speak the few words he had to say in behalf of the memory of his dead friend. He said:

"'I cannot refrain from taking part in this meeting, and yet I cannot say anything satisfactory to the bench and the bar. Between Mr. Brown and myself existed the most intimate relations, and I am justified in saying that I knew him thoroughly. I rise to say only that of his beauty of character and patriotism the whole truth will never be told. A bold and ripe scholar and an orator and patriot who thought always of his country and not of himself, and a stainless gentleman,—all these he was. I can say no more of him. I loved him too dearly and I knew him too intimately. I am therefore only listening to his praise from the lips of others.'

"Henry Hazlehurst, a playmate, schoolfellow, and life-long friend of Mr. Brown, told of his having been associated in his first case with him, and turning to the chairman, he continued:

"'I have often heard you, sir, speak of his distinguished success on that occasion before a judge who is now your own associate in the Supreme Court. It was not the formal and courteous recollection of counsel, but the wise and just appreciation of a man who promised to fill a place that was vacant at the bar. Had he lived, that promise would have been faithfully kept, and as a forensic orator Mr. Brown would have made it our pride to tell of his triumphs. But he did live to advocate the greatest of all causes, pure and just municipal administration, and at a time when every word he spoke brought encouragement and assurance, he won his highest honors. I know of no eulogy now so fitting to be spoken in this distinguished presence as was contained in the message which announced to me his death. The scrap of paper said, "Died at noon." In every sense he died with the freshness of morning upon him, without a disappointment, before envy had time to speak, and while every man's hand was stretched out; at home and among "troops of friends" he passed away. We must not call him dead. Let us say that "at mid-day, on the King's Highway, there met him an angel in the way."'

"President Judge Hare was the next speaker.

"'While this is no ordinary occasion,' he remarked, 'I cannot do more than touch upon its cause. Henry Armitt Brown was a natural-born orator, and possessed all the necessary gifts to persuade and sway his fellow-men. He was a representative man, and one of whom the city was proud. When he rose to speak his first utterances were received with pleasure, and regret followed when he closed.'

"His Honor rehearsed the attending circumstances of Mr. Brown's first public speech, and concluded with :

"'He had a noble purpose to serve the public and his fellows, and with his accomplishments what might he not have accomplished?'

"George T. Bispham followed in a brief speech, closing with the following tribute:

"'I never knew a man for whose friendship so many men were eager, or one whose friendship when gained was so valuable. His loss to the bar and his friends is irreparable.'

"Samuel W. Pennypacker spoke as follows:

"'It was my fortune to have been nearer to Mr. Brown than perhaps any other of his friends among the young bar during the preparation of his last and probably his greatest work. After he had been invited to make the oration at Valley Forge, which he considered to be the most important of all the Pennsylvania celebrations, he came to me because of my acquaintance with the locality. Together, only four months ago, we examined the entrenchments there and rode to the Paoli and the Warren Tavern, and following the track of the British army, crossed the Schuylkill at Girdont Ford. Together, little more than two months ago, we read over the completed oration. The assistance I was able to give him was little indeed, but the opportunity it afforded me of getting a closer insight into his character I shall always cherish among the happiest memories of my life. The Valley Forge oration is beyond question the finest which the Centennial anniversaries called forth, and as an artistic production is a marvel. With patient industry and a determination born of enthusiasm he thoroughly mastered the subject,—topographically and historically. With clear insight he caught the true inspiration of the scenes of that dreary winter. A more beautiful picture than his contrast between the ragged Continentals upon the bleak hills and the royalists amid the luxury of the city could not be limned. And for two hours and a half the people, at the close of a wearisome day of exercises, stood up and listened. A very capable historical critic has said to me that there is no more that can be added to the story of Valley Forge. And hereafter, in the ages to come, when men look back with veneration towards the heroes who suffered and died there, the young orator, whose earnestness to do justice to their memories so sadly shortened his own career, cannot be forgotten. Surely some of their renewed glory belongs to him. The sorrow which I feel in his early death is partly a selfish grief, partly regret at his broken hopes, now forever ended here, but beyond all, the loss to my native State. We have many men who are capable and pure, but they have eaten of the lotos and the spear has dropped from their nerveless hands. With his strength and his ambition he could not have been kept from the national councils; but he is dead, and the fruits we were promised we shall never gather.'

" Judge Biddle recounted the circumstances of an appeal made by Mr. Brown before him in mitigation of a certain sentence:

" 'I was not swayed in my judgment by the appeal,' said the judge, 'but I could not fail but recognize its beauty and pathos. A great distinctive characteristic of Mr. Brown was his manliness. He took his views and shaped his course from the earlier statesmen of the country, and if he had been spared he would have met many of the issues of the day.'

" Judge Peirce followed.

" He remarked: 'Mr. Brown had the courage of his

convictions,—a rare quality,—and was the steadfast opponent of corruption and wrong. In the death of such a
man the community has sustained a loss, but the example
of his life is not lost, and, though dead, he yet should
speak from the grave and move young men to fill the
break left vacant, and this being done it cannot be said
that he died in vain.'

"John J. Ridgway closed the addresses of the day, re-
counting the circumstances attending the illness of the
deceased, and spoke eloquently of his manliness and purity
of purpose.

"The following despatch from Mr. McClure was read
by Mr. Lewis Waln Smith:

"'MINNEQUA, August 22.

"'JAMES H. HEVERIN,—I cannot be present to join the
members of the Philadelphia bar on Saturday in giving
expression to the profound sense of bereavement that the
untimely death of Henry Armitt Brown has created in
the circle of his professional brethren. He will be lamented
as the most gifted of all his associates, and he will long
live in friendship's memories as one of the bravest, noblest,
and best of men.

"'A. K. McCLURE.'

"The meeting then adjourned."

The subjoined brief piece came out in the *Sunday
Transcript:*

"Mr. Brown was a politician in the true sense of the
term, and none the less so because he ignored the primaries
and sought only to enforce his views when the candidates
were selected and were before the people for election or
rejection. His oratory and his masterly command of the

language enabled him to discuss issues and questions in terse and vigorous English, but he failed to recognize that higher duty of the citizen,—to attend the delegate elections. Again and again has Mr. Brown denounced in scathing phrases the supineness of the voters who allowed their delegates to be selected without their knowledge and without their sanction. But did he ever go down to the depths and seek to discover the true cause of all the political woes which he depicted in such glowing language? No. He was a dilettante. He preferred, like many others, to discuss the evils above without reference to those below the surface, and took no active part in that department where delegates are made or elected and where candidates are selected."

The following, under the heading "The Honor that Endures," from the *Philadelphia Times*, August 26, is in some sort a reply to the above:

"The tributes of many of the partisan organs to the integrity, attainments, and political efforts of the late Henry Armitt Brown must attract the attention of intelligent readers. He was of the class of resolute men against whose teachings in modern politics the mere partisan organs were tuned to their steadiest pitch, and the triumph of his dream of a purified political system was what they most adroitly and persistently antagonized, and what they most feared as the inevitable end of their mission. The journal that was ever to the front in the effort to prove that Mr. Brown was always doing the right thing at the wrong time and in the wrong way, and which has long been trained to the obedience that treated every appeal for reform as an affront to the party, now tells how the time might have come when Mr. Brown would have spoken for Philadelphia in Congress, and felicitates itself on the promise of such honors in store for the one for whom every good citizen mourns to-day. Doubtless the time would have come, but it would have been only when machine politicians and machine organs had perished from our contests. The *Sunday Transcript,* with more candor, strikes the average distinction between the faithful and eloquent reformer and the leaders he antagonized, as it explains what it regards as the failure of Mr. Brown as a politician by reminding us that he failed to attend the primary elections. Doubtless Henry Armitt Brown did not trouble himself to attend political primaries, and none could better explain why he so abstained than the shrewd and well-schooled leader in such contests who presides over the editorial columns of that journal. Mr. Brown was no novice in anything of which patient research, keen observation, and intelligent appreciation of men could advise him, and he well knew that a half-score of regular primary managers would carry any precinct at a primary conflict against five times their number of men of the faith of Mr. Brown, even if all of them voted solid for desired candidates. He was not a great man in the battles where chicanery and brute force were the implements of warfare, and therefore 'he failed to recognize that higher duty of the citizen,—to go to the delegate elections.' In that regard 'he was a dilettante,' because he knew no arts but those of honesty, manly effort, and unswerving devotion to the right.

"Looking back over the local battles of Philadelphia during the last ten years, no one man has commanded such enduring tributes from his antagonists as has Henry Armitt Brown; and those who hasten to judge his campaigns as failures in practical results are strangely insensible to the living witnesses and varied evidence about them. There has not been a great movement against official wrong and

for a better rule in city, State, and nation, that has not inspired the matchless eloquence of the fallen champion of
reform, and slowly but surely his efforts were ripening into
fruition. Compare the authority of Philadelphia to-day,
with the authority that defiantly ruled when he first braved
power and resentment to demand fidelity and competency
in public trust, and there can be none so blind as not to
appreciate the high measure of practical success that crowned
his brave and patriotic efforts. To the young men of the
nation, and especially of his native city, the courage and
struggles and success of this young man will stand out in
singleness of grandeur as the example of a life that left his
community and his country better than he found it. Others
won honors which they denied to his conceded merits, but
when they and their unseemly honors shall have reached
generous forgetfulness, it will be remembered how, in the
dark days of misrule, one voice, more eloquent than all
others, gave silvered lining to the clouds, and made justice
and integrity respected in the councils of our rulers."

Omitting other notices from papers all over the country, we give this letter, which appeared in the *Nation* of
August 29:

"To the Editor of the Nation.

"Sir,—The death of Henry Armitt Brown, which this
community so deeply deplores, is really a public calamity;
and, even while our grief is freshest and keenest, I cannot
forbear from stating to the readers of the *Nation* some of
the qualities which compelled us to regard him as a man
who gave great promise of future usefulness.

"He was a ripe scholar, not only in the classics, in history, philosophy, and literature, but he also spoke and

wrote modern languages with unusual accuracy and elegance. He possessed special aptitude for society, and was the centre of every social gathering of which he was a part by the charm of his conversation. He was a clear and forcible writer, using his brilliant rhetoric and his admirable gift of humor only when they were aids to the enforcement of his argument. He was entitled to be called, without any exaggeration, an accomplished orator. His judgment in political matters was so excellent that he could foresee and describe many of the grave misfortunes which would follow the attempt to consider as judicial the functions of the returning boards of Florida and Louisiana. His sense of honor was so delicate that he forbade his friends to solicit office for him, declaring that he could not enjoy it unless it were freely conferred, upon the ground of his fitness for it.

" And above and beyond all these claims to our regard, the words which Mr. Burke wrote of his dead son exactly describe him,—' He was made a public creature.' His guiding and controlling purpose was to try to make the government of his country purer and stronger and better in all ways than he found it. I need hardly add that he was the instinctive foe of all manner of baseness and corruption in our politics, or that he was as chivalric in uttering his convictions as he was conscientious in forming them. The simple truth is that he never had any trouble in choosing the right side of any political questions, for he never regarded it as a possible aid of his own ambition, but simply in its relation to the public welfare, and the causes he championed furnish the best evidence of the manner of man he was: municipal reform, honest money, civil service reform, revenue reform, the restoration of fraternal feelings between all sections of the country, and the use of the lessons of the Revolution for the elevation of the spirit of our public life; for these great labors he was thoroughly equipped, and to them, if he had been spared to us, he would have devoted his life.

" These are the reasons why we who knew and loved him feel sure that not only this city and State, but the whole country has suffered in his untimely death, for, unfortunately, these other words of Mr. Burke are also applicable: ' At this exigent moment the loss of a finished man is not easily supplied.'

"WAYNE MACVEAGH.

"PHILADELPHIA, August 28, 1878."

From the proceedings of the Massachusetts Historical Society, at their meeting September 12, 1878, we make this extract:

" The president (Hon. Robert C. Winthrop) then said:

"' Before turning to other topics, I am unwilling to omit the opportunity of mentioning another loss to historical literature, which has occurred within a few weeks past.

"' I had made a memorandum, in my notes for the present meeting, to ask the concurrence of the council of our society in proposing the name of Henry Armitt Brown, of Philadelphia, as one of our corresponding members, and I have no reason to doubt that he would have been nominated to-day.

"' He will be remembered by many of us as the eloquent young Philadelphian who came on as a delegate to our Centennial Tea-Party Celebration, in December, 1873, and made an admirable address at Faneuil Hall on that occasion. In the following year he delivered a really brilliant historical discourse in Carpenters' Hall, Philadelphia, on the one hundredth anniversary of the meeting of the old Congress of 1774, which deservedly attracted great attention.

"'In December last he delivered another historical oration, of hardly inferior interest, at Burlington, New Jersey, in commemoration of the settlement of that place by the Quakers. More recently still, he had been engaged to deliver the orations on the Centennial Anniversary of Valley Forge, on the 19th of June last, and of the Battle of Monmouth, on the 29th of the same month.

"'As the result of the fulfilling of the first of these engagements, and preparing for the second, he was struck down with a fever, from which he did not recover.

"'He died on the 21st of August last, in the thirty-fourth year of his age.

"'Mr. Brown has always kindly sent me everything which he printed, and I have never failed to read whatever he sent; and I know of no young man or old man, of his period, who has exhibited greater power or skill in working up the historical materials which he labored with so much zeal and enthusiasm in collecting. He was an orator of no second class, and his sketches and illustrations of the scenes and events which he depicted were most felicitous and impressive.

"'Had his life and health been prolonged, he could hardly have failed to rise to great distinction ; and his death at so early an age, and after such signal evidences of his taste and talent for historical research and description, entitle him to be remembered in our records, though it be too late to inscribe his name on our rolls.

"'I am glad to observe a statement in the papers that his anniversary addresses are to be made up into a memorial volume.'"

In his annual message, in January, 1879, Governor Hartranft made a graceful allusion to three Pennsylvanians who had died during the previous year,—H. A. Brown, Bayard Taylor, and Morton McMichael. He said of the first of these:

"The country has suffered the loss during the year of three distinguished Pennsylvanians. On the 21st day of August, in the thirty-fourth year of his age, Henry Armitt Brown died at Philadelphia. He belonged to public life only in the highest sense of simple citizenship, for he held no office, except the high position of a leader of men, and wielded no authority, except the noble influence of a pure and strong life. At the time of his death he had just completed the masterly orations on Revolutionary events, upon which his reputation as a scholar and orator will eventually rest, after the personal recollections of him have faded into tradition."

The following tribute is from the pen of Mr. George William Curtis:

"The death of Henry Armitt Brown, of Philadelphia, is more than a sorrow to his friends: it is a loss to the country. He was a young man of a lofty sense of political duty and personal honor, of force and purity of character, admirably accomplished, holding sound views upon the most important public questions, and able to maintain them with unusual eloquence and skill. He had, no doubt, the power, also, of scorning the mean aspersions and insinuations, the lies and taunts and ribaldry, which every such man encounters from those whom he disturbs. He was, indeed, a type of the American who best understands the true value of American principles and institutions.

"Mr. Brown did what every young American, and not

least those of fortunate circumstances and of high education, ought to do. He made himself acquainted with public affairs, and he took an active interest in politics. It is not possible, of course, that every man in the country should devote his life, or even a great deal of time, to politics; but he should have sufficient interest and knowledge and independence to exercise a positive and, in the true sense, conservative influence upon them. It is because of a general feeling that men like Mr. Brown can do no good in politics that there are so few men like him in politics. If there really be no need of them in our system, then a republic has no need of its best citizens. But one man like him, earnest, intelligent, sagacious, unselfish, courageous, at once shows by what he does alone how much a hundred such men together might do. Demagogues appeal only to passion and prejudice, swaying the brute force of ignorance, and count upon a numerical majority. Their reasoning or their instinct is, that the mass of men will always be venal and ignorant, and therefore that if a leader would have a majority, he must appeal to the lowest passions. Men like Mr. Brown know that the real justification of a popular government is the fact that brute force is always subordinated to brain force, and that immoral brain force has no advantage even with ignorant people. No man who has ever faced a mob really feared it if he knew that he would be heard. The demagogue, of every kind and degree, therefore, tries to silence his opponent by insult, or threat, or ridicule. He spurts dirty water, believing that a decent man will be unwilling to stand it. But if a man really means to do something, he will not heed blackguards.

"Mr. Brown's abilities, tastes, and circumstances fitted him so well for public life that his death is the loss of a man who might have been of conspicuous service. It is said that a high official position was open to him had he cared for it. But he showed always that his concern was less for office than for a real influence.   And it is always questionable in the case of such men whether they do not lose rather than gain influence by entering official life.   There are obviously two ways of serving the public, either by official action or by criticising properly the tone and methods of official action, and the time and opportunity necessary for the last are not always attainable with proper fidelity to the first. The last is one of the chief functions of the press, and in the degree that it is honestly performed the power and consideration of the press increase.   It was in such subjects that Mr. Brown was interested, and for such debates that he was especially equipped.   We had no personal acquaintance with him that would authorize us to speak of delightful qualities and charms of social intercourse known to us only by report.   But we sincerely deplore in his death the loss of a brave and sincere American, while all who are striving, each in his own way, for

> 'nobler modes of life,
> With sweeter manners, purer laws,'

will surely find an inspiration in the remembrance of this young fellow-laborer."

The thought suggested in the last extract, of the important rôle that the independent political worker may play, expresses one of the rare felicities of Mr. Brown's life. His life conclusively proved that in a free country a man of brains and of character does not need office; and, above all, that he need not be an office-seeker, which trade is the curse of our land.   He testified to the fact that the citizen is a power in himself, and that he requires no position from which to exert his power other than the popular system in which he is set, and which affords him all the opportunity he wants for self-development.

The citizen is the highest object of the republic. He is in fact its noblest product. Men of brains and character are often greater powers as citizens than they would be as rulers. They are raised above the ordinary motives and temptations which assail those in office, and yet, as men of intellectual breadth and moral earnestness, they cannot help studying politics, which is simply the science of men's living together in the State, or in those common relations that promote their best public and private well-being. From such citizens flow the ideas and influences which conserve, purify, and mould political institutions. If, with this genius for independent political thinking, there be combined a positive talent for political and public life, then we have the best possible material for making statesmen.

But if the cultivated portion of the community—what the Germans call *Die Gebildeten*—by the very conditions of their culture are to be shut out of this public life, then it is time to ask to what is education tending, and what is the worth of our higher schools of learning? The progress of science itself does not answer this question. There are interests superior even to the advancement of knowledge. There is a wider interest, a larger and more generous conception of humanity, contained in the idea of the nation, than in the idea of the individual man, however highly developed by culture. The students in our universities should steadfastly resist the narrowing influence of their training in any specific field of knowledge, and should not permit themselves to be reared in that intellectual exclusiveness by which this broader instinct of humanity, this grander idea of public spirit, becomes deadened.

Culture in any genuine field of knowledge ought to have a most liberalizing effect upon the nature; but, unless it be accompanied by other influences, we know that it is very apt to circumscribe rather than enlarge the sympathies; and, in a democracy above all, an aristocracy of learning may be almost as offensive as an aristocracy of rank, or of wealth. But when this wealth of culture, when these rich gifts of knowledge, are meant to be used for the benefit of all, are pervaded by the idea of the public good, then study is lifted into a nobler plane of work; then the higher spirit of humanity comes into it, and the old narrow forms are infused with new life and power.

Young men in our American colleges should, we think, ever look forward to becoming public men, the avowed and recognized servants of the republic; and they should act upon the principle that from the very talents intrusted to them they are expected to become the strong stays and helpers of the commonwealth. By so doing they will follow in his footsteps whose life has been imperfectly set forth in these pages, and who fell on the "high places of the field," to make more room for them to follow.

HISTORICAL ORATIONS.

ORATION

DELIVERED IN

CARPENTERS' HALL,

PHILADELPHIA,

ON

THE ONE HUNDREDTH ANNIVERSARY

OF THE MEETING OF

THE CONGRESS OF 1774.

"It is a tale brief and familiar to all; for the examples by which you may still be happy are to be found not abroad, men of Athens, but at home."

DEMOSTHENES, 3D OLYNTHIAC.

ORATION.

WE have come here to-day in obedience to that natural
impulse which bids a people do honor to its past. We
have assembled to commemorate a great event,—one of the
most famous in our history. In the midst of prosperity
and profound peace, in the presence of the honorable and
honored Vice-President of the United States, of the chosen
rulers of the people, of the members of the present and
other Congresses—the successors of the statesmen of 1774
—of the representatives of the learned professions, and of
every department of human enterprise and industry and
skill, we have gathered beneath this roof to celebrate, with
reverent and appropriate services, the one hundredth anniversary of the meeting of the First Continental Congress.

It is a great privilege to be here, and we have to thank
the Carpenters' Company for it.* The Carpenters' Company of Philadelphia has always been a patriotic body.
In the months which preceded the Revolution it freely
offered its hall for the meetings of the people; and besides
the high honor of having entertained the Congress of 1774,

---

* "The Carpenters' Company of the city and county of Philadelphia" was founded in the year 1724, and has continued to the present moment in activity and vigor. It is made up entirely of Master
Carpenters, who, at the time of their election, have been actively
engaged in business, and numbers now ninety members.

it can point to its having sheltered the Committees of Safety and the Provincial Committee for a long time beneath this roof. The Carpenters' Company of Philadelphia is a very ancient body. It came into existence when George the First was king, when Benjamin Franklin was a printer's lad, and Samuel Johnson was a boy at school. It was founded fifty years before an American Congress met, and it is now half as old again as American independence. And more than this, it is a very honorable body. Its members have been counted among our best citizens for industry and character. Both this hall, in which the nation may be said to have been born, and that other, where in 1776 its articles of apprenticeship were cancelled, are the monuments of its earlier skill, and there are few houses in this City of Homes in which its members have not had a hand. And, after all, how fitting does it seem that the hall of the Carpenters' Company should have been the scene of that event which we have assembled to commemorate! The men of the First Congress were architects themselves; the master-builders of a Republic founded on the equality of man—the highest types of which, in the two struggles through which it has had to pass, have been Benjamin Franklin, the mechanic, and the farmer's lad whose name was Abraham Lincoln. They represented among themselves every rank of life—the lawyer, the merchant, the farmer, the mechanic—and they did more to dignify Labor and advance the cause of Humanity in the seven weeks during which they sat in this place than all the parliaments of the world have done in twice as many centuries. If there be anything good, if there be anything noble, if there be anything precious in the American Revolution, it is just this—that it secured for every man an equal chance. Far wiser than those who have attempted a similar work beneath other skies, the men who achieved that Revolution attacked no vested rights, set up no false notions of equality, nor the oppression of the many for the tyranny of the few, nor did they break the chain that bound them to an honorable past. They sought rather to make Virtue and Intelligence the test of manhood—to strike down Prerogative and Privilege, and open the gates of happiness to all alike. And as I contemplate their glorious struggle at this distance of time, and think of the national life which it has blessed us with—a century of which is surely a great achievement for any people*—I cannot but think it to have been a happy omen that it was inaugurated here. It is impossible, in the time which I can allow myself, to attempt a description of the causes of the Revolution. The

---

* The historian Freeman, writing in 1862, says (History of Federal Government, vol. i. p. 112): "At all events, the American Union has actually secured, for what is really a long period of time, a greater amount of combined peace and freedom than was ever before enjoyed by so large a portion of the earth's surface. There have been, and still are, vaster despotic empires, but never before has so large an inhabited territory remained for more than seventy years in the enjoyment at once of internal freedom and of exemption from the scourge of internal war."

Professor Hoppin, of Yale College, writes me of a conversation he had some years ago with Professor Karl von Raumer, of Berlin: "I asked him what was his opinion as to the perpetuity of republican institutions. He said: 'Under certain conditions fulfilled, they would be more permanent than any other form. But,' said he, starting up from his chair with great energy, 'if they should fail, fifty years of American freedom would be worth a thousand years of Siberian despotism!'"

A similar thought is expressed by Freeman in page 52 of the volume above quoted: "The one century of Athenian greatness, from the expulsion of the Thirty Tyrants to the defeat of Aigospotamos, is worth millenniums of the life of Egypt or Assyria."

duty which I have to discharge is sufficiently difficult. I shall tax your patience, at any rate, I fear (for the trial is rather how little than how much to say), but the story must needs be long, and the occasion seems one of historic dignity.

It was only a month ago that the inhabitants of a little island in the northern corner of the Atlantic Ocean met on their Law Mount and celebrated, with song and saga, their one thousandth anniversary. That hardy race, which counts among its achievements the first discovery of this continent, has witnessed many memorable and strange events. Locked up in snow and ice, protected by the warring elements, it has watched the growth and decay of empires, the rise and fall of nations, the most wonderful changes in every quarter of the globe. But it has seen no spectacle more extraordinary than that which we commemorate to-day, and in all the sterile pages of its thousand years of history it can point to no such achievements as fill up the first century of this younger nation.

The tendency of the American colonies toward union had frequently shown itself before 1774. There was, of course, little sympathy at the outset between the Puritan of New England and the Virginian cavalier, the Roman Catholic of Maryland and the Pennsylvania Quaker. Each had, in times past, suffered at the other's hands, and the smart of their injuries was not soon forgotten. But Time, that great healer, came after a while to efface its sharpness, and when the third generation had grown up, little bitterness remained. For, after all, there is no sympathy like that which is begotten by common suffering. The trials of these men had been much the same. The spirit of persecution had driven forth all alike. Their ideas of liberty—narrow as they were at first—did not materially differ, and their devotion to them had led all alike across the seas. They spoke the same language, inherited the same traditions, revered the same examples, worshipped the same God. Nor had the obstacles which they had overcome been different. Heat and cold, fire and sword, hunger and thirst—they had all experienced these. The Frenchman on the North and the Indian along the Western frontier had constantly threatened them with a common danger, and when the news of Braddock's defeat came down the slopes of the Alleghany Mountains it sent a thrill through hearts in Georgia and New Hampshire, as well as in Pennsylvania and Maryland. As early as the year 1754 the Indian troubles and the necessity for united action had led to the assembling of a convention or council at Albany, at which seven colonies were represented. The scheme for a perpetual union which the genius of Franklin had then devised was not successful, it is true, but the meeting under such circumstances awakened a strong desire for union among his countrymen; and when, in 1765, the times had changed, and the mother-country, victorious over France, turned her hand against her children, the sense of danger found expression in the convention which the Stamp Act brought together in New York. I pass without comment over the years which intervened between 1765 and 1774. The Stamp Act had been repealed, but a succession of severer measures had brought things from bad to worse. Great Britain was in the zenith of her power. The colonies were thirteen in number, and contained about two millions and a half of inhabitants.* Let us, then, in the course of the hour which we are to spend together here, endeavor to go back in imagination to the summer of 1774.

---

* Bancroft's History of the United States, vol. vii. p. 128.

Here in Philadelphia there have been feverish days. The news of the determination of the ministry to shut up the port of Boston, followed, as it is soon after, by the attempt to do away with the ancient charter of Massachusetts, and to remove to Great Britain the trial of offences committed in America, has aroused the patriotic resistance of the whole country. In every town and hamlet, from New Hampshire to the southern boundary of Georgia, bold protests are recorded by the people, and Boston is declared to be suffering in the common cause. The first day of June, when the Port Bill goes into effect, is everywhere kept as a day of fasting and humiliation. Flags are lowered to half-mast, shops shut up, and the places of worship crowded with thoughtful men. Nine-tenths of the houses in Philadelphia are closed in mourning, and the famous bells of Christ Church are muffled in distress. Nor are the fellow-countrymen of the Bostonians content with this manifestation of their sympathy. From every part of the colonies come contributions for the suffering poor. Money, provisions, and articles of clothing pour in from every side. There is but one sentiment in the great majority of the people—a determination to support the men of Massachusetts to the end. They were not unconscious of the dangers of such a course. The disparity between the power of Great Britain and their own was far more apparent to them than it can ever be to us. They saw her the first power of the age—fresh from the memorable wars in which she had destroyed the naval and colonial power of France. The air still rang with the cheers with which they had greeted her successive triumphs, each of which they had come to look upon as their own. Her armies had been victorious in every land, her fleets triumphant on the most distant seas, and whatever of spirit, of courage, and of endurance

they might believe themselves to possess, they had inherited
from her. "We have not fit men for the times," wrote
one of the leading actors in the drama that was about to
begin; "we are deficient in genius, in education, in travel,
in fortune, in everything. I feel unutterable anxiety."*
But there is no thought of yielding in anybody's breast.
"God grant us wisdom and fortitude," writes John Adams,
in June, and he speaks the universal sentiment of his countrymen. "Should the opposition be suppressed, should this
country submit, what infamy and ruin! God forbid! Death
in any form is less terrible."† It was out of this consciousness of weakness that the strength of the Revolution grew.
Had Massachusetts stood alone, had a feeling of strength
seduced the colonies to remain divided, the end would have
been far different. Singly, they would have offered but
a slight resistance—together, they were invincible. And
the blind policy of the English king and ministry steadily
fostered this sentiment of union. The closing of the port
of Boston was intended by its authors to punish Massachusetts alone, but the merchant of Charleston or New York
saw in the act the attempt to exercise a power which might
one day be directed against him, and the Pennsylvanian
could have little feeling of security in submitting his
valued institutions to the mercy of those who sought, by
an act of Parliament, to sweep away the ancient charter of
Massachusetts. The cause of one colony became the cause
of all. The rights of Massachusetts were the rights of
America.

All through the spring and summer there has been earnest consultation. Couriers are riding here and there with
messages from the Committees of Correspondence which,

---

* Works of John Adams, vol. ii. p. 338.   † Ibid.

thanks to Samuel Adams, have been established in every village. A constant interchange of counsels has soon begotten confidence; with better understanding has come a sense of strength. Each colony seems ready for her share of the responsibility, and no town, however feeble, feels alone. Boston is strengthened in her glorious martyrdom as her sister towns reach forth to clasp her shackled hands, and the cry goes forth, at last, for the assembling of a Continental Congress. "Permit me to suggest a general Congress of deputies from the several Houses of Assembly on the Continent,"* John Hancock says on the 4th of March, "as the most effectual method of establishing a union for the security of our rights and liberties." "A Congress, and then an assembly of States,"† cries Samuel Adams, in April, 1773. Here is a call for a general Congress in the newspaper which I hold in my hand—a journal published in Philadelphia on the 11th of October, 1773. "A Congress," suggest the Sons of Liberty of New York in the spring of the following year, and in all parts of the country the cry meets with a response. The first official call comes from Virginia, dated May 28, 1774. On the 20th of that month the Whigs of Philadelphia have met, to the number of three hundred, in the long room of the City Tavern on Second Street, and, after consultation, unanimously resolved that the governor be asked at once to call a meeting of the Assembly of this province, and a Committee of Correspondence be appointed to write to the men of Boston "that we consider them as suffering in the general cause;" "that we truly feel for their unhappy situation;" "that we recommend to them firmness, pru-

---

* Bancroft's History of the United States, vol. vi. p. 508.
† Ibid., p. 456.

dence, and moderation;" and that "we shall continue to evince our firm adherence to the cause of American liberty."*

The messenger who bears this letter finds the country all alive. The Boston Committee sends southward a calm statement of the situation, and asks for general counsel and support. Rumor follows rumor as the days go by, and presently a courier comes riding down the dusty King's Highway from the North, and never draws rein till he reaches the Merchants' Coffee-House, where the patriots are assembled in committee. The intelligence he brings is stirring, for men come forth with flushed cheeks and sparkling eyes. And soon it is on every lip. Behold, great news! Bold Sam Adams has locked the Assembly door on the king's officers at Salem, and the General Court has named Philadelphia and the 1st of September as the place and time for the assembling of a Congress of deputies from all the colonies. Twelve hundred miles of coast is soon aflame. Nor is the enthusiasm confined to youth alone. Hopkins and Hawley in New England, and Gadsden in Carolina, are as full of fire as their younger brethren, and far away, in a corner of the British capital, a stout old gentleman in a suit of gray cloth, with spectacles on his nose, and a bright twinkle in his eye, is steadily preparing for the struggle which he—wise, far-sighted,

---

* *Pennsylvania Packet* for June 6, 1774. The reply to the Bostonians was written by the Rev. Dr. William Smith, first provost of the University of Pennsylvania (who did service afterward as one of the Provincial Convention of 1774). An interesting account of this will be found on pages 41 and 42 of the valuable "Memoir of the Rev. William Smith, D.D.;" for a copy of which I am indebted to its author, Charles J. Stillé, Esq., LL.D., the present provost of the University.

great-souled Franklin—has long foreseen and hoped for. One by one the colonies choose delegates. Connecticut first, Massachusetts next, Maryland the third, New Hampshire on the 21st of July, Pennsylvania on the 22d, and so on until all but Georgia have elected representatives. Yet still king and Parliament are deaf and blind, royal governors are writing: "Massachusetts stands alone; there will be no Congress of the other colonies." Boston lies still, the shipping motionless in her harbor, the merchandise rotting on her wharves; and elsewhere, as of old, the dull routine of provincial life goes jogging on. The creaking stages lumber to and fro. Ships sail slowly up to town, or swing out into the stream waiting for a wind to take them out to sea. Men rise and go to work, eat, lie down and sleep. The sun looks down on hot, deserted streets, and so the long days of summer pass until September comes.

With the first days of the new month there is excitement among the Philadelphia Whigs. All through the week the delegates to Congress have been arriving. Yesterday, Christopher Gadsden and Thomas Lynch, Esquires, landed at the wharf, having come by sea from Charleston, South Carolina; to-day, Colonel Nathaniel Folsom and Major John Sullivan, the delegates from New Hampshire, ride into town.* The friends of liberty are busy. The great coach-and-four† of John Dickinson rolls rapidly through the streets as he hastens to greet the Virginian gentlemen who have just arrived, and in the northern suburbs a company of horsemen has galloped out the old

---

* *Pennsylvania Packet* for August 29, 1774.

† "Mr. Dickinson, the farmer of Pennsylvania, came in his coach, with four beautiful horses, to Mr. Ward's lodgings to see us."—*J. Adams's Works*, vol. ii. p. 360.

King's Road to welcome the delegates from Massachusetts, who have arrived at Frankford, with Sam Adams at their head.*   With Saturday night they are all here, save those from North Carolina, who were not chosen till the 25th, but are on their way.

Sunday comes—the last Sabbath of the old provincial days.   The bells of Christ Church chime sweetly in the morning air, and her aisles are crowded beyond their wont; but the solemn service glides along, as in other days, with its prayer for king and queen, so soon to be read for the last time within those walls; and the thought, perhaps, never breaks the stillness of the Quakers' meeting-house that a thing has come to pass that will make their quiet town immortal.   Then the long afternoon fades away, and the sun sinks down yonder over Valley Forge.

The fifth day of September dawns at last.   At ten in the morning the delegates assemble at the Merchants' Coffee-House.†   From that point they march on foot along the

* J. Adams's Works, vol. ii. p. 357 : "After dinner we stopped at Frankford, about five miles out of town.   A number of carriages and gentlemen came out of Philadelphia to meet us. . . . We were introduced to all these gentlemen, and cordially welcomed to Philadelphia.   We then rode into the town, and, dirty, dusty, and fatigued as we were, we could not resist the importunity to go to the tavern, the most genteel one in America."   The important consequences of this meeting at Frankford are set forth in a letter of Adams to T. Pickering in 1822, printed in a note on page 512 of the same volume.—*Vide,* also, vol. i. p. 151.

† Then called the City Tavern.   It stood on the west side of Second Street, above Walnut, at the corner of Gold Street (or Bank Alley), and had been recently opened by Daniel Smith.   It was already the rendezvous of the Whigs, as the London Coffee-House (still standing), at Front and Market, had long been of the Tory party.—*Vide* Westcott's History of Philadelphia, Philadelphia Library copy, vol. ii. p. 364.

street until they reach the threshold of this hall. And what a memorable procession! The young men cluster around them as they pass, for these are their chosen leaders in the struggle that has come. The women peep at them, wonderingly, from the bowed windows of their low-roofed houses, little dreaming, perhaps, that these are the fathers of a republic for the sake of which their hearts are soon to be wrung and their homes made desolate. Here a royalist —"Tory" he is soon to be called—turns out for them to pass, scarcely attempting to hide the sneer that trembles on his lips, or some stern-browed Friend, a man of peace, his broad-brimmed hat set firmly on his head, goes by, with measured footsteps, on the other side. Yonder urchin, playing by the roadside, turns his head suddenly to stare at this stately company. Does he dream of the wonders he shall live to see? Men whose names his children shall revere through all descending generations have brushed by him while he played, and yet he knows them not. And so along the street, and down the narrow court, and up the broad steps the Congress takes its way.

The place of meeting has been well chosen. Some of the Pennsylvanians would have preferred the State-House, but that is the seat of government, and the Assembly, which has adjourned, has made no provision for the meeting of Congress there. Here, too, have been held the town-meetings at which the people have protested against the acts of Parliament, and the Carpenters' Company, which owns the hall, is made up of the friends of liberty. It has offered its hall to the delegates, and the place seems fit. It is "a spacious hall," says one of them,* and above

---

* John Adams; from whose Journal or Correspondence I have taken the personal descriptions in nearly every instance.

there is "a chamber, with an excellent library," "a convenient chamber opposite to this, and a long entry where gentlemen may walk." The question is put whether the gentlemen are satisfied, and passed in the affirmative; the members are soon seated and the doors are shut. The silence is first broken by Mr. Lynch, of South Carolina. "There is a gentleman present," he says, " who has presided with great dignity over a very respectable society, and greatly to the advantage of America;" and he " moves that the Honorable Peyton Randolph, Esquire, one of the delegates from Virginia, be appointed chairman." He doubts not it will be unanimous. It is so, and yonder " large, well-looking man," carefully dressed, with well-powdered wig and scarlet coat, rises and takes the chair.* The commissions of the delegates are then produced and read, after which Mr. Lynch nominates as secretary Mr. Charles Thomson, "a gentleman," he says, "of family, fortune, and character." And thereupon, with that singular wisdom which our early statesmen showed in their selection of men for all posts of responsibility, the Congress calls into his country's service that admirable man, " the Sam Adams of Philadelphia and the life of the cause of liberty."† While

---

* During the delivery of this address an original portrait of Mr. Randolph hung above the chair in which he sat during the sessions of Congress.

† The Hon. Eli K. Price has kindly sent me the following interesting account of the manner in which this was made known to Mr. Thomson. The allusion in the address " reminded me," writes a lady of Mr. Price's family, Miss Rebecca Embree, " of the great simplicity of that appointment, as I have heard it related by Deborah Logan, wife of Dr. George Logan, of Stenton, viz.: ' Charles Thomson had accompanied his wife on a bridal visit to Deborah Logan's mother, Mary Parker Norris, who resided on Chestnut Street above Fourth, where the custom-house now stands. Whilst there a mes-

preliminaries are being despatched, let us take a look at this company, for it is the most extraordinary assemblage America has ever seen. There are fifty delegates present, the representatives of eleven colonies. Georgia has had no election, the North Carolinians have not yet arrived, and John Dickinson, that "shadow, slender as a reed, and pale as ashes," that Pennsylvania farmer who has sown the seeds of empire, is not a member yet.* Directly in front, in a seat of prominence, sits Richard Henry Lee. His brilliant eye and Roman profile would make him a marked man in any company. One hand has been injured, and is wrapped, as you see, in a covering of black silk, but when he speaks his movements are so graceful and his voice so sweet that you forget the defect of gesture, for he is an orator—the greatest in America, perhaps, save only one. That tall

---

senger arrived inquiring for Mr. Thomson, and informed him that he was wanted at Carpenters' Hall. Being introduced to the company there assembled, he was requested to act as their secretary, which he accordingly did.' "

* Justice is not done nowadays to the patriotic labors of John Dickinson. The effect of his "Farmer's Letters" in preparing the minds of his countrymen for resistance to Great Britain, can hardly be exaggerated, and to him they owed the phrase, " No taxation without representation." When the Congress of 1774 assembled, no man in the colonies was more prominent than the Farmer, and his influence upon its deliberations was very great. On page 13 of the valuable "Early History of the Falls of Schuylkill, etc., etc.," by Charles V. Hagner, Esq., will be found an interesting account, taken partly from the *Pennsylvania Gazette* of May 12, 1768, of the presentation of a laudatory address to Mr. Dickinson by the Society of Fort St. Davids. Other similar addresses were sent to him from various parts of the colonies—one especially worthy of note being signed by Dr. Benjamin Church, John Hancock, Samuel Adams, Dr. Joseph Warren, and John Rowe, and enclosing resolutions adopted at a town-meeting held in Boston.

man with the swarthy face, and black unpowdered hair, is William Livingston of New Jersey—"no public speaker, but sensible and learned." Beside him, with his slender form bent forward, and his face lit with enthusiasm, sits his son-in-law, John Jay, soon to be famous. He is the youngest of the delegates, and yonder sits the oldest of them all. His form is bent, his thin locks fringing a forehead bowed with age and honorable service, and his hands shake tremulously as he folds them in his lap. It is Stephen Hopkins, once Chief Justice of Rhode Island. Close by him is his colleague, Samuel Ward, and Sherman of Connecticut—that strong man whose name is to be made honorable by more than one generation. Johnson of Maryland is here, "that clear, cool head," and Paca, his colleague, "a wise deliberator." Bland of Virginia, is that learned-looking, "bookish man," beside "zealous, hot-headed" Edward Rutledge. The Pennsylvanians are grouped together at one side — Morton, Humphreys, Mifflin, Rhoads, Biddle, Ross, and Galloway, the Speaker of the Assembly. Bending forward to whisper in the latter's ear is Duane of New York—that sly-looking man, a little "squint-eyed" (John Adams has already written of him), "very sensible and very artful." That large-featured man, with the broad, open countenance, is William Hooper; that other, with the Roman nose, McKean of Delaware. Rodney, the latter's colleague, sits beside him, "the oddest-looking man in the world—tall, thin, pale, his face no bigger than a large apple, yet beaming with sense, and wit, and humor." Yonder is Christopher Gadsden, who has been preaching independence to South Carolina these ten years past. He it is who, roused by the report that the regulars have commenced to bombard Boston, proposes to march northward and defeat Gage at once, before his reinforcements can arrive; and when some one timidly says that in the event of war the British will destroy the seaport towns, turns on the speaker, with this grand reply: "Our towns are built of brick and wood; if they are burned down we can rebuild them; but liberty once lost is gone forever." In all this famous company perhaps the men most noticed are the Massachusetts members. That colony has thus far taken the lead in the struggle with the mother-country. A British army is encamped upon her soil; the gates of her chief town are shut; against her people the full force of the resentment of king and Parliament is spent. Her sufferings called this Congress into being, and now lend sad prominence to her ambassadors. And of them surely Samuel Adams is the chief. What must be his emotions as he sits here to-day—he who "eats little, drinks little, and thinks much"*—that strong man whose undaunted spirit has led his countrymen up to the possibilities of this day? It is his plan of correspondence, adopted, after a hard struggle, in November, 1772, that first made feasible a union in the common defence. He called for union as early as April, 1773. For that he had labored without ceasing and without end, now arousing the drooping spirits of less sanguine men, now repressing the enthusiasm of rash hearts, which threatened to bring on a crisis before the time was ripe, and all the while thundering against tyranny through the columns of the *Boston Gazette.* As he was ten years ago he is to-day, the master-spirit of the time—as cool, as watchful, as steadfast, now that the hour of his triumph is at hand, as when, in darker days, he took up the burden

---

* Historical and Political Reflections on the Rise and Progress of the American Rebellion, by Joseph Galloway, London, 1780.

James Otis could no longer bear. Beside him sits his younger kinsman, John Adams, a man after his own heart —bold, fertile, resolute, an eloquent speaker, and a leader of men. But whose is yonder tall and manly form? It is that of a man of forty years of age, in the prime of vigorous manhood. He has not spoken, for he is no orator, but there is a look of command in his broad face and firm-set mouth, that marks him among men, and seems to justify the deference with which his colleagues turn to speak with him. He has taken a back seat, as becomes one of his great modesty—for he is great even in that— but he is still the foremost man in all this company. This is he who has just made in the Virginia Convention that speech which Lynch of Carolina says is the most eloquent that ever was made: " I will raise a thousand men, subsist them at my own expense, and march with them, at their head, for the relief of Boston." These were his words— and his name is Washington. Such was the Continental Congress assembled in Philadelphia.

Its members were met by a serious difficulty at the very outset. The question at once arose, How should their votes be cast—by colonies, by interest, or by the poll? Some were for a vote by colonies; but the larger ones at once raised the important objection that it would be unjust to allow to a little colony the same weight as a large one. " A small colony," was the reply of Major Sullivan, of New Hampshire, " has its all at stake, as well as a large one." Virginia responded that the delegates from the Old Dominion, will never consent to waive her full representa- tion; and one of them went so far as to intimate that if she were denied an influence in proportion to her size and numbers, she would never again be represented in such an assembly. On the other hand, it was confessed to be impossible to determine the relative weight which should be assigned to each colony. There were no tables of population, of products, or of trade, nor had there been a common system in the choice of delegates. Each province had sent as many as it liked—Massachusetts four, South Carolina five, Virginia seven, Pennsylvania eight. In one case they had been chosen by a convention of the people, in another by a general election, in most by the Assembly of the province. There was no rule by which the members could be guided. Nor was this the only point of difference among the delegates. On no one thing did they seem at first sight to agree. Some were for resting their rights on an historical basis—others upon the law of nature. These acknowledged the power of Great Britain to regulate trade —those denied her right to legislate for America at all. One would have omitted the Quebec Bill from the list of grievances—another held it to be of them all the very worst. Some were for paying an indemnity for the destruction of the tea—others cried out that this were to yield the point at once. One was defiant, a second conciliatory; Gadsden desired independence; Washington believed that it was wished for by no thinking man.

It was with a full sense of the diversity of these views, of the importance of a speedy decision, and of the danger of dissension, that the Congress reassembled the next morning.

When the doors had been closed, and the preliminaries gone through with, it is related that an oppressive silence prevailed for a long time before any man spoke. No one seemed willing to take the lead. It was a season of great doubt and greater danger. Now, for the first time perhaps, when the excitement of the assembling had passed away, and reflection had come to calm men's minds, the members realized completely the importance of their acts. Their countrymen watched and waited everywhere. In the most distant hamlet beyond the mountains, in the lonely cabin by the sea, eyes were turned to this place with anxious longing, and yonder, in the North, the brave town lay patient in her chains, resting her hopes for deliverance upon them. And not Boston only, nor Massachusetts, depended upon them. The fate of humanity for generations was to be affected by their acts. Perhaps in the stillness of this morning hour there came to some of them a vision of the time to come. Perhaps to him, on whose great heart was destined so long to lie the weight of all America, it was permitted to look beyond the present hour, like that great leader of an earlier race when he stood silent, upon a peak in Moab, and overlooked the Promised Land. Like him, he was to be the chosen of his people. Like him, soldier, lawgiver, statesman. Like him, he was destined to lead his brethren through the wilderness; and, happier than he, was to behold the fulfilment of his labor. Perhaps, as he sat here in the solemn stillness that fell upon this company, he may have seen, in imagination, the wonders of the century that is complete to-day. If he had spoken, might he not have said: I see a winter of trouble and distress, and then the smoke of cannon in the North. I see long years of suffering to be borne, our cities sacked, our fields laid waste, our hearths made desolate; men trudging heavily through blood-stained snow, and wailing women refusing to be comforted. I see a time of danger and defeat, and then a day of victory. I see this people, virtuous and free, founding a government on the rights of man. I see that government grown strong, that people prosperous, pushing its way across a continent. I see these villages become wealthy cities; these colonies great States;

the Union we are about to found, a power among the nations; and I know that future generations shall rise up and call us blessed.

Such might have been his thoughts as these founders of an empire sat for a while silent, face to face. It was the stillness of the last hour of night before the morning breaks; it was the quiet which precedes the storm.

Suddenly, in some part of this hall a man rose up. His form was tall and angular, and his short wig and coat of black gave him the appearance of a clergyman. His complexion was swarthy, his nose long and straight, his mouth large, but with a firm expression on the thin lips, and his forehead exceptionally high. The most remarkable feature of his face was a pair of deep-set eyes, of piercing brilliancy, changing so constantly with the emotions which they expressed that none could tell the color of them. He began to speak in a hesitating manner, faltering through the opening sentences, as if fully convinced of the inability, which he expressed, to do justice to his theme. But presently, as he reviewed the wrongs of the colonies through the past ten years, his cheek glowed and his eye flashed fire and his voice rang out rich and full, like a trumpet, through this hall. He seemed not to speak like mortal man, thought one who heard him ten years before in the Virginia House of Burgesses; and a recent essayist in a leading English Review has spoken of him as one of the greatest orators that ever lived.* There was no report made of his speech that day, but from the notes which John Adams kept of the debate, we may learn what line of argument he took. He spoke of the attacks made upon America by the king and ministry of Great Britain, counselled a union in the

---

* Essays, by A. Hayward, Esq., Q. C., 3d series, p. 50.

general defence, and predicted that future generations would quote the proceedings of this Congress with applause. A step in advance of his time, as he had ever been, he went far beyond the spirit of the other delegates, who, with the exception of the Adamses and Gadsden, did not counsel or desire independence. "An entire new government must be founded," was his cry; "this is the first in a never-ending succession of Congresses," his prophecy. And gathering up, as it was the gift of his genius to do, the thought that was foremost in every mind about him, he spoke it in a single phrase: "British oppression has effaced the boundaries of the several colonies; I am not a Virginian, but an American."

My countrymen, we cannot exaggerate the debt we owe this man. The strength of his intellect, the fervor of his eloquence, the earnestness of his patriotism, and the courage of his heart placed him in the front rank of those early patriots, and he stands among them the model of a more than Roman virtue. His eloquence was one of the chief forces of the American Revolution—as necessary to that great cause as the intelligence of Franklin, the will of Samuel Adams, the pen of Thomas Jefferson, or the sword of Washington. In such times of a nation's trial there is always one voice which speaks for all. It echoes the spirit of the age—proud or defiant, glad or mournful, now raised in triumph, now lifted up in lamentation. Greece stood on the Bema with Demosthenes; indignant Rome thundered against Catiline with the tongue of Cicero. The proud eloquence of Chatham rang out the triumphs of the English name, and France stood still to hear her Mirabeau. Ireland herself pleaded for liberty when Henry Grattan spoke, and the voice of Patrick Henry was the voice of America, struggling to be free!

Rest in peace, pure and patriotic heart! Thy work is finished and thy fame secure. Dead for three-quarters of a century, thou art still speaking to the sons of men. Through all descending time thy countrymen shall repeat thy glowing words, and, as the pages of their greatest bard kept strong the virtue of the Grecian youth, so from the grave shalt thou, who "spoke as Homer wrote,"* inspire in the hearts of men to be, that love of liberty which filled thine own!

Great as were at first the differences of interest and opinion among the members of the Congress of 1774, there were none which their patriotic spirits could not reconcile. It was the salvation of the Americans that they had chosen for their counsellors men who believed, with Thomas Jefferson, that "the whole art of government consists in the art of being honest,"† and who were enthusiastic lovers of their country. No matter how strong had been their individual opinions, or how dear the separate interests involved, there seemed to these men no sacrifice too great to make for the common cause. As the debates progressed, different views were reconciled and pet theories sacrificed to the general judgment. Day after day they became more united and confidence increased. "This," wrote John Adams on the 17th of September, "was one of the happiest days of my life. In Congress we had noble sentiments and manly eloquence. This day convinced me that America will support the Massachusetts or perish with her."‡ After a full and free discussion, in which the subject was considered in all its aspects, it was decided that each colony was entitled

---

* Memoir of Thomas Jefferson, vol. i. p. 3.

† Ibid., p. 115.

‡ Journal of John Adams, vol. ii. p. 380.

to a single vote. By this means the integrity of the provinces was preserved, and out of it grew the theory, so familiar to us, of the sovereignty of the State. It was next agreed upon to rest the rights of the colonies on an historical basis. By this wise determination the appearance of a revolution was avoided, while the fact remained the same. Nor was there a sudden break in the long chain of the nation's history; the change was gradual, not abrupt. The common law of England, under the benign influence of which the young colonies had grown up, remained unchanged, and when, in less than two years, the Declaration of Independence created a new government, the commonwealth quietly took the place of king. The revolution was then complete; the struggle which followed was merely to secure it; and the American grew strong with the belief that it was his part to defend, not to attack—to preserve, not to destroy; and that he was fighting over again on his own soil the battle for civil liberty which his forefathers had won in England more than a century before. We cannot too highly prize the wisdom which thus shaped the struggle.

Having decided these points, the Congress agreed upon a declaration of rights. First, then, they named as natural rights the enjoyment of life, liberty, and fortune. They next claimed, as British subjects, to be bound by no law to which they had not consented by their chosen representatives (excepting such as might be mutually agreed upon as necessary for the regulation of trade). They denied to Parliament all power of taxation, and vested the right of legislation in their own Assemblies. The common law of England they declared to be their birthright, including the rights of a trial by a jury of the vicinage, of public meetings, and petition. They protested against the maintenance in the colonies of standing armies without their full consent, and against all legislation by councils depending on the Crown. Having thus proclaimed their rights, they calmly enumerated the various acts which had been passed in derogation of them. These were eleven in number, passed in as many years—the Sugar Act, the Stamp Act, the Tea Act, those which provided for the quartering of the troops, for the supersedure of the New York Legislature, for the trial in Great Britain of offences committed in America, for the regulation of the government of Massachusetts, for the shutting of the port of Boston, and the last straw, known as the Quebec Bill.

Their next care was to suggest the remedy. On the 18th of October they adopted the articles of American Association, the signing of which (on the 20th) should be regarded as the commencement of the American Union. By its provisions, to which they individually and as a body solemnly agreed, they pledged the colonies to an entire commercial non-intercourse with Great Britain, Ireland, the West Indies, and such North American provinces as did not join the Association, until the acts of which America complained were all repealed. In strong language they denounced the slave-trade, and agreed to hold non-intercourse with all who engaged therein. They urged upon their fellow-countrymen the duties of economy, frugality, and the development of their own resources; directed the appointment of committees in every town and village to detect and punish all violators of the Association, and inform each other from time to time of the condition of affairs; and bound themselves, finally, to carry out the provisions of the Association by the sacred ties of " virtue, honor, and love of country."

Having thus declared their rights, and their fixed determination to defend them, they sought to conciliate their English brethren. In one of the most remarkable state papers ever written, they called upon the people of Great Britain, in a firm but affectionate tone, to consider the cause for which America was contending as one in which the inhabitants of the whole empire were concerned, adroitly reminding them that the power which threatened the liberties of its American, might more easily destroy those of its English subjects. They rehearsed the history of their wrongs, and " demanded nothing but to be restored to the condition in which they were in 1763." Appealing at last to the justice of the British nation for a Parliament which should overthrow the "power of a wicked and corrupt ministry," they used these bold and noble words: " Permit us to be as free as yourselves, and we shall ever esteem a union with you to be our greatest glory and our greatest happiness; we shall ever be ready to contribute all in our power to the welfare of the empire; we shall consider your enemies as our enemies, your interests as our own. But if you are determined that your ministers shall sport wantonly with the rights of mankind,—if neither the voice of justice, the dictates of the law, the principles of the constitution, nor the suggestions of humanity can restrain your hands from shedding blood in such an impious cause—we must then tell you that we will never submit to be hewers of wood or drawers of water for any ministry or nation in the world."

In an address to the people of Quebec they described the despotic tendency of the late change in their government effected by the Quebec Bill, which threatened to deprive them of the blessings to which they were entitled on becoming English subjects, naming particularly the rights of representation, of trial by jury, of liberty of person and *habeas corpus*, of the tenure of land by easy rents instead of oppressive services, and especially that right so essential " to the advancement of truth, science, art, and morality," " to the diffusion of liberal sentiments" and " the promotion of union"—" the freedom of the press." " These are the rights," said they, " without which a people cannot be free and happy," and " which we are, with one mind, resolved never to resign but with our lives." In conclusion, they urged the Canadians to unite with their fellow-colonists below the St. Lawrence in the measures recommended for the common good. They also prepared letters to the people of St. John's, Nova Scotia, Georgia, and East and West Florida, who were not represented in this Congress, asking for their co-operation and support.

Nor was anything omitted by these men which could soften the hearts of their oppressors. Declining to petition Parliament, they had addressed themselves to the people, recognizing in them for the first time the sovereign power. They now decided to petition the king. In words both humble and respectful, they renewed their allegiance to his crown, detailed the injuries inflicted on them by his ministers, and besought his interference in their behalf. " We ask," they said, " but for peace, liberty, and safety. We wish not a diminution of the prerogative, nor do we solicit the grant of any new right in our favor. Your royal authority over us and our connection with Great Britain, we shall always carefully and zealously endeavor to support and maintain." Solemnly professing that their " counsels were influenced by no other motive than a dread of impending destruction," they earnestly besought their " Most Gracious Sovereign" " in the name of his faithful people in America," " for the honor of Almighty God," " for his own glory," " the interest of his family," and the good and welfare of his kingdom, to suffer not the most sacred "ties to be further violated" in the vain hope " of effects" which, even if secured, could "never compensate for the calamities through which they must be gained."

There remained now for the Congress but one thing to do—to render to its countrymen an account of its stewardship. In a long letter to their constituents, the delegates gave a summary of their proceedings, of the difficulties they had encountered, the opinions they had formed, the policy they had agreed to recommend, and, with a mournful prophecy of the trials that were at hand, urged their fellow-countrymen "to be in all respects prepared for every contingency." Such were, in brief, the memorable state papers issued by the First Continental Congress. And, terrible as were the dangers which seemed to threaten them from without, its members were to be subjected to a trial from within. On the 28th of September, Joseph Galloway of Pennsylvania, submitted to the Congress his famous plan.* A man of talent and address, at one time high in the opinion and confidence of Franklin, he stood at the head of the Pennsylvania delegation. The Speaker of the House of Assembly, he had wielded great influence in the policy of the province. Cold, cautious, and at heart a thorough royalist, he determined, if possible, to nip the patriotic movement in the bud. Seconded by Duane of New York, he moved that the Congress should recommend the establishment of a British and American government, to consist of a President-General, appointed by the king, and a Grand Council, to be chosen by the several Legislatures; that the Council should have co-ordinate powers with the British

---

* *Vide* Tucker's History, vol. i. p. 111 ; Sabine's American Loyalists, vol. i. p. 309 ; John Adams's Works, vol. ii. p. 389.

House of Commons, either body to originate a law, but the consent of both to be necessary to its passage; the members of the Council to be chosen for three years, the President-General to hold office at the pleasure of the king. Here, then, was an ingenious trap in the very path of the infant nation. Some men, and good ones, too, fell into it. The project was earnestly supported by Duane. The younger Rutledge thought it "almost perfect," and it met with the warm approbation of the conservative Jay. But wiser men prevailed. The Virginian and Massachusetts members opposed it earnestly. Samuel Adams saw in it the doom of all hope for liberty, and Henry condemned in every aspect the proposal to substitute for "a corrupt House of Commons" a "corruptible" legislature, and intrust the power of taxation to a body not elected directly by the people. His views were those of the majority, and the dangerous proposition met with a prompt defeat. The Suffolk County resolutions, adopted on the 9th of September, at Milton, Massachusetts, had reached Philadelphia and the Congress on the 17th, and awakened in every breast the warmest admiration and sympathy. Resolutions were unanimously adopted, expressing these feelings in earnest language, recommending to their brethren of Suffolk County "a perseverance in the same firm and temperate conduct," and urging upon the people of the other colonies the duty of contributing freely to the necessities of the Bostonians. There now came a still more touching appeal from Massachusetts. "The governor," it said, "was suffering the soldiery to treat both town and country as declared enemies;" the course of trade was stopped; the administration of law obstructed; a state of anarchy prevailed. Filled with the spirit which, in olden times, had led the Athenians to leave their city to the foe and make their ships their country, this gallant people promised to obey should the Congress advise them to "quit their town;" but if it is judged, they added, that "by maintaining their ground they can better serve the public cause, they will not shrink from hardship and danger."* Such an appeal as this could not have waited long for a worthy answer from the men of the First American Congress. The letter was received upon October 6th. Two days later the official journal contains these words: "Upon motion it was resolved that this Congress approve the opposition of the inhabitants of the Massachusetts Bay to the execution of the late acts of Parliament; and if the same shall be attempted to be carried into execution, all America ought to support them in their opposition." "This," says the historian, "is the measure which hardened George the Third to listen to no terms."† In vain conciliation and kind words; in vain all assurances of affection and of loyalty. The men of Massachusetts are traitors to their king, and the Congress of all the colonies upholds them in rebellion. "Henceforth," says Bancroft, "conciliation became impossible."

Having thus asserted their rights to the enjoyment of life, liberty, and fortune; their resistance to taxation without representation; their purpose to defend their ancient charters from assault; having denounced the slave-trade in

---

* The spirit of this people is reflected in a letter from Boston, printed in the *Pennsylvania Packet* for October 10, 1774, describing a conversation which the writer had with a fisherman. "I said: 'Don't you think it time to submit, pay for the tea, and get the harbor opened?' 'Submit? No. It can never be time to become slaves. I have yet some pork and meal, and when they are gone I will eat clams; and after we have dug up all the clam-banks, if the Congress will not let us fight, I will retreat to the woods; I am always sure of acorns!'"

† Bancroft's History of the United States, vol. vii. p. 145.

language which startled the world, and recognized, for the first time in history, the People as the source of Authority; having laid the firm foundations of a Union based upon Freedom and Equality—the First Congress passed out of existence on the 26th of October, after a session of two and fifty days. Half a hundred men, born in a new country, bred amid trials and privations, chosen from every rank of life, untried in diplomacy, unskilled in letters, untrained in statecraft, called suddenly together in a troubled time to advise a hitherto divided people, they had shown a tact, a judgment, a self-command, and a sincere love of country hardly to be found in the proudest annals of antiquity. And their countrymen were worthy of them. If the manner in which they had fulfilled their duties had been extraordinary, the spirit with which their counsels were received was still more remarkable. In every part of the country the recommendations of the Congress were obeyed as binding law. No despotic power in any period of history exercised over the minds and hearts of men a more complete control. The Articles of Association were signed by tens of thousands, the spirit of Union grew strong in every breast, and the Americans steadily prepared to meet the worst. The stirring influence of this example penetrated to the most distant lands. "The Congress," wrote Dr. Franklin from London in the following winter, "is in high favor here among the friends of liberty."* "For a long time," cried the eloquent Charles Botta, "no spectacle has been offered to the attention of mankind of so powerful an interest as this of the present American Congress."† "It is impossible," says the Scotch writer,

---

* Letter to Charles Thomson, 5th February, 1775; Watson's Annals of Philadelphia, vol. i. p. 421.

† Otis's Botta, vol. i. p. 128.

Grahame, " to read of its transactions without the highest admiration."* "There never was a body of delegates more faithful to the interests of their constituents," was the opinion of David Ramsay, the historian.† " From the moment of their first debates," De Tocqueville says, " Europe was moved."‡ The judgment of John Adams declared them to be, " in point of abilities, virtues, and fortunes, the greatest men upon the continent."§ Charles Thomson, in the evening of his well-spent life, pronounced them " the purest and ablest patriots he had ever known ;"‖ and, in the very face of king and Parliament, the illustrious Chatham spoke of them the well-known words : " I must avow and declare that in all my reading of history—and it has been my favorite study ; I have read Thucydides and admired the master states of the world—that for solidity of reasoning, force of sagacity, and wisdom of conclusion, under such a complication of circumstances, no nation or body of men can stand in preference to the General Congress assembled in Philadelphia."¶ Long years have passed, and there have been many changes in the governments of men. The century which has elapsed has been crowded with great events, but the calm judgment of posterity has confirmed that opinion, and mankind has not

---

* History of the United States, by James Grahame, LL.D., vol. ii. p. 496.

† History of the American Revolution, by David Ramsay, M.D., vol. i. p. 174.

‡ La Démocratie en Amérique, by Alexis de Tocqueville, vol. iii. p. 182.

§ John Adams's Letters to his Wife, vol. i. p. 21.

‖ Field-Book of the Revolution, by B. J. Lossing, vol. ii. p. 60, note.

¶ Speech in Favor of the Removal of Troops from Boston, January 20, 1775.

ceased to admire the spectacle which was once enacted here. "But that you may be more earnest in the defence of your country," cried the great Roman orator, speaking in a vision with the tongue of Scipio, "know from me that a certain place in heaven is assigned to all who have preserved, or assisted, or improved their country, where they are to enjoy an endless duration of happiness. For there is nothing which takes place on earth more acceptable to the Supreme Deity, who governs all this world, than those councils and assemblies of men, bound together by law, which are termed states; the founders and preservers of these come from heaven, and thither do they return."* The founders and preservers of this Union have vanished from the earth, those true lovers of their country have long since been consigned into her keeping, but their memory clings around this place, and hath hallowed it for evermore. Here shall men come as to a sanctuary. Here shall they gather with each returning anniversary, and as the story of these lives falls from the lips of him who shall then stand where I stand to-day, their souls shall be stirred within them and their hearts be lifted up, and none shall despair of the Republic while she can find among her children the courage, the wisdom, the eloquence, the self-sacrifice, the lofty patriotism, and the spotless honor of those who assembled in this hall an hundred years ago.

The conditions of life are always changing, and the experience of the fathers is rarely the experience of the sons. The temptations which are trying us are not the temptations which beset their footsteps, nor the dangers which threaten our pathway the dangers which surrounded them. These men were few in number, we are many.

---

* Cicero, De Re Publica, lib. vi.; Somnium Scipionis, ? iii.

They were poor, but we are rich. They were weak, but we are strong. What is it, countrymen, that we need to-day? Wealth? Behold it in your hands. Power? God hath given it you. Liberty? It is your birthright. Peace? It dwells among you. You have a government founded in the hearts of men, built by the people for the common good. You have a land flowing with milk and honey; your homes are happy, your workshops busy, your barns are full. The school, the railway, the telegraph, the print-ing-press have welded you together into one. Descend those mines that honeycomb the hills! Behold that com-merce whitening every sea! Stand by your gates and see that multitude pour through them from the corners of the earth, grafting the qualities of older stocks upon one stem, mingling the blood of many races in a common stream, and swelling the rich volume of our English speech with varied music from an hundred tongues. You have a long and glorious history, a past glittering with heroic deeds, an ancestry full of lofty and imperishable examples. You have passed through danger, endured privation, been acquainted with sorrow, been tried by suffering. You have journeyed in safety through the wilderness and crossed in triumph the Red Sea of civil strife, and the foot of Him who led you hath not faltered nor the light of His countenance been turned away! It is a question for us now, not of the founding of a new government, but of the preservation of one already old; not of the forma-tion of an independent power, but of the purification of a nation's life; not of the conquest of a foreign foe, but of the subjection of ourselves. The capacity of man to rule himself is to be proven in the days to come—not by the greatness of his wealth, not by his valor in the field, not by the extent of his dominion, not by the splendor of his genius. The dangers of to-day come from within. The worship of self, the love of power, the lust of gold, the weakening of faith, the decay of public virtue, the lack of private worth—these are the perils which threaten our future; these are the enemies we have to fear; these are the traitors which infest the camp; and the danger was far less when Catiline knocked with his army at the gates of Rome than when he sat smiling in the Senate House. We see them daily face to face—in the walk of virtue, in the road to wealth, in the path to honor, on the way to happiness. There is no peace between them and our safety. Nor can we avoid them and turn back. It is not enough to rest upon the past. No man or nation can stand still. We must mount upward or go down. We must grow worse or better. It is the Eternal Law—we cannot change it. Nor are we only concerned in what we do. This government, which our ancestors have built, has been "a refuge for the oppressed of every race and clime," where they have gathered for a century. The fugitive of earlier times knew no such shelter among the homes of men. Cold, naked, bleeding, there was no safety for him save at the altars of imagined gods. I have seen one of the most famous of those ancient sanctuaries. On a bright day in spring-time I looked out over acres of ruin. Beside me the blue sea plashed upon a beach strewn with broken marble. That sacred floor, polished with the penitential knees of centuries, was half hidden with heaps of rubbish and giant weeds. The fox had his den among the stones, and the fowl of the air her nest upon the capitals. No sound disturbed them in their solitude, save sometimes the tread of an adventurous stranger, or the stealthy footfall of the wild beasts and wilder men that crept down out of the surrounding hills under cover of the night. The god had vanished, his seat was desolate, the oracle was dumb. Far different was the temple which our fathers builded, and "builded better than they knew." The blood of martyrs was spilled on its foundations, and a suffering people raised its walls with prayer. Temple and fortress, it still stands secure, and the smile of Providence gilds plinth, architrave, and column. Greed is alone the Tarpeia that can betray it, and vice the only Samson that can pull it down. It is the Home of Liberty, as boundless as a continent, "as broad and general as the casing air;" a "temple not made with hands;" a sanctuary that shall not fall, but stand on forever, founded in eternal truth!

My countrymen: the moments are quickly passing, and we stand like some traveller upon a lofty crag that separates two boundless seas.

The century that is closing is complete. "The past," said your great statesman, "is secure." It is finished, and beyond our reach. The hand of detraction cannot dim its glories nor the tears of repentance wipe away its stains. Its good and evil, its joy and sorrow, its truth and falsehood, its honor and its shame, we cannot touch. Sigh for them, blush for them, weep for them, if we will; we cannot change them now. We might have done so once, but we cannot now. The old century is dying, and they are to be buried with him; his history is finished, and they will stand upon his roll forever.

The century that is opening is all our own. The years that lie before us are a virgin page. We can inscribe it as we will. The future of our country rests upon us—the happiness of posterity depends on us. The fate of humanity may be in our hands. That pleading voice, choked with the sobs of ages, which has so often spoken unto ears of stone, is lifted up to us. It asks us to be brave, benevolent, consistent, true to the teachings of our history—proving "divine descent by worth divine." It asks us to be virtuous, building up public virtue upon private worth ; seeking that righteousness which exalteth nations. It asks us to be patriotic—loving our country before all other things; her happiness our happiness, her honor ours, her fame our own. It asks us in the name of Justice, in the name of Charity, in the name of Freedom, in the name of God!

My countrymen: this anniversary has gone by forever, and my task is done. While I have spoken the hour has passed from us ; the hand has moved upon the dial, and the Old Century is dead. The American Union hath endured an hundred years! Here, on this threshold of the future, the voice of humanity shall not plead to us in vain. There shall be darkness in the days to come; Danger for our Courage; Temptation for our Virtue; Doubt for our Faith ; Suffering for our Fortitude. A thousand shall fall before us and tens of thousands at our right hand. The years shall pass beneath our feet, and century follow century in quick succession. The generations of men shall come and go; the greatness of Yesterday shall be forgotten To-day, and the glories of this Noon shall vanish before To-morrow's sun ; but America shall not perish, but endure, while the spirit of our fathers animates their sons!

"THE SETTLEMENT OF BURLINGTON."

AN ORATION

Delivered in that City December 6, 1877,

in commemoration of

THE TWO HUNDREDTH ANNIVERSARY

OF ITS SETTLEMENT

BY THE PASSENGERS OF THE GOOD SHIP KENT, WHO
LANDED AT RACCOON CREEK, AUGUST 16, O. S., AND LAID OUT
THE TOWN ON CHYGOE'S ISLAND "TOWARDS
YE LATTER PART OF YE 8TH
MONTH," 1677.

ORATION.

THERE are few events in American history more interesting than that which we commemorate to-day. There are few stories more honorable than that which I shall have to tell. The sun which has broken through the clouds of this morning with such unexpected and auspicious splendor, has rarely looked down upon an anniversary more worthy to be observed than this which marks the peaceful planting of a people—the founding of a free and happy commonwealth. The life of old Burlington has been a modest one. She sings no epic-song of hard-fought fields and gallant deeds of arms; she tells no tales of conquest, of well-won triumphs, of bloody victories. Seated in smiling meadows and guarded by the encircling pines, her days have been full of quietness and all her paths of peace. The hand of Time has touched her forehead lightly. The centuries have flown by so softly that she has hardly heard the rustle of their wings. The stream of years has flowed before her feet as smoothly as the broad bosom of her own great river by whose banks she dwells. But her history is none the less worthy to be remembered, for it is full of those things which good men rejoice to find in the character of their ancestors—of a courage meek but dauntless, a self-sacrifice lowly but heroic, a wisdom humble and yet lofty, a love of humanity that nothing could quench, a devotion to liberty that was never shaken, an unfaltering and childlike faith in God. And it is right that it be remembered by those who enjoy the blessings which such qualities have won. "I wish," wrote one who had witnessed the beginning, describing in her old age the dangers and trials of her youth, " I wish they that come after may consider these things."* Seven-score years have gone since that was written. The heart that held that hope has long been still. The hand that wrote those words has been motionless for more than a century, and the kindred to whom they were addressed have vanished from the earth. But here to-day in that ancient town, strangely unaltered by the changes of two centuries—here amid scenes with which those venerable eyes were so familiar—we who have "come after" have assembled to fulfil that pious wish, to "consider those things" with reverence and gratitude, and take care that they be held hereafter in eternal remembrance and everlasting honor.

The causes which led to the event which it is my duty to describe to-day are to be found in one of the most interesting periods of English history. The attempt of Charles I. to secure for the Crown a power which not even the pride of Henry VIII. had claimed, had ended in disastrous failure. Conquered by his people, the unfortunate monarch had paid for his folly with his life—a victim less of political hatred than of that personal distrust which his frequent want of faith had planted in the breast of friends and foes—and England was nominally at peace. In reality, however, she continued in commotion. The excesses into which their triumph over their king and his party not un-

---

* Account of Mary Murfin Smith in Baxter and Howe's New Jersey Historical Collection, p. 90. Mrs. Smith came over with her parents while yet a child. She was drowned in 1739.

naturally led the victors were soon over, and already, in 1650, the reaction had set in which was destined to lead the country backward to the Restoration. But the passions into which the civil wars had thrown all classes would not easily cool. The struggle of the Cavalier and the Round-head was not like that in which two great sections of a vast country—each in itself a unit—are pitted against each other. It aroused feelings far more personal and bitter. Families were divided among themselves, and every man was in arms against his neighbor. No single county had borne the brunt of a war which had involved all alike, ravaged the whole country, and brought desolation to half the hearths in England; and, though peace might be proclaimed, some of the spirits which it had called up would not down even at the bidding of such a man as Cromwell. Feared at home and abroad, and armed with an authority which belonged less to his office than to himself, the victor of Worcester could govern his turbulent countrymen, but pacify and unite them he could not. It might have been possible had their differences been simply political, but a deeper feeling entered into all the actions of that time. It was the age of politico-religious fanaticism. The Cavalier and the Roundhead, the Royalist and the Republican, had they been nothing more, might have been made to sit down in peace together under a liberal and strong government, which, though it represented the peculiar ideas of neither, expressed in its actions many of the views of both. But Baptist, Presby-terian, and Independent, Protestant and Roman Catholic no man could reconcile, and between the many sects which the spirit of free inquiry had bred in the heat of those fanatic days the most vigorous ruler England had ever seen had hard work to keep the peace. It is not easy in these colder, calmer times to understand the polemic spirit of that age. It had arisen suddenly and grown with amazing speed, and the transition from the manners of the time when the graceful Buckingham had set the fashion to those of a day in which the psalm-singing soldier of Cromwell stood guard before Whitehall, was as extraordinary as it had been startling and abrupt. Religion now was the mainspring of men's actions, the subject of their talk, the basis of their politics, the object of their lives. It is strange that religious liberty remained yet to be contended for. Too near to the Reformation to have escaped its spirit, and not far enough from Philip and Mary's day to have forgotten the crimes committed in their name—of which indeed he had had beneath his eyes a constant reminder in the scenes of which Holland had been the theatre for more than sixty years—the Englishman of 1650 was sincerely and aggressively a Protestant, and it might naturally have been expected that religious freedom would in his mind have gone hand in hand with the civil liberty for which he had recently gained such splendid and substantial triumphs. But such was not the case. Free from political tyranny from within, he would not brook even the semblance of interference in religious matters from without, but, in the fierce controversies of Englishmen with each other, liberty of conscience meant to the zealous theologian of that day—when all men claimed to be theologians—only the right of all other men to yield their own opinions and agree with him. It was soon observed that the sincere bigotry of the Roman Catholic and the proud intolerance of the English Churchman had only given place to a fervent but narrow piety, which, like them, would brook no opposition, mistook differences of opinion for hostility, and watched all other creeds with a jealous and unchristian eye. Forgetful of the truth that all cannot think alike, mixing essentials and non-essentials in blind confusion, and armed with the cant and loose learning of the day, men went forth to controversy as the knights errant of an earlier and more chivalric, but not more zealous, age went forth to battle. Each sect became a political party, and every party a religious sect. Each in its turn, according to its power, persecuted the others, and all united to persecute the Quakers.

I have no time to-day to describe the rise of the Society of Friends. Considered only as a political event and in its bearing upon the struggle for civil and religious liberty, it is a strange chapter in the history of progress, and it is one of the peculiar glories of those whom the world calls Quakers, that without justice to their achievements such a history would be incomplete.* It was in the midst of the stormiest years of the civil war that George Fox began his ministry. An humble youth watching his flocks by night in the fields of Nottingham, he had heard, as he believed, the voice of God within him, and seen afar off the star that was to become the beacon of his chosen people. That light shining impartially on all; that voice speaking to the hearts of all alike; God and the soul of man in close communion—the Creator and the humblest of his creatures face to face—here was at last the scheme of a spiritual democracy striving to lead all men in a single pathway, and unite the nations under the same promise of salvation. A mystery even to himself, and believing that he was divinely appointed, Fox went forth to preach to his countrymen the new gospel founded on freedom of conscience, purity of life, and the equality of man.† The times were

---

* *Vide* Bancroft's History of the United States, vol. ii. chap. xvi.

† *Vide* Fox's Life, Barclay's Apology, Gough and Sewell, Besse, and Penn's Witness.

ripe for such a mission. The public mind was like tinder, and the fire that came from the lips of the young enthusiast soon set England in a blaze. The people flocked to hear him, and his enemies became alarmed. Here was not only a new religious creed, but a dangerous political doctrine. Here was an idea, that, once embodied in a sect, would strike a blow at caste and privilege, and shake the very foundations of society. But nothing availed to tie the tongue of Fox or cool the fervor of his spirit. Threatened, fined, and beaten, he turned neither to the right hand nor to the left. Often imprisoned, he was released only to set forth again undaunted.

His followers rapidly increased, and the sober yeomanry of England began to abandon all and follow him. At Cromwell's death the Quakers were already a numerous people. At the Restoration they had grown to dangerous proportions. Obnoxious naturally to all parties, there were reasons why they incurred especial hatred. Their refusal to fight, to take an oath, to pay tithes or taxes for the repairs of churches, or acknowledge the authority of the priesthood, their determination to worship God publicly and proclaim the truth abroad, aroused the hatred of the Church, angered all other sects, and brought against them the penalties of the existing law, while their simple but unwavering determination not to take off their hats, " not for want of courtesy," as they said, but as a symbol of their belief in man's equality, gained for them the suspicious hostility of those whose privileges such a principle would utterly destroy.

Against them, therefore, was directed the vengeance of all parties and of every sect. Under all governments it was the same, and the Quaker met with even worse treatment from the Puritan government of New England than he had received from either the stern republican of Cromwell's time or the gay courtier of the Restoration. Though his hand was lifted against no man, all men's were laid heavily on him. Everywhere he was exposed to persecution and nowhere understood. His religion was called fanaticism, his courage stubbornness, his frugality avarice, his simplicity ignorance, his piety hypocrisy, his freedom infidelity, his conscientiousness rebellion. In England the statutes against Dissenters, and every law that could be twisted for the purpose, were vigorously enforced against him.* Special ones were enacted for his benefit, and even Charles II., from whose restoration they, in common with all men, expected some relief—good-natured Charles, who in general found it as hard to hate his enemies as to remember his friends; too indolent, for the most part, either to keep his word or lose his temper—took the trouble to exclude the Quakers by name from all indulgence.† During the Long Parliament, under the Protectorate, at the Restoration—for more than thirty years—they were exposed to persecution, fined, turned out-of-doors, mobbed, stoned, beaten, set in the stocks, crowded in gaols in summer, and kept in foul dungeons without fire in the winter-time, to be released at last and sold into colonial bondage.‡ But though they fought no fight, they kept the faith. Whatever history may record of their lives; whatever learning may think of their attainments; whatever philosophy may say of their intelligence; whatever theology may hold about their creed; whatever judgment a calmer posterity, in the light of a

---

* *Vide* Bancroft's History of the United States, vol. ii. chap. xvi.

† Letter of the King to the Massachusetts Government.

‡ *Vide* Williamson's North Carolina. In one vessel, in March, 1664, sixty Quaker convicts were shipped for America. *Vide* also Besse and Fox's Journal, Anno 1665.

higher civilization and a freer age, may pass upon their actions, none can deny that they were men who sought the faith with zeal, believed with sincerity, met danger with courage, and bore suffering with extraordinary fortitude. Gold had no power to seduce, nor arms to frighten them. "They are a people," said the great Protector, "whom I cannot win with gifts, honors, offices, or places."* Dragged from their assemblies, they returned; their meeting-houses torn down, they gathered on the ruins. Armed men dispersed them, and they came together again. Their enemies "took shovels to throw rubbish on them, and they stood close together, willing to be buried alive witnessing the Lord." † And when in one of their darkest hours their comrades lay languishing in prison, the rest marched in procession to Westminster Hall to offer themselves to Parliament as hostages for their brethren.

I know of few things in the history of the English race more noble than this act. No poet has made it the subject of his eulogy, and even the historians of civil and religious liberty have passed it by. But surely never did the groined arches of that ancient hall look down upon a nobler spectacle. They had seen many a more splendid and brilliant one, but none more honorable than this. They had looked down on balls and banquets, and coronations and the trial of a king, but never, since they were hewn from their native oak, did they behold a sight more honorable to human nature than that of these humble Quakers grouped below. They had rung with the most eloquent voices that ever spoke

---

* Bancroft's History of the United States, vol. ii. p. 345; Fox's Journal, p. 162.

† Bancroft's History of the United States, vol. ii. p. 355; Barclay, 356, 483, 484.

the English tongue, but never heard before such words as these. (Let me repeat them here to-day, for among those that spoke them were men that founded Burlington): "In Love to our Brethren," they say to Parliament, "that lie in Prisons and Houses of Correction and Dungeons, and many in Fetters and Irons, and have been cruelly beat by the cruel Gaolers, and many have been persecuted to Death and have died in Prisons, and many lie sick and weak in Prison and on Straw," we "do offer up our Bodies and Selves to you, for to put us as Lambs into the same Dungeons and Houses of Correction, and their Straw and nasty Holes and Prisons, and do stand ready a Sacrifice for to go into their Places, that they may go forth and not die in Prison as many of the Brethren are dead already. For we are willing to lay down our Lives for our Brethren and to take their Sufferings upon us that you would inflict on them. . . . And if you will receive our Bodies, which we freely tender to you, for our Friends that are now in Prison for *speaking the Truth* in several places; for *not paying Tithes;* for *meeting together* in the Fear of God; for *not Swearing;* for *wearing* their *Hats;* for *being accounted as Vagrants;* for *visiting Friends,* and for Things of a like Nature. We, whose Names are hereunto subscribed, being a sufficient Number, are waiting in Westminster-hall for an Answer from you to us, to answer our Tenders and to manifest our Love to our Friends and to stop the Wrath and Judgment from coming to our Enemies."*

Well done, disciple of the shoemaker of Nottingham! No prince or king ever spoke braver words than these! What matter if your Parliament send back for answer sol-

---

* *Vide* Preface to Joseph Besse's Sufferings of the Quakers, vol. i. p. iv.

diers with pikes and muskets to drive you out into the street? Go forth content! What if your brethren languish and die in gaol? You shall not long be parted. What if the times be troubled and nights of sorrow follow days of suffering? They cannot last forever. What if the heathen rage and the swords of the wicked be drawn against you? The peace within you they cannot take away. The world may note you little and history keep no record of your life. Your kindred may pass you by in silence and your name be unremembered by your children. No man may know your resting-place. But what of that? You have done one of those things that ennoble humanity—and by One, at least, who saw it, you will not be unrewarded nor forgotten!

Such was the condition of affairs when the opportunity of the Quakers arose out of the necessities of their enemies. Between the Dutch New Netherlands and the English colony of Virginia lay a noble river draining a fertile and pleasant land. Hudson had discovered it in 1609, and the following year the dying Lord de la Warr had bequeathed to it his name. For thirty years the three Protestant nations of Europe had contended for its shores, each victorious in its turn, until, at length, the dominion of the Dutchman and the Swede came to an end forever, and the flag of England floated in triumph over their few and feeble settlements.*

It was at this time, in the year 1664, that the Duke of York, afterward James II., eager to mend his fortunes, persuaded King Charles II. to give him a large share of

---

* I cannot but regret the necessity which compelled me to pass by in a paragraph the forty years which followed the expedition of Captain Mey. Some future historian of Pennsylvania will find them full of fascinating materials. Isaac Mickle's "Reminiscences of Old Gloucester" is well worth reading in this connection.

the newly-acquired territory in America. It was hardly yet subdued, but Charles carelessly complied. In a patent, the date of which reveals the duke's haste to secure the grant, the king conveyed to his brother all that territory which may be roughly described as lying between Delaware Bay and the Canadian border. Hardly had the ink become dry upon this parchment when James himself, in consideration of "a competent sum of money," sold what is now known as New Jersey to two of his friends, Sir George Carteret and Lord Berkeley. England was now full of colonization schemes. The rude interruption of the civil war was over, and men began to remember the days when Smith and Raleigh were wont to return from America with glowing descriptions of what they had seen in that mysterious country. A sterner age had followed, and few now perhaps cherished the golden visions which had led those brilliant adventurers into the exploits which have immortalized their names, but there still lived in the Englishman of the seventeenth century the love of adventure, and the desire to spread the dominion of the Crown, and America lay before him an attractive field. The failure of Sir Edmund Ployden to carry out his romantic and fantastic plan of building up a power called New Albion, of which he assumed in advance the title of Earl Palatine,* taught an unheeded lesson, and dreams of future empire continued to dazzle many an English mind. But years passed by without result. Carteret, the younger of the new proprietors, managed to plant some settlements in Eastern Jersey, where to this day the city of Elizabeth perpetuates the name of his

---

* *Vide* Mickle's Reminiscences of Old Gloucester, p. 24. Beauchamp Plantagenet's Description of New Albion, in the Philadelphia Library.

accomplished wife, and a few Englishmen from Connecticut found a precarious foothold on the banks of the Delaware, but for the most part all attempts to encourage immigration ended in expensive failure. As it had been with Massachusetts it was with Pennsylvania and the Jerseys. The foot of the adventurer was not suffered to rest in peace upon soil destined by the Almighty for a nobler purpose than to enrich the unworthy or mend the broken fortunes of an English nobleman. The fingers which had grasped so eagerly the choice places of the New Continent were quickly to be loosened, and the wilderness kept ready as a place of refuge for an oppressed and persecuted people.

After ten years of thankless efforts and unprofitable ownership, and too old to hope for a realization of his plans, my Lord Berkeley became anxious to be rid of his province, and offered it for sale. The opportunity was a rare one for the Quakers. To America they had naturally looked as a place to which they might escape and bear with them in peace their peculiar principles and creed. In that distant country they might, it seemed to them, worship God according to their consciences. Three thousand miles of sea (ten times as great a distance then as now) would lie between them and their enemies, and in the wilderness, at least, with trial and privation would dwell peace.

For a while, indeed, they were deterred by a sentiment that was natural to men of English blood. Persecution, thought some of them, ought not to be avoided. The trials, the sufferings, the dangers to which they were exposed it was their duty to meet, and not to shun. Let us endure these things for the glory of the truth, and not try, like cowards, to avoid them. Let us bear this burden ourselves, nor leave it for others to take up. This unwillingness to flee before the face of persecution held them for some time resolute and firm. But, at length, another sentiment prevailed. It sprang from the thought that others were destined to come after them. There is nothing more remarkable in the history of this country than the fact that those who settled it seem everywhere alike to have been moved by the belief that they acted, not for themselves, but for posterity. Not for himself alone did the Pilgrim embark upon the Mayflower: not for himself alone did the Puritan seek a shelter on the bleak shores of Massachusetts: not for himself only did Roger Williams gather his little colony at the head of Narragansett Bay; and the same faith that he was building in the wilderness a place of refuge for the oppressed forever led the stern Quaker out of England. Not for us, but for the sake of them that shall come after us. This was the faith that sustained them without a murmur through all the horrors of a New England winter; that kept their courage up while the Connecticut Valley rang with the war-whoop of the Indian; that raised their fainting spirits beneath the scorching rays of a Southern sun; that made them content and happy in the untrodden forest of New Jersey.

"The settlement of this country," writes one who witnessed it, "was directed by an impulse on the spirits of God's people, not for their own ease and tranquillity, but rather for the posterity that should be after them."*

Proud may we justly be, Americans, of those who laid the foundations of our happiness. I know of no people who can point to a purer and less selfish ancestry—of no nation that looks back to a nobler or more honorable origin.

There were many reasons why our forefathers, when at

---

* Thomas Sharp's Memoir in Newton Monthly Meeting Records. *Vide* Bowden's History of Friends, p. 16.

last they had convinced themselves that it was right for them to emigrate, should have turned their eyes upon New Jersey. The unrelenting Puritan had long ago shut in their faces the doors of Massachusetts Bay and Plymouth Colony. New York had already been appropriated by the Dutch, and the followers of Fox could find little sympathy among those who had established settlements within the wide borders of the Old Dominion. Besides, George Fox himself had travelled across New Jersey two or three years before. He had seen the beauty of the South River and the majestic forests that lined its shores. The Swedes and Dutch upon its banks were few in number and of a peaceful disposition, and the Indians, its natives, were noted for their gentleness. The river of Delaware was universally described as a " goodly and noble river"—the soil was rich and fertile, the " air," as was soon to be written, was " very delicate, pleasant, and wholesome, the heavens serene, rarely overcast, bearing mighty resemblance to the better part of France."* Just at this time the property of Lord Berkeley was offered for sale. The wealthier men among the Friends saw the opportunity, and Edward Byllynge and John Fenwick became its purchasers. A devoted Friend, Byllynge had been one of those who offered themselves as hostages at Westminster in 1659. He had suffered like all the rest, but had continued to be thought a man of property. But times were hard, and when the conveyance came to be made the name of John Fenwick, as trustee, was substituted for that of Byllynge, and after a little while all the interest of the latter was given up for the benefit of creditors to three trustees, Gawen Lawrie, Nicholas Lucas,

---

* Gabriel Thomas's Description of Pennsylvania and West Jersey, published in 1698, p. 7.

and William Penn. Now for the first time in American history appears the name of that great man whom, in the words of Lord Macaulay, who viewed him with mistaken and unfriendly eye, "a great Commonwealth regards with a reverence similar to that which the Athenians felt for Theseus and the Romans for Quirinus."* It is interesting to remark, as one reads of the reluctance with which he assumed this task, how directly Penn's connection with the settlement of Burlington led to the founding of Pennsylvania.

It was now the year of Grace 1675. John Fenwick, a soldier of the civil war and now a Quaker (whose memory has been recently preserved by the pen of a Jerseyman†), soon set sail with his family and a small company of Friends. Entering the Capes, after a prosperous voyage, he landed on the eastern shore at a "pleasant, rich spot," to which, in memory of its peaceful aspect, he gave the name of Salem—an appellation which that quiet town has continued to deserve even unto this day. Two years of comparative inaction followed. Troublesome disputes between Fenwick and Byllynge, which it required all the authority and address of Penn to settle, threatened destruction to the colony. But at length these came to an end, and the settlement began in earnest. There were important things to be done at the beginning. First, the province had to be divided by agreement with the owner of the other half, and this was not accomplished until 1676. A line was provided to be drawn northward from Egg Har-

---

* Macaulay's History of England, vol. i. p. 394.

† Hon. John Clement, of Haddonfield, New Jersey, to whom I am indebted for kind suggestions in the preparation of this address. A full account of the relations of Fenwick and Byllynge may be found in his valuable History of Fenwick's Colony.

bor to the Delaware, dividing the province into two. The eastern part was taken by Sir George Carteret; the other by the trustees, who gave it the name of West New Jersey. Penn and his agents next divided their share into one hundred parts, of which they assigned ten to Fenwick and ninety to the creditors of Byllynge. But their most important duty was to frame a constitution for the new country. This was no easy task. None of these men were legislators. Neither by birth nor election had they enjoyed the advantages of experience in the legislative bodies of their country. They were not generally men of reading or education (with the exception of Penn), nor of that training which is usually essential to true statesmanship. Nor in those days had the making of free constitutions been a frequent task. He who attempted it entered an unknown and dangerous country, full of disappointments. Lucas and Lawrie were men of business little known; Penn was a youth of two-and-thirty, and among all their associates there were few who had knowledge and none who had experience of Statecraft. But they were animated by the truest spirit of philanthropy, by the sincerest love of liberty, by the warmest devotion to what they understood to be the command of God. And they were, after all, worthy to lay the foundations of a free and humane government. Independence of thought, Freedom of person, Liberty of conscience: these were the things they all believed in, and for them they were ready to make any sacrifice. For liberty they had suffered each and all. For it, men like them had scorned danger and gone chanting into battle. For the sake of it they had even welcomed the horrors of civil war. For it they had charged their brethren at Naseby and ridden rough-shod over their kindred upon Marston Moor. And now they were ready, if the day were lost at home, to abandon all and seek it beyond the sea. On liberal principles, then, did they naturally determine to build up their new government in the wilderness, where, a century afterward, their children, for whom they were making so many sacrifices, were destined to fight over again the same battle with an equal courage and devotion. Little did they dream—those stern yet gentle men of peace—when they gave to their infant Commonwealth freedom from all taxation except what its own Assemblies should impose, that a hundred years later England would rise up, sword in hand, to take it back; that for the sake of a principle, which they never thought to call in question, the little town which they were about to found would one day tremble at the roar of contending cannon, and the banks of Delaware be stained with English blood! Could they have been permitted to foresee the struggle that was yet to come they could not more wisely have prepared posterity to meet it. First, they created an Executive and Legislative power; the former to be chosen by the latter, the Assembly by the people, voting to be by ballot, and every man capable to choose and to be chosen. Each member of the Assembly they agreed "hath liberty of speech," and shall receive for wages *one* shilling a day, "that thereby he may be known as the *servant* of the people." No man shall be imprisoned for debt nor; without the verdict of a jury, deprived of life, liberty or estate, "and all and every person in the province shall, by the help of the Lord and these fundamentals, be free from oppression and slavery." The Indian was to be protected in his rights and the orphan brought up by the State. Religious freedom in its broadest sense was to be secured, and no one "in the least punished or hurt, in person, estate or privilege, for the sake of his opinion, judgment, faith, or worship toward God in matters of religion; for no man nor number of men upon earth have power to rule over men's consciences."*   "Such," writes one who, though an alien to their blood and of an hostile creed, could do them justice, "is an outline of the composition which forms the first essay of Quaker legislation, and entitles its authors to no mean share in the honor of planting civil and religious liberty in America."†   Happy would it have been for the children of those simple-minded men had they never departed from ideas so true, so wise, and so humane!

The authors of this document, adopted and signed on the 3d of March, 1676, seem to have seen the goodness of their handiwork.   "There," they cry in words which are at once a prophesy and a confession of faith, " we lay a foundation for after-ages to understand their liberty, as men and Christians, that they may not be brought in bondage but by their own consent.   *For we put the power in the people."*‡

So much, then, for this government on paper.   Where now are the men to put it into execution?   They come from two different parts of England.   Among the creditors of Byllynge were five Friends who dwelt in Yorkshire. Persecutions had been very severe in that county, and York Castle at one time contained a large number of prominent Friends.§   Among these latter were five heads of families

---

* Smith prints this remarkable document in full in the appendix to his History of New Jersey, p. 512.

† History of the United States, by James Grahame, LL.D., vol. i. p. 475.

‡ Letter of Penn and the others to Hartshorne, London, 6th mo. 26, 1676; Smith's History of New Jersey, p. 80.

§ William Clayton, Richard Hancock, John Ellis, Richard Guy, and Richard Woodmancy were in York Castle at different times between 1660 and 1677; Christopher Wetherill in Beverley Gaol in 1660.   *Vide* Besse, *passim.*

who were glad to join the creditors of Byllynge in their new plan for settling West Jersey, and a company was speedily formed among them, which was known as the Yorkshire Company. It was thus that the names of Clayton, Ellis, Hancock, Helmsley, Stacy, and Wetherill first came to be transported into Jersey. Meantime another company was forming in the vicinity of London. Men came from different parts of England to join its ranks; William Peachy, fresh from his trial at Bristol and under sentence of banishment as a convict for attending "meetings;" John Kinsey, of Hadham in Hertfordshire, himself a prisoner a few years before, and marked among these settlers of Burlington as the first to die; John Cripps, twelve days in a cell in Newgate for "keeping his hat on in a bold, irreverent manner" when the Lord Mayor passed by into Guildhall; Thomas Ollive, familiar with the inside of Northampton Gaol; John Woolston, his companion in that prison, and Dr. Daniel Wills, tried for banishment for a third offence, and thrice in prison for holding meetings in his house.* The last three were all men of note, and their joining the London Company had great influence on its history. In the little town of Wellingborough, the home of Ollive, and near which the others dwelt, there was a monthly meeting. Here Dewsbury, in 1654, had converted many to the Truth, and here he had been mobbed and thrown in gaol. By the spring of 1677 his disciples had become numerous in Northamptonshire, and nowhere, per-

---

* *Vide* Besse's Sufferings, where these facts are all set forth with painful particularity. The names of nearly all the early settlers of Burlington can be found in that record of persecution. I doubt if there has ever been another town of which so many of its citizens had been in gaol. Certainly no other can speak of the matter with so much honest pride.

haps, had the propriety of going to America been more earnestly discussed. "Many who were valuable," says an old account, "doubting, lest it should be deemed flying from persecution." In the midst of this discussion, he, who had converted so many in the place twelve years before, gathered the faithful about him and bade them go. "The Lord," he said, "is about to plant the wilderness of America with a choice vine of noble seed, which shall grow and flourish." Let His servants depart thither and they shall do well. "I see them, I see them, under His blessing, arising into a prosperous and happy state."* And so it came about that many of that little band followed the lead of Thomas Ollive and Dr. Daniel Wills, and turned their faces toward London.

The preparations are now made and the time for departure is at hand. The two companies have appointed commissioners to govern them—Joseph Helmsley, Robert Stacy, William Emley, and Thomas Foulke, for the Yorkshire people; Thomas Ollive, Daniel Wills, John Penford, and Benjamin Scott, for the London purchasers. They have secured a staunch ship, under the command of an experienced seaman, and she is now lying ready in the Thames. With what feelings does this band of self-devoted exiles go on board! Does any one of the half million souls in the great metropolis notice the little company of English yeomen, as, laden with their scanty store of household stuff and leading their wives and children by the hand, they shake the dust of England from their feet and clamber on the deck? Does any one foresee, as he looks with pride on

----

* Life of William Dewsbury; Account of James and William Brown in Nottingham, Pennsylvania, Monthly Meeting Records. *Vide* also The Friend, vol. 23, pp. 443, 451.

the forest of masts and yard-arms that stretches from London Tower to London Bridge, that of all the ships that move to and fro beneath him, or lie at anchor in the crowded Thames, but one shall be remembered? It is not that big merchantman, fast to yonder wharf, discharging the rich cargo she has just brought from the Indies; nor this gallant vessel that, as she swings with the tide, turns to him a hull scarred with many a Dutch or Spanish broadside; nor yet the stately ship that, at this moment, comes slowly up, under full sail, from Gravesend. Long after these and they that sailed them shall have been forgotten, the happy citizens of a free commonwealth in a distant land shall speak with affectionate remembrance of the good ship "Kent" and "Master Godfrey Marlow!" Obscure and unnoticed and, perhaps on that account undisturbed, all are at last on board. They have taken leave of their country; it remains only to say farewell to their King. It is a pleasant day in the opening summer, and London is full of gayety. The banquets at Whitehall have never been more brilliant, and the King, in spite of French victories and Popish plots and Quaker persecutions, is as gay as ever. What cares good-natured Charles, or my lady of Cleveland, or his Lordship of Buckingham if the public mind be full of discontent and the public coffers empty and the prestige of England be threatened both on sea and land? The weather is fine, the French gold still holds out, and the charms of Her Grace of Portsmouth are as fresh as ever. The bright sun and the pleasant air tempt His Majesty upon the water and he passes the afternoon floating in his barge. The Thames is full of shipping, for at this time London has no rival in commerce but Amsterdam, and the King amuses himself watching the vessels as they come to and fro. Suddenly the barge approaches a ship evidently about to sail. Something attracts the King, and draws him near. A group of men and women are on the deck, plain in appearance, sombre in dress, quiet in demeanor. They are of the yeoman class chiefly, and the gay courtiers wonder what attracts the attention of the King. The two strangely different vessels come together, and for a moment those widely separated companies are face to face. Charles, with that pleasant voice that could heal with a friendly phrase the wounds inflicted by a lifetime of ingratitude, inquires who they are. "Quakers, bound to America!" is the reply. There is a pause for an instant, and then the King, with a royal gesture, flings them his blessing, and Charles II. and his Quaker subjects have parted forever.* Each to his fate according to his manner. "Now," said old Socrates to his weeping friends, "it is time to part, you to life and I to death—which of the two things is the better is known only unto God."† And now the wind is fair and the tide is full and the steeples of London are sinking in the west. Farewell, broad fields of Norfolk and pleasant Kentish woods! Farewell, ye Yorkshire moors and sloping Sussex downs! Farewell, old mother England! Our feet shall never tread upon your shores again. Our eyes shall never more behold your face; but from our loins a greater Britain shall arise to bless a continent with English law and English liberty and English speech!

On the 6th of August (old style), 1677, there is excitement on the Kent. The voyage has been fair, but the

---

* *Vide* Smith's History of New Jersey, p. 93 : "King Charles the Second in his barge, pleasuring on the Thames, came alongside, seeing a great many passengers, and, informed whence they were bound, asked if they were all Quakers, and gave them his blessing."

† Plato's Apologia, cap. **xxxiii.**

ocean is wide and full of perils, and all are longing for the land. Suddenly a faint line appears on the horizon. Slowly it rises from the sea until at last the straining eyes of the Kent's passengers can make out land. It is a low, sandy beach projecting far into the sea. By and by behind it appears the faint blue of distant hills, and at last the clear outlines of a well-wooded shore. The old ship turns to the northwest and enters the mouth of a beautiful bay. This is the first view of the Western World—the harbor of New York. The object the emigrants have in view in coming here is to wait upon Sir Edmund Andros, the Duke of York's lately appointed governor of his. territory.* According to the commissioners go on shore. Andros receives them coldly. They inform him of their purpose to settle on the Delaware. He feigns an ignorance of their authority. They remind him of the law, and repeat how the land in West Jersey was granted by the King to his brother, by the Duke to Carteret and Berkeley, and by them to their grantors. It is of no use. "Show me a line from the Duke himself," says Andros. They have neglected this precaution. Upon which the governor forbids them to proceed, and when remonstrated with, touches his sword significantly. Here is a new and unexpected trouble, and it is no comfort to learn that John Fenwick is at the moment a prisoner in New York for attempting his settlement at Salem without the Duke's authority. Suddenly their perplexity is unexpectedly relieved. If they will take commissions from him Sir Edmund will allow them to set sail, but they must promise to write to England and abide by the result. Anxious to escape from the dilemma they accept the proposal; Fenwick is released at the same time,

---

* Smith's History of New Jersey, p. 93.

and they set sail for the Delaware. On the 16th day of August—about the 26th according to our style—they reach the site of New Castle, and presently—two hundred and thirty in number—land at the mouth of Raccoon Creek.[*] The few settlements of the Dutch and Swedes have hardly changed the original appearance of the country, and they find themselves on the borders of a wilderness. The Swedes have a few houses at the landing-place, and in these and in tents and caves our new-comers take temporary lodging. It is a change from the snug homes to which they have been accustomed, and the fare they find is rough, but there is no murmuring among them. "I never heard them say," wrote one of their number, who had herself exchanged a pleasant home in England for a cave—"I never heard them say 'I would I had never come,' which it is worth observing, considering how plentifully they had lived in England."[†] But they were not given to complaining, and

---

[*] Smith's History, p. 93.

[†] Barber and Howe's Historical Collection, p. 90. "My friend William John Potts, Esq., of Camden, New Jersey, an indefatigable antiquary, whose acquaintance with early history has been of the greatest assistance to me, writes : ' Some of them were obliged to live in caves, owing to the scarcity of houses. Similar instances occurred in the first settlement of Philadelphia. I have the honor to descend from a cave-dweller myself. The most noted instance of this I think you will find in Barber and Howe, under Columbus, where it is mentioned that in that part of Burlington County Thomas Scattergood, whose benevolent name still flourishes among us, brought up nine children in a cave.' Like Mr. Potts, I can count a cave-dweller among my ancestors. One of them sailed up Dock Creek, now Dock Street, and landing, lived in a cave below Second Street while his house was building. No less a person than Francis Daniel Pastorius lived in a cave in October, 1683. These caves were excavations in the banks, roofed and faced with logs overlaid with sod or bark, or

moreover the autumn is at hand. Without delay the commissioners set out to examine the country and settle the terms of purchase with the Indians. Accompanied by Swedish interpreters they buy three tracts—from the Assanpink to the Rancocas, from Rancocas to Timber Creek, and from Timber Creek to Old Man's Creek.* The Yorkshire purchasers choose the former as their share; the London decide to settle at Arwaumus, near the present Gloucester; and Daniel Wills orders timber to be felled and grass to be cut in preparation for the winter.

But a second thought prevails. Why should we separate? We have passed through many perils together, we are few in number, the forests are thick and full of savages; let us build a town in company. It is at once agreed upon. Where shall it be? Old Man's Creek is too near John Fenwick's colony; Assanpink is too far; the mouth of the Rancocas is a marsh. None of these points will do. About six miles above the last-named creek, within the limits of the Yorkshire tenth, there are two islands. One, called "Matiniconk," lies in the middle of the river, which here turns suddenly to the south, and forms a little bay. The other lies close against the Jersey shore, from which it is separated only by a narrow creek where the tide ebbs and flows, and is known as "Jegou's Island." It has taken this name not from an Indian chief, as is at first supposed, but from a Frenchman who lately lived at "Water-Lily Point."† On this neck of land between the Asiskonk

---

plastered with clay."—*Vide* Watson's Annals of Philadelphia, vol. i. p. 171.

* The list of articles paid for the land can be found in Smith's History of New Jersey, p. 95, note.

† In an unpublished lecture delivered in 1870, the Rev. William Allen Johnson, formerly rector of St. Mary's, has solved these two

Creek and the Delaware River, opposite Matiniconk, three Dutchmen settled long before the surrender to the English. Their rights were recognized by Governor Carteret in 1666, and soon afterward sold to Peter Jegou, who, about 1668, armed with a license from the same authority, built on the point, hard by the water-side, a log house after the Swedish fashion.* It was the only tavern in this part of the country. And it was well placed, for at this point the narrow foot-path which leads through the woods from the banks of the North River comes out upon the Delaware, and those who journey from Manhattan toward Virginia, must cross the latter river at this point. This is the place which Governor Lovelace meant when in expectation of a journey thither some years ago, he directed one of his servants to "go with the horse allotted by the captain, as speedily as you can, to Navesink, and thence to the house of Mr. Jegoe, right against Matiniconk Island, on Delaware River, where there are persons ready to receive you."† But the journey was not undertaken, for somehow or other Jegou became an object of hatred to the Indians, and recently (in 1670) they have plundered him and driven him away. His house

---

questions, which so long puzzled the local antiquary: "Chygoe," he says, is a misspelling of the name of Jegou, and "Lazy" or "Leazy" Point—which he has found spelled in five different ways —a corruption of the Dutch word Lisch, Pond- or Water-Lily. I have no doubt of the correctness of this simple explanation. Water-Lily Point would not be an inappropriate name for the place to-day. Mr. Johnson's lecture was the result of much labor and careful examination. The credit of settling these points belongs entirely to him.

* Record of Upland Court, 9th mo. 25, 1679; Memoirs of Historical Society of Pennsylvania, vol. vii. p. 140.

† For this I am indebted to the discoveries among the Records at Albany of the Rev. W. A. Johnson.

was empty and deserted five years ago, as is mentioned by a very noted traveller. After a day's journey of fifty miles without seeing man or woman, house or dwelling-place, he says, " at night, finding an old house which the Indians had forced the people to leave, we made a fire and lay there at the head of Delaware Bay. The next day we swam our horses over the river, about a mile, twice, first to an island called Upper Dinidock, and then to the mainland, having hired Indians to help us over in their canoes." This is especially interesting, for the name of that traveller was George Fox.*

" Matiniconk" lies too far from the mainland, but Jegou's Island is a very fit place for a town. It is about a mile long and half as wide. It lies, as I have said, on the only path between the North River and the South, and the channel in front of it is deep enough for ships of large burden. Its soil is rich, its meadows rank with grass, its trees tall and luxuriant, and its green and sloping bank destined to be always beautiful. The decision in its favor is soon made, and the emigrants, embarking in small boats, ascend the Delaware.

Tinakonk, the residence of the ancient Swedish Governors; Wickakoe, a small settlement of that people, close to the high bluff called " Coaquannock," " a splendid site for a town ;" Takona, an ancient Indian town, and the mouth of the Rancocas, or " Northampton River," are passed in turn. It is already late in October, and the wild landscape lies bathed in the mellow glory of the Indian summer. Beneath a sky more cloudless than English eyes have been wont to see, waves the primeval forest clad in the rainbow garments of the Fall. No sound breaks the stillness save the plash

---

* Fox's Journal, 7th mo. 10, 1672

of the oars in the water or the whistling of the wings of the wild-fowl that rise in countless numbers from the marshes. The air is full of the perfume of grapes, that hang in clusters on the banks and climb from tree to tree, and the sturgeons leap before the advancing prow. The startled deer stands motionless upon the beach; and hidden in the tangled thickets the Indian gazes in silent wonder at the pale-faced strangers who have come to take his place in the land of his fathers. Presently the river seems suddenly to come to a stop. On the left is a gravel beach. In the distance in front, is an island, with a steep red bank washed by the rushing stream and pierced with swallows' holes. To the right, a bit of marsh, the mouth of a silvery creek, a meadow sloping to the shore, and then a high bank lined with mulberries and sycamores and unutterably green. For the first time, and after so many days, the eyes of its founders have rested upon Burlington!

Among them was a youth of one-and-twenty. The first of his race to be born in the Quaker faith, he had grown up amid persecution and been familiar with suffering from his boyhood. A child of tender years he had, wonderingly, followed his family, driven from their old home for conscience' sake, and among his earliest recollections was the admonition of his dying father to seek a refuge beyond the sea. Beside him was the English maiden who, in a short time, in the primitive meeting-house made of a sail taken from the Kent, was to become his wife. Little that youthful pair imagined, as they gazed for the first time on Jegou's Island, that at the end of two centuries, one of their name and lineage, looking back to them over the graves of five generations of their children, would stand here in old Burlington to-day, and lift his voice in commemoration of an event in which they were then taking an humble but honorable part!*

Among those who landed on the bank at Burlington on that autumn day was Richard Noble, a surveyor. He had come with John Fenwick two years before, and his profession had naturally made him familiar with the country. To him was at once committed the duty of laying out the town—a labor in which William Matlack and others of the young men assisted.† A broad and imposing main street was opened through the forest, running at right angles to the river, southward into the country. It is probable that it did not at first extend very far past the place at which we are gathered now. Another, crossing it, ran lengthwise through the middle of the island, and a third was opened on the bank. The town thus laid out was divided into twenty properties—ten in the eastern part for the Yorkshire men, and ten in the western for the London proprietors. All hands went at once to work to prepare for the winter. Marshall, a carpenter, directed the building, and the forests began to resound with the blows of his axe. A clearing

---

* James Browne, the fourth son of Richard and Mary Browne, of Sywell, in Northamptonshire, was born on the 27th of 3d month, 1656. His father, whom William Dewsbury had converted in 1654–5, died in 1662, before which time the family had removed to Puddington, in Bedfordshire. James remained at Burlington but a short time, settling in 1678 at Chichester or Markus Hook, in Pennsylvania. On the 8th of the 6th month, 1679, he married, at Burlington, Honour, the daughter of William Clayton (one of the Yorkshire purchasers and a passenger with his family in the Kent). He lived on his place, called "Podington," on Chichester Creek, until 1705. when he gave it to his son William and removed "into the wilderness." He died at Nottingham, Pennsylvania, in 1716.

† William Matlack's affidavit, stating these facts, is to be found in Book A, in the Surveyor-General's office in Burlington.

was made on the south side of the main street, near Broad, and a tent pitched there as a temporary meeting-house. In a short time the settlement began to have the appearance of a town, and, when worthy of a name, in memory of a village in old Yorkshire, was christened "Burlington."* The dwellings were at first caves, dug in the banks and faced with boards, or shanties of the most primitive description. They were not built of logs, as is popularly believed. ·It is to the Swede alone that we owe the "block-house" of our early Indian wars and the "log cabin" of political campaigns. Two Dutch travellers who saw Burlington when it was two years old, say on this point that "the English and many others have houses made of nothing but clapboards, as they call them here. They make a wooden frame, as in Westphalia and at Altona, but not so strong, then split boards of clapwood like coopers' staves, though unbent, so that the thickest end is about a little finger thick, and the other is made sharp like the end of a knife. They are about five or six feet long, and are nailed on with the ends lapping over each other. . . . When it is cold and windy the best people plaster them with clay."† From these details we can imagine the homes of our first settlers, "many of whom," says one of them, "had been men of good estate." That they remembered their English homes

---

* Smith says it was first called New Beverley, and next, Bridlington, and by the latter name it appears on Holme's Map, dated 1682. I find, however, that the earliest letters written from the place (several within a week or two of the beginning of the town) are dated at "Burlington." Bridlington and Burlington are the same name, and the latter is a very old form of the word. Richard Boyle was created Earl of *Burlington* in 1663.

† Journal of Dankers and Sluyter in 1679, published by Long Island Historical Society, vol. i. pp. 173–175.

with fond affection is proved in many ways. Wills gave to one portion of the neighborhood the name of his native " Northampton," which it bears to-day, and the township of " Willingborough," where many of you dwell, recalls the home of Ollive. " York" Street is close at hand, though the bridge that bore that name has disappeared; and what boy is there in Burlington to-day that has not thrown a line from " London" bridge? " Oh, remember us," they write to their friends in England, " for we cannot forget you; many waters cannot quench our love nor distance wear out the deep remembrance. . . . Though the Lord hath been pleased to remove us far away from you, as to the ends of the earth, yet are we present with you. Your exercises are ours; our hearts are dissolved in the remembrance of you."

But though their thoughts turned fondly to England and their brethren, they did not repine. They found the country good; " so good," wrote one as early as the 6th of November, 1677, " that I do not see how reasonably it can be found fault with. The country and air seem very agreeable to our bodies, and we have very good stomachs to our victuals. Here is plenty of provision, of fish and fowl and good venison, not dry, but full of gravy. And I do believe that this river of Delaware is as good a river as most in the world." " I like the place well," said another, three days afterward; " it's like to be a healthful place and very pleasant to live in." A report having spread in England that the water and soil were bad, and danger to be feared from bears, wolves, rattlesnakes, and Indians—the first, but not the last time that Burlington has been slandered—six of the leading settlers indignantly deny its truth, declaring that " those that cannot be contented with such a country and such land as this is are not worthy to come here." " I affirm," said one, " that these reports are not true, and fear they were spoke from a spirit of envy. It is a country that produceth all things for the support and sustenance of man. I have seen orchards laden with fruit to admiration ; their very limbs torn to pieces with the weight, and most delicious to the taste and lovely to behold. I have seen an apple-tree from a pippin kernel yield a barrel of curious cyder, and peaches in such plenty that some people took their carts a peach gathering. I could not but smile at the conceit of it. I have known this summer forty bushels of bold wheat from one bushel sown. We have from the time called May till Michaelmas great store of very good wild fruits—strawberries, cranberries, and whortleberries, very wholesome. Of the cranberries, like cherries for color and bigness, an excellent sauce is made for venison and turkeys. Of these we have great plenty, and all sorts of fish and game. Indeed the country, take it as a wilderness, is a most brave country, and," he adds, in words that you may make use of to the world yourselves to-day, " whatever envy or evil spies may speak of it, I could wish you all here."* From the Indians these settlers experienced little trouble. The Mantas, it is true, who dwelt hard by, had committed a murder at Matiniconk and plundered poor Jegou some years before the arrival of the Kent, but these were exceptional instances. The Leni Lenape were a peaceful race. Upright in person and straight of limb, their fierce countenances of tawny reddish-brown belied a gentle nature. Grave even to sadness, courteous to strangers and respectful to the old, never in haste to speak, and of cool, deliberate temper, this mysterious people easily forgave injury and never forgot kindness—more than repaying the benevolent

---

* Smith's History of New Jersey contains these letters.

humanity of the settlers of Burlington by a forbearing friendship that lived as long as they. At the same time at which the savages of Virginia were punishing cold-blooded murder with passionate bloodshed, and scourging with fury every plantation from the Potomac to the James, and on the northern sky the light of blazing villages, from one end of New England to the other, marked the despairing vengeance of King Philip, the banks of Delaware smiled in unbroken peace, and their simple-hearted native, conscious of the fate that would speedily overtake his people—which no one foretold sooner or more touchingly than he—was saying in a council here in Burlington: "We are your brothers, and intend to live like brothers with you. We will have a broad path for you and us to walk in. If an Indian be asleep in this path, the Englishman shall pass him by and do him no harm; and if an Englishman be asleep in it, the Indian shall pass him by and say: 'He is an Englishman—he is asleep—let him alone.' The path shall be plain; there shall not be in it a stump to hurt the feet."*

The soil fertile, the climate healthy, the situation good, and the Indian friendly, the little settlement soon became a prosperous colony. Ships began to come with emigrants from different parts of England. The Willing Mind, from London, with sixty passengers; the "Flieboat" Martha, from the older Burlington, with one hundred and fourteen; the Shield, from Hull, and several more beside. It is this

---

* Smith's History of New Jersey, p. 100, and 136, note; Bancroft, vol. ii. p. 102, *et seq.; Idem.*, p. 216. "When six of the hostile chieftains presented themselves as messengers to treat of a reconciliation, in the blind fury of the moment they were murdered." This was in 1675. The war in Virginia continued more than a year afterwards. King Philip's "rebellion" broke out in June, 1675. He was killed in August, 1676.

last one of which the story is told that tacking too near the high shore called "Coaquannock," her masts caught in an overhanging tree, and her passengers, unconscious of the Philadelphia that was soon to be, were struck by the beauty of the site, and spoke of its fitness for a town.* The forests were felled and farms sprang up in all directions. Ollive's new mill, on the "Mill Creek" that runs into Rancocas, was quickly built. The trade with Barbadoes was begun by Mahlon Stacy and others as early as the winter of 1679–80, whose "ketch of fifty tons" met with the good fortune their enterprise deserved. By an Act of Assembly in the following year, "all vessels bound to the province" were "obliged to enter and clear at" its "chief town and head," "the port of Burlington," and at the same time two annual fairs were provided for in the market street, "for all sorts of cattle and all manner of merchandise."† But in the bustle of the growing town and the attractions of an opening trade, other things were not forgotten. The first act of the meeting was to provide for the collections of money once a month for "ye support of ye poor," and the next to consider "selling of rum unto Indians," and whether it "be lawful att all for friends pfessing truth to be concerned in itt." It has been said that the Quaker has never been the friend of education. These at least are two honorable truths in the history of Burlington: That there, before 1690, William Bradford found work and welcome for his printing-press ;‡ and her

---

* Watson's Annals of Philadelphia, vol. i. p. 10.

† Leaming and Spicer's Laws of New Jersey, p. 435; Hazard's Annals of Pennsylvania, vol. i. p. 537.

‡ My authority for this statement was the following: "At A yearly meetinge held at Burlington in west new Jersey the 10th of the 7th month 1690: An Account beinge giuen heere that seuerall particular

people—before William Penn had ever set foot on American soil—commemorated the fifth anniversary of their settlement by consecrating "to the use of the public schools" the broad acres of Matiniconk, and have kept them piously devoted to that purpose from that day to this.*

How fortunate would it have been, my friends of Burlington, if the spirit had moved one of these early settlers to have given posterity a sketch of the daily life of the

---

friends haue engaged themselues to raise A considerable sum of money for the encouragement of the printer to continue the press heere: it is Agreed that it bee recommend to each quarterly meetinge belonging to this meetinge." The Hon. John William Wallace, who is an authority on these matters, and has given especial attention to the life of the printer William Bradford (*vide* his valuable Address on the subject in New York in May, 1863), has called my attention to the following extract from the Salem Monthly Meeting Minute Book No. 1: "whereas in the month Called nouember: 1689: A gratuity was giuen to William bradford printer that hee should continue his press in philadelphia it being forty pound A yeare from and After the date hereof, for Seuen years;" and adds, "on 5th mo. 26th 1689 Bradford, being then in Philada., gaue notice to Friends of his purpose to go to *England* and got a *bene decessit* accordingly. Now, by the above extract the meeting in 1689 gaue (actually gaue, it would seem) a gratuity to Bradford to 'continue' his press in Philadelphia for seven years from that time. We have in 1688 and also in 1693 books printed by him in Philadelphia. In 1690 he established a paper-mill on the Wissahickon. It would seem, therefore, that the word 'heere' does not mean here in Burlington, but here in America, or hereabouts and within the jurisdiction of the Quakers assembled at Burlington." I agree with Mr. Wallace that "this, I fear, hardly makes out the case for our dear old town of Burlington;" but I leave the passage in the text to stand as spoken, with this correction in a note. The town was not, in all probability, the scene of Bradford's labors, as I thought at the time I said so, but the townsfolk are entitled to the credit which I claimed for them just the same.

* Act of Assembly, September 28, 1682.

young colony!   How delightful to have been able to see, as with the eye of a contemporary, the infant town!   The forest of oak and sassafras, and birch and maple encircling the island; the broad main street cut through the clearing, and but lately freed from stumps; the clap-board houses beginning to rise on every side; Samuel Jennings's, on the corner of Pearl Street, the new Governor, "a man of both spiritual and worldly wisdom, a suppressor of vice and an encourager of virtue;"* and Thomas Gardiner's next, where the meetings are held till the new place of worship can be built.   It is at one of these, perhaps, that the Labadists dine in 1679, on their way to Tinicum and Upland.   "The Quakers," they write, "are a very worldly people.   On the window we found a copy of Virgil, as if it had been a common hand-book, and Helmont's book on medicine!"   How pleasant, too, to walk in imagination along the bank of the newly-surveyed river lots and admire the good ship Shield, as she lies in the stream, moored by a long rope to a leaning buttonwood† that stands by the water's edge, or watch yonder canoe as it comes swiftly across the river laden with the fat carcass of a noble buck!   The village is full of cheery noise, the constant sound of the hammer and the saw, and every now and then a crash like distant thunder tells of the falling of some giant tree.   Now, perhaps, a horn blown from Thomas Gardiner's calls the town-meeting together, to appoint ten men to help lay out the town's share of a road through the wilderness to Salem, or four of the proprietors to get to work to drain

---

* Robert Proud, quoted by Bowden in his History of Friends.

† Tradition says that this is the gigantic tree in front of Governor Franklin's house (now torn down) about which the "witches used to dance."

the meadows, or solemnly resolve "that the townfolk meet
at five o'clock the next morning to go and clear the brush
upon the island." It may be market day, and here are
Indians with venison and turkeys and plenty of wild fruit
for sale; or, yonder on a stump, Ollive, the magistrate,
holds his rustic court, and, while his neighbors stand reverently by, dispenses impartial justice. The Sabbath morning comes to begin the busy week, and the little town is
still. The hammer and the saw are laid aside, and the axe
rests undisturbed against the tree. All is so quiet that the
rustling of the dead leaves can be heard as they fall through
the frosty air, and the cawing of the crows as they rise from
their roost in the distant pines. No sentinel, with leathern
doublet, his matchlock resting in the hollow of his arm,
stands guard by yonder house, or watches with suspicious
eye, his hand upon his cutlass, the curious savage who
walks unbidden to the door. Within is gathered a little
company, seated in solemn silence or listening with rapt
attention as one of their number, with rude but reverent
manner, and perhaps unlettered speech, talks of the Inner
Light and of the goodness of Him who placed them in the
wilderness and protects them there.

A simple anecdote recorded by a descendant, and, until
now, forgotten for a century, is worthy of remembrance:*
"Tradition delivers," he says, "that when Thomas Ollive
acted in the quadruple character of governor, preacher,
tanner, and miller, a customer asked, 'Well, Thomas, when
can my corn be ground?' 'I shall be at the Assembly next

---

* My friend Brinton Coxe, Esq., to whom I am under many obligations for kind and intelligent assistance in gathering materials,
has given me this, which he found in a MS. note written by R. Smith
in 1796 on page 573 of his copy of Leaming and Spicer.

Third-day,' replied the good man, 'and I will bring it for thee behind me on my horse.'" Such were your governors in those early days! O rara temporum simplicitas!

What wonder then that the seed planted by those hands took root and brought forth fruit an hundred-fold! What wonder that the strong right arm of men like this conquered the forest and made the wilderness to bloom! What wonder that as this godly people looked back to those days beyond the stormy sea their hearts were stirred within them and they cried: "Blessed be the God of Abraham, of Isaac, and of Jacob that has called us not hither in vain!" "He was with us and is with us; yea, he hath made our way for us and proved and confirmed to us his word and providence!" "The desert sounds; the wilderness rejoices, a visitation outwardly and inwardly is come to America; God is Lord of all the earth and at the setting of the sun will his name be famous."*

My countrymen: Since those words were spoken and this town was built two hundred years have come and gone. The seed that could blossom in the dense thickets of New Jersey and find a root among the rocks of Plymouth has planted a continent with liberty and law. The light that glimmered on the Delaware and lit the cold waves of Boston Bay, was but the dawn of that advancing age whose morning beams now shine with impartial splendor upon all mankind. Your fathers' prayers are granted, and their prophecy fulfilled! Here on the threshold of your history I needs must stop. My task is finished, and my duty done. How could I hope to tell the story of two centuries? How dear old St. Mary's Church was founded in Queen Anne's reign.

---

* Letter of William Penn and others, 1st month, 1683. *Vide* Bowden's History of Friends, vol. i. p. 20.

How in colonial days great men as Governors lived in Burlington; how Council and Assembly met in the now vanished court-house, before whose door one day George Whitefield preached; how, in a darker time, the Hessians camped in a meadow beyond Yorkshire Bridge; how the Whigs knocked one night at Margaret Morris's door, and the Tory parson hid trembling in the "auger hole;" how patriotic gondolas bombarded Burlington, and managed to hit a house at Broad and York Streets; how, in the following year, the British in their turn opened the cannonade, and after an hour's fire knocked a hole in Adam Shepherd's stable near the wharf; how things were quiet for a little while till Light-Horse Harry Lee came thundering in.*

And what can I hope to say, in the last moments of so long a speech, of the inhabitants of a city whose life has not been more peaceful than her sons illustrious. From the beginning to the end, in times of the Colony, the Province, and State, it has always been the same. Here were the famous printers, Bradford the pioneer, and Isaac Collins, who published the first Jersey newspaper.† Here dwelt

---

* James Craft's Journal, Hist. Mag., vol. i. p. 300, Boston, 1857: "6th mo. 16th, 1770, Geo. Whitefield, the Great Calvinistic Preacher, preacht before the Court House. Great Audience. Deal of humor. 12th mo. 11th, 1776, sad work this day. The Hessians came. Town fired on by gondolas. Nobody hurt, altho' large and small shot was fired plenty and in all directions. 5th mo. 10, 1778. British came back (from Bordentown) and O what a whipping our poor town got, tho' through blessing nobody hurt. Bullets and every kind of shot showered down upon us for hours. 12th mo. 16th, 1778, Lee's troop of horse at Burlington." For an amusing account of Dr. Odell's adventure in the hidden chamber called the "Auger hole," see Dr. Hill's excellent History of the Church in Burlington, p. 321. *Vide* Barber and Howe's Historical Collection, pp. 94, 95.

† Of Bradford I have spoken in an earlier note. Isaac Collins was a man of great prominence in the Colony. He was appointed Co-

Judge Daniel Coxe, who planned a union for the Colonies full thirty years ere Franklin thought of it, and half a century before the Revolution.*   Here came Elias Boudinot, the President of Congress, to pass the evening of his well-spent life; and in the spacious garden of his house some of you may have seen his daughter and her friend, those venerable women who had borne the names of William Bradford and Alexander Hamilton.†   Here, on a Saturday morning, weary with walking "more than fifty miles," clad "in a working dress," his "pockets stuffed out with shirts and stockings," a boy of seventeen came trudging into town.   Nobody noticed him, except to smile perhaps, save an old woman who talked to him kindly and sold him gingerbread.   Years afterward he came again to print the money of the Province and become the friend of all the great men who dwelt in Burlington, for by that time the world had begun to hear of Benjamin Franklin.‡   Two

---

lonial printer in 1770, and issued the first number of the *New Jersey Gazette* on December 5, 1777.

* In the preface to his "Description of Carolana, &c., &c.," published in London in 1722.   He was the son of Daniel Coxe, of London, the Proprietary Governor, and was a Judge of the Supreme Court.   The Coxe family was long prominent in the history of Burlington and West Jersey.   ·

† Elias Boudinot was President of Congress in 1782, and Director of the Mint under General Washington's administration.   He was the first President, and in conjunction with his friend and kinsman Mr. Wallace, the originator of the American Bible Society.   His daughter and only child married the Hon. William Bradford, Attorney-General in Washington's cabinet.   Alexander Hamilton had been a friend in the family of Mr. Boudinot in his boyhood, and the colleague of his son-in-law in the cabinet.   The friendship between the widows of those two remarkable men, both so untimely cut off in their prime, continued to the end of their long lives.

‡ Bigelow's Franklin's Autobiography, pp. 110 and 163.

other boys belong to Burlington. Born side by side, beneath adjoining roofs, close to this spot where you are gathered now, both became sailors; but of different destinies. The elder, after a brief but brilliant life, fell in disastrous battle on the deck with the immortal cry upon his lips of "Don't give up the ship!" The younger lived to a green and vigorous old age, to make those Jersey names of Fenimore and Cooper famous forever in American literature!* Count this array of native or adopted citizens: Ellis and Stockton and Dutton and Sterling and Woolman and the mysterious Tyler; Franklin, the Tory governor, and Temple, his accomplished son; Samuel Smith, the historian, and Samuel J. Smith, the poet; William Coxe, the pomologist, and John Griscom, the friend of learning; Shippen and Cole in medicine, and Dean and the Gummeres in education; Bloomfield and McIlvaine and Wall in politics, and at the bar, Griffith, Wallace, Reed, two generations of the McIlvaines and four of the name of Kinsey, and those great masters of the law, Charles Chauncey and Horace Binney.† Read the long list of teachers of religion;

---

* James Fenimore Cooper in a published letter dated 1844 said: "I was born in the last house but one of the main street of Burlington as one goes into the country. There are two houses of brick stuccoed, built together, the one having five windows in front and the other four, the first being the last house in the street. In this house dwelt Mr. Lawrence, my old commander, Captain Lawrence's father, and in the four-window house my father."

† Charles Ellis, Samuel Stockton, and Thomas Dutton were prominent citizens in Burlington half a century ago; the latter in connection with John Griscom, LL.D., W. R. Allen, and Thomas Milnor, was active in founding the Public Schools, and the names of all of them are honorably borne in Burlington to-day. James Sterling was a famous merchant—his store at the corner of Broad and Main Streets was known from Sussex to Cape May. James Hunter Sterling is

I name the dead alone—Grellet and Cox and Hoskins and Mott and Dillwyn among Friends, and in the Church

---

remembered as the benefactor of the Library, to whom we owe the handsome building. Richard Tyler was an accomplished Englishman of wealth and evidently of rank, who settled in Burlington early in this century. There was some mystery about his life which has never been solved. It has been conjectured that he was a relative of Warren Hastings. John Woolman, the famous Quaker preacher, was a Burlington County man, and the name has existed there for the past two centuries; the late Burr Woolman and his son Franklin Woolman, Esq., have both been Surveyor-Generals of West Jersey. Governor William Franklin lived in the large house on the bank afterward occupied by Charles Chauncey as a summer residence, and torn down in 1873. His son, Temple, lived in elegant retirement with his books, and died at Franklin Park on the Rancocas, about six miles out of town. Samuel Smith, the historian, was long Treasurer of the Province. A notice of him has recently appeared as a preface to a second edition of his history, published in 1877, and an interesting paper on this subject of Samuel J. Smith and his writings can be found at page 39 of vol. ix. of the Proceedings of the New Jersey Historical Society. Both are by John Jay Smith, Esq. Dr. William Coxe was quite famous as a pomologist about the beginning of this century, and Griscom's Travels was a noted and much read book. Dr. Edward Shippen lived many years in the house occupied for nearly fifty years by the late Joseph Askew in Ellis Street at the end of Broad. Dr. Nathaniel W. Cole was an excellent citizen and a physician of great skill and experience. James Dean, LL.D., Professor of Mathematics in Vermont University ; John Gummere, the author of works on Astronomy, Surveying, etc., and Samuel R. Gummere, of others on Oratory, Geography, etc., are honored names in the history of Education. "Gummere's schools" had a famous reputation forty years ago. Joseph Bloomfield, a soldier of the Revolution and long Governor of the State, lived in the large house on Main Street known by his name. Joseph McIlvaine was United States Senator in 1820, Garret D. Wall in 1834, and his son James W. Wall in 1860. William Griffith was a most accomplished lawyer and stood at the head of the bar. He was one of John Adams's "Midnight Judges ;" Joshua Maddox Wallace, also at one

Talbot, the missionary, the witty Odell, the venerable Wharton, the saintlike McIlvaine, and that princely prelate —the most imposing figure of my boyish memories—

time Judge of the Pleas of Burlington County, was a very distinguished man, the co-worker of Mr. Boudinot in the Bible Society. He was the father of another well-known lawyer, John B. Wallace, and the grandfather of two others whose names are prominent in American legal literature—John William Wallace, lately the Reporter of the United States Supreme Court, and Horace Binney Wallace. Bowes Reed was a brother of General Joseph Reed, Washington's Aide-de-Camp. Joseph McIlvaine, the Senator, was also distinguished at the Bar and the father of Bloomfield McIlvaine, whose early death alone prevented his taking the front rank in the profession. The Kinsey family has been remarkable in the law. John Kinsey, the son of the first-comer, was noted in provincial history as a leader of the profession ; John Kinsey, his son, was Chief Justice of Pennsylvania and died in 1750 ; James Kinsey, his grandson, was Chief Justice of New Jersey, and the late Charles Kinsey, his great-grandson, was an eminent and learned lawyer. Mr. Chauncey and Mr. Binney lived for many summers side by side on the bank, the latter at the corner of Wood Street, in the house owned by the late Edward B. Grubb.

There are many other names which one might speak of and which ought to be remembered ; Samuel Emlen, Elihu Chauncey, who lived where the College stands to-day, Charles Read, Judge of Admiralty before the Revolution, and Andrew Allen the grandson of Chief-Justice Allen, "a most accomplished man," at one time British Consul at Boston, but after 1812 a resident of Burlington, in the house where St. Mary's Hall was afterwards erected, were all men whose names ought not to be forgotten. Barbaroux and Benoist were Frenchmen of family and fortune who settled in Burlington after the troubles in San Domingo. Both of these families lived on the bank. John Michael Hanckel was the Principal of the Academy: "His talents," said Rev. Dr. Wharton in his epitaph, "were of the first order." He died at twenty-nine. In an humbler walk in life were Thomas Aikman, the Sexton and Undertaker, Ben Shepherd, and Captain Jacob Myers of the "Mayflower," a well-known character.

whose tongue alone could have done justice to this anniversary !*

Now as I speak of them under the inspiration of these memories I seem to feel the touch of vanished hands and hear the sound of voices that are still. Before me rise the scenes of other days. I see the brilliant Wall; the rough and ready Engle; the venerable Grellet; Allen, your Mayor for quarter of a century; the little form, too small for such a heart, of William Allinson; the white head of Thomas Milnor; the well-beloved face of Cortlandt Van Rens-

----

* John Cox, John Hoskins, Richard Mott, and George Dillwyn were eminent as preachers. Stephen Grellet had an extraordinary life; born a nobleman, he escaped from France during the terrors of 1793 and became a Missionary among Friends. *Vide* his life, published by Benjamin Seebohn, London. He was a man of excellent talents, and great purity and benevolence. Dr. Hill's book, to which I have referred before, contains the best account of Talbot, Odell, and Wharton. The Rt. Rev. Charles Pettit McIlvaine, D.D., LL.D., D.C.L., Bishop of Ohio, was certainly one of the most distinguished prelates in the Episcopal Church. He was born at the northwest corner of Broad and Main Streets. His father, the Senator, was a son of Colonel Joseph McIlvaine of the Revolution. His wife was a daughter of Dr. William Coxe. I cannot condense into a note any expression which would convey to those who never knew him the place which Bishop Doane filled in Burlington between 1840 and 1859. Riverside was an Episcopal palace, filled always with distinguished men from home and abroad, among whom the host was an acknowledged chief. Burlington College was in the beginning of an apparently flourishing life. St. Mary's Hall was a successful institution. St. Mary's was the cathedral church of the Diocese, and on every occasion, ecclesiastical, collegiate, social, political, on Commencement Day, at Christmas, on the Fourth of July, the Bishop was a prominent and attractive figure. I shall never forget the wondering admiration with which I used to look at him; and the fascination of his manner—for no one had the gift of charming the young more than he—lingers with me still.

selaer; and the splendid countenance and manly form of him—the friend of many here—whose name I dare not trust myself to speak ! And you, too—friends of my boyhood's days, whom death has crowned with an immortal youth—you, young defenders of my country's honor—Grubb, Chase, Barclay, Baquet, and Van Rensselaer—on such a day as this you, too, shall be remembered !*

---

* These names need no explanatory note to-day, but I must not forget that a generation is rapidly approaching to whom they will seem as shadowy as do to me most of those which I have mentioned in the preceding paragraph. James W. Wall, often the candidate of his party for Congress and a Senator for a short time in 1860, was a man of brilliant talents, a witty poet, a graceful writer, and an orator of no little power. Frederick Engle, who died a Rear Admiral of the United States Navy, was a gallant and distinguished sailor. Of the venerable and excellent Grellet I have already spoken ; he lived in Main Street, next the alley called Library Street, opposite Governor Bloomfield's. When it was known that perhaps " Friend Grellet would preach," there were many of the world's people at meeting. I have heard him, and recall a tall slender figure speaking with strong French accent, and with French rather than Quaker warmth and vehemence. William R. Allen was a strong man in every sense ; he made himself felt in the community in many ways. The name of Allinson is honorably remembered. David Allinson was a publisher and Samuel a brewer ; William J. was a druggist and apothecary ; he was active in all that concerned the good of Burlington, and was a great benefactor of the Library and other institutions. He had much literary taste, and great antiquarian knowledge and zeal. Thomas Milnor was another excellent man, whose name should not be forgotten. Of the Rev. Dr. Cortlandt Van Rensselaer all Burlingtonians have pleasant memories. His activity in all good works outside of his church, of which he may be called the founder, as well as in it, endeared him greatly to the community. He was a very distinguished minister in the Presbyterian Church, and a man of great learning and culture. Frederick Brown of Philadelphia built his house called " Summer Home " in 1847, and made it his place of refuge from the cares of an active life, as labor-

My countrymen: The age that saw the birth of Burlington has passed away. The passions that raged about her cradle have long been dead. The furies of contending creeds have been forgotten, and Quaker and Presbyterian, Churchman and Catholic, rest in her bosom side by side. The twin sycamores by yonder meeting-house stand guard above a soil enriched with the bones of six generations of your kindred, and the spire of old St. Mary's springs from a doubly consecrated mould. The tree, the ancient church, the pleasant field, the flowing river—these shall endure, but you shall pass away. The lifeless thing shall live and the deathless die. It is God's mystery; we cannot solve it.

---

ious as it was singularly useful, until his death in 1864. Here were the extensive graperies filled with well-selected vines, the orchards of dwarf pears, the rare plants and flowers, and the choice trees in which he took such genuine delight and which must ever be associated in his children's minds with the memories of a perfectly happy childhood.

> " Ille te mecum locus et beatæ
> Postulant arces ; ibi tu calentem
> Debitâ sparges lacrimâ favillam
> *Patris* amici."

There are other names which ought to be remembered on such anniversaries, but those of Isaac Parker Grubb, Richard Chase, Mark Wilkes Collet Barclay, Francis Baquet, and Cortlandt Van Rensselaer, Jr., I love especially to recall. They all died in the active service of their country during the Rebellion. Three of them " with their bodies bore the brunt of battle, and after a short and quickly decided crisis of their fate, at the height of glory, not of fear, yielded up their lives!" Of all it is true that, in those other words of Pericles, " they laid down their bodies and their lives for their country, and therefore as their private reward they receive a deathless fame and the noblest of sepulchres, not so much that in which their bones are entombed as that in which their glory is preserved to be had in everlasting remembrance on all occasions, whether of speech or action."

That change that has come to all must come to you—and long before this story shall be told again, you will have followed the footsteps of your fathers. But still on the banks of Delaware shall stand your ancient town. Time shall not harm her nor age destroy the beauty of her face. Wealth may not come to her, nor power, nor fame among the cities of the earth; but civil freedom and liberty of conscience are now her children's birthright, and she rests content. Happy, indeed, if they can exclaim, with each recurring anniversary, as their fathers did two hundred years ago: "We are a family at peace within ourselves!"*

---

* Wrote William Penn and others in the 1st month (March), 1683: "Dear friends and brethren, we have no cause to murmur; our lot is fallen every way in a good place, and the Son of God is among us. We are a family at peace within ourselves, and truly great is our joy therefore." I add an amusing quotation from old Gabriel Thomas. Writing in 1698 he says: "Of *Lawyers* and *Physicians* I shall say nothing, because this Country is very Peaceable and Healthy; long may it so continue and never have occasion for the Tongue of the one, nor the Pen of the other, both equally destructive to Men's Estates and Lives; besides forsooth they, Hang-Man like, have a License to Murder and Make Mischief."

ORATION

AT

VALLEY FORGE,

June 19, 1878,

THE ONE HUNDREDTH ANNIVERSARY OF THE DE-
PARTURE OF THE ARMY OF THE REVOLUTION
FROM WINTER QUARTERS AT THAT PLACE.

ORATION.

—

IT is an honor to be here to-day. It is a privilege to behold this anniversary. This unusual spectacle, these solemn services, these flags and decorations, this tuneful choir, this military array, this distinguished company, this multitude darkening all the hillside, proclaim the general interest and attest its magnitude. And it is proper to commemorate this time. One hundred years ago this country was the scene of extraordinary events and very honorable actions. We feel the influence of them in our institutions and our daily lives, and it is both natural and right for us to seek, by some means, to mark their hundredth anniversaries. Those moments are passing quickly. Lexington, Bunker Hill, Germantown, Saratoga, have gone by already. Monmouth, Stony Point, Eutaw, and York-town are close at hand. It is eminently fit that we should gather here.

I cannot add to what has already been said about this place. The deeds which have made it famous have passed into history. The page on which they are recorded is written. We can neither add to it nor take away. The heroic dead who suffered here are far beyond our reach. No human eulogy can make their glory greater, no failure to do them justice make it less. Theirs is a perfect fame —safe, certain, and complete. Their trials here secured the happiness of a continent; their labors have borne fruit

303

in the free institutions of a powerful nation; their examples give hope to every race and clime; their names live on the lips of a grateful people; their memory is cherished in their children's hearts and shall endure forever. It is not for their sakes then, but for our own, that we have assembled here to-day. This anniversary, if I understand it right, has a purpose of its own. It is duty that has brought us here. The spirit appropriate to this hour is one of humility rather than of pride, of reverence rather than of exultation. We come, it is true, the representatives of forty millions of free men by ways our fathers never dreamed of, from regions of which they never heard. We come in the midst of plenty, under a sky of peace, power in our right hand and the keys of knowledge in our left. But we are here to learn rather than to teach; to worship, not to glorify. We come to contemplate the sources of our country's greatness; to commune with the honored past; to remind ourselves, and show our children that Joy can come out of Sorrow, Happiness out of Suffering, Light out of Darkness, Life out of Death.

Such is the meaning of this anniversary. I cannot do it justice. Would that there could come to some one in this multitude a tongue of fire—an inspiration born of the time itself, that, standing in this place and speaking with the voice of olden time, he might tell us in fitting language of our fathers! But it cannot be. Not even now—not even here. Perhaps we do not need it. Some of us bear their blood, and all alike enjoy the happiness their valor and endurance won. And if my voice be feeble, we have but to look around. The hills that saw them suffer look down on us; the ground that thrilled beneath their feet we tread to-day; their unmarked graves still lie in yonder field; the breastworks which they built to shelter them

surround us here! Dumb witnesses of the heroic past, ye
need no tongues! Face to face with you we see it all:—
this soft breeze changes to an icy blast; these trees drop
the glory of the summer, and the earth beneath our feet is
wrapped in snow. Beside us is a village of log huts—
along that ridge smoulder the fires of a camp. The sun
has sunk, the stars glitter in the inky sky, the camp is
hushed, the fires are out, the night is still. All are in
slumber save when a lamp glimmers in a cottage window,
and a passing shadow shows a tall figure pacing to and fro.
The cold silence is unbroken save when on yonder rampart,
crunching the crisp snow with wounded feet, a ragged
sentinel keeps watch for Liberty!

The close of 1777 marked the gloomiest period of the
Revolution. The early enthusiasm of the struggle had
passed away. The doubts which the first excitements
banished had returned. The novelty of war had gone, and
its terrors become awfully familiar. Fire and sword had
devastated some of the best parts of the country, its cities
were half ruined, its fields laid waste, its resources drained,
its best blood poured out in sacrifice. The struggle now had
become one of endurance, and while Liberty and Independence seemed as far off as ever, men began to appreciate the
tremendous cost at which they were to be purchased. The
capture of Burgoyne had, after all, been only a temporary
check to a powerful and still unexhausted enemy.* Nor

---

* Such at least was the opinion of Lafayette (Memoirs, vol. i. pp. 34
and 35). A friend to whom Mr. Brown read this oration, pointed out
the fact that the capture of Burgoyne's army had been considered
by all the latest and most accurate historians as the undoubted turning-point of the war, and that Creasy had included the battle of
Behmus's Heights in the fifteen *decisive battles of the world.* Mr.
Brown said that although it had undoubtedly proved so, he felt

was its effect on the Americans themselves wholly beneficial. It had caused the North to relax, in a great measure, its activity and vigilance, and, combined with the immunity from invasion which the South had enjoyed, " to lull asleep two-thirds of the continent." While a few hundred ill-armed, half-clad Americans guarded the Highlands of the Hudson, a well-equipped garrison, several thousand strong, lived in luxury in the city of New York.* The British fleet watched with the eyes of Argus the rebel coast. Rhode Island lay undisputed in their hands; Georgia, Virginia, and the Carolinas were open to their invasion, and as incapable of defence as Maryland had been when they landed in the Chesapeake. Drawn upon for the army, the sparse population could not half till the soil, and the savings of laborious years had all been spent. While the miserable paper currency which Congress, with a fatal folly never to be absent from the counsels of men, continued to issue and call money, obeyed natural rather than artificial laws and fell four hundred per cent., coin flowed to Phila-delphia and New York, and in spite of military orders and civil edicts, the scanty produce of the country followed it. Nor could the threatened penalty of death restrain the evil. Want began to be widely felt, and the frequent proclama-tions of the British, accompanied with Tory intrigue and abundant gold, to have effect. To some, even of the wisest,

---

that in picturing the feeling of the day he was justified in using the impression left on the mind of so distinguished an actor as Lafay-ette; but that, when the oration was printed, he would add a note that would protect him from any criticism prompted by the suppo-sition, that biased by local prejudice, he had spoken lightly of a brilliant event which occurred in a neighboring State, in order to give prominence to the trials of Valley Forge.—Ed.

* *Vide* Lafayette's Memoirs, vol. i. pp. 34 and 35.

the case was desperate. Even the elements seemed to combine against the cause. A deluge prevented a battle at the
Warren Tavern; a fog robbed Washington of victory at
Germantown; and at last, while the fate of America hung
on the courage, the fortitude, and the patriotism of eleven
thousand half-clothed, half-armed, hungry Continentals,
who, discomforted but not discouraged, beaten but not disheartened, suffering but steadfast still, lay on their firelocks
on the frozen ridges of Whitemarsh, a British army, nineteen thousand five hundred strong, of veteran troops, perfectly equipped, freshly recruited from Europe, and flushed
with recent victory, marched into winter quarters in the
chief city of the nation.

Philadelphia surely had never seen such gloomy days as
those which preceded the entry of the British. On the
24th of August the American army marched through the
length of Front Street;* on the 25th the British landed at
the Head of Elk. Days of quiet anxiety ensued. On
the 11th of September, as Tom Paine was writing a letter
to Dr. Franklin, the sound of cannon in the southwest interrupted him.† From morning until late in the afternoon
people in the streets listened to the dull sound like distant
thunder.‡ About six o'clock it died away, and the straining
ear could catch nothing but the soughing of the wind.
With what anxiety men waited—with what suspense!
The sun sank in the west, and the shadows crept over the
little city. It was the universal hour for the evening meal,
but who could go home to eat? Men gathered about the
State House to talk, to conjecture, to consult together, and

---

* Saffell's Records of the Revolutionary War, p. 333.
† Pennsylvania Magazine, vol. ii. p. 283.
‡ Watson's Annals of Philadelphia, vol. ii. p. 283.

the women whispered in little groups at the doorsteps, and craned their necks out of the darkened windows to look nervously up and down the street. About eight o'clock there was a little tumult near the Coffee House. The story spread that Washington had gained a victory,* and a few lads set up a cheer. But it was not traced to good authority, and disappointment followed. By nine in the evening the suspense was painful. Suddenly, far up Chestnut Street, was heard the clatter of horses' feet. Some one was galloping hard. Down Chestnut like an arrow came at full speed a single horseman. He had ridden fast, and his horse was splashed with foam. Hearts beat quickly as he dashed by; past Sixth Street, past the State House, past Fifth, and round the corner into Fourth. The crowd followed, and instantly packed around him as he drew rein at the Indian Queen.† He threw a glance at the earnest faces that were turned toward his, and spoke: "A battle has been fought at the Birmingham Meeting-House, on the Brandywine; the army has been beaten; the French Marquis Lafayette shot through the leg. His Excellency has fallen back to Chester; the road below is full of stragglers." And then the crowd scattered, each one to his home, but not to sleep. A few days followed full of contradictory stories. The armies are manœuvring on the Lancaster Road. Surely Washington will fight another battle. And then the news came and spread like lightning —Wayne has been surprised and his brigade massacred at the Paoli, and the enemy are in full march for Philadelphia; the Whigs are leaving by hundreds; the authorities are going; the Congress have gone; the British have

* Irving's Washington, vol. iii. p. 202.
† Watson's Annals, vol. ii. p. 283.

arrived at Germantown.* Who can forget the day that followed?

A sense of something dreadful about to happen hangs over the town. A third of the houses are shut and empty. Shops are unopened, and busy rumor flies about the streets. Early in the morning the sidewalks are filled with a quiet, anxious crowd. The women watch behind bowed windows with half curious, half frightened looks. The men, solemn and subdued, whisper in groups: "Will they come to-day?" "Are they here already?" "Will they treat us like a conquered people?" It was inevitable since the hot-bloods would have war. Sometimes the Tory can be detected by an exultant look, but the general sentiment is gloomy.† The morning drags along. By ten o'clock Second Street from Callowhill to Chestnut, is filled with old men and boys. There is hardly a young man to be seen. About eleven‡ is heard the sound of approaching cavalry, and a squadron of dragoons comes galloping down the street, scattering the boys right and left. The crowd parts to let them by, and melts together again. In a few minutes far up the street there is the faint sound of martial music and something moving that glitters in the sunlight. The crowd thickens, and is full of hushed expectation. Presently one can see a red mass swaying to and fro. It becomes more and more distinct. Louder grows the music and the tramp of marching men, as waves of scarlet, tipped with steel, come moving down the street. They are now but a square off—their bayonets glancing in perfect line, and steadily advancing to the music of "God Save the King."§

---

* Miller's Diary, given in Watson's Annals, vol. ii. p. 68.
† Morton's Diary, Pennsylvania Magazine, vol. i. p. 8.
‡ Ibid., p. 7.
§ Reed's Life of Reed, vol. i. p. 315.

These are the famous grenadiers. Their pointed caps of red, fronted with silver, their white leather leggins and short scarlet coats, trimmed with blue, make a magnificent display. They are perfectly equipped and look well fed and hearty.* Behind them are more cavalry. No, these must be officers. The first one is splendidly mounted and wears the uniform of a general. He is a stout man with gray hair and a pleasant countenance,† in spite of the squint of an eye which disfigures it. A whisper goes through the bystanders: "It is Lord Cornwallis himself." A brilliant staff in various uniforms follows him, and five men in civilian's dress. A glance of recognition follows these last like a wave along the street, for they are Joseph Galloway, Enoch Story, Tench Coxe, and the two Allens—father and son—Tories, who have only dared to return home behind British bayonets.‡ Long lines of red coats follow till the Fourth, the Fortieth, and the Fifty-fifth regiments have passed by. But who are these in dark blue that come behind the grenadiers? Breeches of yellow leather, leggins of black, and tall, pointed hats of brass, complete their uniform. They wear moustaches and have a fierce foreign look, and their unfamiliar music seems to a child in that crowd to cry "Plunder! plunder! plunder!" as it times their rapid march.§ These are the Hessian mercenaries whom Washington surprised and thrashed so well at Christmas in '76. And now Grenadiers and Yagers, horse, foot, and artillery that rumbles along making the windows

---

* Watson's Annals, vol. ii. p. 284.　　　　　† Ibid., p. 289.

‡ It has been said that with others Tench Coxe went out to meet Howe to ask him to protect the city. His conduct, however, was such that he was attainted of treason, and it is also true that he surrendered himself and was acquitted.—Ed.

§ Watson's Annals, vol. ii. p. 283.

rattle, have all passed by. The Fifteenth Regiment is drawn up on High Street, near Fifth; the Forty-second Highlanders in Chestnut, below Third, and the artillery is parked in the State House yard.* All the afternoon the streets are full—wagons with luggage lumbering along, officers in scarlet riding to and fro, aids and orderlies seeking quarters for their different officers. Yonder swarthy, haughty-looking man, dismounting at Norris's door, is my Lord Rawdon. Lord Cornwallis is quartered at Peter Reeve's in Second, near Spruce, and Knyphausen at Henry Lisle's, nearer to Dock Street, on the east. The younger officers are well bestowed, for Dr. Franklin's house has been taken by a certain clever Captain Andre.† The time for the evening parade comes, and the well-equipped regiments are drawn up in line, while slowly to the strains of martial music the sun sinks in autumnal splendor in the west. The streets are soon in shadow, but still noisy with the tramping of soldiers and the clatter of arms. In High Street, and on the commons, fires are lit for the troops to do their cooking, and the noises of the camp mingle with the city's hum. Most of the houses are shut, but here and there one stands wide open, while brilliantly-dressed officers lounge at the windows or pass and repass in the doorway. The sound of laughter and music is heard and the brightly-lit windows of the London Coffee House and the Indian Queen tell of the parties that are celebrating there the event they think so glorious; and thus, amid sounds of revelry, the night falls on the Quaker City. In spite of Trenton and Princeton and Brandywine; in spite of the wisdom of Congress and the courage and skill of the commander-in-chief; in spite of the bravery and

---

* Watson's Annals, vol. ii. p. 287.   † Ibid., p. 289.

fortitude of the Continental army, the forces of the king
are in the Rebel capital, and the "all's well" of hostile
sentinels keeping guard by her northern border passes
unchallenged from the Schuylkill to the Delaware.

What matters it to Sir William Howe and his victorious
army if rebels be starving and their ragged currency be
almost worthless?   Here is gold and plenty of good cheer.
What, whether they threaten to attack the British lines or
disperse through the impoverished country in search of
food?   The ten redoubts that stretch from Fairmount to
Cohocsink Creek are stout and strongly manned, the river
is open, and supplies and reinforcements are on the way
from England.   What if the earth be wrinkled with frost?
The houses of Philadelphia are snug and warm.   What if
the rigorous winter have begun and snow be whitening the
hills?   Here are mirth and music, and dancing and wine,
and women and play, and the pageants of a riotous capital!
And so with feasting and with revelry let the winter wear
away!

The wind is cold and piercing on the old Gulf Road, and
the snow-flakes have begun to fall.   Who is this that toils
up yonder hill, his footsteps stained with blood?   "His
bare feet peep through his worn-out shoes, his legs nearly
naked from the tattered remains of an only pair of stockings, his breeches not enough to cover his nakedness, his
shirt hanging in strings, his hair dishevelled, his face wan
and thin, his look hungry, his whole appearance that of a
man forsaken and neglected."*   On his shoulder he carries
a rusty gun,† and the hand that grasps the stock is blue with

---

* Diary of Albigence Waldo, kept at Valley Forge.   Historical
Magazine, vol. v. p. 131.

† Kapp's Life of Steuben, p. 117.

cold. His comrade is no better off, nor he who follows, for both are barefoot, and the ruts of the rough country road are deep and frozen hard. A fourth comes into view, and still another. A dozen are in sight. Twenty have reached the ridge, and there are more to come. See them as they mount the hill that slopes eastward into the Great Valley. A thousand are in sight, but they are but the vanguard of the motley company that winds down the road until it is lost in the cloud of snow-flakes that have hidden the Gulf hills. Yonder are horsemen in tattered uniforms, and behind them cannon lumbering slowly over the frozen road, half dragged, half pushed by men. They who appear to be in authority have coats of every make and color. Here is one in a faded blue, faced with buckskin that has once been buff. There is another on a tall, gaunt horse, wrapped "in a sort of dressing-gown made of an old blanket or woollen bed cover."* A few of the men wear long linen hunting shirts reaching to the knee, but of the rest no two are dressed alike—not half have shirts, a third are barefoot, many are in rags.† Nor are their arms the same. Cow-horns and tin boxes they carry for want of pouches. A few have swords, fewer still bayonets.‡ Muskets, carbines, fowling-pieces, and rifles are to be seen together side by side.

Are these soldiers that huddle together and bow their heads as they face the biting wind? Is this an army that comes straggling through the valley in the blinding snow? No martial music leads them in triumph into a captured capital. No city full of good cheer and warm and comfortable homes awaits their coming. No sound keeps time to their steps save the icy wind rattling the leafless branches

---

* Kapp's Life of Steuben, p. 118.
† Memoirs of Lafayette, vol. i. p. 19.
‡ Life of Steuben, p. 118.

and the dull tread of their weary feet on the frozen ground. In yonder forest must they find their shelter, and on the northern slope of these inhospitable hills their place of refuge. Perils shall soon assault them more threatening than any they encountered under the windows of Chew's house or by the banks of Brandywine. Trials that rarely have failed to break the fortitude of men await them here. False friends shall endeavor to undermine their virtue and secret enemies to shake their faith; the Congress whom they serve shall prove helpless to protect them, and their country herself seem unmindful of their sufferings; Cold shall share their habitations, and Hunger enter in and be their constant guest; Disease shall infest their huts by day, and Famine stand guard with them through the night; Frost shall lock their camp with icy fetters, and the snows cover it as with a garment; the storms of winter shall be pitiless —but all in vain. Danger shall not frighten nor temptation have power to seduce them. Doubt shall not shake their love of country nor suffering overcome their fortitude. The powers of evil shall not prevail against them, for they are the Continental Army, and these are the hills of Valley Forge!

It is not easy to-day to imagine this country as it appeared a century ago. Yonder city, which now contains one-fourth as many inhabitants as were found in those days between Maine and Georgia, was a town of but thirty thousand men, and at the same time the chief city of the continent. The richness of the soil around it had early attracted settlers, and the farmers of the Great Valley had begun to make that country the garden which it is to-day; but from the top of this hill one could still behold the wilderness under cover of which, but twenty years before, the Indian had spread havoc through the back settlements on the Lehigh and the

Susquehanna. The most important place between the latter river and the site of Fort Pitt, "at the junction of the Ohio," was the frontier village of York, where Congress had taken refuge. The single road which connected Philadelphia with the Western country had been cut through the forest to Harris's Block House but forty years before. It was half a century only since its iron ore had led to the settlement of Lancaster, and little more than a quarter since a single house had marked the site of Reading. The ruins of Colonel Bull's plantation, burned by the British on their march, lay in solitude on the hills which are covered to-day with the roofs and spires of Norristown ;* and where yonder cloud hangs over the furnaces and foundries of Phœnixville, a man named Gordon, living in a cave, gave his name to a crossing of the river.† Nor was this spot itself the same. A few small houses clustered about Potts's Forge, where the creek tumbled into the Schuylkill, and two or three near the river bank marked the beginning of a little farm. The axe had cleared much of the bottom lands and fertile fields of the Great Valley, but these hills were still wrapped in forest that covered their sides as far as the eye could reach. The roads that ascended their ridge on the south and east plunged into densest woods as they climbed the hill, and met beneath its shadow at the same spot where to-day a school-house stands in the midst of smiling fields. It is no wonder that the Baron De Kalb, as he gazed on the forest of oak and chestnut that covered the sides and summit of Mount Joy, should have described the place bitterly as "a wilderness."‡

---

* Historical Collections of Pennsylvania, by Sherman Day, p. 499.

† Annals of Phœnixville, by S. W. Pennypacker, p. 174.

‡ Life of General Baron De Kalb, by Frederick Kapp, p. 128.

But nevertheless it was well chosen.   There was no town
that would answer.   Wilmington and Trenton would have
afforded shelter, but in the one the army would have been
useless, and in the other in constant danger. Reading and
Lancaster were so distant that the choice of either would
have left a large district open to the enemy, and both, in
which were valuable stores, could be better covered by an
army here.   Equally distant with Philadelphia from the
fords of Brandywine and the ferry into Jersey, the army
could move to either point as rapidly as the British themselves, and while distant enough from the city to be safe
from surprise or sudden attack itself, it could protect the
country that lay between, and at the same time be a constant
menace to the capital.   Strategically, then, the General could
not have chosen better.   And the place was well adapted
for the purpose.   The Schuylkill, flowing from the Blue
Hills, bent here toward the eastward.   Its current was
rapid, and its banks precipitous.   The Valley Creek, cut-
ting its way through a deep defile at right angles to the
river, formed a natural boundary on the west.   The hill
called Mount Joy, at the entrance of that defile, threw out
a spur which, running parallel to the river about a mile,
turned at length northward and met its banks.   On the one
side this ridge enclosed a rolling table land; on the other it
sloped sharply to the Great Valley.   The engineers under
Du Portail marked out a line of entrenchments four feet
high, protected by a ditch six feet wide, from the entrance of
the Valley Creek defile, along the crest of this ridge until
it joined the bank of the Schuylkill, where a redoubt marked
the eastern angle of the encampment.   High on the shoulder
of Mount Joy a second line girdled the mountain, and then
ran northward to the river, broken only by the hollow
through which the Gulf Road descended to the Forge.

This hollow place was later defended by an abattis and a triangular earthwork.

A redoubt on the east side of Mount Joy commanded the Valley road, and another behind the left flank of the abattis, that which came from the river, while a star redoubt on a hill at the bank acted as a tête-de-pont for the bridge that was thrown across the Schuylkill. Behind the front and before the second line the troops were ordered to build huts for winter quarters. Fourteen feet by sixteen, of logs plastered with clay,* these huts began to rise on every side. Placed in rows, each brigade by itself, they soon gave the camp the appearance of a little city. All day long the axe resounded among the hills, and the place was filled with the noise of hammering and the crash of falling trees. "I was there when the army first began to build huts," wrote Paine to Franklin. "They appeared to me like a family of beavers, every one busy; some carrying logs, others mud, and the rest plastering them together. The whole was raised in a few days, and it is a curious collection of buildings in the true rustic order."† The weather soon became intensely cold. The Schuylkill froze over, and the roads were blocked with snow, but it was not until nearly the middle of January that the last hut was built and the army settled down into winter quarters on the bare hillsides. Long before that its sufferings had begun.

The trials which have made this place so famous arose chiefly from the incapacity of Congress. It is true that the country in the neighborhood of Philadelphia was well-nigh exhausted. An active campaign over a small extent of territory had drawn heavily on the resources of this part

---

* Sparks's Writings of Washington, vol. v. p. 525.
† Pennsylvania Magazine, vol. ii. p. 294.

of Pennsylvania and the adjacent Jersey. Both forces had fed upon the country, and it was not so much disaffection (of which Washington wrote) as utter exhaustion which made the farmers of the devastated region furnish so little to the army. Nor would it have been human nature in them to have preferred the badly printed, often counterfeited, depreciated promise to pay, of the Americans, for the gold which the British had to offer. In spite of the efforts of McLane's and Lee's Light Horse and the activity of Lacey, of the militia, the few supplies that were left went steadily to Philadelphia, and the patriot army remained in want. But the more distant States, north and south, could easily have fed and clothed a much more numerous army. That they did not was the fault of Congress. That body no longer contained the men who had made it famous in the years gone by. Franklin was in Paris, where John Adams was about to join him. Jay, Jefferson, Rutledge, Livingston, and Henry were employed at home. Hancock had resigned. Samuel Adams was absent in New England. Men much their inferiors had taken their places.*

The period, inevitable in the history of revolutions, had arrived, when men of the second rank came to the front. With the early leaders in the struggle had disappeared the foresight, the breadth of view, the loftiness of purpose, and the self-sacrificing spirit belonging only to great minds which had marked and honored the commencement of the struggle. A smaller mind had begun to rule, a narrower view to influence, a personal feeling to animate the members.† Driven from Philadelphia, they were in a measure disheart-

---

* P. S. Duponceau, quoted in Kapp's Steuben, p. 100.

† These views are expressed in Hamilton's letter to Clinton, February 7, 1778. *Vide* History of the Republic of the United States, vol. i. p. 422.

ened, and their pride touched in a tender spot. Incapable of the loftier sentiments which had moved their predecessors, they could not overcome a sense of their own importance and the desire to magnify their office. Petty rivalries had sprung up among them, and sectional feeling, smothered in '74, '75, and '76, had taken breath again, and asserted itself with renewed vigor in the recent debates on the confederation. But if divided among themselves by petty jealousies, they were united in a greater jealousy of Washington and the army. They cannot be wholly blamed for this. Taught by history no less than by their own experience, of the dangers of standing armies in a free State, and wanting in modern history the single example which we have in Washington of a successful military chief retiring voluntarily into private life, they judged the leader of their forces by themselves and the ordinary rules of human nature. Their distrust was not unnatural nor wholly selfish, and must find some justification in the exceptional greatness of his character.

It was in vain that he called on them to dismiss their doubts and trust an army which had proved faithful.* In vain he urged them to let their patriotism embrace, as his had learned to do, the whole country with an equal fervor. In vain he pointed out that want of organization in the army was due to want of union among them. They continued distrustful and unconvinced. In vain he asked for a single army, one and homogeneous. Congress insisted on thirteen distinct armies, each under the control of its particular State. The effect was disastrous. The personnel of the army was continually changing. Each State had its own rules, its own system of organization, its own plan of

---

* Sparks's Writings of Washington, vol. v. p. 328.

making enlistments. No two worked together—the men's terms even expiring at the most delicate and critical times. Promotion was irregular and uncertain, and the sense of duty was impaired as that of responsibility grew less. Instead of an organized army, Washington commanded a disorganized mob. The extraordinary virtues of that great man might keep the men together, but there were some things which they could not do. Without an organized quartermaster's department the men could not be clothed or fed. At first mismanaged, this department became neglected. The warnings of Washington were disregarded, his appeals in vain. The troops began to want clothing soon after Brandywine. By November it was evident that they must keep the field without blankets, overcoats, or tents. At Whitemarsh they lay, half clad, on frozen ground. By the middle of December they were in want of the necessaries of life.

"We are ordered to march over the river," writes Dr. Waldo, of Colonel Prentice's Connecticut Regiment, at Swede's Ford, on December 12. "It snows—I'm sick—eat nothing—no whiskey—no baggage—Lord—Lord—Lord! . . . Till sunrise crossing the river, . . . cold and uncomfortable."* "I'm sick," he goes on two days after, in his diary, "discontented and out of humor. Poor food—hard lodging—cold weather—fatigued—nasty clothes—nasty cookery . . . smoked out of my senses . . . I can't endure it. . . . Here comes a bowl of soup, . . . sickish enough to make a Hector ill. Away with it, boy—I'll live like the chameleon, on air."† On the 19th of December they reached Valley Forge. By the 21st even such a bowl of soup had become a luxury. "A general cry," notes Waldo again,

---

* Historical Magazine, vol. v. p. 131.   † Ibid.

" through the camp this evening: . . . 'No meat, no meat.' The distant vales echoed back the melancholy sound: 'No meat, no meat.' "* It was literally true. On the next day Washington wrote to the President of Congress: "I do not know from what cause this alarming deficiency, or rather total failure of supplies, arises, but unless more vigorous exertions and better regulations take place in that line immediately this army must dissolve. I have done all in my power by remonstrating, by writing, by ordering the commissaries on this head, from time to time; but without any good effect, or obtaining more than a present scanty relief. Owing to this the march of the army has been delayed on more than one interesting occasion in the course of the present campaign; and had a body of the enemy crossed the Schuylkill this morning (as I had reason to expect from the intelligence I received at four o'clock last night), the divisions which I ordered to be in readiness to march and meet them could not have moved."† Hardly was this written when the news did come that the enemy had come out to Darby, and the troops were ordered under arms. " Fighting," responded General Huntington when he got the order, " will be far preferable to starving. My brigade is out of provisions, nor can the commissary obtain any meat."‡ " Three days successively," added Varnum, of Rhode Island, " we have been destitute of bread, two days we have been entirely without meat."§ It was impossible to stir. And "this," wrote Washington, in indignation, brought forth the only commissary in camp, "and with him this melancholy and alarming truth that he had not a single

---

* Historical Magazine, vol. v. p. 132.
† Sparks's Writings of Washington, vol. v. p. 193.
‡ Ibid., foot-note.   § Ibid., foot-note.

hoof to slaughter, and not more than twenty-five barrels of flour."*   "I am now convinced beyond a doubt that unless some great and capital change suddenly takes place in that line this army must inevitably be reduced to one or other of these three things—starve, dissolve, or disperse, in order to obtain subsistence."†

But no change was destined to take place for many suffering weeks to come. The cold grew more and more intense, and provisions scarcer every day. Soon all were alike in want. "The colonels were often reduced to two rations and sometimes even to one. The army frequently remained whole days without provisions," is the testimony of Lafayette.‡ "We have lately been in an alarming state for want of provisions," says Colonel Laurens, on the 17th of February.§ "The army has been in great distress since you left," wrote Greene to Knox nine days afterwards; "the troops are getting naked. They were seven days without meat, and several days without bread. . . . We are still in danger of starving. Hundreds of horses have already starved to death."|| The painful testimony is full and uncontradicted. "Several brigades," wrote Adjutant-General Scammel to Timothy Pickering, early in February, "have been without their allowance of meat. This is the third day."¶ "In yesterday's conference with the General," said the Committee of Congress sent to report, writing on the 12th of February, "he informed us that some brigades had been four days without meat, and that even the common soldiers had been at his quarters to make known their wants."

---

* Sparks's Writings of Washington, vol. v. p. 197.   † Ibid.

‡ Memoirs of Lafayette, vol. i. p. 35.

§ Correspondence of Col. John Laurens, p. 126.

|| Life of Knox, by Drake, pp. 55–6.

¶ Life of Pickering, vol. i. p. 204.

"Should the enemy" attack the camp successfully, "your artillery would undoubtedly fall into their hands for want of horses to remove it. But these are smaller and tolerable evils when compared with the imminent danger of your troops perishing with famine, or dispersing in search of food."* " For some days past there has been little less than a famine in the camp," writes Washington to Clinton; "a part of the army has been a week without any kind of flesh, and the rest three or four days."† Famished for want of food, they were no better off for clothes. "The unfortunate soldiers were in want of everything. They had neither coats, hats, shirts, nor shoes," wrote the Marquis de Lafayette.‡ "The men," said Baron Steuben, "were literally naked, some of them in the fullest extent of the word."§ " 'Tis a melancholy consideration," were the words of Pickering, "that hundreds of our men are unfit for duty only for want of clothes and shoes."‖ Hear Washington himself on the 23d of December: " We have (besides a number of men confined to hospitals for want of shoes, and others in farm-houses on the same account), by a field return, this day made, no less than two thousand eight hundred and ninety-eight men now in camp unfit for duty, because they are barefoot, and otherwise naked."¶ " Our numbers, since the 4th instant, from the hardships and exposures they have undergone, (many having been obliged for want of blankets to sit up all night by fires instead of taking rest in a natural and common way,) have decreased two thousand men."** By the 1st of February that number

---

* Reed's Life of Reed, vol. i. p. 362.
† Sparks, vol. v. p. 239.　　　　　　‡ Memoirs, vol. i. p. 35.
§ Kapp's Life of Steuben, p. 118.
‖ Life of Pickering, vol. i. p. 201.　　¶ Sparks, vol. v. p. 199.
** *Vide* Sparks, ibid.

had grown to four thousand, and there were fit for duty but five thousand and twelve, or one-half the men in camp. "So," in the words of the Hebrew prophet, "they labored in the work, and half of them held the spears from the rising of the morning till the stars appeared."

Naked and starving in an unusually rigorous winter, they fell sick by hundreds. From want of clothes "their feet and legs froze till they became black, and it was often necessary to amputate them."*   Through a want of straw or materials to raise them from the wet earth (I quote again from the Committee of Congress) "sickness and mortality have spread through their quarters to an astonishing degree." The smallpox has broken out. "Notwithstanding the diligence of the physicians and surgeons, of whom we hear no complaint, the sick and dead list has increased one-third in the last week's return, which was one-third greater than the week preceding, and from the present inclement weather will probably increase in a much greater proportion."† Well might Washington exclaim: "Our sick naked, and well naked, our unfortunate men in captivity naked!"‡ "Our difficulties and distresses are certainly great, and such as wound the feelings of humanity."§ Nor was this all.   What many had to endure beside, let Dr. Waldo tell: "When the officer has been fatiguing through wet and cold, and returns to his tent to find a letter from his wife filled with the most heart-aching complaints a woman is capable of writing, acquainting him with the incredible difficulty with which she procures a little bread for herself and children; that her money is of very little consequence

---

* Memoirs of Lafayette, vol. i. p. 35.
† Reed's Life of Reed, vol. i. p. 361.
‡ Sparks, vol. v. p. 207.   § Ibid.

to her—concluding with expressions bordering on despair of getting sufficient food to keep soul and body together through the winter, and begging him to consider that charity begins at home, and not suffer his family to perish with want in the midst of plenty—what man is there whose soul would not shrink within him? Who would not be disheartened from persevering in the best of causes—the cause of his country—when such discouragements as these lie in his way, which his country might remedy if it would?"*

Listen to his description of the common soldier: "See the poor soldier when in health. With what chearfullness he meets his foes, and encounters every hardship! If barefoot, he labours thro' the Mud and Cold with a Song in his mouth extolling War and Washington. If his food be bad, he eats it notwithstanding with seeming content, blesses God for a good Stomach, and Whisles it into digestion. But harkee! Patience a moment! There comes a Soldier," "and crys with an air of wretchedness and dispair: 'I'm Sick; my feet lame; my legs are sore; my body cover'd with this tormenting Itch; my Cloaths are worn out; my Constitution is broken; my former Activity is exhausted by fatigue, hunger, and Cold; I fail fast; I shall soon be no more! And all the reward I shall get will be, 'Poor Will is dead!'"† And in the midst of this they persevered! Freezing, starving, dying, rather than desert their flag they saw their loved ones suffer, but kept the faith. And the American yeoman of the Revolution remaining faithful through that winter is as splendid an example of devotion to duty as that which the pitying ashes of Vesuvius have preserved through eighteen centuries in the figure of the

---

* Historical Magazine, vol. v. p. 131.   † Ibid., p. 169.

Roman soldier standing at his post, unmoved amid all the
horrors of Pompeii. "The Guard die, but never surrender," was the phrase invented for Cambronne. "My comrades freeze and starve, but they never forsake me," might
be put into the mouth of Washington.

"Naked and starving as they are," writes one of their
officers, we "cannot enough admire the incomparable patience and fidelity of the soldiery that they have not been
ere this excited by their sufferings to a general mutiny and
desertion."*   "Nothing can equal their sufferings," says the
Committee, "except the patience and fortitude with which
they bear them."†   Greene's account to Knox is touching:
"Such patience and moderation as they manifested under
their sufferings does the highest honor to the magnanimity
of the American soldiers. The seventh day they came before
their superior officers and told their sufferings as if they had
been humble petitioners for special favors. They added that
it would be impossible to continue in camp any longer without support."‡   In March Thomas Wharton writes in the
name of Pennsylvania: "The unparalleled patience and
magnanimity with which the army under your Excellency's
command have endured the hardships attending their situation, unsupplied as they have been through an uncommonly
severe winter, is an honor which posterity will consider as
more illustrious than could have been derived to them by a
victory obtained by any sudden and vigorous exertion."§   "I
would cherish these dear, ragged Continentals, whose patience
will be the admiration of future ages, and glory in bleeding

---

* Sparks's Writings of Washington, vol. v. p. 239.
† Reed's Life of Reed, vol. i. p. 361.
‡ Life of Greene, by Prof. G. W. Greene, vol. i. p. 563.
§ Correspondence of the Revolution: Sparks, vol. ii. p. 83.

with them," cried John Laurens in the enthusiasm of youth.* "The patience and endurance of both soldiers and officers was a miracle which each moment served to renew," said Lafayette in his old age.† But the noblest tribute comes from the pen of him who knew them best: " Without arrogance or the smallest deviation from truth it may be said that no history now extant can furnish an instance of an army's suffering such uncommon hardships as ours has done and bearing them with the same patience and fortitude. To see men without clothes to cover their nakedness, without blankets to lie on, without shoes (for the want of which their marches might be traced by the blood from their feet), and almost as often without provisions as with them, marching through the frost and snow, and at Christmas taking up their winter quarters within a day's march of the enemy, without a house or a hut to cover them till they could be built, and submitting without a murmur, is a proof of pa tience and obedience which in my opinion can scarce be paralleled."‡ Such was Washington's opinion of the soldiers of Valley Forge.

Americans, who have gathered on the broad bosom of these hills to-day: if heroic deeds can consecrate a spot of Earth, if the living be still sensible of the example of the dead, if Courage be yet a common virtue, and Patience in Suffering be still honorable in your sight, if Freedom be any longer precious and Faith in Humanity be not banished from among you, if Love of Country still find a refuge among the hearts of men, take your shoes from off your feet, for the place on which you stand is holy ground!

And who are the leaders of the men whose heroism can

---

* Correspondence of John Laurens, p. 136.

† Memoirs, vol. i. p. 35.   ‡ Sparks, vol. v. p. 329.

sanctify a place like this? Descend the hill and wander through the camp. The weather is intensely cold and the smoke hangs above the huts. On the plain behind the front line a few general officers are grouped about a squad whom the new inspector, the German baron, is teaching some manœuvre. Bodies of men here and there are dragging wagons up hill (for the horses have starved to death) or carrying fuel for fires, without which the troops would freeze.* The huts are deserted save by the sick or naked, and as you pass along the street a poor fellow peeps out at the door of one and cries: "No bread, no soldier!"

These are the huts of Huntington's brigade of the Connecticut line;† next to it those of Pennsylvanians under Conway. This is the Irish-Frenchman soon to disappear in a disgraceful intrigue. Here in camp there are many who whisper that he is a mere adventurer, but in Congress they still think him "a great military character." Down towards headquarters are the Southerners commanded by Lachlin McIntosh, in his youth "the handsomest man in" Georgia. Beyond Conway, on the hill, is Maxwell, a gallant Irishman, commissioned by New Jersey. Woodford of Virginia, commands on the right of the second line, and in front of him the Virginian Scott. The next brigade in order are Pennsylvanians—many of them men whose homes are in this neighborhood—Chester county boys and Quakers from the Valley turned soldiers for their country's sake. They are the children of three races—the hot Irish blood mixes with the colder Dutch in their calm English veins, and some of them—their chief, for instance—are splendid fighters. There he is at this moment riding up the hill from his quarters in the valley. A man of medium height

---

* Reed's Life of Reed, p. 362.
† Map in vol. v. of Sparks's Washington.

and strong frame, he sits his horse well and with a dashing
air. His nose is prominent, his eye piercing, his complexion
ruddy, his whole appearance that of a man in splendid
health and flowing spirits. He is just the fellow to win by
his headlong valor the nickname of "The Mad." But he
is more than a mere fighter. Skilful, energetic, full of resources and presence of mind, quick to comprehend and
prompt to act, of sound judgment and extraordinary courage, he has in him the qualities of a great general, as he
shall show many a time in his short life of one-and-fifty
years. Pennsylvania, after her quiet fashion, may not
make as much of his fame as it deserves, but impartial
history will allow her none the less the honor of having
given its most brilliant soldier to the Revolution in her
Anthony Wayne. Poor of New Hampshire, is encamped
next, and then Glover, whose regiment of Marblehead
sailors and fishermen manned the boats that saved the
army on the night of the retreat from Long Island.
Learned, Patterson, and Weedon follow, and then at the
corner of the entrenchments by the river is the Virginian
brigade of Muhlenberg. Born at the Trappe, close by,
and educated abroad, Muhlenberg was a clergyman in Virginia when the war came on, but he has doffed his parson's
gown forever for the buff and blue of a brigadier. His
stalwart form and swarthy face are already as familiar to
the enemy as they are to his own men, for the Hessians are
said to have cried, "Hier kommt Teufel Pete!"* as they
saw him lead a charge at Brandywine. The last brigade is
stationed on the river bank, where Varnum and his Rhode
Islanders, in sympathy with young Laurens, of Carolina,
are busy with a scheme to raise and enlist regiments of

---

* Greene's Life of Greene, vol. i. p. 452.

22

negro troops.* These are the commanders of brigades. The major-generals are seven. Portly William Alexander, of New Jersey, who claims to be the Earl of Stirling, but can fight for a republic bravely, nevertheless; swarthy John Sullivan, of New Hampshire, a little headstrong, but brave as a lion; Steuben, the Prussian martinet, who has just come to teach the army; De Kalb—self-sacrificing and generous De Kalb—whose honest breast shall soon bear eleven mortal wounds, received in the service of America; Lafayette, tall, with auburn hair, the French boy of twenty with an old man's head, just recovering from the wounds of Brandywine; and last and greatest of them all, Nathaniel Greene, the Quaker blacksmith from Rhode Island, in all great qualities second only to the Chief himself. Yonder is Henry Knox of the artillery, as brave and faithful as he is big and burly; and the Pole, Pulaski, a man " of hardly middle stature, of sharp countenance and lively air."† Here are the Frenchmen, Du Portail, Dubryson, Duplessis, and Duponceau. Here are Timothy Pickering and Light Horse Harry Lee, destined to be famous in Senate, Cabinet, and field. Here are Henry Dearborn and William Hull, whose paths in life shall one day cross again, and John Laurens and Tench Tilghman, those models of accomplished manhood, destined so soon to die!

Does that silent boy of twenty, who has just ridden by with a message from Lord Stirling, imagine that one day the doctrine which shall keep the American continent free from the touch of European politics shall be forever associated with the name of James Monroe? Does yonder tall,

---

* Correspondence of John Laurens, p. 108. Historical Research respecting Negroes as Slaves, Citizens, and as Soldiers, Livermore, p. 151.

† Waldo, Historical Magazine, vol. v. p. 171.

awkward youth in the Third Virginia, who bore a musket
so gallantly at Brandywine, dream as he lies there shiver-
ing in his little hut on the slopes of Mount Joy that in the
not distant future it is he that shall build up the jurispru-
dence of a people, and after a life of usefulness and honor
bequeath to them in the fame of John Marshall the precious
example of a great and upright Judge? Two other youths
are here—both of small stature and lithe, active frame—of
the same rank and almost the same age, whose ambitious
eyes alike look forward already to fame and power in law
and politics.   But not even his own aspiring spirit can foretell the splendid rise, the dizzy elevation and the sudden
fall of Aaron Burr—nor can the other foresee that the time
will never come when his countrymen will cease to admire
the genius and lament the fate of Alexander Hamilton!

And what shall I say of him who bears on his heart the
weight of all? Who can measure the anxieties that afflict
his mind? Who weigh the burdens that he has to bear?
Who but himself can ever know the responsibilities that rest
upon his soul? Behold him in yonder cottage, his lamp
burning steadily through half the winter night, his brain
never at rest, his hand always busy, his pen ever at work;
now counselling with Greene how to clothe and feed the
troops, or with Steuben how to reorganize the service; now
writing to Howe about exchanges, or to Livingston about
the relief of prisoners, or to Clinton about supplies, or to
Congress about enlistments or promotions or finances or the
French Alliance; opposing foolish and rash counsels to-day,
urging prompt and rigorous policies to-morrow; now calm-
ing the jealousy of Congress, now soothing the wounded
pride of ill-used officers; now answering the complaints of
the civil authority, and now those of the starving soldiers,
whose sufferings he shares, and by his cheerful courage

keeping up the hearts of both; repressing the zeal of friends to-day, and overcoming with steadfast rectitude the intrigues of enemies in Congress and in camp to-morrow; bearing criticism with patience, and calumny with fortitude, and, lest his country should suffer, answering both only with plans for her defence, of which others are to reap the glory; guarding the long coast with ceaseless vigilance, and watching with sleepless eye a chance to strike the enemy in front a blow; a soldier subordinating the military to the civil power; a dictator, as mindful of the rights of Tories as of the wrongs of Whigs; a statesman, commanding a revolutionary army; a patriot, forgetful of nothing but himself; this is he whose extraordinary virtues only have kept the army from disbanding, and saved his country's cause. Modest in the midst of Pride; Wise in the midst of Folly; Calm in the midst of Passion; Cheerful in the midst of Gloom; Steadfast among the Wavering; Hopeful among the Despondent; Bold among the Timid; Prudent among the Rash; Generous among the Selfish; True among the Faithless; Greatest among good men, and Best among the Great—such was George Washington at Valley Forge.

But the darkest hour of night is just before the day. In the middle of February Washington described the dreadful situation of the army and "the miserable prospects before it" as "more alarming" than can possibly be conceived, and as occasioning him more distress "than he had felt"* since the commencement of the war. On the 23d of February, he whom we call Baron Steuben, rode into camp;† on the 6th Franklin signed the Treaty of Alliance at Versailles.

Frederick William Augustus Baron von Steuben was a native of Magdeburg, in Prussia. Trained from early life

---

* Sparks, vol. v. p. 239.   † Kapp's Life of Steuben, p. 104.

to arms, he had been Aide to the Great Frederick, Lieuten-
ant-General to the Prince of Baden, Grand Marshal at the
Court of one of the Hohenzollerns, and a Canon of the
Church. A skilful soldier, a thorough disciplinarian, a
gentleman of polished manners, a man of warm and generous heart, he had come in the prime of life and vigor to
offer his services to the American people. None could have
been more needed or more valuable at the time. Congress
sent him to the camp, Washington quickly discerned his
worth, and in a little time he was made Major-General and
Inspector of the Army. In an instant there was a change
in that department. A discipline unknown before took
possession of the camp. Beginning with a picked company
of one hundred and twenty men, the Baron drilled them
carefully, himself on foot and musket in hand. These,
when they became proficient, he made a model for others,
and presently the whole camp had become a military school.
Rising at three in the morning, he smoked a single pipe
while his servant dressed his hair, drank one cup of coffee,
and, with his star of knighthood gleaming on his breast,
was on horseback at sunrise, and, with or without his suite,
galloped to the parade. There all day he drilled the men,
and at nightfall galloped back to the hut in which he made
his quarters, to draw up regulations and draft instructions
for the inspectors under him.* And thus day after day,
patient, careful, laborious, and persevering, in a few months
he transformed this untrained yeomanry into a disciplined
and effective army. There have been more brilliant services rendered to America than these, but few perhaps more
valuable and worthier of remembrance. Knight of the
Order of Fidelity, there have been more illustrious names

* Kapp's Life of Steuben, p. 130.

than thine upon our lips to-day.   Like many another who
labored for us, our busy age has seemed to pass thee by.
But here, at least, when, after a Century, Americans gather
to review their Country's history, shall they recall thy unselfish services with gratitude and thy memory with honor!

And surely at Valley Forge we must not forget what
Franklin was doing for his country's cause in France.   It
was a happy thing for the Republican Idea that it had a
distant continent for the place of its experiment.   It was a
fortunate thing for America that between her and her
nearest European neighbor lay a thousand leagues of sea.
That distance—a very different matter from what it is to-
day—made it at the same time difficult for England to
overcome us, and safe for France to lend us aid.   From an
early period this alliance seemed to have been considered by
the Cabinet of France.   For several years secret negotiations
had been going on, and in the fall of 1777 they became
open and distinct, and the representatives of both nations
came face to face.   There was no sympathy between weak
and feeble Louis and his crafty Ministers on the one side
and the representatives of Democracy and Rebellion on the
other; nor had France any hopes of regaining her foothold
on this Continent.   The desire of her rulers was simply to
humiliate and injure England, and the revolution in America seemed to offer the chance.   Doubtless they were influenced by the fact that the cause of America had become
very popular with all classes of the French people, impressed to a remarkable degree with the character of Dr.
Franklin, and stirred by the contagious and generous example of Lafayette.   Nor was this popular feeling merely
temporary or without foundation.   Long familiar as he
had been with despotism in both politics and religion, the
Frenchman still retained within him a certain spirit of

liberty which was stronger than he knew. His sympathies naturally went out toward a distant people engaged in a gallant struggle against his hereditary enemies, the English; but besides all that, there was in his heart something, he hardly knew what, that vibrated at the thought of a freedom for others which he had hardly dreamed of and never known. Little did he or any of his rulers foresee what that something was. Little did France imagine, as she blew into a flame the spark of Liberty beyond the sea, that there was that within her own dominions which in eleven years, catching the divine fire from the glowing West, would set herself and Europe in a blaze! Accordingly, after much doubt, delay, and intrigue, during which Franklin bore himself with rare ability and tact, Treaties of Amity, Commerce, and Alliance were prepared and signed. The Independence of America was acknowledged and made the basis of alliance, and it was mutually agreed that neither nation should lay down its arms until England had conceded it. A fleet, an army, and munitions were promised by the King, and, as a consequence, war was at once declared against Great Britain.

We are accustomed to regard this as the turning-point in the Revolutionary struggle. And so it was. But neither the fleet of France nor her armies, gallant as they were, nor the supplies and means with which she furnished us, were as valuable to the cause of the struggling country as the moral effect, at home as well as abroad, of the Alliance. Hopes that were built upon the skill of French sailors were soon dispelled, the expectations of large contingent armies were not to be fulfilled, but the news of the French Alliance carried into every patriotic heart an assurance that never left it afterward and kept aroused a spirit that henceforward grew stronger every year. Says the historian

Bancroft: "The benefit then conferred on the United States was priceless." And "so the flags of France and the United States went together into the field against Great Britain, unsupported by any other government, yet with the good wishes of all the peoples of Europe."* And thus illustrious Franklin, the Philadelphia printer, earned the magnificent compliment that was paid him in the French Academy: "Eripuit fulmen cœlo, sceptrumque tyrannis."

And all the while, unconscious of the event, the winter days at Valley Forge dragged by, one after another, with sleet and slush and snow, with storms of wind, and ice and beating rain. The light-horse scoured the country, the pickets watched, the sentinels paced up and down, the men drilled and practised, and starved and froze and suffered, and at last the spring-time came, and with it stirring news. Greene was appointed Quartermaster-General on the 23d of March, and under his skilful management relief and succor came. The Conciliatory Bills, offering all but independence, were received in April, and instantly rejected by Congress, under the stirring influence of a letter from Washington, declaring with earnestness that "nothing short of independence would do," and at last, on the 4th of May, at eleven o'clock at night, the news of the French treaty reached the Head-Quarters.

On the 6th, by general orders, the army, after appropriate religious services, was drawn up under arms, salutes were fired with cannon and musketry, cheers given by the soldiers for the King of France and the American States, and a banquet by the General-in-Chief to all the officers, in the open air, completed a day devoted to rejoicing.† "And all

---

* History of the United States, vol. ix. pp. 505–6.
† Correspondence of John Laurens, p. 169.

the while," says the English satirist, "Howe left the famous camp of Valley Forge untouched, whilst his great, brave, and perfectly appointed army, fiddled and gambled and feasted in Philadelphia. And by Byng's countrymen triumphal arches were erected, tournaments were held in pleasant mockery of the Middle Ages, and wreaths and garlands offered by beautiful ladies to this clement chief, with fantastical mottoes and poesies announcing that his laurels should be immortal."* On the 18th of May (the day of that famous festivity) Lafayette took post at Barren Hill, from which he escaped so brilliantly two days afterwards. At last, on the 18th of June, George Roberts,† of Philadelphia, came galloping up the Gulf Road covered with dust and sweat, with the news that the British had evacuated Philadelphia. Six brigades were at once in motion—the rest of the army prepared to follow with all possible despatch early on the 19th. The bridge across the Schuylkill was laden with tramping troops. Cannon rumbled rapidly down the road to the river. The scanty baggage was packed, the flag at Head-Quarters taken down, the last brigade descended the river bank, the huts were empty, the breastworks deserted, the army was off for Monmouth, and the hills of Valley Forge were left alone with their glory and their dead. The last foreign foe had left the soil of Pennsylvania forever. Yes, the last foreign foe! Who could foretell the mysteries of the future? Who foresee the trials that were yet to come? Little did the sons of New England and the South, who starved and froze and died here in the snow together, think, as their eyes beheld for the last time the little flag that meant for them a com-

---

* Thackeray's Virginians, chap. xci.
† Sparks's Writings of Washington, vol. v. p. 409.

mon country, that the time would come when, amid sound of cannon, their children, met again on Pennsylvania soil, would confront each other in the splendid agony of battle! Sorrow was their portion, but it was not given them to suffer this. It was theirs to die in the gloomiest period of their country's history, but certain that her salvation was assured. It was theirs to go down into the grave rejoicing in the belief that their lives were sacrifice enough, blessedly unconscious that the Liberty for which they struggled demanded that three hundred thousand of their children should with equal courage and devotion lay down their lives in its defence. Happy alike they who died before that time and we who have survived it! And, thank God this day, that its shadow has passed away forever. The sins of the fathers, visited upon the children, have been washed away in blood—the sacrifice has been accepted— the expiation has been complete. The men of North and South whose bones moulder on these historic hillsides did not die in vain. The institutions which they gave us we preserve—the Freedom for which they fought is still our birthright—the flag under which they died floats above our heads on this anniversary, the emblem of a redeemed, regenerate, reunited country. The union of those States still stands secure. Enemies within and foes without have failed to break it, and the spirit of faction, from whatever quarter or in whatever cause, can no more burst its holy bonds asunder, than can we separate in this sacred soil the dust of Massachusetts and that of Carolina from that Pennsylvania dust in whose embrace it has slumbered for a century, and with which it must forever be indistinguishably mingled!

Such, then, is the history of this famous place. To my mind it has a glory all its own! The actions which have made it famous stand by themselves. It is not simply because they were heroic. Brave deeds have sanctified innumerable places in every land. The men of our revolution were not more brave than their French allies, or their German cousins, or their English brethren. Courage belongs alike to all men. Nor were they the only men in history who suffered. Others have borne trial as bravely, endured with the same patience, died with as perfect a devotion. But it is not given to all men to die in the best of causes or win the greatest victories. It was the rare fortune of those who were assembled here a hundred years ago that, having in their keeping the most momentous things that were ever intrusted to a people, they were at once both faithful and victorious. The army that was encamped here was but a handful, but what host ever defended so much? And what spot of Earth has had a farther reaching and happier influence on the Human Race than this?

Is it that which the traveller beholds when from Pentelicus he looks down on Marathon? The life of Athens was short, and the Liberty which was saved on that immortal field she gave up ingloriously more than twenty centuries ago. The tyranny she resisted so gallantly from without, she practised cruelly at home. The sword which she wielded so well in her own defence she turned as readily against her children. Her civilization, brilliant as it was, was narrow and her spirit selfish. The boundaries of her tiny state were larger than her heart, whose sympathy could not include more than a part of her own kindred. Her aspirations were pent up in herself, and she stands in history to-day a prodigy of short-lived splendor—a warning rather than example.

Is it any one of those, where the men of the Forest Cantons fell on the invader like an avalanche from their native Alps and crushed him out of existence? The bravery of the Swiss achieved only a sterile independence, which his native mountains defended as well as he, and he tarnished his glory forever when the sword of Morgarten was hawked about the courts of Europe, and the victor of Grandson and Morat sold himself to the foreign shambles of the highest bidder.

Or is it that still more famous field, where the Belgian lion keeps guard over the dead of three great nations? There, three and sixty years ago yesterday, the armies of Europe met in conflict. It was the war of giants. On the one side England, the first power of the age, flushed with victory, of inexhaustible resources, redoubtable by land and invincible by sea; and Prussia, vigorous by nature, stronger by adversity, hardened by suffering, full of bitter memories and hungry for revenge; and, on the other, France, once mistress of the Continent, the arbiter of nations, the conqueror of Wagram and Marengo and Friedland and Austerlitz—spent at last in her own service, crushed rather by the weight of her victories than by the power of her enemies' arm—turning in her bloody footsteps, like a wounded lion, to spring with redoubled fury at the throat of her pursuers. Behold the conflict as it raged through the long June day, while all the world listened and held its breath !

The long lines of red, the advancing columns of blue, the glitter of burnished steel, the roll of drums, the clangor of trumpets, the cheering of men, the fierce attack, the stubborn resistance, the slow recoil, the rattle of musketry, the renewed assault, the crash of arms, the roar of cannons, the clatter of the charging cavalry, the cries of the combatants, the clash of sabres, the shrieks of the dying, the confused retreat, the gallant rally, the final charge, the sickening repulse, the last struggle, the shouts of the victors, the screams of the vanquished, the wild confusion, the blinding smoke, the awful uproar, the unspeakable rout, the furious pursuit, the sounds dying in the distance, the groans of the wounded, the fall of the summer rain, the sighing of the evening breeze, the solemn silence of the night. Climb the steps that lead to the summit of the mound that marks that place to-day. There is no spot in Europe more famous than the field beneath your feet. In outward aspect it is not unlike this which we behold here. The hills are not so high nor the valleys so deep, but the general effect of field and farm, of ripening grain and emerald woodland, is much the same. It has not been changed. There is the chateau of Hougomont on the west and the forest through which the Prussians came on the east; on yonder hill the Emperor watched the battle; beneath you Ney made the last of many charges —the world knows it all by heart. The traveller of every race turns toward it his footsteps. It is the most celebrated battle-field of Europe and of modern times.

But what did that great victory accomplish? It broke the power of one nation and asserted the independence of the rest. It took from France an Emperor and gave her back a King, a ruler whom she had rejected in place of one whom she had chosen, a Bourbon for a Bonaparte, a King by divine right for an Emperor by the people's will. It revenged the memory of Jena and Corunna, and broke the spell that made the fated name Napoleon the bond of an empire almost universal; it struck down one great man and fixed a dozen small ones on the neck of Europe. But what did it bequeath to us besides the ever-precious example of heroic deeds? Nothing. What did they who conquered there achieve? Fame for themselves, Woe for the vanquished, Glory for England, Revenge for Prussia, Shame for France, nothing for Humanity, nothing for Liberty. Nothing for Civilization, nothing for the Rights of Man.

One of the great Englishmen of that day declared that it had turned back the hands of the dial of the World's progress for fifty years. And, said an English poetess:—

"The Kings crept out again to feel the sun.

The Kings crept out—the peoples sat at home,
And finding the long invocated peace
A pall embroidered with worn images
Of rights divine, too scant to cover doom
Such as they suffered,—curst the corn that grew
Rankly, to bitter bread, on Waterloo."

My countrymen: For a century the eyes of struggling nations have turned toward this spot, and lips in every language have blessed the memory of Valley Forge! The tide of battle never ebbed and flowed upon these banks. These hills never trembled beneath the tread of charging squadrons nor echoed the thunders of contending cannon. The blood that stained this ground did not rush forth in the joyous frenzy of the fight; it fell drop by drop from the heart of a suffering people. They who once encamped here in the snow fought not for conquest, not for power, not for glory, not for their country only, not for themselves alone. They served here for Posterity; they suffered here for the Human Race; they bore here the cross of all the peoples; they died here that Freedom might be the heritage of all. It was Humanity which they defended; it was Liberty herself that they had in keeping. She that was sought in the wilderness and mourned for by the waters of Babylon—that was saved at Salamis and thrown away at Chæronea; that was fought for at Cannæ and lost forever at Pharsalia and Philippi—she who confronted the Armada on the deck with Howard and rode beside Cromwell on the field of Worcester—for whom the Swiss gathered into his breast the sheaf of spears at Sempach, and the Dutchman broke the dykes of Holland and welcomed in the sea—she of whom Socrates spoke, and Plato wrote, and Brutus dreamed and Homer sung—for whom Eliot pleaded, and Sydney suffered, and Milton prayed, and Hampden fell! Driven by the persecution of centuries from the older world, she had come with Pilgrim and Puritan, and Cavalier and Quaker, to seek a shelter in the new. Attacked once more by her old enemies, she had taken refuge here. Nor she alone. The dream of the Greek, the Hebrew's prophecy, the desire of the Roman, the Italian's prayer, the longing of the German mind, the hope of the French heart, the glory and honor of Old England herself, the yearning of all the centuries, the aspiration of every age, the promise of the Past, the fulfilment of the Future, the seed of the old time, the harvest of the new—all these were with her. And here, in the heart of America, they were safe. The last of many struggles was almost won ; the best of many centuries was about to break ; the time was already come when from these shores the light of a new Civilization should flash across the sea, and from this place a voice of triumph make the Old World tremble, when from her chosen refuge in the West the spirit of Liberty should go forth to meet the Rising Sun and set the people free!

Americans : A hundred years have passed away and that Civilization and that Liberty are still your heritage. But think not that such an inheritance can be kept safe without exertion. It is the burden of your Happiness, that with it Privilege and Duty go hand in hand together. You cannot shirk the Present and enjoy in the Future the blessings of the Past. Yesterday begot To-day, and To-day is the parent of To-morrow. The Old Time may be secure, but the New

Time is uncertain. The dead are safe; it is the privilege of the living to be in peril. A country is benefited by great actions only so long as her children are able to repeat them. The memory of this spot shall be an everlasting honor for our fathers, but we can make it an eternal shame for ourselves if we choose to do so. The glory of Lexington and Bunker Hill and Saratoga and Valley Forge belongs not to you and me, but we can make it ours if we will. It is well for us to keep these anniversaries of great events. It is well for us to meet by thousands on these historic spots. It is well to walk by those unknown graves or follow the windings of the breastworks that encircle yonder hill. It is well for us to gather beneath yon little fort, which the storms of so many winters have tenderly spared to look down on us to-day. It is well to commemorate the past with song and eulogy and pleasant festival—but it is not enough.

If they could return, whose forms have been passing in imagination before our eyes; if in the presence of this holy hour the dead could rise and lips dumb for a century find again a tongue, might they not say to us: You do well, Countrymen, to commemorate this time. You do well to honor those who yielded up their lives in glory here. Theirs was a perfect sacrifice, and the debt you owe them you can never pay. Your lines have fallen in a happier time. The boundaries of your Union stretch from sea to sea. You enjoy all the blessings which Providence can bestow; a peace we never knew; a wealth we never hoped for; a power of which we never dreamed. Yet think not that these things only can make a nation great. We laid the foundations of your happiness in a time of trouble, in days of sorrow and perplexity, of doubt, distress, and danger, of cold and hunger, of suffering and want. We built it up by virtue, by courage, by self-sacrifice, by unfailing patriotism, by unceasing vigilance. By those things alone did we win your liberties; by them only can you hope to keep them. Do you revere our names? Then follow our example. Are you proud of our achievements? Then try to imitate them. Do you honor our memories? Then do as we have done. You yourselves owe something to America, better than all those things which you spread before her with such lavish hand—something which she needs as much in her prosperity to-day, as ever in the sharpest crisis of her fate! For you have duties to perform as well as we. It was ours to create; it is yours to preserve. It was ours to found; it is yours to perpetuate. It was ours to organize; it is yours to purify! And what nobler spectacle can you present to mankind to-day, than that of a people honest, steadfast, and secure—mindful of the lessons of experience —true to the teachings of history—led by the loftiest ex-amples and bound together to protect their institutions at the close of the Century, as their fathers were to win them at the beginning, by the ties of "Virtue, Honor, and Love of Country"—by that Virtue which makes perfect the happiness of a people—by that Honor which constitutes the chief greatness of a State—by that Patriotism which survives all things, braves all things, endures all things, achieves all things—and which, though it find a refuge no-where else, should live in the heart of every true American!

My Countrymen: the century that has gone by has changed the face of Nature and wrought a revolution in the habits of mankind. We to-day behold the dawn of an extraordinary age. Freed from the chains of ancient thought and superstition, man has begun to win the most extraordinary victories in the domain of Science. One by one he has dispelled the doubts of the ancient world.

Nothing is too difficult for his hand to attempt—no region too remote—no place too sacred for his daring eye to penetrate. He has robbed the Earth of her secrets and sought to solve the mysteries of the Heavens! He has secured and chained to his service the elemental forces of Nature—he has made the fire his steed—the winds his ministers—the seas his pathway—the lightning his messenger. He has descended into the bowels of the Earth and walked in safety on the bottom of the sea. He has raised his head above the clouds and made the impalpable air his resting-place. He has tried to analyze the stars, count the constellations, and weigh the Sun. He has advanced with such astounding speed that, breathless, we have reached a moment when it seems as if distance had been annihilated, time made as naught, the invisible seen, the inaudible heard, the unspeakable spoken, the intangible felt, the impossible accomplished. And already we knock at the door of a new century which promises to be infinitely brighter and more enlightened and happier than this. But in all this blaze of light which illuminates the present and casts its reflection into the distant recesses of the past, there is not a single ray that shoots into the Future. Not one step have we taken toward the solution of the mystery of Life. That remains to-day as dark and unfathomable as it was ten thousand years ago.

We know that we are more fortunate than our fathers. We believe that our children shall be happier than we. We know that this century is more enlightened than the last. We hope that the time to come will be better and more glorious than this. We think, we believe, we hope, but we do not know. Across that threshold we may not pass; behind that veil we may not penetrate. Into that country it may not be for us to go. It may be vouchsafed to us to behold it, wonderingly, from afar, but never to enter in. It matters not. The age in which we live is but a link in the endless and eternal chain. Our lives are like the sands upon the shore; our voices like the breath of this summer breeze that stirs the leaf for a moment and is forgotten. Whence we have come and whither we shall go not one of us can tell. And the last survivor of this mighty multitude shall stay but a little while.

But in the impenetrable To Be, the endless generations are advancing to take our places as we fall. For them as for us shall the Earth roll on and the seasons come and go, the snowflakes fall, the flowers bloom, and the harvests be gathered in. For them as for us shall the Sun, like the life of man, rise out of darkness in the morning and sink into darkness in the night. For them as for us shall the years march by in the sublime procession of the ages. And here, in this place of Sacrifice, in this vale of Humiliation, in this valley of the Shadow of that Death, out of which the Life of America rose, regenerate and free, let us believe with an abiding faith, that to them Union will seem as dear and Liberty as sweet and Progress as glorious as they were to our fathers and are to you and me, and that the Institutions which have made us happy, preserved by the virtue of our children, shall bless the remotest generations of the time to come. And unto Him, who holds in the hollow of His hand the fate of nations, and yet marks the sparrow's fall, let us lift up our hearts this day, and into His eternal care commend ourselves, our children, and our country.

ORATION

COMPOSED TO BE DELIVERED AT

FREEHOLD, NEW JERSEY, JUNE 28, 1878,

THE ONE HUNDREDTH ANNIVERSARY

OF THE

BATTLE OF MONMOUTH.

ORATION.

It is your fortune, men of Monmouth, to dwell upon historic ground. Yonder by the sea are the hills on which Hendrik Hudson gazed before he beheld the great river which still bears his name. Around you are the towns and villages whose settlements recall the days of Carteret and Berkeley. The name of your pleasant country takes the imagination back to the gay court of Charles the Second and his favorite and ill-fated son—and year after year you gather the ripened grain from one of the most famous fields in the long fight for Liberty. Your sires were a patriotic race. When the struggle with Great Britain had begun and the gallant town of Boston lay suffering and in chains, the men of Monmouth County sent on October 12, 1774, twelve hundred bushels of rye and fifty barrels of rye meal to their suffering brethren, with a letter in which I find these words: "We rely under God upon the firmness and resolution of your people, and earnestly hope they will never think of receding from the glorious ground they stand upon while the blood of Freedom runs in their veins."* So wrote the Jerseymen of Monmouth in the beginning of the trouble, and when the war broke out they

---

* Collections of Massachusetts Historical Society, 4th Series, vol. iv. p. 110.

did not wait for their enemy to come, but armed themselves and went to meet him.

Sons of such sires, in full enjoyment of all they gained for you, you can celebrate with a light heart to-day, the 28th of June. The glory of that day belongs to all your countrymen alike, but the place that witnessed it belongs to you. The place—the time—this inspiring throng, would stir colder blood than his who speaks to you; and even if all else were calm within me, here and now I must still feel tingling within my veins the drops of blood which I inherit from one whose patriotic heart boiled within him at the hedgerow on the Parsonage farm an hundred years ago. And I must not forget that my duty is chiefly introductory. My task to-day is to describe the battle. It is hard to describe a fight, especially one so full of strange and contradictory stories, nor is it easy to cram into an hour's speech the deeds of a day so long and glorious. With me you shall fight that battle over again. Others shall follow me to charm you with their eloquence, but for the hour that I stand here to-day, the Battle of Monmouth shall be the orator. I pray you, then, my countrymen, to listen, and to give me your attention and your patience.

The British and American armies during the winter of 1777–78 presented the most extraordinary contrast in military history. The troops of Washington were encamped in huts at Valley Forge, without clothes, or shoes, or blankets, and some of the time without food even of the simplest kind. The army of Howe lay snugly ensconced in Philadelphia, protected by strong entrenchments, thoroughly equipped, well fed, well clothed, and in direct communication with New York and England. At one time the hardships of the winter had reduced the Americans from eleven or twelve thousand to five thousand and twelve men.

The British marched into Philadelphia with more than nineteen thousand, and at no time had less than twelve ready for the field.* "Two marches on the fine Lancaster road," said Lafayette, " by establishing the English in the rear of" the American " right flank, would have rendered their position untenable, from which, however, they had no means of retiring. The unfortunate soldiers were in want of everything. . . . From want of money they could neither obtain provisions nor any means of transport." They " frequently remained whole days without" food. " The sight of their misery prevented new engagements—it was almost impossible to levy recruits."† From December till the middle of March their situation continued to be desperate, and at any time during that period resistance to a vigorous attack by Sir William Howe would have been impossible. But that which rendered their sufferings so severe, protected them. The weather was extremely cold, the ice immensely thick, the highways blocked with snow. Philadelphia furnished attractive quarters—it would be as easy to disperse the rebels next week as to-morrow. They had been often beaten in the field, and could be at any time—their submission was simply a question of a few months—it would be best to wait till spring. So reasoned the English commander, and the opportunity slipped by forever. Little did he understand the value to the rebels of those winter days. Little did he know while his officers feasted and gambled and rioted in Philadelphia, that yonder up the Schuylkill those ragged, half-starved rebels were drilling and practising and growing into an effective and veteran army. January and February

---

* In March, 1778, they were nineteen thousand five hundred and thirty strong. *Vide* Sparks, vol. v. p. 542.

† Memoirs of Lafayette, vol. i. p. 35.

went by while the British were amusing themselves and the Americans working hard; March and April came and went, and still there were feasting and frolic in Philadelphia, and fasting and labor at Valley Forge. But the change had come. Greene had been appointed Quartermaster, Steuben Inspector, the intrigues of Mr. Conway and his friends been exposed and brought to naught, the last attempt at conciliation without independence had been rejected by the Congress, and with the early days of May had arrived the news of the alliance of America and France. It was a rude awakening for the British army after its winter's debauch to find itself master solely of the ground it occupied, the King respected only where his army was— the rebels stronger and better disciplined than ever, and encouraged by the news from Europe that seemed to loyal ears so distressing. The campaign of 1777 had accomplished nothing—the victories of Howe had been fruitless —the defeats of Burgoyne disastrous—the winter in the rebel capital fatal to the royal cause. Not one prediction of loyal prophets had come true. Defeat had neither disheartened nor destroyed the rebel army—the loss of the capital had transferred to a distant village instead of dispersing the Continental Congress—the power of the Rebellion remained unbroken, its heart alive, its limbs more vigorous than ever. In a word, Philadelphia had proved a second Capua, and the saying of shrewd Franklin had come true: "Sir William Howe had not taken Philadelphia—Philadelphia had taken Sir William Howe."*

The announcement of the treaty between France and the Americans, followed by the news of a declaration of war

---

* Parton's Life of Franklin, vol. ii. p. 281. There quoted from Bowring's Bentham, vol. x. p. 527.

against Great Britain, was of sinister importance to the British in Philadelphia. Threatened by a hostile army, and surrounded as they were by an enemy's country, a French fleet at the mouth of the Delaware would put them in great peril. The time for conquest had gone by; it had become now a question of escape and safety. The season was too far advanced for an attack on the camp at Valley Forge. The army of Washington had been largely increased, and his naturally strong position strengthened since the winter ceased. The country swarmed with scouts and partisans and spies. The vigilance of the Americans was untiring: McLane and Harry Lee kept the neighborhood of the city in constant agitation—the banks of the Delaware might at any time intercept the shipping—the French fleet would perhaps soon arrive—to remain in Philadelphia would increase the danger. What was to be done? An escape to New York across the Jerseys seemed the only chance, and the sooner that was attempted the better. On the 11th of May, Howe announced to the army his departure for Europe and the appointment of Sir Henry Clinton to the command.* On the 14th it was ordered that the heavy baggage should be made ready.† On the 20th the "several corps were directed to put on board their transports every kind of baggage they could possibly do without in the field,"‡ and five days later—"to send on board their baggage-ships the women and children and the men actually unfit to march."§ The preparations for departure were rapidly and well made, and on the 17th of

---

* Manuscript Orderly Book of the British Army found on the field of Monmouth. A transcript is in the Library of the Historical Society of Pennsylvania.

† Ibid.   ‡ Ibid.   § Ibid.

June, at four in the morning, Lieutenant-General Knyphausen and General Grant crossed the river with a large division and all the wagons and baggage.* At daybreak on the 18th the remainder of the army followed them. The departure was hurried and almost noiseless.† The troops marched down toward League Island and were ferried over to Gloucester Point. "They did not go away," wrote an eye-witness, " they vanished."‡ It must have seemed so to some of them who came near being left behind. The Hon. Cosmo Gordon, on that memorable morning, rose for an instant into the notice of posterity, as he sprang out of bed, belated, and hurried to the wharf in search of a boat to take him into Jersey. Hardly had he found one and started for the other side when Allen McLane's light-horsemen came galloping into town.§ That night the British army encamped at Haddonfield.|| It consisted of about fourteen thousand men. A few of the Hessians, the sick, the camp-followers, and the Tory refugees, of whom there were a number, had embarked on the ships in the river destined for New York. Notwithstanding the strict and repeated orders to the contrary, the camp-followers were numerous, and the train of baggage nearly twelve miles long.¶ On the morning of the 19th Clinton moved with three brigades to Evesham, eight miles from Haddonfield,

* Manuscript Orderly Book, *supra*, p. 355.

† Bell's Journal: New Jersey Historical Society's Proceedings, vol. vi. p. 15.

‡ Du Simitiere to Colonel Lamb. *Vide* Life of John Lamb, p. 213.

§ Recollections of a Lady: Watson's Annals of Philadelphia, vol. ii. p. 286.

|| Bell's Journal: New Jersey Historical Society's Proceedings, vol. vi. p. 15.

¶ Clinton's Letter to Lord George Germaine: Lee Papers, vol. ii. p. 463.

Leslie commanding the advance, and Knyphausen following
with the Hessians and two brigades of British.* The
country had by this time become alarmed. The militia
had sprung to arms in all quarters of the State. Familiar
as they had been with the presence of the enemy from the
beginning of the war, the Jerseymen had become proficient
in partisan warfare. The State was thoroughly patriotic.
It had suffered more perhaps than any other from the dep-
redations of the enemy. Beginning in 1776, the armies
had crossed and re-crossed from the Hudson to the Delaware, and at no period of the struggle was the soil of New
Jersey destined to be free from the irruptions of the British. The wise and patriotic Livingston, who was then the
governor, had foreseen the danger of a new invasion, and
prepared to meet it, and the tramp of Clinton's army was
the signal at which the armed yeomen sprung as it were out
of the very ground. Philemon Dickinson, of Trenton,
their commander, prepared to harass the enemy at every
point, and detached bodies were ordered to break the
bridges in their way and hang upon their flanks and rear.
Hardly had the advance-guard left Haddonfield, on the
19th, before it was attacked by a body of militia, and a
sharp skirmish followed.† On the 20th Clinton reached
Mount Holly,‡ on the 22d the Black Horse, seven miles
farther on.§ At five in the morning of the 23d he moved
to Crosswicks.|| A lively skirmish delayed him at the
bridge across the creek; but the next day he arrived at
Allentown.¶ Up to this point the British commander
had been uncertain whether to push to New York by the
way of Brunswick, or turn eastward and seek the protection

* Bell's Journal: New Jersey Historical Society's Proceedings,
vol. vi. p. 15.

  † Ibid.   ‡ Ibid.   § Ibid., p. 16. || Ibid.   ¶ Ibid.

of the fleet at Sandy Hook. The information which he gained at Crosswicks decided him. The whole American army had crossed the Delaware and was advancing in his front.*

Washington had lost no time. Convinced that the British would soon evacuate Philadelphia and try to cross the Jerseys,† he had issued orders to prepare for the contingency nearly three weeks before. For the past fortnight he had had everything in readiness.‡ On the 18th of June, at eleven A.M., the news reached him that the enemy had gone.§ At three o'clock Charles Lee, with Poor's, Huntington's, and Varnum's brigades, crossed the Schuylkill in full march for Coryell's Ferry, and at five Wayne followed with three brigades of Pennsylvanians.‖ The Jersey brigade of Maxwell had already been ordered to join General Dickinson and co-operate in his efforts to detain the enemy.¶ On the 19th Washington followed with the whole army.** The heat was intolerable, the weather rainy, and the roads bad.†† It was not until the 21st that the army was safely over the river and encamped in Jersey.‡‡ The British were approaching Crosswicks. The country was alive with rumors and excitement. The enemy were reported to be in force, with

---

* Clinton's Letter to Lord George Germaine. *Vide* Lee Papers, vol. ii. p. 462.

† Sparks's Washington, vol. v. pp. 374, 376, 380, 381, 387.

‡ Lee Papers, vol. ii. pp. 406–408.

§ Sparks's Washington, vol. v. p. 409.

‖ Diary of Joseph Clark: New Jersey Historical Society's Proceedings, vol. vii. p. 106.

¶ Sparks's Washington, vol. v. pp. 386–7.

** Washington to his brother: Ibid., p. 431.

†† Washington to President of Congress, June 28, 1778: Ibid., p. 420.

‡‡ Washington to his brother: Ibid., p. 431.

an immense baggage-train and a host of followers, who committed all sorts of depredations as they marched.* Accounts of plundered farms and burned homesteads came thick and fast. Their slow advance led Washington to think that they wished a general action and sought to draw him into the low country to the south and east. Detaching Morgan with six hundred men to reinforce Maxwell and watch them close at hand, he marched to Hopewell, where he remained until the 25th.† Summoning a council of war, he put the question whether a battle should be fought. Greene, Lafayette, Du Portail, and Wayne urged, as one of them has told us, "that it would be disgraceful and humiliating to allow the enemy to cross the Jerseys in tranquillity"‡—that his rear might be attacked without serious risk, and that he ought to be followed closely, and advantage taken of the first favorable opportunity to attack him. But the majority held other views.§ It was argued that much was to be lost by defeat and little gained by victory. That the French alliance insured the final triumph of the cause, and it would only be a risk to attempt a battle with the British army, which several declared had never been so excellent or so well disciplined. This view prevailed chiefly because of the earnest eloquence and great reputation of him who urged it on the council.|| Charles Lee, the second in command, was a native of England, and about forty-seven years of age. An ensign in the British army at twelve, he had risen to be lieutenant-colonel. He had served in the old French war, and in Portugal against the Spanish, and at

---

* See letter in "Pennsylvania Packet" of July 14, 1778.

† Sparks's Washington, vol. v. p. 422.

‡ Memoirs of Lafayette, vol. i. p. 51.   § Ibid.

|| Ibid., p. 50. Also Sparks, vol. v. p. 552.

one time had been a major-general in the Polish service. Of unquestioned bravery, he had distinguished himself by several exploits, which his excessive vanity would not suffer to be forgotten. Taken at his own estimation rather than at his real value, as such a man is apt to be, he had won without a stroke of his sword the most exaggerated reputation among the Americans for military genius and experience. A soldier of fortune, he cared little at heart for the principles for which the colonies were contending, as the selfish terms on which he entered their employment showed, but he had rendered the cause essential service, and enjoyed a reputation second only to that of Washington. Indeed, there were many who, a little while before, would have been glad to have seen the names reversed, and some who still felt with an anonymous writer, when at the moment that Washington's virtues were keeping the army together at Valley Forge, he cried for "a Gates, a Lee, or a Conway." Accustomed to be revered as an authority, Lee spoke with earnestness and even eloquence. He had lately returned from more than a year's captivity. He was acquainted with the character of Clinton. He knew the efficiency of the British army—he had had great experience in war. His courage was known, his character trusted, his fidelity unquestioned, his arguments ingenious, his language eloquent. His views prevailed, and it was decided only to harass the enemy. Charles Scott of Virginia was sent forward to join Dickinson, and the army marched to Kingston.* But after the council had dissolved Hamilton, Lafayette, and Greene urged more vigorous measures; some of the others changed their minds—the chief himself inclined to run the risk, and it was decided to seek battle.†

* Sparks's Washington, vol. v. p. 423.
† Memoirs of Lafayette, vol. i. p. 51.

Accordingly, on the 25th, three thousand men were ordered to join Scott and approach the enemy.* The command of this body naturally belonged to Lee. But disgusted at the altered plan, that officer declined to undertake it, and it was given to Lafayette. Hardly had the latter marched, however, when Lee changed his mind. The detachment was a separate command—he would be criticised if he allowed a junior to assume it—he besought Washington to let him have it after all.† Disturbed by this and anxious not to wound Lafayette, the Commander-in-Chief settled the difficulty by giving Lee a thousand men, with orders to overtake the former, when his seniority would give him command of the whole.‡

This was on the 26th of June. On the morning before, the British march at five o'clock had revealed what Sir Henry Clinton had decided to do. Finding Washington approaching, he turned eastward and made for Sandy Hook. Sending the baggage forward under Knyphausen, he followed slowly with the main part of his army.§ On the 27th he encamped at Monmouth Court-House.|| Meantime the Americans had not been idle. All the way from Crosswicks, Dickinson and Morgan had hung upon the British flanks.¶ The main American army had been detained at Cranberry by rain, and the advance retarded by want of provisions (Wayne's detachment obliged to halt at mid-day

---

* Lee Papers, vol. ii. p. 413. Also Lafayette's Memoirs, vol. i. p. 51.

† Lee Papers, vol. ii. p. 417.

‡ Sparks, vol. v. pp. 418–19.

§ Clinton to Lord George Germaine. *Vide* Lee Papers, vol. ii. p. 462.

|| Manuscript Orderly Book.

¶ Washington to President of Congress. *Vide* Sparks, vol. v. p. 424.

on the 26th because it was "almost starving"),* but on the morning of the 27th Lafayette and Lee effected a junction† between Cranberry and Englishtown. The two armies were now less than five miles apart. It was evident to the commanders of both that the last moment for a battle had arrived. A few miles beyond Monmouth the British would reach the high ground of Middletown, when it would be impossible to cut them off and dangerous to follow.‡ If a blow was to be struck, now or never was the time. The orders of Washington were explicit. On the afternoon of the 27th he sent for Lee and the brigadiers of his command, told them he wished the enemy to be attacked next morning, and desired General Lee to concert with his subordinates some plan of action. Five o'clock was named as the time for a conference, but when the officers called, Lee dismissed them with the remark that it was not possible to make a plan beforehand.§ The advance lay for the night at Englishtown, the main body of the Americans three miles farther to the westward. The British were encamped along the road, their right resting on the forks of the roads to Middletown and Shrewsbury, the baggage in charge of the Hessians placed near the Court-House, the left extending toward Allentown about three miles.|| The little village of Monmouth Court-House had grown up at the intersection of three roads—

---

* Hamilton to Washington : Lee Papers, vol. ii. p. 420.

† Ogden's Testimony : Ibid., vol. iii. p. 65.

‡ Sparks, vol. v. p. 425.

§ Testimony of Generals Scott and Wayne : Lee Papers, vol. iii. pp. 2, 4. [The "Lee Papers" to which frequent reference is made in this oration are papers relating to Lee's trial by court-martial, published by the New York Historical Society.—Ed.]

|| Sparks, vol. v. p. 424.

that on which the British were marching, another which led northward toward Amboy, and a third which came from Englishtown and Cranberry. A few houses clustered about the wooden Court-House, which stood on the spot where we are gathered to-day. Long settled as the country had been, much of it remained uncleared. The undulating plain through which the road ran northeastwardly to Middletown was open, but the way to Cranberry soon after leaving the Court-House plunged into woods, which lined it for several miles.

It was the night of Saturday, the 27th of June. Imagine, if you can, the scene: the little village about the Court-House, full of soldiers in scarlet—the baggage-wagons drawn together in the open ground to the southward—the crackling of the fires as the troops get supper—the neighing of many horses picketed along the road—here an officer riding by, there a guard marching to its post—the hum of voices—the innumerable noises of the camp growing fainter as the evening draws on—and at last the quiet of the summer night, broken only by the steady footfalls of the sentinels and the barking of a dog at some distant farm-house or the stamping of some restless horse. Who can foresee that to-morrow a deed shall be done that shall consecrate for all time this quiet Jersey village, and that the benedictions of a grateful people shall descend forever upon Monmouth Court-House!

By ten o'clock all is hushed. It is a hot night, without a breath of wind. The woods in the northwest are as still as death, their leaves drooping and motionless, and the summer sky is unobscured by a single cloud. A sharp lookout is kept down the road and on the edge of the woods towards Englishtown, for in the afternoon a deserter has come in with the information that "the rebels are extended along our left flank, and are very numerous."*   But the darkness passes without the sign of an enemy.   At the early dawn there is bustle and noise in the camp about the Court-House.   The reveille sounds and the Hessians are astir.   The air is full of the noise of neighing horses and chattering men.   The baggage-wagons begin to move into the road to Middletown, the line of march is formed, and as the sun rises, about half-past four, Knyphausen's division has begun to move.†   Five o'clock comes, and with it daylight.   The fresh breath of the morning is pleasant after the hot night, but the cloudless sky and the heavy air promise a trying day.   All along the road the camp is stirring, the different regiments forming into line—the Light Infantry and Hessian Grenadiers on the right, the Guards, the First and Second Grenadiers, the Highlanders, the loyal battalions, and the Queen's Rangers each in turn.   At six the hot day has begun, but it is nearly eight before the column has started.   It is a splendid sight, and one that this quiet county will never see again, this perfectly-appointed army moving with its long train of artillery and baggage along the road.   Here is the Hessian: "a towering, brass-fronted cap, mustaches covered with the same material that colors his shoes, his hair, plastered with tallow and flour, tightly drawn into a long appendage reaching from the back of his head to his waist, his blue uniform almost covered by the broad belts sustaining his cartouch-box, his brass-hilted sword, and his bayonet; a yellow waistcoat with flaps, and yellow breeches met at the knee by black

---

* Bell's Journal : New Jersey Historical Society's Proceedings, vol. vi. p. 17.

† Testimony of Captain Mercer: Lee Papers, vol. iii. p. 102 ; also Clinton's Letter to Lord George Germaine, vol. ii. p. 463.

gaiters—thus heavily equipped,"* he moves "like an automaton" down the road. See the British Grenadier, tall and stalwart, with smooth-shaven face and powdered hair, on his head a pointed cap of black leather fronted with a gilded ornament—his coat of scarlet, with collar and cuffs of buff trimmed with red—a broad, white leather strap over the left shoulder carrying his cartridge-box—one over the right bears his bayonet-scabbard which hangs at his left thigh, and where they cross on his breast there is a plate of brass with the number of his regiment. His breeches of white are protected by long black leggins.† The accoutrements of all are in perfect order, their equipment complete, and one after another the regiments break into column and march toward the east. The sun has already risen above the high ground near the sea, the birds that have been twittering in the branches have ceased to sing—Knyphausen with the long train of heavily lumbering baggage has crossed the open plain, and still the lines of scarlet are passing by the little Court-House. Where are the Americans?—the chance to fight a battle is almost gone.

Somewhere in that still and silent wood Dickinson's militia have been watching through the night. With the first noise in the British camp they are alert. No movement of the enemy escapes them, and as Knyphausen begins his march a messenger gallops off at full speed through the woods. He dashes into camp at five o'clock. An order is at once sent to General Lee to follow and attack "unless there should be very powerful reasons to the

---

* Dunlap's History of the American Theatre, London, vol. i. pp. 85–6.

† Moorsom's History of the Fifty-second Regiment.

contrary,"* and the main army is ordered under arms. Meantime Lee has his detachment ready. Butler of Pennsylvania with two hundred men marches first; Scott's brigade and a part of Woodford's, about six hundred, follow; Varnum's brigade, under Lieutenant-Colonel Olney, six hundred strong; Wayne's detachment of one thousand; Scott with another of fourteen hundred, and Maxwell with about one thousand bringing up the rear. Distributed among these are twelve pieces of artillery.† At seven o'clock the advance has reached the old Presbyterian Church on the side of the road, east of Englishtown, and is distant from the British about three miles. A road nearly straight leads from this point to the Court-House. Let us take a look at the country that lies between. It is a rolling country, well covered with timber. Just beyond the Church, as one goes towards Monmouth, the road descends a hill and crosses a morass, through which a stream of water flows toward the south and west. A long causeway of logs has made the place passable,‡ and on the eastern side the hill rises quickly to a considerable elevation. The road now continues through a piece of timber, which is large and heavy on the left, but just beyond the edge of it, on the right, are the open fields of three farms, known as Tennent's, Wikoff's, and Carr's. The two latter are divided by a deep ravine, which crosses the road at right angles, about half-way between the causeway and the Court-House. The wood on the left extends almost to the village, and covers the side of a bluff which forms the western

---

* Testimony of Lieutenant-Colonel Meade: Lee Papers, vol. iii. pp. 7, 8; also of Captain Mercer, p. 102.

† Testimony of Wayne: Ibid., p. 22.

‡ Ralph Schenck's statement. *Vide* Historical Magazine, 1861, vol. v. p. 220.

boundary of the plain of Monmouth. Beneath this bluff, running due north from the Court-House, is a deep and almost impassable morass. There are but three houses between the Church, at which the advance has halted, and the village, the first called the Parsonage, in the open field, just after one ascends the hill, and the second and third, known as Wikoff's and Carr's, on the western and eastern sides of the ravine that separates them. The morass westward of the Parsonage begins more than a mile to the northeast, and, following the stream which makes it, sweeps around between the hills to the southeast, where it joins another that runs westwardly. It is a bog a couple of hundred yards in width, deep and impassable, save at the causeway. The distance from the Court-House to the ravine between Carr's house and Wikoff's is about a mile; to the causeway, across the large morass, a trifle more than two miles. Such is the country that separates the armies.* As the advance under Lee approaches the long causeway, a few scattering shots are heard and it is halted. Scott's brigade have advanced up the morass, the rest formed upon the western hill.† A few of Dickinson's militia, down the road toward the Court-House, have encountered a flanking party of the British. As the troops halt, a stout, ruddy-faced officer rides up. It is Anthony Wayne, whom Lee has summoned to command the advance. There is a report that the enemy are near. Wayne takes his spy-glass, but can discover only a party of the country people.‡ Dickinson comes in haste to Lee. He is sure that the enemy are marching from the Court-House. Lee doubts the story, but orders a brigade to form at the left, facing a road by which Dickinson expects the enemy.§

---

* Map in Carrington's Battles of the American Revolution.

† Wayne's Testimony: Lee Papers, vol. iii. p. 18.   ‡ Ibid.   § Ibid.

But the intelligence is contradictory, and, after a few minutes' delay, Lee in impatience pushes the troops forward across the causeway.

Down the road toward the Court-House they move rapidly, marching briskly in spite of the heat, which by this time has become oppressive. They are a sad contrast to the well-equipped enemy they go to meet. They have no uniforms. Linen shirts and coats of butternut, home spun, and made, and dyed, are the best among them, and few have these. "They are so nearly naked that it is a shame to bring them into the field,"* says Major Jameson of Maryland, and Lee complains that they have no uniforms, colors, or marks to distinguish the regiments from each other. But they march well and with a soldierly air, thanks to the training of Steuben at Valley Forge. About half-past eight o'clock they approach the Court-House. The rear-guard of the British has passed through it, but a party of both infantry and horse are drawn up in the open ground to the northwestward.† The Americans halt under cover of the woods, and Lee and Wayne ride forward to reconnoitre. A messenger stops Lee, and Wayne goes on alone.‡ There appear to be about five hundred foot, and in front of them three hundred horsemen—the famous Queen's Rangers Hussars, under the command of Lieutenant-Colonel Simcoe.§ Wayne orders Butler out of the woods into the open close to the Court-House. The enemy slowly retire as the Americans approach. A few of Butler's men fire, and the Rangers fall back with the infantry pre-

---

* Bland Papers, vol. i. p. 97.

† Wayne's Testimony: Lee Papers, vol. iii. p. 18.   ‡ Ibid.

§ Simcoe's Journal, p. 68; also Bell's Journal: New Jersey Historical Society's Proceedings, vol. vi. p. 17.

cipitately into the village.* Long shall that spot be neglected and forgotten, but the time shall come when, on another 28th of June, the sons of America, beneath peaceful skies, shall build with pious services upon that sloping field a monument to mark forever the place where the first shot was fired and the Battle of Monmouth was begun! And now, as the enemy are apparently moving rapidly off into the plain, Butler files to the left of their left flank, and sends word to Wayne that the enemy are retreating.† The General, in reply, gallops up and halts the Pennsylvanians in the edge of a wood, close to the Court-House, from which they can see the British in regular order, horse, foot, and artillery, retreating toward the eastward. It is evident that they are leaving the ground in haste. Meantime the detachments of Scott, Grayson, and Varnum have halted on the side of the morass which bounds the plain of Monmouth,‡ half a mile or more to the northward of the position of Wayne and Butler. From all these points the enemy can be seen moving rapidly out of the village across the open plain.§ Hot-headed Wayne grows impatient. At the edge of the wood he has found a place where the morass can be crossed, and orders Butler forward. At the same moment a swarthy man on horseback gallops up to Lee. He has been near the enemy, and is sure they are a rear-guard of only one thousand men—considerably separated from the main body. He offers to take a detachment and double their right flank. It is black David Forman—commander of

---

* Butler's Testimony: Lee Papers, vol. iii. p. 44.

† Ibid.

‡ Scott's Testimony: Ibid., vol. iii. p. 28; also Grayson's, p. 36; Olney's, p. 127; Lee's, p. 182.

§ Wayne's Testimony: Ibid., p. 20.

the Monmouth County militia—the terror of the Tories.* Lee spitefully replies, "I know my business," and Foreman retires in disgust.† But what is that business? Surely not to let the enemy move away under his guns as if upon parade. The precious moments are flying—the Rangers in the rear-guard are half a mile out of the village already, continuing their march, when Captain Mercer, of Lee's staff, rides up to him. He has been down the road toward the Court-House, and has seen a large encampment of the enemy, which they have just left, for the chairs are standing and water lies there freshly spilt; a countryman tells him that there is a strong force, about two thousand, still behind the Court-House.‡ "Then I shall take them," says Lee,§ and orders the detachments on the left to march into the plain, to turn their right. They quit the woods, descend the bluff, cross the morass, and advance nearly half a mile into the plain—Grayson's in advance, Jackson's a hundred yards behind, Scott's next to Jackson's, and Maxwell's Jerseymen in the rear, on the outer edge of the morass. Wayne is now far in front in the open ground. On his right, on a little elevation, he has posted Eleazer Oswald, with two guns.‖ Varnum's brigade, of the Rhode Island line, is on the left, Butler's regiment in front, in the rear of all Wesson, Livingston, and Stewart. Suddenly the enemy halt and form in line of battle. A regiment of cavalry supported by infantry advance towards Butler, and several guns to the eastward open fire. Oswald replies effectively with his two pieces on the height, and Butler prepares to receive an attack. Down come the British cavalry in full charge.

---

* Barber and Howe's Historical Collection of New Jersey, p. 346.
† Foreman's Testimony : Lee Papers, vol. iii. p. 25.
‡ Mercer's Testimony : Ibid., p. 106.   § Ibid.
‖ Oswald's Testimony : Ibid., pp. 132–3.

Butler reserves his fire till they are near, when a well-directed volley breaks them, and they retire in disorder through the infantry, throwing them into confusion.* At this the British suddenly turn back and march towards the Court-House. They appear very strong; it is evident that the whole rear division has returned to prevent a demonstration against the baggage. Wayne sends to Lee for more troops. Lee answers that it is a feint,† and that he does not wish the enemy to be vigorously attacked until his flank is exposed. The British approach the Court-House in great force. Lee directs Lafayette to fall back to the Court-House with the brigade of Varnum, and Stewart's and Livingston's regiments.‡ Wayne, meantime, is chafing with impatience. The enemy are crossing his front—he cannot get troops enough to strike them with effect, and Oswald's ammunition has given out.§ Just at this moment General Scott rides up—a hot-headed Virginian, as gallant and full of fight as Wayne himself. From his command on the left, far out in the plain, he has seen the troops under Lafayette apparently retreating toward the Court-House. Alarmed at this, and having tried in vain to get his cannon across the morass, he has ordered his men to retire behind it and form in the woods beyond, from which they came. Here he has left them, and galloped down to learn what is the matter.‖. Wayne is in equal wonderment. One of his aides has just come from General Lee with the startling information that the whole right is falling back in haste from the Court-House; but he brings no orders. Together Scott and

---

* Butler's Testimony: Lee Papers, vol. iii. p. 44; also Wayne's, p. 20.

† Lee's Defence: Ibid., p. 194.

‡ Lafayette's Testimony: Ibid., p. 12.

§ Oswald's Testimony: Ibid., p. 134.

‖ Scott's Testimony: Ibid., p. 28.

Wayne ride there. The troops have already left. Wayne
sends an aide to Lee to beg that they might be ordered back
to the place from which they had retired, the enemy being
still a mile away. Major Fishbourne returns. He has found
General Lee, whose only answer is that he will see General
Wayne himself.* It is now about eleven o'clock. Furious
with disappointment, Wayne sends a third time. Will not
General Lee halt the main body to cover the retreat of General Scott? His aides return without an answer;† the troops
are still retiring in some confusion nearly a mile in the rear,
in front of the ravine by Carr's House. The enemy are
close at hand. Wayne orders Butler out of the plain in
haste,‡ while he and Scott watch in the orchard near the
village. At this moment up gallops Richard Meade. He
is an aide of Washington's, and has ridden forward by the
General's orders at the first sound of the cannonading. He
has met the troops retreating in disorder near the defile by
Carr's House. There he has found General Lee, who tells
him that they are all in confusion, but has no message for
the Commander-in-Chief. Meade gallops to the village;
the enemy are there, and already the head of their column
appears this side the Court-House.§ Scott hurries to his
command,|| while Wayne retires slowly with Meade toward
Carr's House, pursued by the enemy's horsemen. The
British advance is now between Scott and the retreating
troops with Lee and Lafayette. A rapid march through
the woods to the northward alone enables the former to

---

* Fishbourne's Testimony: Lee Papers, vol. iii. pp. 47–8; also
Scott's, p. 28; and Wayne's, p. 21.

† Lee Papers, vol. ii. p. 440.

‡ Letter of Scott and Wayne to Washington: Ibid.

§ Meade's Testimony: Ibid., vol. iii. p. 63.

|| Letter of Scott and Wayne to Washington: Ibid., vol. ii. p. 440.

rejoin the army.* He comes out into the large morass, and crosses it far to the north and eastward of the old Presbyterian Church. Meantime, what has become of General Lee? When the enemy first turned back in force he was on the left, watching, with the intention of turning their right flank. Observing them to approach in force, he directed the troops on the right to retire and form near the Court-House. Arrived there, and finding the position less strong than he supposed, he gave orders to fall back.† Confusion followed. The heat was intense. The men were nearly fainting with fatigue. The horses of the aides-decamp could hardly stand.‡ Orders that were given were not delivered, and orders were delivered that had never been given by the General. Contradictory directions made matters worse. Near Carr's House a regiment was posted at a fence, and presently withdrawn. Du Portail insisted that the position here was a strong one. Lee declared that it was execrable, and commanded by an eminence on the British side.§ Back the troops kept falling—forming now in line, and the next minute ordered to retire. No one knew why or whither, nor did Lee take pains to check the disorder. The officers were furious, the men dejected. There had been no fighting to speak of—the enemy did not seem dangerously strong—the chance to fight him on good terms had appeared so favorable.;—it was inexplicable. It is now nearly twelve o'clock. In front of the ravine near Carr's House there is a temporary halt. General Lee him-

---

* Cilley's Testimony : Lee Papers, vol. iii. p. 33.

† Lee's Defence: Ibid., p. 183.

‡ Mercer's Testimony : Ibid., p. 111; Stewart's Testimony, p. 40; Tilghman's Testimony, pp. 80-2.

§ Du Portail's Testimony: Ibid., p. 139; also Lee's Defence, p. 184.

self orders Jackson's Massachusetts regiment to form behind a fence, but hardly has it done so when he commands it to retire beyond the ravine.* A part of Varnum's brigade halts for ten minutes in an orchard, but the enemy coming on rapidly, they too retire beyond the ravine.† As the troops are falling back a countryman rides up to General Lee. It is Peter Wikoff, who lives in the farm-house between the Parsonage and Carr's. He knows the country well—what can he do? Lee asks him where there is a strong position to which the army can retire. He points to the west and south. But there is an almost impassable morass in the way. It can be crossed on logs. Too late to make a bridge. Beyond the causeway then there are high hills. Lee urges him to ride back and halt some regiment on the ground.‡ He gallops off at speed. All is disorder, the troops retiring rapidly, so fagged with the heat that many faint. Here is Olney, with the Rhode Islanders, crossing the ravine; yonder, near Carr's House, is Stewart of Pennsylvania, keeping his panting men together;§ the gallant Ramsey is close at hand;‖ Maxwell has crossed the ravine, and is forming his Jerseymen in the woods on the north of the road;¶ while Oswald tries to get his guns across the defile.**

All is in uproar and confusion; shouts of go back! go back! drive on! drive on!†† are heard above the din, and all the while the dropping fire of musketry in the rear shows that the enemy is close at hand. Five thousand men

---

* Jackson's Testimony: Lee Papers, vol. iii. p. 124.

† Olney's Testimony: Ibid., p. 127.

‡ Wikoff's Deposition: Ibid., pp. 172–3.

§ Stewart's Testimony: Ibid., p. 40.

‖ Oswald's Testimony: Ibid., p. 136.

¶ Maxwell's Testimony: Ibid., p. 92.

** Oswald's Testimony: Ibid., p. 135.

†† Jackson's Testimony: Ibid., p. 124; also Ogden's, p. 134.

have fallen back in disorder nearly two miles, in the face of a constant and vigorous pursuit. It is extraordinary that there is no panic. But both men and officers are too angry to be frightened; there is no breaking of the ranks; no running among the troops—it is a sullen retreat. The men halt at the first order, form like veterans, and only retire when commanded to do so. Some faint with heat and fall. All are panting for water—the sweat streaming from them, their tongues dry and swollen, their faces flushed, their eyes bloodshot. The horses are completely broken down. Many refuse to carry their riders, and half of the officers are on foot. And so through the hot wood and beneath the blazing sun, down one side of the ravine and up the other, the regiments of Lee's command fall back in disorder along the road and through the fields of Wikoff's farm, towards the long causeway across the wide morass, on the way to Englishtown.

The day that promised so well has begun in disaster. The Americans are in full retreat without a fight. Grayson's Marylanders and Patton's North Carolinians are about to cross the causeway—a part of Jackson's Massachusetts regiment, under Lieutenant-Colonel Smith, are close behind them. Ogden's and Shreve's Jerseymen are descending the hill—the heights are covered with the retreating regiments. When suddenly down the western hill, toward the causeway, come at full speed two horsemen. They are Fitzgerald and Harrison, of the Commander-in-Chief's staff.* Riding with him, near the Presbyterian Church, they have met a countryman on horseback. He has come, he says, from near the Court-House, and has heard that our people were retreating. General Washington refuses to believe him, for he

---

* Tilghman's Testimony: Lee Papers, vol. iii. p. 80.

has heard no sound except a few discharges of cannon more than an hour before. The man points to a fifer, who has come up breathless. Yes, says the fifer, in affright, the Continental troops are in retreat. Vexed at the story, which he cannot believe, the General orders the man into a light horseman's charge and hurries forward.* Fifty paces down the road he meets some stragglers—one of them has come from the army. All the troops, he says, are falling back. The thing looks serious, but still the General will not believe it true. He sends Harrison and Fitzgerald forward to ascertain the facts. As they descend the hill they encounter Grayson's men. Captain Jones declares that the troops behind are in the same condition as his own.† Lieutenant-Colonel Parke's men are in disorder.‡ William Smith, of Jackson's regiment, cannot imagine why they have retreated; he has lost but a single man.§ Beyond the causeway is Aaron Ogden, "exceedingly exasperated," declaring with an oath that "the troops are fleeing from a shadow."‖ Shreve, of the next Jersey regiment, smiles bitterly; he has retreated by order, but he knows not why. Rhea, his lieutenant-colonel, cannot understand it, nor where to go.¶ Howell, his major, has never seen the like;** and on the height General Maxwell confesses that he is wholly in the dark.†† The aides push on toward Carr's House. Here Mercer, of Lee's staff, says with warmth to Harrison, that if he will ride to the Court-House he will find reason enough in the numbers of the enemy;‡‡ but Wayne declares that it is

---

* Harrison's Testimony: Lee Papers, vol. iii. p. 72; also Tilghman's, p. 78.

† Harrison's Testimony: Ibid., p. 72.

‡ Ibid. § Ibid., p. 73. ‖ Ibid. ¶ Ibid.

** Tilghman's Testimony: Ibid., p. 80.

†† Harrison's Testimony: Ibid., p. 73. ‡‡ Ibid.

impossible to tell the cause of the retreat, for a very select body of men have this day been drawn off from troops far inferior in number.* And all this while General Lee sits for twenty minutes by a fence, without giving an order or making an attempt to stop the enemy.† One of the French engineers comes to Fitzgerald—the ground he thinks very advantageous for stopping the enemy; he begs for two pieces of cannon. Oswald has but four pieces left, the others have retreated with their brigades, and his men are so fatigued with heat that they are dropping beside the guns. But he will post them here, and open on the enemy as they approach from the village.‡ On come the British through the open fields, in perfect order, marching in two columns, their artillery and horse between them, and Lee retires hastily with some scattered troops beyond the ravine. They are within quarter of a mile—the American rear just crossing the ravine. The case is desperate. "The most sanguine hope," says young Laurens, who has seen it all, "scarcely extends . . . to an orderly retreat."§ It is an awful moment for America. Was it for this that these gallant fellows bore the dull tortures of the winter? Was it for this that they have trudged through pouring rain and torrid sun—now ankle-deep in mud and now with their feet buried in the burning sand? Was it for this that they have covered Charles Lee with confidence and honor, and gone forth under him from happy homes to meet the proudest army in the world?

But see yonder in the west—beyond the long causeway the troops have stopped retreating! Grayson and Patton

---

* Harrison's Testimony: Lee Papers, vol. iii. p. 74.

† Meade's Testimony: Ibid., p. 64.

‡ Oswald's Testimony: Ibid., pp. 135-6.

§ Ibid., vol. ii. p. 450.

have halted half-way up; on this edge of the morass Ogden and Shreve are falling into line,* and on the crest of the distant hill are the heads of columns, apparently advancing. There is a sudden halt as down the hill dashes a tall horseman. A group of officers try to follow, but he rides too fast. Over the bridge and up the road he rushes like the wind, his horse in a lather of sweat as he drives the rowels in. Up the hill he comes as fast as his horse can run, his manly figure and perfect horsemanship commanding admiration; his face flushed with excitement, his lips compressed, his often languid eye flashing an angry fire, his usually white brow as black as night. See him as he dashes through the lines—great as he is, never greater than to-day—checking the retreat by his very presence, arresting disaster by a glance, and in an instant changing defeat to victory! On a sudden he reins his foaming horse, and Washington and Lee are face to face. As it was three-and-twenty years ago, it is to-day; as on the banks of Monongahela so on the heights of Freehold. It is the Englishman that shall be beaten and the American that shall cover his retreat; it is the Regular that shall run and the Provincial that shall stand his ground; it is Lee that shall lose the day; it is Washington that shall save the army! And what a contrast!—the one thin as a skeleton, his features plain, his eyes prominent, his nose enormous, his whole appearance singular and unprepossessing; the other broad, with an open countenance and manly air, his figure that of an accomplished gentleman, his gestures graceful, his presence strangely commanding and impressive. They are almost the same age, but Lee looks old and wrinkled, while Washington appears in the prime of unusual health and

---

* Tilghman's Testimony: Lee Papers, vol. iii. pp. 80–1.

vigor. And thus for the last time they sit looking at each other. But for a moment only, for the indignation of Washington has burst restraint. " What, sir, is the meaning of all this?" he asks, in a tone of thunder. "Sir, sir," stammers the other, and is dumb. " I desire to know, sir, the meaning of this disorder and confusion," repeats Washington, his aspect in his anger really terrible to see. Lee answers confusedly—his orders have been misunderstood or disobeyed, particularly by General Scott. He did not choose to beard the whole British army with troops in that condition, and finally that the whole thing was against his opinion. " Whatever your opinion may have been, sir, I expected my orders to have been obeyed." " These men cannot face the British grenadiers." " They can," cried Washington, as he spurred away—" they can do it, and they shall !"* Indeed there is not a moment to be lost. Harrison comes up from Carr's House with the news that the enemy are but fifteen minutes off, in great strength, approaching rapidly.† Washington hurriedly examines the ground as Tilghman goes for Lieutenant-Colonel Rhea, who knows it well.‡ It seems fit to make a stand upon, and the British must be stopped till the main army can be formed. Yonder are Walter Stewart and Nathaniel Ramsey coming out of the ravine. The General hastens to them. On them, he says, he shall depend to give the enemy a check ;§ and under Wayne's eye, who arrives at the moment, the two regiments are formed in the woods on the left.‖ Wash-

---

* This account of the meeting of Washington and Lee is gathered from the following authorities : Meade's Testimony, Lee Papers, vol. iii. p. 64 ; also McHenry's, p. 78 ; Tilghman's, p. 81 ; Lee's Defence, p. 191 ; Papers relating to the Maryland Line ('76 Soc. Pub.), p. 104.

† Tilghman's Testimony : Lee Papers, vol. iii. p. 81.   ‡ Ibid.

§ Harrison's Testimony : Ibid., p. 75.   ‖ Ibid.; also Wayne's, p. 22.

ington calls for artillery. Oswald's pieces have gone by.
He orders them back at once and posts them on the
right,* with Livingston's regiment to support them.† By
this time the British have entered the wood in front of
Stewart and Ramsey; their guns open from the centre
and their cavalry are beginning to traverse the ravine.
The Battle of Monmouth has begun. Having made
this hurried disposition of his troops, Washington hastens
to the right. Here, close to Oswald's cannon, Lee and
stout Henry Knox are watching the movements of the
British. "Will you command here, or shall I?" the
Chief demands of Lee. "If you will, I will go to the
rear and form the army." "I will," is the answer, "and
will be one of the last men off the field."‡ With a
word to Knox for more artillery, Washington gallops to
the rear. The sharp fire of musketry on the left, with
the skilful practice of Oswald's cannoneers, have checked
pursuit. The British halt and bring their guns to the
front. A precious ten minutes has been gained. Meantime, in the rear, the army is coming up. The General is
already across the causeway and is forming the men rapidly
upon the height. It is a splendid position, the hills in
semicircle rising steeply from the marsh in front, which
can only be crossed by the narrow causeway. Greene is on
the right, Stirling well posted on the left; the practised eye
of Steuben places the cannon skilfully, while Lafayette, on
the crest of the ridge, commands the second line. The
Frenchman, Duplessis de Manduit, is sent with six pieces
to Comb's Hill, more than half a mile on the extreme right,

---

* Fitzgerald's Testimony: Lee Papers, vol. iii. pp. 69, 70.

† Mercer's Testimony: Ibid., p. 113.

‡ Hamilton's Testimony: Ibid., p. 59; also Knox's, p. 156; Shaw's,
p. 159; Mercer's, p. 113.

whence he can enfilade the enemy as they advance.* The troops move into place with the precision of trained soldiers, better even, says Hamilton, who watches them, than the British themselves;† the guns are posted, and it is just in time. For the light-horse have crossed the ravine and threaten Oswald's guns, and on the left Stewart and Ramsey's men come slowly out of the woods fighting inch by inch, Americans and British mixed up together as they come.‡ By Knox's order Oswald falls back a hundred yards, repeatedly unlimbering his guns and firing as he retreats. The crackling of the musketry is heavy, like a thousand bonfires, and every now and then a discharge from the artillery checks the red-coats and throws them into confusion. Wikoff's fields are spotted with dead men; brave Ramsey is down wounded and a prisoner;§ Fitzgerald has been hit, and John Laurens slightly, as his horse falls dead beneath him.|| Slowly the Americans recede, and as slowly the British advance. And now they have reached the line between the Wikoff and the Tennent farms—a fence grown up with weeds and bushes and small trees that runs right across the line of the retreat. A small man rides up to Olney, who commands Varnum's brigade, and points to the hedge-row.¶ He is a youth of two-and-twenty, with sharp features and a brilliant eye. His manner is earnest, and he speaks with an authority far beyond his years. It is Lieutenant-Colonel Alexander Hamilton. The Rhode

---

* Barber and Howe's Historical Collection of New Jersey, p. 337.

† Lee Papers, vol. ii. p. 470.

‡ Mercer's Testimony: Ibid., vol. iii. p. 113.

§ Life of Knox, p. 57.

|| Correspondence of John Laurens, p. 197.

¶ Hamilton's Testimony: Lee Papers, vol. iii. p. 60; also Olney's, p. 127.

Islanders throw themselves behind the hedge-row,* while Knox, without a minute's delay, posts two guns on a little knoll a few paces in the rear. The British are within a dozen rods, advancing to the charge. A volley cracks from the hedge-row, and the guns behind open at short range. The enemy recoils; the infantry give place to the light-horsemen, who charge up within forty yards, but are driven back with heavy loss. On come the foot again, when suddenly the guns of Duplessis on Comb's Hill open a cross-fire upon the right, and they stagger and fall back. The hedge-row is still held—the field in front strewn with dead, the rattle of musketry is incessant, the cannon shake the very earth. But the left is turned—Olney's men have begun to fall behind the hedge—Hamilton is down, his horse shot dead, but he gathers himself up, bruised and hurt.† The enemy have the woods on the left—their cavalry are threatening the right—their front line is nearly at the hedge —they outnumber the Rhode Islanders ten to one. Knox withdraws the guns; the Continentals leave the hedge-row; and, covered by the heavy cannonade from the hills in the rear, the whole body descends in pretty good order and crosses the long causeway.‡ It is after two o'clock. The British are masters of the woods on the right and the open fields up to the hedge-row.

But where is Wayne? The old Tennent Parsonage and barn lie in a hollow about a hundred yards westward of the hedge-row. Behind them ascends a ridge, which presently falls rapidly to the morass in front of Greene. Here in an orchard behind the barn and Parsonage, about three hundred yards in advance of the main army, Wayne awaits

---

* Knox's Testimony: Lee Papers, vol. iii. p. 158.
† Hamilton's Testimony: Ibid., p. 61.
‡ Olney's Testimony: Ibid., p. 128.

attack.* He has a few hundred Pennsylvanians under William Irvine and Thomas Craig, a Virginia regiment, and several pieces of artillery. Clinton has now brought up the flower of his army, and while his batteries engage the Americans on the distant heights he orders the grenadiers to dislodge Wayne. In splendid array his veterans advance, their scarlet coats in perfect line, their bayonets gleaming in the sunshine. Down they come toward the exposed position where the Pennsylvanians lie. A terrific fire opens on them, and they stagger and fall back. They rally, reform, and advance again to the attack. A second volley greets them, and they are driven back blinded and broken toward the cover of the woods. And all the while the cannon on both sides is thundering away. Daniel Morgan hears it yonder at Shumais Mills.† He has sent to Lee for orders, but can get none, and there, useless, he passes the long afternoon pacing like a lion in a cage. Clinton now tries to turn the left. The Highlanders attack Lord Stirling furiously, but his batteries check them, and his infantry advance and drive them back. Lieutenant-Colonel Aaron Burr pursues them into the meadow, but an order halts him in the open ground; his brigade suffers heavily—his horse is shot, and Rudolph Bunner, lieutenant-colonel of the Pennsylvania line, is killed.‡ Attempting to turn, the right meets with no better

* The authorities for placing Wayne at the Parsonage with Pennsylvania and Virginia troops, are Langworthy's Memoir of Lee, p. 17; Kapp's Life of Steuben, p. 161; Wayne's Letters, *vide* Lee Papers, vol. ii. p. 448, vol. iii. p. 241; Clark's Letter to Lee, ibid., p. 232; and Letters of General William Irvine, Pennsylvania Magazine, vol. ii. pp. 147–8. In the first of Wayne's letters referred to he says, "Pennsylvania showed the Road to Victory."

† Graham's Life of Morgan, p. 211.

‡ Davis's Memoirs of Burr, vol. i. pp. 127–8.

fate.　Wayne must be driven from his ground or the King's army must retire.

On the ridge, behind the orchard, Wayne has two cannon posted.　Their fire is most effective, but the men who serve them are fearfully exposed, and have fallen one by one; they are worked now with half the requisite force, and still the men are dropping.　Suddenly as the British approach, a matross in the act of ramming the charge throws up his arms and falls headlong to the ground.　The gun is useless and must be withdrawn, for there is none to take his place. Aye, but there is, for, yonder, rushing to the front, behold a woman!　The wife of the fallen matross, she has been to the creek for water to keep the sponge wet.　Seeing her husband fall, she dashes forward, snatches up the rammer, and drives it home with the vigor of a veteran.　A moment and the priming is ready—another, and the gun belches forth in the very faces of the British.　There she stands, black with powder, in the blinding smoke, the shot raining about her, the dead and wounded at her feet, plying the rammer with a furious energy, and keeping that heated gun busy at its deadly work!　And there in the midst of that conflict, the figure of Molly Pitcher, the woman cannoneer of Monmouth, goes down to history.　But see, Sir Henry is ready for his final effort.　From the woods on the northeast, across the open ground before the hedge-row, in the face of a heavy cannonade from the Americans on Comb's Hill, the grenadiers advance.　Veterans of many a well-won field, they move steadily to the attack.　The picked men of the Royal army, perfect in equipment and in the practice of arms, and never more magnificent or better handled than to-day, they sweep onward toward the little Parsonage and barn.　It is a moment of dreadful suspense to the patriots upon the heights.　Surely the Pennsylvanians will be swept like chaff before them. Nearer and nearer they come, in "magnificently stern array" of glowing scarlet and glittering steel, their bayonets fixed, advancing silently without a shot, while the cannon on the distant hills shakes the earth beneath their feet. Who is there to resist them? A few hundred Pennsylvanians drawn up in a little orchard and behind a wooden barn and farm-house—a handful of yeomen in their shirt-sleeves, armed with old-fashioned muskets, awaiting the charge of the British grenadiers. The odds against the Americans are fearful, as the well-trained enemy sweeps down. But not a man among them moves. Somewhere in that orchard is Anthony Wayne himself, watching the foe with steady glance, his teeth set, his cheek flushed. "Wait," he tells his men, "till they are close at hand, and then pick off the king birds."*

On comes the unbroken column, apparently resistless, in the full blaze of the afternoon's sun. In front, in the splendid uniform of a lieutenant-colonel, is their commander, Henry Monckton, the Viscount Galway's son, waving his sword and calling on the grenadiers to "charge." They have swept through the open field, they have passed the hedge-row, they have begun to descend the slope beyond, their pace quickens, the front rank has almost reached the barn—the whole column is in full charge. There is a moment of suspense. And then, with a crash, a sheet of flame from Parsonage and barn and fence and orchard leaps forth to meet them, and in an instant a dense cloud of smoke has hidden them from view. A moment later the cloud has broken, and here and there glimpses can be seen

---

* King's Address. *Vide* New Jersey Historical Society's Proceedings, vol. iv. p. 139.

of men in deadly combat—red-coated grenadiers and yeomen in shirt-sleeves mixed in inextricable confusion. See as the smoke lifts, Wayne's men have leaped the fence coatless, their sleeves rolled up,* and dashed into the mêlée, and yonder in the hollow of the field they are fighting hand to hand with bayonet thrust and clubbed guns over a lifeless body. It is his who a moment ago cheered on his men to victory—his breast bloody with wounds, his scarlet coat stained and torn as the fight rages about him. Now his men press forward, and again are driven back, as the Americans from barn and orchard throw themselves headlong into the struggle. The cracking of the musketry is incessant—the cries of the combatants can be heard, and all the while, above the din, the guns upon the heights keep up "the heaviest cannonading ever heard in America." And now beyond the rim of smoke the grenadiers are falling back in groups together, broken and confused. The Americans have Monckton's body and are driving his men before them in retreat. Back up the sloping field—through the broken hedge-row—across the open ground—toward the woods beyond, faster and faster go the British—in confused mass, their ranks broken—their battalions shattered—their leader killed! At last—at last—in open ground and hand to hand the ragged rebels have withstood and beaten the British grenadiers!

The day is now spent; the American position can neither be turned nor taken; the British left is threatened, and the whole army cooped up on the right—there is nothing for Clinton to do but to retire. Already his troops have left the woods in front of Stirling—the centre has repassed the

---

* Statement of John Crolius, *vide* Dawson's Battles of the American Revolution, vol. i. p. 409.

ravine in front of Carr's House—the horsemen have turned their backs—the whole army is retreating. Down from the heights come the Americans in pursuit, and over the hot fields filled with the bodies of the dead. The word goes back to Steuben to bring up fresh men, for the enemy are retreating in confusion, and though Lee, then at the rear, declares that it cannot be true, the old veteran hastens to obey.* Before he has arrived the enemy are strongly posted on the ground beyond the ravine, and it is nearly seven o'clock. Washington prepares to resume the offensive, but both sides are tired out. And there through the sultry twilight the two armies lie watching each other, panting and exhausted, with only the defile between them.† The fields are strewn with coats, cartouch-boxes, and guns, the ground torn up with shot, the trees shattered with the marks of cannon-balls. The Americans hold the field of battle, but the British present a sullen and threatening front. The shadows creep out of the west—the steam rises from the hollows—the sun, like a ball of fire, has disappeared—the sultry twilight has faded—the hot night has begun. The dead lie where they fell, the wounded groan and gasp for air—in the woods, by the hedge-row, in the marsh, on the trodden field—and the tired living sink on their arms to sleep. Poor's sentinels, close to the enemy, are watching their right—Woodford's guarding their left.‡ Beneath a tall tree Washington and Lafayette, wrapped in a single cloak, lie down to rest.§ A solemn silence has followed the tumult of the day, and so the long hours of the night pass by.

With the first streak of dawn the men are under arms.

---

* Kapp's Life of Steuben, p. 163.
† Correspondence of John Laurens, p. 198.
‡ Washington to President of Congress, July 1.
§ Lafayette's Memoirs, vol. i. p. 54.

Poor pushes his brigade across the ravine, Woodford advances on the left, and the whole army awaits the signal for attack. But still no sound comes from the British camp. And look, for the sun is up, the fields in front are deserted; the cannon that frowned across the ravine at nightfall have disappeared; the red-coats have vanished in the night. Four of their officers and forty men lie wounded in their empty camp. In the darkness, in the shadows of the night, the Royal army has stolen away.* The Battle of Monmouth has been fought and won!

During the midnight hours Clinton has withdrawn in stealth to join his baggage in the hills of Middletown. Without cavalry, pursuit is useless. The British reach Sandy Hook on the 30th, and Washington advances to Brunswick and White Plains.

With the events that followed I have not to do. We all know the result: how the allied attack on Rhode Island was a failure, and how the British remained quiet in New York until December, when they departed to invade the South.

But the excitements of the affair of Monmouth ceased not with the battle. The singular conduct of General Lee —his disrespectful letters to the Commander-in-Chief—his trial—the confused and conflicting testimony—his able and ingenious defence (often inconsistent and based on afterthought though it was)—his conviction and his sentence— gave rise to bitter controversy for years to come. Many were convinced that he was guilty of greater offences than those with which he had been charged; some held him innocent, and even deserving of high praise. It is probable that he was in some degree innocent, and, at the same time, in greater measure guilty. It is clear that Wash-

---

* Correspondence of John Laurens, p. 198.

ington's order to attack left him full discretion. It is evident that an engagement in the plain would have been unwise, and that Lee's opinion of the position near the Court-House was a sounder one than Wayne's. It is probable that a well-managed retreat, drawing the British into the ground they finally occupied, and providing for the main army to receive them there, might have resulted in a battle disastrous to the enemy; but nothing before, or during, or after his retreat suggests that any such plan had entered the mind of General Lee. He made no plan of action in advance. He communicated none to his brigadiers at any time. He withdrew his right in haste when the enemy approached, but gave his left no orders. He fell back to Carr's House in confusion, which he saw but did not try to check. His directions to those about him were contradictory; to those at a distance he had none to give. His talk with Wikoff showed that he thought to make a stand, but knew neither when nor where to do it, and from the beginning to the end he sent no word to Washington of what was taking place. It was his fault that his command acted without a head; it was his fault that the enemy had to be stopped at a disadvantage to get time to form the main army, even for defence; and if it was his plan to draw Clinton into a trap, as he asserted, and in the same breath denied, in his defence, he took no pains to make that plan successful or avert the disaster, which every moment, under his eyes, threatened to be more complete and overwhelming. And it is certain that his subsequent conduct cannot be excused. His behavior to Congress was undignified and weak; his attacks on Washington ill-natured and contemptible; and his death—sudden and speedy as it was— was too tardy for his fame.

The generation that knew Charles Lee was too much

interested in the events in which he was an actor to form an accurate estimate of his character or sit in judgment on his life. The century that has intervened has cooled forever the passions that stirred the bosoms of his friends and enemies. We can judge him with calmness and impartiality; for to us he is simply a figure in our early history. And we know him better than our fathers did. They may have seen that, like Gates, he feared the British grenadiers, and could not persuade himself that the raw levies of Congress could stand up against them. They may have thought that, like others besides Gates, he was jealous of Washington, and did not wish him victory. They may have suspected that he was annoyed that his advice had been overruled, and did not wish an attack, made in spite of it, to be successful. But they did not understand, in the face of many signs, that his heart was not in their struggle; and they did not know, as we do, that when a prisoner in New York, on the 25th of March, 1777, this second in command of their armies had written and submitted to the British general an elaborate plan for the subjection of America. Side by side with that paper, in Lee's unmistakable handwriting, and endorsed by Howe's secretary "Mr. Lee's Plan,"* the most elaborate defence of his conduct here at Monmouth falls broken to the ground. His motives may have been humane, his desire to prevent bloodshed earnest, his wish to reunite the mother-country and the colonies sincere; but the act was that of a traitor, and on this spot, identified with the last scene of his career, it is more charitable than just, to grant to a name and memory associated with such a deed, the mercy of oblivion.

----

* *Vide* Treason of Charles Lee, by George II. Moore, New York, 1860.

The battle of the 28th of June was famous for many things. It was there that Charles Lee ended his career. It was there that the last great battle of the war was fought—from this to Yorktown the conflicts were on a smaller scale. And it was there that the American first showed himself a finished soldier. Courage he had exhibited enough already, but for the task which he had undertaken untrained valor was not enough. The audacious spirit which led the half-armed farmers of Massachusetts to seize the hill beyond Charlestown neck, at night, and throw up a rude breastwork within half a cannon-shot of a British fleet and army—the headlong daring of Arnold at Quebec and Behmus's Heights —the splendid gallantry of Christopher Greene behind the intrenchments at Red Bank—the intrepidity of Wayne leading his forlorn hope up the heights of Stony Point—the rash valor of Ethan Allen in the gates of Ticonderoga— the reckless bravery of Sergeant Jasper on the ramparts of Fort Moultrie, were but examples of an almost universal courage. But even this, splendid as it was, would not have availed alone through seven years of constant and often disastrous fighting. It was the calm and reflecting courage of the soldier trained in the school of trial—that could fall back without disorder, retreat without panic, endure suffering without a murmur, and bear defeat with patience. It was the long suffering of Valley Forge bearing its fruit in the veteran-like courage of Monmouth, that saved Civil Liberty for both continents alike.

And never were the soldierly qualities of Washington displayed more brilliantly than here. "I never saw the general to so much advantage," wrote Hamilton to Boudinot; "his coolness and firmness were admirable."* "His

* Lee Papers, vol. ii. p. 469.

presence stopped the retreat," said Lafayette; "his dispositions fixed the victory—his fine appearance on horseback, his calm courage, roused to animation by the vexations of the morning, gave him an air best calculated to arouse enthusiasm."* The general voice of his countrymen confirmed the judgment of Hamilton when he wrote: "America owes a great deal to General Washington for this day's work—a general rout, dismay, and disgrace would have attended the whole army in any other hands but his."†

From this time forward there was no longer question who should be Commander-in-Chief. One after another his enemies disappeared—Lee was suspended from command, Conway returned to France, Mifflin left the service. Gates was overthrown at Camden. It was he alone who had kept the army together at Valley Forge—it was he alone who had saved the day at Monmouth—it is he alone that shall win the liberties of this struggling people. Soldier and statesman, for five-and-twenty years the central figure in his country's history, he shall appear to posterity as he did to Lafayette that day, who thought, as he watched the splendid figure dashing along the forming lines, that never before or since had he beheld "so superb a man."‡ The affair of Monmouth was in some respects a drawn battle. The report which Clinton wrote conveyed the idea that he had accomplished all he wished—beaten the provincials and continued on his way to take advantage of the moonlight, although the fact was, that the moon on that night was but four days old. Many in England recognized the truth about the battle, for we find Horace Walpole writing shortly afterwards, "The undisciplined courtiers speak of it in

---

* Memoirs of Lafayette, vol. i. p. 34, foot-note. Bruxelles, 1837.
† Lee Papers, vol. ii. p. 470.
‡ Recollections of Geo. W. P. Custis, p. 221.

most dismal terms." "If I guess right, Washington was ill served, and thence, and by the violent heats, could not effect all his purposes; but an army on a march through a hostile country that is twice beaten back—which is owned—whose men drop down with heat, have no hospitals, and were hurrying to a place of security, must have lost more than three hundred and eighty men ;"* and he adds later, with a sneer, "The Royal army has gained an escape."† But the Americans claimed it with enthusiasm as a victory. It was true that the enemy had escaped. It was true that the fruits belonged rather to Clinton than to Washington, for the purpose of the one had failed, and that of the other been accomplished. But it was evident to all men that the days of the superiority of the British army were over. The Continentals had encountered the grenadiers in the open field, and under disastrous circumstances, and had withstood and even repulsed them. After a whole day's fighting it had been the British who fell back, and the Americans who kept the field—and this time it had been the Rebels who had wished to renew the battle, and the Regulars who had refused it. The fact that the enemy had escaped made little difference to the enthusiastic Americans. He had been beaten fairly, and that was glory enough. The Congress was in ecstasy—the Whigs jubilant. Wrote Washington himself, "From an unfortunate and bad beginning it turned out a glorious and happy day."‡ "The behavior of the officers and men in general was such as could not easily be surpassed. Our troops, after the first impulse from mismanagement, behaved with more

* Walpole to Rev. Wm. Mason, August 14, 1778. *Vide* Correspondence, vol. ii. p. 13.

† Walpole to Sir H. Mann. Ibid., vol. iii. p. 96.

‡ Washington to his Brother: Sparks, vol. v. p. 431.

spirit and moved with greater order than the British troops," were the words of Hamilton. Said General William Irvine, " It was a most glorious day for the American arms."* "Indeed," wrote Knox, "it is very splendid. The capital army of Britain defeated and obliged to retreat before the Americans, whom they despised so much." " The effects of the battle will be great and lasting. It will convince the enemy that nothing but a good constitution is wanting to render our army equal to any in the world."† As for Wayne, whose "good conduct and bravery," in the words of Washington, " deserve particular commendation,"‡ he could not contain himself. " Tell those Philadelphia ladies," he wrote to a friend, " who attended Howe's assemblies and levees, that the heavenly, sweet, pretty redcoats, the accomplished gentlemen of the guards and grenadiers, have been humbled on the plains of Monmouth. The Knights of the Blended Roses and of the Burning Mount have resigned their laurels to rebel officers, who will lay them at the feet of those virtuous daughters of America, who cheerfully gave up ease and affluence in a city for liberty and peace of mind in a cottage."§

Such, my countrymen, is the history of this famous fight. The years that have gone by have left no trace of it upon your soil. The fields are changed, the morass has become a pleasant meadow, the woods have fallen, the ancient Parsonage has gone. And they who struggled here, grenadier and Continental, veteran in scarlet and yeoman in rags, have all passed away forever; they who fought against us and they who fought to make us free, old and young alike,

---

* Hamilton to Boudinot. *Vide* Lee Papers, vol. ii. p. 470.
† Life of Knox, pp. 57–9.
‡ Washington to President of Congress, July 1.
§ Moore's Life of Wayne, pp. 64–5.

great man and humble, he whose fitting sepulchre is his country's heart and they who, in unmarked graves in yonder field, have long since mouldered into dust—the nameless dead, who died for you and me. Father, son, and grandchild, they have descended to the grave, and of all that knew and loved them in their prime, not one survives. The peaceful plough passing through your fields may uncover rusted ball, or broken bayonet, or mouldering skull, or crumbling skeleton. But the wild fury of the fight has gone; the struggling host has vanished; the loud-mouthed cannon are forever dumb. Another sound is rising in the land. It comes from town and hamlet, from marts of commerce and from haunts of trade, from workshop and from forge, from field and mine, from forest, hill, and stream. It tells of joy and gladness, of content and peace, of well-stored granaries and happy homes. It tells of a people virtuous and free, a government rooted in the hearts of men. It is a nation's prayer, a people's cry, a song of Hope and Prophecy.

And from these hills to-day a voice goes forth to meet it. Americans, it seems to say, as with your fathers shall it be with you. Faith, Courage, Fortitude, Virtue, and Love of Country can win you battles now as well as then. Defeat may still lead the way to Victory and suffering to Happiness. And when the night cometh and the shadows fall, remember that the sun that went down at Valley Forge was the same that arose above the Heights of Freehold.

THE END.